# CALIPHATE

## Tom Kratman

CALIPHATE

Copyright © 2008 by Tom Kratman

A Baen Books Original
Baen Publishing Enterprises
P.O. Box 1403
Riverdale, NY 10471
www.baen.com

ISBN: 978-1-4391-3342-2

Cover art by Kurt Miller

First Baen paperback printing, March 2010

Distributed by Simon & Schuster
1230 Avenue of the Americas
New York, NY 10020

Library of Congress Cataloging-in-Publication Data:
2008002986

Printed in the United States of America

10 9 8 7 6 5 4 3 2 1

# Dedication

For the defiant Oriana Fallaci, for the brave Bat Yeor,
and for the insightful Claire Berlinski.

# PROLOGUE

Hidden in the grass, the hare froze as the shadow passed over it. Even with its little brain, still it knew that the shadow was not just some passing puff of cloud. It was too small, too quick, too purposeful. And, too, something in the half-seen glimpse of the dark outline undulating over the uneven ground told of a raptor soaring above.

The hare was a naturally shy and timid creature, rarely venturing out into the meadows and pastures that covered the land. But this was spring. Instinct told the animal to find a mate. Instinct ruled. It could hardly help itself from gamboling about in search of a female.

It had found one, too, or thought it had. When he'd approached, though, the female had slapped him repeatedly to drive him away. Either she didn't want him for a mate or she wasn't quite ready yet. No matter to the

1

hare, it would hang around until the female was in a more accommodating and receptive frame of mind. He could still smell her; she wasn't far. Time, it had seemed, was on his side.

But there was that shadow overhead.

The raptor's eyes were large and keen. With them she saw her lifetime mate, even at his scouting distance. Though she was the better hunter, still the pair took turns, scouting and driving, diving and killing. Now it was the mate's turn to scout.

From her high post she thought she'd seen prey, some smallish brown animal. A hare, she thought. *Good eating . . . and the young hunger.*

She'd turned in her flight then and lost sight of the thing. It couldn't have gone far though. There . . . *Yes, there,* it probably was, down there in the patch of grass. It was rare to find grass so thick now, what with the depredations of the goats. The raptor thought only of the advantages to hunting that lack of cover provided. It never considered what would happen when there was no grass anymore, nor anything else for the prey to eat. In this, at least, the raptor and its master—the man below on horseback with the outstretched arm and the thick, heavy glove—were in agreement: Let the future take care of itself; live for today.

The raptor—it was a golden eagle—gave a cry. *Eeek . . . eeek . . . eeek.* This told her mate all he needed to know.

The hare heard the cry and began to tremble with fright. Should it move from its hide and open itself up to attack from above? Should it stay there and risk being isolated, uncovered and caten? And then there was the female to think about. Where was she? The male thought it could still smell her. Was she, too, hiding and trembling?

The male hare wasn't concerned with protecting the female. It would have gladly offered her up to the raptors' feast if only it had known how. Yes, the urge to mate was strong. But the urge to live was stronger still and another mate could probably be found. It would probably have offered up its own offspring rather than face the ripping talons and tearing beak.

The female gave another cry, subtly different from the first. She saw, with satisfaction, her mate swoop down with a terrorizing cry of his own. *Aha . . . there's the prey!* She swooped, exulting in her own ferocity.

*How the contemptible thing tries to avoid me, to save its miserable life. No use, little one, for the God of Eagles has placed you here for me.*

The eagle's feathers strained as they bent under the braking maneuver. Then came the satisfying strike of talons, the delightful spray of blood and the high pitched scream, so like a baby of one of the bipeds that dominated the ground here and guarded the goats that consumed the grass.

The female called to her mate. *Eeek . . . ee-ee-eeek. Come and feast, my love.*

Slowly the trembling subsided. The hare wasted no tears for the one that might have been its mate. Though the female was dead, the male would live, for the nonce. It would feed, even as the raptors fed on the corpse of the female.

How much better then, a man than a hare?

# PART I

# CHAPTER ONE

Where now is the ancient wealth and dignity of the Romans? The Romans of old were most powerful; now we are without strength. They were feared; now it is we who are fearful. The barbarians paid them tribute; now we are the tributaries of the barbarians. Our enemies make us pay for the very light of day and our right to life has to be bought. Oh, what miseries are ours! To what a state we have descended! We even have to thank the barbarians for the right to buy ourselves off them. What could be more humiliating and miserable?
—Salvian of Marseilles, 5th Century AD

Grolanhei, Province of Affrankon, 12 Safar, 1527 AH (23 March, 2103)

"Wonderful strike!" applauded the man on horseback, slapping the stock of the rifle in the saddle holster at

the horse's right. Mohammad was his name, though, as
Mohammad was the most common name in Europe, this
was less than significant, individually. "Wonderful strike,
Rashid," he repeated. A third man, Bashir, agreed.

Bashir's rifle was in his arms. It was hardly necessary.
The *Nazrani* were like rabbits and no man needed a rifle
to ward off rabbits. Even so, the presence of the weapon,
and its display, was a badge of the superiority of the
faithful and the inferiority—the *helpless* inferiority—of
the infidel. Virtually all of the masters carried them
almost all the time they were in public. There was quite
a lively trade in personal arms, too. Nearly every town
with any numbers of the faithful had a shop full of shotguns, rifles, and even automatic weapons for sale.

Rashid, their companion, just nodded. Like Mohammad and Bashir, Rashid also sat astride a horse, in his
case a magnificent white animal. In truth, Rashid's attention was not on the birds, nor even on their prey. Rather,
he watched the little hamlet of Grolanhei, part of his
personal domain as one of the tax gatherers for the emir-
ate of Kitznen.

Grolanhei did *not* have an arms dealer.

*All my little helpless rabbits,* Rashid thought. *All you
disgusting filthy* Nazrani *are my prey.*

As light skinned and blue eyed as the wretched here-
tics that peopled the town, still Rashid more resembled
his hawks than he did them. His eyes were bright, keen
and avaricious; his nose a beak jutting from his face.
Inside, too, he resembled a hawk, all fierce and selfish
appetite, all blood-lust and drive to dominate.

Every year, at tax time, Rashid made sure to collect a
few children in lieu of the taxes he deliberately set too
high. He received a direct bounty from the *bundejaysh*,

the army, for the boys he collected for the Corps of Janissaries. The girls went on the market to whosoever might want a female child for service. Sometimes that service was domestic. Other girls, especially the prettiest ones, could be sold for other purposes.

*But the bastard* Nazrani *hide their women and girls now,* Rashid mentally cursed. *It's become altogether too difficult to tell which of their little bitches might fetch a decent price. Shameful for them to pervert the law like that. Bastards.*

"Stop being such a *girl*, Petra," the young boy said to his sister as the two watched the bird of prey swoop and strike.

Petra bint Minden, aged six, had shuddered at the swooping hawk's cry. She shuddered again, shielding her eyes with tiny hands, as the hare screamed out in pain and terror. Barely, she forced her fingers apart to see the eagle carry off its limp and bloody prey. Again she shuddered, pleased that *she* was not so small as to be the prey of a raptor.

Petra felt her brother tug at her arm. His voice commanded, "Come *on*. The masters are coming. And we're almost late for school."

Turning away from the pasture where the eagle had struck, Petra followed after her brother on little legs. It was hard to keep up, what with the enveloping cloth sack the girl wore that covered her from head to heel. The covering was whole, though her mother had spent long hours patching and mending it. For it wasn't the law that required Petra to be so enclosed; she was too young for it to matter.

Rather, she wore the burka at her mother's insistence. As the mother had said, "Some of the masters take a long view of things. You're a beautiful child, Petra, though you're too young to know what that means. Even so, no sense in letting them see you and put you on a list for when you've turned nine."

Behind her, Petra heard a horse neigh, the sound echoed by several more of them. Turning quickly, she spied a group of three riding across the bare and open field. Two held their arms out, she saw, as another twirled something overhead. Two great hunting birds came to rest on the outstretched arms, one of them bearing the corpse of the hare. Petra knew they must be from the masters; *Nazrani* weren't allowed to ride horseback.

"Come along, Petra," insisted her older brother, Hans. Hans was nine, big for his age and strong. He was her protector and the hero of Petra's existence. Like his sister, the boy was blond with bright blue eyes. Folk of the town were already whispering that he was sure to be gathered for the janissaries within a few years. Unlike their father, Hans was too young to have the bowed back of the *dhimmi*, those who submitted by treaty to the rule of the masters, their taxes, and their laws.

There were several *orta* of janissaries in the old al Harv barracks set roughly between the town of Grolanhei and the larger one of Kitznen. They sometimes came to the smaller town to drink forbidden beer or make use of the town's dozen or so whores. (For the janissaries were well disciplined and rarely indulged in rape.) Petra found their black uniforms with silver insignia strangely compelling.

"Come along," Hans commanded again, grabbing her by her arm and pulling her back to the town that edged the open field. "We don't want them to notice us."

Bad things, so it was whispered, sometimes happened to blond and blue-eyed children who attracted the notice of the masters. Petra shuddered again and followed her brother, stopping only once more to turn and peer at the magnificent horsemen.

The way to school, up the cobblestoned Haupstrasse, led past a fountain and a crumbling monument, a painted wall, which listed the names of the town's war dead going back centuries. No names had been added to the monument in over one hundred and fifty years. Few of those old names were visible now. The picture, painted on a wall over the town fountain, was of an angel lifting a fallen soldier to Heaven. It was part of the back of the Catholic church. As such, under the rules of protection imposed by the masters, the treaty of *dhimmitude*, neither it, nor the church, could be repaired.

It didn't really matter anyway. Petra couldn't read yet, though Hans was trying to teach her, no matter that the law forbade it. Left to the masters she would never learn to read. She was, after all, a mere female. In their view, her ultimate value was in her body, in the pleasure it might someday bring to a man, in the household work she would do, and in the children she would bear. For all practical purposes, she—like virtually all the females of the Caliphate, to include the Moslem ones—was considered to be not much more than a donkey who could speak and bear children.

Instead, her school taught her only basic theology—to include, by law, a theology not her own—and homemaking, as well as the rules under which she must live out her life. That last was a part of that theology not her own.

As she had nearly every day since she had learned to walk, Petra looked without understanding at the wretched and abandoned memorial, then turned and

continued on her way. She expressly did not look across
the street from the monument to the crude wooden gallows where the remains of two teenaged boys swung in
the breeze by ropes around their stretched necks. The
boys were dressed in girls' clothing, minus the hijab.

Petra had known both boys. Their names were—had
been— Martin Müller and Ernst Ackermann. She, like
the other women and girls of the town, had cried when
the masters took the boys and hanged them before the
crowd last Sunday after church. The dry-eyed Catholic
priest had stood by and blessed the masters' work. The
boys would sway there, if history was a guide, until the
following Sunday, just before church. (For while the
masters had firm rules for the timing of the burial of
their own dead, *Nazrani* bodies could be left unburied
for educational reasons.)

Petra remembered the pleading as the executioner
had forced the boys onto the stools under the gallows'
crosspiece, the tears on the boys' faces as they were
noosed and then the flailing legs, the eyes bugging and
the tongues swelling out past blackening lips. That's why
she couldn't look; she remembered it too well.

She didn't know why the boys had been executed.
They'd always seemed very nice to her, especially nice
in comparison to most of the other boys of the town, her
Hans, only, excepted. After the hanging, all the girls had
agreed that, among a pretty rowdy lot, those two had
been much kinder and more decent to them than were
any of the other boys of the town. Indeed, they'd been so
sweet that they might almost have been girls themselves.

There was too much in the world that Petra really
didn't understand. Shaking her head, she followed her
brother to the small schoolhouse where she would spend

half her day before hurrying home to help mother with the daily chores.

At the schoolhouse, Petra and Hans split up, he going in by the front door, she walking around back to the girls' entrance. Inside, she doffed her coat and her confining burka, hung them on her own peg, and walked into the classroom. A set of solid and pretty much soundproof walls separated the girls, all in one room, from the boy's seven classes. That was not so bad, really. Though the classroom was overcrowded, a little, education for girls wasn't mandatory and so there were only about a fifth as many girls in the school as boys.

Sister Margarete, the sole teacher for the girls of the town, was old enough to have learned to read as a girl herself. What would happen to the girls, once she died, the nun didn't know. The masters had granted the church a local exemption to the strictures against educating Christian females, but it was at best a partial and limited exemption. Margarete didn't know if it stretched enough to provide a replacement for herself once she'd gone to her final reward.

Tapping a wooden pointer on the podium, Sister Margarete directed the girls to sit, then began with a review of the previous day's lesson:

"We must pay the *jizya* . . . we must submit to the Sharia . . . Slavery is a part of *jihad* and *jihad* a part of Islam . . . we must cover ourselves in accordance with the Sharia . . . We must submit to our fathers and husbands or any other masters the Almighty may decree for us . . . No one not of the True Faith may ride a horse or an automobile, except at the order of one of the faithful . . ." Petra knew what an automobile was but had only seen one occasionally in her life. She knew no one who had ever ridden one. . . . "No Christian may live in a house better, larger or higher than any lived in by a Moslem . . . In a court of Sharia a Christian's testimony" —Petra wasn't too sure what "testimony" meant—"counts for only half that of a Moslem, and a woman's for only half a man's. . . . No Christian or Jew"—Petra had no clue what a Jew was, either—"may possess a weapon . . . If the masters demand silver we must humbly offer gold . . . If a master wishes to fill our mouths with dirt we must open them to receive it . . . "

Along with the others, Petra recited. Like the other young girls, she didn't understand more than half of what she recited meant. Maybe it would come in time; she knew she was only six and that older people understood more than she did. Besides, her town was entirely Catholic, for the most part ruling itself. The Moslems all lived far away in the provincial capital of Kitznen or with the janissaries at the barracks of al Harv.

"Okay, children, school's over," announced Sister Margerete as she stood near the door. "You older girls, don't forget your burkas. Though you are not of the masters still you are subject to the same rules as the Moslem women."

This only made sense. How, after all, was one of the masters to have any peace at home if the shameless Christian hussies had more privileges than their own wives and daughters? Even many of the younger girls, such as Petra, wore burkas for the same reasons Petra's mother had for forcing it on her daughter.

School got out early. School, for girls, *always* got out early. After all, most of what they needed to know in this year of someone else's Lord, 1527, they would learn better at their mothers' knees than in a school. Pulling on her gray covering, Petra filed out with the other girls. Since Hans would be several hours more, Petra walked home alone. She took back streets, dirty and muddy, rather than the cobblestoned main street. That way she didn't have to walk by the swaying and soon to be rotting bodies of Martin and Ernst.

As she walked, Petra chanced to look to her right, out into the open fields. A small herd of goats was out there, property of one of the masters in Kitznen, no doubt. The goats were eating the shoots from a field of barley.

# Imperial Military Academy, West Point, New York, 26 March, 2106

"Knock it off on the Area!" the corporal bellowed. Immediately, some fifty-odd stamping cadets took themselves out of step and ceased their illicit, cadenced marching on the asphalt. Hours were punishment, to be walked alone and not marched as a group.

*Fun while it lasted, for some constrained values of "fun,"* thought the gray-clad, overcoated, white-crossbelted, biochemistry major and Cadet First Classman John Hamilton. (Hamilton, despite being a first classman, was also Cadet *Private*, but that was a different story, an altogether sadder story, involving an illicit tryst in a little-used alcove down in the Sinks.)

Hamilton was a native of Maine. He'd had an ancestor, as a matter of fact, in the famous 20th Maine, during the Civil War—a Canadian who'd come south from New Brunswick to enlist and decided to stay on after the war. (Though one couldn't tell from his color or his eyes, he'd also had an ancestor from Toronto who'd enlisted in Company G of the equally famous 54th Massachusetts. That might have accounted for the wave in his hair.) For more than four centuries, in every generation that was called, Hamilton's generations had answered. He'd answered, too.

Coming to a halt a few yards from the stone wall of Bradley Barracks, Hamilton transferred his rifle—now, in an exercise in deliberate anachronism, a reproduction Model 1861 Springfield—from one shoulder to the other, turned about, and began walking in the other direction.

Already, Hamilton could hear the plaintive cries of "Odinnn!" arising from the surrounding barracks to echo off the stone walls.

Much like the empire it supported and defended, the school had grown considerably from its rather humble beginnings. For example, while its first class, that of 1806, had graduated and commissioned fifteen cadets, the current class, that of 2106, was more than one hundred times greater. The Class of 2106 was expected to send forth some fifteen hundred and twenty-seven newly commissioned second lieutenants, or roughly one-fortieth of all new officers accessed by the Army in this year.

*Or*, thought the gray-clad Cadet John Hamilton, as he paced off his four hundred and seventy-seventh hour of punishment tours, *One—thousand, five hundred and twenty-six if I get too many more demerits. I must be a shoo-in for the Martinez Award by now. If, that is, I don't get found*—booted from the Academy—*on demerits.*

As West Point traditions went, the Martinez Award was, at about one hundred years since founding, relatively new. Like being the goat—the last ranking man or woman of the class—it was a distinction not avidly sought. Still, there had been a fair number of general officers who had, in their time, been recipients of the award, just as there had been through history a fair number of goats who rose to stars, George Edward Pickett (1849) and George Armstrong Custer (1861) being neither the least significant nor the most successful among them.

Hamilton, though, wasn't interested in stars. He wasn't really all that interested in the Army, certainly not as a career. If he ever had been, the Imperial Military Academy had knocked such ambition out of him. Instead, he saw it as a way to pay for school and to serve out his mandatory service obligation. Whether that service would see him on the coasts of the Empire's British allies, more or less comfortably, if chillily, watching the Moslem janissaries across the Channel, or hunting *Luminosos* or *Bolivanos* in the mountains or jungles of the South American Territories, or policing the Philippine Islands, or any of the dozens of other places across the globe where the Empire held or fought for sway, he couldn't predict.

*Anything, Lord, anything but freezing my balls off hunting Canadians in northern Quebec or Ontario,* please. *I'm too tall and skinny for the cold. Even Chechnya on the exchange program would be better.*

"Ooodddiiinnn!" sounded again from out the barracks windows.

Hamilton already had his branch assignment, infantry. Yet he lacked for a unit assignment still, and that must depend on the latest casualty figures and some schooling. As a matter of fact, he wouldn't find out his first assignment until he graduated Ranger School—assuming he did, of course; many did not—just before reporting in for the Basic Course at either Fort Benning (Light Infantry and Suited Heavy Infantry Officers Basic Course) or Fort Bliss (Mechanized Infantry Officer Basic Course) or Fort Stewart (Constabulary Infantry Officers Basic Course). And even then it might change if casualties in, say, Mindanao suddenly soared.

*And the casualty lists are never short,* Hamilton mused. *They never have been; not in my lifetime, anyway.* He stopped, again facing a stone wall, then transferred his rifle and executed an about face. *Then again, when you've got a population of your own in excess of five hundred million, and control more than another billion, what's a few thousand a month? Except that one of them, sometime in the next five years, might be me. Oh, well . . . buy your ticket and take your chances. And it isn't as if we've a lot of choice about fighting. Maybe once we had that kind of choice. Not anymore.*

Hamilton took a surreptitious glance overhead. Yes, clouds were gathering. The prayers were working. *Perhaps no parade tomorrow.*

"OOODDDIIINNN!"

One of the nice things about walking hours in the Area was that it gave one time to think, though the weather could sometimes be all that one was able to think about. Weather permitting though, and today was merely brisk rather than outright miserable, one could really do some interior soul searching and reflection. Hamilton wondered, sometimes, if he didn't court demerits just so he could have that time alone.

*I wonder what it was really like here, before the Empire. The histories don't discuss it much, beyond showing the before and after pictures of Los Angeles, Boston, and Kansas City. I've read the Constitution, all through the Thirty-Sixth Amendment, but the words don't really give me a feel for what it was like back then. Different . . . it must have been different. Did Free Speech really mean people were free to criticize the wars of defense? To protest them in public? Did Freedom of Religion accept even the enemy here? Well, that was before the Three Cities. Was military service really voluntary? For everybody? How the Hell could they maintain the hundred divisions we need that way? Then again, did we need a hundred divisions the old way? But after we were hit here, did we have any choice, really?*

Despite being at war, and having been at war—even if it wasn't always recognized as such—for over a century, the emphasis at the IMA was still more on "Academy" than on "Military." Even so, there was a fair amount of military training, some practical, some theoretical. Hamilton had signed up for several practical electives over the last two academic years. One of these was "The Fighting Suit," the basic equipage of the Suited Heavy Infantry. (And, yes, when Hamilton had been the roughly four-millionth to publicly note the convenient acronym that came along with Suited Heavy Infantry Troops, he'd been slugged with a whopping forty hours of walking the Area.)

In any case, the Exo wasn't really a suit, not in the sense that it covered its wearer completely. Rather, it was an exoskeleton to which some considerable degree of armor protection could be added, at a cost in speed, range and supplies carried.

"Remember, it's not a cure-all," the sergeant-instructor, Master Sergeant Webster, had told the cadets the first day of class. Grizzled and old, Webster was the color of strong coffee. He was, so far as Hamilton could tell, the platonic ideal of a noncommissioned officer as such existed in the mind of God: tough, dedicated, no nonsense, and with just enough sense of humor to be, or at least *seem*, human.

"The suit is a bludgeon, not a rapier. It can get you to the objective," Webster had added. "It can get you there reasonably fresh and well supplied, but without much armor. Or it can get you across the objective, with full armor and reduced supply. Or it can do both if, and only if, something else carries you to near the objective.

"It's also a guarantee that, if you wear it while setting up an ambush somewhere in the Caucasus, the enemy will smell it from a mile away and never come near you. So why bother? And if you think you can use it for a recon patrol, I'll also guarantee you that the enemy will *hear* it from half a mile away. So why bother?"

"Because with full armor and a winterizing pack it will keep me warm while hunting Canadian rebels in Northern Ontario?" Hamilton had suggested, one inquisitive finger in the air.

"Mister Hamilton," Sergeant Webster had answered, "there is no such thing as a 'Canadian.' There are Americans. Then there are imperial subjects. There are also rebels, allies, and enemies. *No* Canadians, however. Write yourself up for an eight and four: minor lack of judgment."

*Story of my life*, Hamilton thought. *Ask a question; get some time in the Area. Try to think and—*

The thought was interrupted by the Area sergeant. "Attention on the Area. The hour is over. Fall out and fall in on your company areas."

Young Cadet John Hamilton, and many another, hastened to get on with something that passed for a more normal and fruitful life.

*Why the fuck didn't I apply to Annapolis? I love boats. I grew up around boats. But nooo. Family tradition was Army and so I just had to follow along. Jackass.*

"What will kill or take out an exoskeleton?" Webster asked rhetorically, after the class had taken seats. His finger pointed, "Mr. Hamilton?"

"Kill the man wearing it, Sergeant."

"How? Ms. Hodge."

That cadet, cute, strawberry blonde and—Hamilton reluctantly admitted—probably tougher than he was, answered. "Without armor, Master Sergeant, shooting the wearer in a vital organ is sufficient. Assuming armor is worn, however, the armor can be penetrated by a .41-caliber or better uranium or tungsten discarding sabot projectile. The joints are subject to derangement by large explosive devices or near-impacting heavy artillery or mortar fire. The power pack can similarly be fractured or penetrated. This will also contaminate the exoskeleton such that it cannot again be worn short of depot level decontamination. If the enemy is very clever, and the situation on the ground very bad, it can be worn out of power—"

"At which point," Webster interrupted, "you will have made a present of some very expensive gear to some very bad people. Very good, Cadet Hodge."

Hamilton leaned over and whispered in Hodge's ear, "Ass kisser."

"Better his than yours," Hodge whispered back. "*He* probably washes."

Webster, more amused than anything, let the byplay go without comment. He continued with the lesson, "The point is, however, that almost anything that will kill you in your bare skin *can* kill you while wearing the exoskeleton, even with maximum armor. It's just harder to do.

"However, unlike armored personnel carriers and infantry fighting vehicles, the Exo allows the member of a unit to take maximum advantage of small bits of cover and concealment. It does not, individually, present as tempting and lucrative a target as a tracked vehicle carrying nine to twelve men. This is true even though at half a million IND"—Imperial New Dollars—"each, nine Exos cost slightly more than one infantry fighting vehicle. Men are not potatoes, after all. Their lives matter."

Webster noticed Hodge fidgeting in her chair. "You had a question, Ms. Hodge?"

"Not a question, Master Sergeant, just an observation. Whatever the cost, whatever the risks and whatever the downsides, the Exo makes sense for me because I'm a woman. Nothing else allows me to be a full equal of men in combat."

"Not quite, Ms. Hodge," Webster corrected. "Because you're the bottleneck . . . not you, personally; I mean women are the bottleneck . . . in the production of the next generation, the Exo cannot *reduce* your overall value to that of a man."

"God knows, *I* value you, sweetie," Hamilton said, no longer in a whisper but at least *sotto voce*.

Webster's voice thundered, "Mr. Hamilton, write yourself up for another eight and four: public display of affection."

## Grolanhei, Province of Affrankon, 2 Shawwal, 1530 AH (1 October, 2106)

"*Jizya!*" demanded Rashid, the tax gatherer, his fist pounding the old oaken table in the Minden's kitchen. But for his beak of a nose, the gatherer did not look noticeably different from the *Nazranis*. Rashid's ancestors had converted early and then married into the dominant group.

"But, sir," Petra's father began to explain, "the harvest has been bad this year. The early frost . . . the rain . . . "

"Silence, pig of an infidel!" The *jizya* is a head tax. It is flat. It is fixed." *Fixed by me.* "It makes no account of the piddling troubles Allah sends you filth to encourage you to give up your decayed and false faith."

Seeing that Minden was still minded to dispute the collection, the tax gatherer's lip curled in a sneer. Cutting off further discussion, he said, "You realize, do you not, that the *jizya* is what permits you the status of *dhimmis*? That without it, without the pact, the *dhimma*, we are in a state of war, of holy war, of *jihad* with you and yours? That your lives are forfeit? Your property forfeit?"

"But . . . please, sir . . . "

Being inside the walls of her own home, Petra was uncovered. Neither she, nor her·mother, had anticipated the arrival of the taxman today. Indeed, they'd all been so distraught and overworked with the gathering of the very skimpy harvest, they'd not thought of much of anything but how they were going to eke out an existence over the winter. They had to hope others had had better luck this year. If it was a question of letting the *Nazrani* farmers eat, or taking the food to feed their own, the masters had no compunction about letting filthy *Nazrani* starve.

Though only nine, and though she feared hunger as much as the next, Petra was ashamed to see her father beg. She was ashamed of his *dhimmi* status, now that she'd grown and learned enough to understand what that meant. She was ashamed of her people who submitted to this humiliation. And, when the tax gatherer looked over at her—more accurately, so she saw, looked her over—she was ashamed of herself. She remembered something Sister Margerete had told her class:

"Mohammad consummated his marriage with his favorite wife, Aisha, when she was nine years old."

Petra hadn't quite understood what "consummated" meant.

"Mark down the boy for gathering to the janissaries," Rashid told the chief of his four guards. "Take the girl now.

"And next year, you filthy swine, when I come for our taxes and demand silver, you had best give me gold or you'll see yourselves joining your daughter on the auction block."

One of Rashid's guards went to Petra. He took handcuffs and a chain from a pouch that hung at his side. The cuffs he ratcheted shut around her wrists, tightly enough to make her wince. The chain he attached to the cuffs.

Hans lunged. "Get your hands off my sister!"

The guard with Petra ignored the boy; that's what the other guard was for. That other guard caught Hans halfway through his lunge, wrapping one arm around the boy's waist. He then put Hans' feet back on the floor, stood and slapped him across the face several times, hard enough to stun and draw blood. The guard then knocked the boy down as his mother wailed and his stoop-shouldered father hung his head in helpless shame.

Petra, who had begun to cry when the cuffs were put on her, screamed when she saw her brother hurt. A slap from Rashid—hard enough to hurt without damaging the merchandise—quieted her.

She was sobbing as they led her away for her first ride in an automobile.

A crowd gathered outside the Minden's hovel, curious but too frightened to help. After all, what help could they give in a country no longer their own?

# Interlude

Kitzingen, Federal Republic of Germany,
9 April, 2003

"No blood for oil! No blood for oil!"

It wasn't a huge crowd, gathered under the crooked-topped tower that was the town's most well-known symbol and landmark. No larger than one might expect in a small city like Kitzingen, the crowd, a mixture of Germans and Moslem guest workers and residents, legal or otherwise, chanted, "No to war . . . no war for oil . . . "

Of the Germans, some were principled pacifists, some leftists of various stripes. Some were just young boys gravitating to young girls. Of the Moslems, few if any had any connection to terrorism. They did, of course, have some connection to their fellow Moslems, wherever they might live. And some of those fellow Moslems had been and were plainly on the target list for the armed forces of the United States.

The television cameras ate it up.

The demonstrators had been more enthusiastic earlier in the year, back when it had still seemed possible to dissuade the United States from the illegal, immoral, imperialist venture its despised President seemed set on. That possibility had proved illusory.

Today was a particularly unpleasant one for them as all the newspapers were carrying photographs of the American military helping a less passive crowd in Baghdad pull down a giant statue of the dictator, Saddam Hussein. Most of the crowd found the pictures, as they found the easy American success and the Iraqis' rapturous welcome, "annoying."

Gabrielle von Minden was annoyed, certainly. She stood in the snowy cold of an early German spring holding a protest sign. It wasn't the cold that annoyed her though. Rather, like the rest of the crowd, what annoyed, or infuriated, was that their best hopes for an Anglo-American defeat in Iraq had been blighted. It was just so . . . *unfair*. Bastard Americans. How she hated those arrogant bastards.

*No, that's not true,* she corrected herself. *I hate their government and the power they wield. The Americans I've known, even the soldiers, were mostly pretty nice people. I mustn't forget that; it is a government and a set of policies I loathe. I must not ever let myself begin to loathe an entire people.*

That said, or thought, Gabrielle didn't feel the need for restraint in her message of protest. Lifting her sign high and waving it, she increased the volume of her chant, *"Kein Blut für Oel. Kein Blut für Oel. Kein Blut . . . "*

Later, chilled to the bone and shivering, Gabrielle and several friends repaired to a nearby coffee shop. It seemed like half the protestors had had the same idea. It was not a large coffee shop and still it held them all easily. That, too, was a little annoying.

*Ah, well,* Gabrielle thought, *maybe I can't save the world but at least I can try.*

She smiled up at the waiter, a handsome, olive-skinned boy about her own age, and gave her order. "And please, might I have some cognac in the coffee?"

"Will Asbach-Uralt do, miss?" the waiter asked.

"Wonderfully," Gabi answered.

Mahmoud didn't feel any of the irritation many of his co-religionists might have felt at being asked to serve alcohol. His Islam was pretty nominal. In fact he was known to take a drink himself from time to time.

And why not? He'd *come* to Germany to escape from Islam.

"Surely then, miss," he answered, returning her smile. "Right away."

Gabrielle looked at the waiter, saw that his name tag read, "Mahmoud," and thought, *Yum.*

# CHAPTER TWO

"They [those who claim Islam is against slavery] are merely writers. They are ignorant, not scholars . . . Whoever says such things is an infidel. Slavery is a part of Islam. Slavery is part of jihad, and jihad will remain as long there is Islam."

> —Sheik Saleh Al-Fawzan, Saudi cleric, author of the bestselling textbook, *al Tawheed* (Monotheism) and imam of the Prince Mataeb Mosque, Riyadh, 2003 (circa 1423 AH)

Kitznen, Province of Affrankon, 4 Shawwal, 1530 AH (3 October, 2106)

"Nobody's going to bid on a crying girl," the auctioneer-*cum*-slave dealer said to Petra, lifting her chin with the quirt he'd carried for so long he was hardly aware of it as anything but an extension of his right hand. "Or, at least, nobody you would *want* to bid on you. Do you understand me, girl?"

Lips crinkling and quivering with deepest sorrow, Petra sniffed and rubbed at her face, trying to push back the tears. She nodded her head three or four times, briskly, and answered, "I'll . . . try. But I miss my *famileee.*" The last word ended in a wail that Petra, herself, cut off abruptly. "I'll try," she said.

The auctioneer smiled at her and answered her nod with one of his own. He'd seen it so many times before. *And yet slaves must come from somewhere. They don't replace themselves, generally. This child, at least, has a chance of finding a* reasonably *happy position. How much worse for the ones who are older, the ones over nine?*

"That's a good girl," he said. "I'll tell you what; let's make a deal. If you can stop crying I'll do my best to get you into a decent family that won't make you work too hard and won't beat you. And—" the auctioneer reached into a pocket of his robe and pulled out a bar of *halawa*, waving it slightly under Petra's nose—"if you'll show me how well you can smile, I'll give you this."

Petra hadn't been fed since being taken from her family. Though the slaves were watered, feeding slaves who weren't expected to be here in the stables long was something of a wasted and unnecessary expense. She licked her lips at the sight of the bar of honey-sweetened, crushed sesame.

"Can you smile for me?"

Slowly, and with difficulty, Petra forced her face into something that was approximately a smile.

"There's a good girl!" the auctioneer congratulated, patting her gently on the head. He took her little hand in his own larger one and placed the sweet in it. "Here, this may help you keep that pretty smile."

"What's the reserve on this one?"

The speaker was a Moslem, Abdul Mohsem, a man, a merchant, in his late thirties, with a substantial roll of prosperity-born fat about his middle. Stealing a glance upward from where she knelt on the straw of her cell, Petra thought he looked kindly, despite the rifle slung across his back.

Few of the *Nazrani* in the province even had the wherewithal to buy a slave. Fewer still were interested, though some were, notably the brothel keepers. These sometimes took a chance on a pretty girl, even if she was still far too young to put to service. Abdul Mohsem knew this, and hated the idea.

True to his word, the slave dealer had sought out a decent family for the girl. Indeed, he'd sought out the most decent patriarch he knew in the community.

"Ten gold dinar," the slaver answered, then, seeing that Adbul didn't blanch, added, "plus twenty silver dirhem."

Abdul Mohsem scowled, inducing the dealer to further amend, "But for you, just ten gold dinar."

"Ten gold dinar seems fair," Abdul said, "but I wasn't scowling over the price; I was scowling over the fact."

"The fact?"

"Facts, actually. One, that we sell young girls and, two, that if I don't buy this one she'll end up in a brothel."

"It is not for us to forbid what Allah permits," answered the dealer, who considered himself, not without reason, to be a pious man.

"Neither does Allah *require* of us everything that he permits," observed Abdul Mohsem, still scowling.

To that the dealer shrugged. It was not for him to question the words or the workings of the Almighty. "Do you want the girl or not?" he asked.

Without answering, Abdul Mohsem knelt down and pushed aside Petra's long blond hair. With his thumb he brushed off a smudge on the girl's cheek.

"Would you like to come home with me, and become a companion to my daughter, Besma?" he asked, smiling.

Shyly and fearfully, forcing a smile, Petra nodded.

"Be happier, girl," Abdul chided. "We'll not work you too hard, nor force you to give up your faith. And my Besma is sweet, if maybe a little too strong-willed. You'll like her. And it's better than the alternative."

Of that, Petra had little doubt, even if she was hazy on the details.

Leading Petra by the hand, Adbul Mohsem brought her through the Marktplatz, past a dozen or so tables where men chatted while sipping at thick Turkish coffee. Ultimately they arrived at a large house guarded by a doorkeeper in one of the town's better residential neighborhoods.

The doorkeeper nodded respectfully at Abdul Mohsem, smiled down at the girl, and then held the heavy oaken door open for them. Abdul Mohsem's was a happy household; smiles were not rare.

"Besma!" the patriarch called, "Besma, light of my life and pearl of my heart, come here."

Petra heard the pitter-patter of feet little or no larger than her own, coming down a hallway to the expansive foyer in which she stood with her new master. She soon caught sight of a girl, about her own size if a little older, very pretty with huge brown eyes and slightly olive skin. The girl's smile was brilliant, and why not? "Besma" meant "smile."

Besma took one look at Petra and began to dance around the foyer, shouting, "Oh! Oh! Oh! Oh, Father, a *friend* for me! Oh, she's beautiful; she's wonderful! And I've been so *lonely*. Thank you! Thank you! *Thank you!*"

Seeing Besma jumping and twisting in the air, her feet kicking lightly, set Petra to laughing, shyly at first but growing with each new step, leap, twist and kick. Finally, worried that she might offend, she covered her mouth and forced herself to seriousness, pushing her chin down to her chest.

Besma, however, was having none of *that*. She stopped her dancing, walked over to Petra and took her by the hand. "I only have one sister," the Moslem girl said, "Aisha. And she's a lot older than me, with her own family now. I miss having a sister at home. Will you be like my sister?"

## Fort Benning, Georgia, 5 October, 2106

Cars were no longer a matter of right for an American. Between the strains of the war, the taxes, the limits on gaseous and liquid fuel and the priority the military had on it, not all Americans could afford an automobile. Of those who could, not all were permitted to own one. The country had changed in many ways over the last ninety years, and many of those changes were not for the better.

As a military officer, Hamilton was in the privileged class. He *could* have a car. He was allowed to have one, though, not for his own pleasure and convenience.

Rather, he was allowed to have one to take care of military business at personal expense and to ensure he could make it in to his unit in the event of an alert.

The car drove itself, leaving Hamilton free to interlace the fingers of both hands between his head and the headrest, and simply to relax. After the last couple of months, relaxation was something he would never take for granted again.

The car—it was a two-seat, multifuel job made down in Guadalajara to a Japanese design—left the strong smell of overdone french fries behind it.

"Building Four coming up on the left," the vehicle announced.

Hamilton glanced leftward out the window and smirked at the bronze statue in front of the main academic building on the post. The building dated back to 1964 and had seen many renovations in its time. The last one had, with something less than full success, attempted to make the thing match the more tasteful architecture of the Infantry Center's early days, all stucco and red tile.

The statue, bronze and about as old as the building, was of a lieutenant in the act of leading his men forward. The lieutenant wore a helmet of a design obsolete more than a century past. One hand gripped an even older style rifle while the other gestured onward, poised forever at about neck level.

"I've had this shit up to here, too, buddy," Hamilton whispered.

He'd graduated from the Imperial Military Academy, though it had been touch and go the last month, with most of his free time spent walking off his myriad sins. He'd won the Martinez Award, too, as everyone had predicted. Then, to everyone's shock, Hamilton had finished Ranger School as the Distinguished Honor Graduate. This was no mean feat in a class that size or with competition that fierce. As such, under the regulations, he'd had his choice of branch and chosen Suited Heavy Infantry. He *really* didn't want to freeze his ass off hunting the northern rebels he still—punishment tours or not— thought of as *Canadians.*

On the other hand, Hamilton had lost forty pounds in the school, half wrecked his health, and damaged both knees. Fortunately, he'd done non-suited jump school a couple of years prior. Otherwise, he thought, he'd probably not have made it. His knees really were a mess and five hundred deep knee bends followed by a five- to seven-mile run were not a formula for success.

*Fortunately, suits don't jump as a rule. Better, they take a load off my ever-so-fucked up knees.*

On its own, the car queried the nearby parking lots and determined that there was a spot reasonably convenient to the building's main entrance. It sent out the signal to claim the spot, then turned left, left again, then right and entered the lot. On its own, it parked, raising the "driver" side door and shutting down the engine. It would secure itself once Hamilton had exited.

Taking only his government issue Mark XVII tactical handheld with him—the thing was light and only seven millimeters by twenty by twenty centimeters, EMP hardened and with holographic screen and virtual keyboard—Hamilton walked as briskly as sore knees would permit from the lot, around the building, and in through the flag-flanked main entrance.

There he was met by a sergeant first class sitting at a desk. The sergeant held out one hand and requested, "Orders, please, sir."

Hamilton reached into a breast pocket then withdrew and passed over an identity card. This the sergeant laid down on a gray-colored panel. Instantly a scaled-down picture of Hamilton appeared above the gray pad, flanked by various copies of orders on one side, and disciplinary and academic records on the other.

"Ohhh," the sergeant said. "*You're* the Martinez Award winner. We've heard all *about* you, sir."

Hamilton sighed. *Make DHG out of Ranger School and nobody cares. Set a record for walking the Area and nobody forgets.*

"Yeah, that was me, Sergeant."

The sergeant—Hamilton saw that his name was Moore—stood and held out his hand. "Sir, if you don't mind, I'd like to shake your hand. I figure nobody who hasn't got what it takes could piss off that many people and still graduate from the IMA."

Flattered, Hamilton shook Moore's hand, but countered, "It isn't like I pissed all those people off deliberately, Sergeant."

"I know, sir. I'm sure you didn't. But when a man has a talent like yours . . . well . . . that talent is just gonna shine through.

"Computer," Moore said.

"Yes, Sergeant Moore?" the machine answered.

"Log this officer in. Do we have his billet?"

"Lieutenant Hamilton is assigned to Room 217, Olson Hall, Sergeant. It is a single with a private bath and maid service. The room has been notified to admit him. His inprocessing schedule has been downloaded to his Mark XVII, along with the academic schedule for the first two weeks."

"Only two weeks?" Hamilton asked.

The sergeant shrugged. "Sir . . . this isn't the IMA or even Ranger School where everything goes right pretty much all the time. This is the Regular Army and if you can follow a plan for ten days you're doing pretty well. Two weeks is actually pretty optimistic."

"But . . ."

"War is chaos, sir, and we practice chaos every day. That's *our* unique talent."

Back in the car, Hamilton let it drive again. Though he'd been at Benning for two months now, all that time had been in Ranger School. He didn't know his way around.

This was wise, letting the car drive. There's no particular and necessary logic to the way the military designates buildings, fields, ranges and such. Sometimes they have both names and numbers; other times not. Sometimes, they're numbered in accord with when they were built. Sometimes they *were* so numbered, but the numbers were changed. Sometimes they're numbered by blocks. The names can change to suck up to the latest political figure or general officer.

Most of the time, you're doing well if "Building 398" and "Building 399" are within a mile of each other. *Chaos: it's what's for breakfast.*

Olson Hall, an old barracks used for the last century and a half as a bachelor officers quarters, or BOQ, had somehow kept its number, Building 399, for well over a century. Where Building 4, the main academic building, had had a facelift that didn't quite take, Olson Hall still reflected the look of solid military efficiency it had been born with. Brick, built in a quadrangle open to the west, the living space was stretched around broad interior-facing, railed walkways. The only elevator was industrial, not passenger; those lazy lieutenants could just walk upstairs.

*Which is fine,* Hamilton agreed, as he trudged up the broad concrete steps carrying *four* bags full of uniforms and the minimum necessary other gear, *a little exercise never hurt anybody . . . but my fucking knees are killing me.*

Arriving at the second floor, Hamilton's nose was assailed by a mix of esoteric foodstuffs in preparation mixed in with the marginally washed bodies of some of the sepoy officers—foreigners selected to lead some of the empire's foreign volunteers—who trained at Benning. These sort were often quite good, Hamilton understood. Some said that their ideas of personal hygiene did not always match those of the American citizen officers among whom they were billeted. More objective sources had told Hamilton that people with different diets will smell different, no matter their personal hygiene habits.

There were enough breakable objects in the bags that just dropping them was a poor idea. Instead, he bent at the waist and the knees to lower the two handheld ones to the concrete. Then, straightening—*ouch*—he reached up and lifted the third. This one he'd had balanced on the back-borne fourth and held steady with the pressure of his head. After lifting it overhead, he placed it, too, on the deck. The last (and curiously enough the Army was still issuing green duffle bags with shoulder straps) he took off one strap at a time.

His other personal belongings, books, dress uniforms and such, would arrive sometime in the next few days. He'd have to call to arrange a drop off and authorize the room to accept it.

"Welcome, Lieutenant Hamilton, to Olson Hall," said the room. "If you would place your palm on the gray panel to the right of the door and look with both eyes directly into the scanner above and to the left of that . . . "

As the palm and retinal scanner recorded and verified his identity, Hamilton heard a familiar feminine voice say, "About time you showed up."

"Hodge, you look like hell," Hamilton said, as the two sat at a table down in the bar just off the lobby of Olson Hall. "Your skin's a mess. You've lost what? Twenty pounds?"

"Twenty-five. And you think you look any better? They starved you worse than they did me."

"True," he agreed, "but not for as long. And it doesn't matter if *my* tits disappeared. I didn't have any to begin with."

"Never mind," she said, tilting her glass towards him. "They'll grow back. And drink up. I'll start looking better, I promise." She tilted her head to one side. "Did I ever tell you you're an asshole?" she asked.

"Many times."

"Did I ever tell you that you're a *cute* asshole?"

## Kitznin, Affrankon, 5 Shawwal, 1530 AH (4 October, 2106)

Besma was awakened by crying. Worse than crying, really; what she heard was a brokenhearted sobbing severe enough to shake her little bed. Tossing the covers off, she put her feet on the floor and walked on cat feet to the source, an even smaller bed at the foot of her own.

"Petra, are you all right?" she asked. The sobbing grew, if anything, worse.

"I m-m-miss my mommy. I m-m-miss my daddy. And I w-w-want my brother, Hans. They didn't even let me take m-m-my d-d-dolly!"

Besma wasn't much older than Petra. She hadn't a clue about any clinical theories on what to do with a child who's been dragged from her home and sold as a slave. She did, however, have a good heart, a naturally kind and sympathetic heart. She spent some time stroking the hair of the weeping slave, then laid her own dark head down on Petra's lighter one. Finally, when those things did no good, she just wrapped the little *Nazrani* in a hug and joined her in her sobs.

The next day Besma cornered the groundskeeper, another slave though he was a Moslem from Mauretania, and asked him, "Ishmael, will you escort me to the town my new friend came from? She left some things behind and I'd like to get them for her."

"Ohhh, Miss Besma," Ishmael shook his brown head, frowning, "I don't know about that. I've still got hedges to trim and the garden plot needs weeding and . . . "

From a fold in her garment Besma drew out five silver dirhem, a gift from her father on the last Ramadan and all the money she had. She knew Ishmael had been working to buy his freedom for years, for as long as she could remember, in fact. She also knew that her father was quite liberal about letting his slaves buy their freedom, subtracting a percentage of the value of the work done from the purchase price and asking only for the difference. Lucky was the slave that found his way to Abdul Mohsem's household.

"I can always ask Rafi to fill in for me," Ishmael announced, his frown changing instantly to a smile.

"Tomorrow, though, all right? Rafi's so stupid it will take me half a day to teach him what he has to do over a single day. And then I'll have to work half the night to fix the mistakes the idiot boy will have made before your father sees them."

Besma nodded quickly. A deal was a deal and she was certain Ishmael would keep his end of the bargain.

In a different part of the city, back at the auction house, Rashid counted out the additions to his wealth.

"It's a dirty business, Rashid," the slave dealer said, "you setting the *jizya* so high these people can't pay. Aren't you worried about getting caught?"

"Why should the caliph care?" Rashid asked. "It's not like these *Nazrani* filth have any value."

"But they *do*," the slave dealer said. "Other than the *zakat* they're virtually the only ones who pay any tax. It's only their sons who are suitable and legal for the corps of janissaries. If you haven't noticed, *they* do most of the work."

Rashid shrugged. "If Allah wants them to disappear, they'll disappear. If he wants them to continue to exist and to continue in their heresy, they will. Nothing you or I can do will change that."

"As you say," the slave dealer conceded. "Do you have any special plans for the extra money?"

"No, not really. Why?"

"I've got a line on some truly prime females from Slo but the price tag is a little high for me."

"Halvsies?" Rashid asked.

"That would be acceptable."

## Room 217, Olson Hall, Fort Benning, 6 October, 2106

"My, that was nice," whispered Hamilton to the ceiling.

"About time you showed up," had led to a bear hug, Hamilton picking Hodge up and swinging her around in full circle before setting her on her feet again. A bear hug had led to talk. Talk, as it will, led the two lieutenants downstairs to the bar almost directly beneath. That had led to some serious drinking, the more serious after four years of the anally tight control of the Imperial Military Academy and two months, in his case, and three, in hers, of far worse deprivation in Ranger School. Drinks were there. Rooms were there. Bodies were there. Attraction, apparently, was there as well. It had seemed only natural to put two and two, or—more technically speaking—one and one, together. Several times.

"I wonder if we'll be in the shit over this," Hamilton mused further.

He didn't expect an answer but got one anyway. Speech still a little slurred, Laurie Hodge answered, "No, dipshit, we're lieutenants, not cadets. We can fuck if we want to. Be unnatural if we didn't. I mean, *Jesus*, 'a man who won't fuck won't fight.' Don't you read *any* history?"

## Grolanhei, Affrankon, 7 Shawwal, 1530 AH (6 October, 2106)

"I have read the histories," Ishmael said, "but *Il hamdu lilah*; the *Nazrani* actually live like this?"

Ishmael led a cloth-wrapped Besma to the front door of Petra's family's home—hovel would have been more accurate—in the town. The slave had a point. The town, whatever it might once have been, had grown decrepit over the years. The asphalt of that portion of the road they trod was sufficiently broken up that the cobblestones underneath it would have been an improvement. The houses were small, dirty and unpainted. Animals—to include disgusting pigs and dogs— wandered free. Worst of all were the people. They, walking with uncertain, shuffling steps, kept their heads down. Even the grubby-faced children seemed to understand their second-class status.

*Or do they look and act like that because we're here,* Besma wondered. An unpleasant aroma reached the girl's nose. *They* might *look and act like that because we're here, but that smell is something that was here already. Maybe I shouldn't feel so bad that Petra is with me.*

Ishmael stopped a passerby and asked, "Where can we find the house of the little girl who was taken as a slave recently?"

Still keeping eyes carefully focused on the ground—yes, Ishmael was obviously a slave but he was equally obviously a *Muslim* slave and thus far above any *Nazrani*—the townsman pointed with one hand, saying, "Down that street. Just before the old train station. On the left."

"*Shokran, sayidi,*" Ishmael answered. From his point of view; well, yes, they *were* stinking *Nazrani* but *he* was a slave. And politeness cost nothing.

"Come, Miss Besma," he directed, leading the way.

"Is this the house . . . the former house . . . of Petra bint Minden?" Ishmael asked.

The door, hung on leather hinges, was only slightly ajar, just enough for one eye to peek through. The door started to open, then stopped.

"Wait," said a woman's voice, closing it again.

When the door opened again, fully this time, the woman had covered her hair and the lower half of her face. "What about my daughter?"

Besma pushed past Ishmael and said, "She's with us now. But she told me she'd left behind her doll and . . . "

"She's with *you* now?" the *Nazrani* woman repeated. "Who are 'you'?"

"I'm Besma bint Abdul Mohsem. My father is a merchant . . . not a slave dealer; he doesn't sell people."

Backing away from the door with unsteady steps the woman sat heavily into a roughhewn chair. "You mean my daughter was not sold to . . . to . . . ?"

"She's with us," Besma repeated. She saw that the woman's eyes were red and puffy as if she'd been crying for days. "She's fine but she misses her family and her dolly. So I came to get it for her. I can't be away from home very long," the girl added.

"Her dolly? *Yes*, her dolly!" the woman said, excitedly. "Please wait . . . just a minute, please."

She immediately raced from the room, disappearing somewhere into the back of the hovel. Besma heard scuffling of feet and the opening and slamming of trunks. When the woman came back she had a doll in her hands, but also a bundle of clothing, ratty clothing, to be honest, in her arms. She was also accompanied by a boy who looked enough like Petra that he just had to be her brother.

As the mother turned the bundle of loosely gathered clothes over to Ishmael, Hans pressed an old leather bound volume into Besma's hands.

"It's our great-grandmother's journal," he explained. "They won't let me take it where I'm going soon. Petra can't read it yet but . . . "

"I can read," Besma said. "My father insisted. I can teach her."

## Room 217, Olson Hall, Fort Benning, 6 October, 2106

"Yes, I read history," Hamilton said to the form lying next to him on the narrow, issue bed. "But, no, I never read that."

"Patton . . . in Italy, I think, during the Second World War," Hodge explained.

"Okay, if you say so. But I'd like to see the history book you dug that little tidbit out of."

"It was down in the library back at IMA. *Deep* down," she amended.

"Yes, but in the sober . . . *okay*, the seriously hungover, light of day, we're still—"

"—no longer cadets," Hodge interrupted. "Not in either's chain of command. Free and over twenty-one. Adults. Moreover, there'll be no punishment tours for you from getting blown by the first captain."

"Hey, at least the first captain was female. That isn't always the way it works." Hamilton laughed aloud. "You know what, Laurie?"

"No, what?"

"She wasn't worth it. Unlike say, you, she gave lousy head. Mechanical, you know. All technique and no feeling."

"That's what I heard . . . from more people than you would care to imagine."

"Jealous, are we?" Hamilton smirked.

"Not anymore," she answered, turning to face him.

# Interlude

Kitzingen, Federal Republic of Germany,
16 April, 2003

Tikrit had fallen the previous day, totally eliminating any chance that Saddam Hussein might defeat, or even slow down, the American-led invasion. Gabrielle was of mixed feelings about that. The fighting was over, she thought, and civilian casualties would stop. These were unquestionably good things. But the Americans had not been humbled; America bestrode the world like a colossus. There was no way that could be good.

She saw the waiter from the previous week, Mahmoud, at this week's protest. He stood out for at least four reasons. One was that there were many fewer people; most of the stalwarts who could be counted on for this sort of thing were disillusioned and heartsick, and saw no reason to contest a *fait accompli*. Another was that he wasn't carrying a sign; indeed he was sitting down sipping a beer, a Kesselring, on this fine spring morning. The third was that he had a look of wry amusement written across his face. He didn't really seem to be part of the demonstration at all. The fourth was that, as she had thought when she had first seen him, *Yum*.

Gabrielle walked over and sat down. Well, she *was*, after all, a very modern girl.

"It's pretty hopeless, isn't it," she said, meaning the protest.

"Beyond hopeless," Mahmoud agreed, still smiling wryly. If he meant the protest he didn't specify. "If I cared it would be humiliating."

"You don't care?" she asked. "You don't care about the hundreds and thousands of innocent people hurt and killed?"

"Don't you care about the tens and hundreds of thousands killed by the former regime or the even greater number who will now be saved?" he countered.

"But—"

"Never mind," he interrupted. The look of wry amusement disappeared. "I can't care because I can't do anything about any of it. What the Americans don't know, though, is that neither can they. The Arab world is a mess . . . beyond redemption. There is nothing anyone can do to change it. All you can hope for is to escape. That's why I came here. I don't even want to *be* an Arab anymore."

"You are Arab?" Gabrielle asked. "I would have thought Turkish."

He shook his head. "No, not a Turk. I'm from Egypt."

Ah, well, that was okay. Gabrielle hadn't known many Egyptians but those she had known seemed among the gentlest and most reasonable of people.

"Moslem, though?" she asked, eyeing the beer.

The wry smile returned as Mahmoud put out one hand, palm down and just above the beer, and wagged it. "If so, not much of one," he shrugged.

*Egypt . . . Egypt. There was a beautiful actor from Egypt . . . very famous. What was that man's name? He looked a little like this one, too.*

Which prompted another thought. "I don't even know your name," she said, which was not strictly true. On the other hand, asking was a way to be friendly.

"Mahmoud," the Egyptian answered. "Mahmoud al Beshay. And . . . ?"

"Gabrielle von Minden."

Mahmoud raised an eyebrow. "Ohhh . . . a 'von.' "

"Not the way you say it. 'Von' hardly means a thing anymore for ninety percent of the people who have it. And for the other ten percent . . . to hell with them. I'm an artist, not an aristocrat."

Mahmoud shrugged. "I'm just a waiter, but I hope to be something more someday. The problem though, is that while I came here to escape, I think I am still stuck with the Bedouin curse."

Gabi raised a quizzical eyebrow. "Curse?" she asked.

"We flee the desert, but we bring it with us wherever we go. I, and many like me, flee the restraints of Islam, yet we bring it with us, wherever we go."

# CHAPTER THREE

Narrated Ibn Abbas:
My mother and I were among the weak and oppressed.
I from among the children, and my mother from among
the women.
   —Imam Muhammad Ibn Ismail Ibn Ibrahim
    Ibn al-Mughirah Ibn Bardiziyeh, al-Bukhari

Kitznen, Affrankon, 7 Shawwal, 1530 AH
(6 October, 2106)

"Ooo, I almost forgot!" Besma exclaimed. Arms flying,
she raced for her burka, lying on a carved wooden trunk
on the opposite side of the room from her bed. She'd
concealed the book Hans had given her in the burka's
folds.

Petra, still clutching her rag doll to her breast, looked on in curiosity until Besma produced the book. "I can't read," she said. "My brother was trying to teach me but we hadn't gotten very far."

"I know. I can teach you. I'd like to teach you."

"You can *read*?" Petra asked, wonder in her voice. "I thought that Muslim girls were forbidden to learn to read."

Besma nodded. "Some *are* forbidden, but it's by their families, or sometimes by the local emirs and sheiks, not by the Quran. My father says that that's wrong, that it's 'improper and impious.' But a lot of people—maybe even most—still forbid their daughters an education in anything but managing a home and family. Some do other things to girls and *those* my father says are worse than impious. He says they're an 'abomination.'"

"What things?" Petra asked

"You don't want to know. Come on," Besma changed the subject, "let's see what new clothes we can put on your dolly."

Besma and Petra leaned against cushions set up against the wall between Besma's bed and her trunk. It was very late and so Besma had a small lamp lit, set into the wall behind them. The flickering flame of the lamp would have made reading the hand-scrawled words in the journal next to impossible except that the writing was so firm and fine. Whoever had written those words must have had very fine motor control of her hands.

"I can't understand any of it," Petra said, her head hanging with shame.

"We'll work on that later. For now, let's just look at the pictures."

"Pictures?"

"Yes. Hand-drawn ones. Whoever wrote this was really good with a pencil. I wish I could draw like that but—"

"—but?"

"A lot of the pictures are of people . . . and animals. We can't draw those. The *mutawa* would cut your skilled hand off if you tried. And even for having them . . ." Besma shuddered.

"What?" Petra asked. "What's wrong? And what are the *mutawa*?"

"You don't see them out of the Moslem towns and cities. The *mutawa* are the police for the prevention of vice and the promotion of virtue. Nobody controls them. My father says that they're lunatics who push everything Allah commanded to the point their rules sicken Allah. For having pictures of living things they'll beat you within an inch of your life. For having pictures like some of the ones drawn in this book they might kill us." Besma suddenly looked shamefaced. "I'm sorry," she apologized. "I looked in the book on the way back from your family's . . . house."

"Show me," Petra said.

## Private Rodger W. Young Range, Fort Benning, Georgia, 10 November, 2106

"Dressed to kill," Hamilton judged as he inspected Hodge's suit. She, and he, and the other two-hundred-and-ten members of the class, were in full up armor. This meant that, besides the close-fitting helmet and facial armor *cum* thermal imager, the neck was protected by a circular guard augmented by woven, silica-impregnated aramid cloth. The torso was covered front and back with four-millimeter liquid metal alloy, below which was a bell-shaped hip-and-groin guard, while greaves and thigh protectors curved from the back of the exoskeleton to encompass those appendages. On the back was worn the pack that provided power, filtered air, cooled or heated the suit wearer, and held the computer that maintained life support and controlled the suit based on physical and verbal commands given by the wearer. Over all were attached various packs and pouches, weapons and sensors.

It had been sixty years since the first practical suit had been developed. In the intervening time some improvements had been made, notably to endurance and coordination, without substantially changing the layout and structure of the suit.

Hamilton inspected digitally, visually and physically. "You're getting a subnominal reading on your left femoral forward pluscle, Laurie. Have the armorer check it after the exercise." He checked in part by having Hodge have her suit do certain things—"Eyes left . . . Eyes right . . . good . . . Deep knee bends . . . good . . . Left arm pushup . . . good . . . Right arm pushup . . . good . . . Jump . . . Jump . . . Jump . . . good . . . Run in place . . . good . . . good . . . hmmm . . . Have the armorer calibrate the gyro . . . seems a little off. . . ." Beyond that, he ran an analysis cable from his own suit, already checked by the platoon leader for the exercise, to hers.

"I feel more like I'm dressed for a funeral, and wearing the coffin," Hodge said.

"Coffin" was a pretty apt description, and not your cheap pine coffin, either. No, no; *this* coffin was the deluxe solid bronze job. All told, between the exoskeleton itself (one hundred and forty-seven pounds, including plastic musculature, or pluscle), the armor (one hundred and twenty-three pounds), power and control pack (sixty-two pounds), weapons, ammunition, communications gear, imaging gear, sensors . . . all in all, it came to just about a quarter of a ton. Add in the one hundred and fifteen pound woman (from eating upwards of ten-thousand calories a day she'd put back most of the twenty-five pounds she'd lost in Ranger School by this time, and even managed to reinflate her breasts) and it amounted to quite a weight. Fortunately, the suit was modular and no single piece (except for the Exo, itself, which could be moved by attaching oneself to it) was so heavy that two fit women couldn't lift and attach it.

And that was for a size small suit. Hamilton's weighed almost a hundred pounds more, having larger pluscles and power pack, and more, but not thicker, armor.

Hamilton checked one last item on his heads-up display and announced, "You can inflate now, Laurie."

Hodge nodded, then made herself go stock still as she said, "Suit . . . inflate shock cushions." From a pump in the back with the power pack the suit began to fill up—to overpressurize, actually—several sets of inflatable cushions. These came in two types and served two purposes. One was to cushion against the shock on direct fire hits, shrapnel and concussion. These were the ones inflating now. The others, however, had already been inflated. It was changes to the pressure in these "cushions" that, once detected by the computer, caused it to apply power to the exoskeletal pluscles that made some of them contract until pressure was equalized. After many different attempts, this had been found to be the most practical for military purposes.

"I read inflation as good," Hamilton announced, thinking *and that's not even counting your tits,* "annnd . . . you're up."

## Kitznen, Province of Affrankon, 13 Duh'l-Qa'dah, 1530 AH (10 November, 2106)

Petra recited from a children's book Besma had saved:
". . . I is for Infidel, burning in Hellfire.

"J is for Jew . . . Besma, what's a Jew?"

The Moslem girl shrugged and shook her head. "I don't know. Demons, I guess. I think there aren't any, anymore. Or at least none near here."

"Okay.

"J is for Jew, whom even the rocks hate.

"K is for Kaffir, enslaved in the jihad.

"L is for liar . . ."

Petra suddenly stopped reading. Her face grew very sad. "That's what the man said who took me from my family, that I was enslaved under *jihad* since my father couldn't pay the tax that allowed us to be *dhimmis*."

"That's just so *wrong*. I'm sorry, Petra."

"It's all right. It wasn't your fault."

"Let's start over at the beginning," Besma suggested, thinking to get Petra's mind away from thoughts of *jihad* and slavery.

The girl thumbed the pages back and started over:

"A is for Americans, devils incarnate . . . Why are the Americans devils, Petra?"

Besma shuddered. "Because they tried to *exterminate* us."


## Private Rodger W. Young Range, Fort Benning, Georgia, 10 November, 2106

"Kill 'em quick, before they get away!"

Hamilton didn't know whose voice it had been, shouting over the comm system. He thought it sounded like

Hodge but, if so, her voice had never been quite so full of passion, not even in bed. He checked his heads-up display to find her position, then looked over to where she stood above a trench, pouring fire down into it. The bullets, all tracers, looked like some alien weapon from a movie about the future.

The range (rather, the range which bore the name) had seen many uses over the years and had once been in a different place. One major use, in the other place, had been as a close assault course. In the original version of this, machine guns had fired at about waist level over the heads of troops crawling forward. Later on, this was deemed too unsafe and the guns were fixed to fire well over the heads of even the tallest man. That this had totally destroyed the already limited moral training value of the range was deemed acceptable by those more concerned with safety statistics than with victory on the battlefield.

They didn't do that anymore, for Suited Heavy Infantry, at least. Now rifles and machine guns, the same kinds as favored by the Moslem enemy across the globe, were aimed by remote control and fired to hit. Since with full-up armor the suits were more or less invulnerable to those rifles and machine guns, it was still a very safe exercise. On the other hand, it was a great way to build confidence in the troops in the armor's ability to withstand direct hits.

While Hodge fanned the trench with lead-tipped flame, Hamilton passed her by, bouncing up and over it and taking a kneeling firing position—trees and sandbags being not as good a protection as four millimeters of liquid metal armor—to begin peppering a bunker farther downrange.

As he did so, Hodge knelt beside him and changed out the helical magazine on her left-wrist borne CCW, or "close combat weapon." Colloquially, among the troops, the things were known as "Slags," as in "Slag 'em,"—turn them into something wet and runny.

Once that was done she took her own weapon, a fifty millimeter semi-automatic grenade launcher, and fired a salvo of four rounds of training practice—it had the same ballistics as a high explosive service round but only as much explosive as one might find in a blasting cap—at the bunker, one of which went directly through the aperture. The bunker decided it was dead and cut off control to the remote operator.

Hamilton directed his comm system, "Closed circuit, me to Hodge," and said, after the beep that indicated the changeover, "Good job, you bloodthirsty bitch. Glad you're on my side."

They both heard, through the platoon net, "Action right. Enemy platoon counterattacking. Kill 'em."

No sooner had they heard this than a flurry of bullets swept over both of them. The suits shrugged those bullets off, but they still had enough energy to rock the two troopers back.

Hodge began slow fire—one round per two seconds—at the advancing robotic targets. As she did, she said, "Closed circuit; me to Hamilton" and then, "Did I ever mention this shit makes me horny?"

## Kitznen, Provence of Affrankon, 13 Duh'l-Qa'dah, 1530 AH (10 November, 2106)

"Now *he*," Besma said, "is a beautiful man."

"Do you suppose he really looked like that?" Petra asked, "Or do you think maybe my great-grandmother sort of . . . what's the word?"

"Idealized?"

"Yes, that one. Do you think she idealized him or did he really look like that?"

"Either way, he's a dream. And there's something about *that*."

"*That*" was a male appendage, plainly visible in the drawing.

To *that* Petra agreed. Mohammad had had a point. Even at nine, a girl is still in good part already a woman.

The drawing the girls were looking at in the journal was labeled "Mahmoud" in the artist's superb handwriting.

"He's one of my people, I think," Besma said.

"Not one of mine, for sure," Petra agreed. "What do you think he was to my great-grandmother?"

"I don't know. Let's try to read some more. Maybe we can find out."

## Private Rodger W. Young Range, Fort Benning, Georgia, 12 November, 2106

"No," Hamilton insisted, "we are *not* going to dump our groin armor so we can fuck."

"Scaredycat," Hodge taunted.

"Nothing of the kind," he answered. "It's just that the thought's preposterous. It'd be like two robots going at it."

Unable to help herself Hodge started to giggle. "It really would look ridiculous. But then, who's going to see?"

"Everybody. We don't have thermal imagers for nothing and the heat waves rising from your hot little ass would be sure to be noticed."

"You think my ass is hot?"

"I think *all* of you is hot, Laurie."

*Some things,* she thought, *are better than sex. Being thought "hot" is sometimes one of them.* "Okay. I'll leave you alone for now. But when we get back to Olson Hall you better show me that you really think all of me is hot."

"Deal," Hamilton agreed.

Though they were lying on their backs in the dirt next to each other, she didn't bother to snuggle in. Hamilton was right; there was something obscene about two robots cuddling.

"You done good, today, Laurie," Hamilton said.

"Thanks. You, too. Though this suit is a damned uncomfortable thing and pretty unflattering to a girl's figure."

At first Hamilton said nothing to that. After a few moments, though, she realized he was laughing.

"What's so funny?"

"Well . . . I was just thinking, a girl in a heavy infantry suit is perfectly dressed under the enemy's law. What's the difference between wearing a burka and wearing Class B armor?"

She thought about that for a few seconds before answering, "I can't kill people as easily wearing a burka."

## Kitznen, Affrankon, 14 Duh'l-Qa'dah, 1530 AH (11 November, 2106)

Ishmael escorted the two burka-clad girls from the house to the market. That was part of his official duty; he didn't hit Besma up for *baksheesh* for it. This was to the good as Besma only had the two dozen *dirhem* she'd begged from her father to buy some new clothes and shoes for the new girl in the house. Her father's wife had objected, and her older stepbrother, Fudail, had sneered, but still her father had given over the money. Besma was, after all, the pearl of his heart.

They went into a women's and girls' shop, a simple door into an old brick building with a sign to one side and the windows painted black. Ishmael had to wait outside with the other various *mahram*, the men suitable as escorts for women because sexual intercourse was prohibited between them and the women escorted.

Ishmael was not exactly in that category. He could legally have had intercourse with either Besma or Petra, had they been married. Ishmael, however, was a eunuch, having been castrated as a boy, just before he was sold. He *couldn't* really be expected to have intercourse with anyone and so was *mahram* as a practical if not a legal matter. Even so, Ishmael's master, Abdul Mohsem, was taking some risk by having him escort the family's womenfolk.

One aspect of that risk was visible just across the street from where Ishmael and the rest of the *mahram* squatted outside the women's store. Ishmael didn't know what the crime was, but he saw a group of *mutaween*, wearing their traditional brown robes, drag a man from another shop and force him up the street to one of the usual sites reserved for executing the judgments of the police for the prevention of vice and the promotion of virtue. There was a stout pole there, affixed into the cobblestones. From the pole hung a looped rope.

The man being forced blubbered and begged for mercy. It was not forthcoming.

First, one of the *mutawa* knocked the man to his back by a blow to the face. Then two others gathered up his legs and lifted them. A fourth dropped a loop of rope over the ankles while a fifth pulled on the rope to raise the feet. Once this was done a sixth lashed the rope to a pintle on the pole. The man's shoes were removed, and the senior of the *mutaween* took a long, stiff but flexible stick from another and bared his right arm to the shoulder.

Even from as far away as he was, Ishmael heard the hiss of the stick. He could have been considerably farther away and still heard the scream of the victim.

The shop was small and the shelves and racks something less than full. Dust gathered here and there showed that the emptiness was not a recent phenomenon. And yet Besma had said that this was one of the better women's shops in the town. Petra assumed this was so, and really didn't even notice the emptiness of the stock or the dust where no stock lay. Her town's one remaining general store had had even less.

"What was that?" Petra asked, as the reverberating sound of a human scream penetrated the shop's black-painted windows.

"The *mutaween*," the shopkeeper answered. "They become more vicious with each passing day. And if you're a poor *Nazrani* minding your own business . . . I'm Muslim and it still makes me sick what they do to the *Nazrani*."

Petra gulped. She was both *Nazrani* and poor. Worse, she was owned. What would they do to *her*?

Besma patted her arm. "Don't worry," she insisted, "I won't let them near you and they wouldn't *dare* touch *me*."

Having had a chance to watch the household for a while by this point, Petra wasn't sure that Abdul Mohsem hadn't doted on Besma so much that she had forgotten her place in the world. After all, their burkas sat on a chair in one corner. Outside was a man who would escort them wherever they went. And she'd seen enough to know that Moslem women, if wealthier, were not even as free as the wretched *Nazrani* girls and women of Grolanhei.

She said nothing, though.

Besma turned her attention to the shopkeeper and said, "My friend needs two new dresses and a pair of shoes."

"Yes, miss. Right away." The shopkeeper measured Petra by eye, then went to a shelf and dusted off some cobwebs. She removed half a dozen ankle length dresses in what she thought was a fair match for size and brought them to the girls.

For the nonce, Petra was able to screen out the screams and sobs coming from outside in her wonder at the fine—she certainly thought it was fine—clothing the shopkeeper began laying out on a table top.


The actual beating was over, though the victim still sobbed loudly. Two of the *mutaween* left, while the rest stood around smoking and, apparently, telling jokes.

"Poor bastard," Ishmael said to no one in particular.

One of the *mahram* smiled, perhaps sadly, and said, "You haven't seen anything yet. Wait."

It wasn't long, so Ishmael saw, before the two *mutaween* who had left returned carrying a large bucket between them.

"Now it gets nasty," the *mahram* who had spoken previously said. "That's ice water. They're going to pour it over his feet."

"What will that do?" Ishmael asked.

"You'll see."

The two *mutaween* lifted the bucket and began to pour water over the bruised soles of the victim's feet. Within a few seconds the crystal clear water running off the feet turned red, even as the victim emitted a scream such as Ishmael couldn't remember having heard since his own castration.

"Does something to the blood vessels, the bones, and the skin," the *mahram* explained. "Regular water wouldn't do; it has to be cold."

"*Il hamdu lillah,* what did he *do* to deserve that?"

The *mahram* looked on Ishmael with something like pity. "You don't get around much do you? The *mutaween* probably demanded a 'donation' which he refused. That would be enough."

Ishmael, even though he thought this an abomination, also thought it very likely as the *mutaween* began circulating about the square shouting, "Donations for the defenders of the faith to continue with their holy work?"

He still had the dirhem he'd been given by Besma. When he dropped one in the cup of a *mutawa,* and got nothing but a dirty look in return, he decided that his feet were more important than a few bits of silver. He turned over all he had. Each tinkle of silver on silver was like a knife to his heart. That money was *freedom* money. And, yet, how much would the *mutaween,* who made a living from robbing others of their freedom, care for the freedom of a castrated slave?

There had been just enough money, after purchasing dress and shoes, to replace Petra's threadbare burka with a new blue one.

"It will match your eyes," Besma assured her, "even if no one but you and I and Ishmael know that it does."

# Interlude

## Kitzingen, Federal Republic of Germany, 11 January, 2004

Mahmoud stretched out on one side of Gabrielle's bed. He'd tried to cover himself partly with the top sheet but she'd insisted on full nudity for her sketch. Having moved the sheet, she'd stepped back, looked him over, then reached out and draped his penis at what she thought was an aesthetically appealing angle.

"Besides," she said, smiling warmly, "I *like* seeing you like this."

It was a strange thing to Gabi, what she'd come to feel for Mahmoud. She was modern and western; casual, recreational sex was no big thing to her. What she felt when she was with Mahmoud was not casual. Rather, it was—though she didn't like the term—something approaching *sacred*.

What he felt for her? Well, he'd never plainly said. His upbringing wouldn't permit it yet. Yet in his every action he proclaimed love. He was putting up with posing for her, after all, even though he hated it.

"I still feel ridiculous," he said, even while putting up with the pose for the sake of love.

"It's for *art*," she insisted. "You'll be famous."

"I don't want to be famous. And my mother will have a stroke if she sees."

"Your mother is kept in purdah, veiled and without a television," Gabrielle countered. "She buys no books; she can't even read. She'll never see."

Mahmoud sighed. When an argument was lost, it was lost. "At least turn on the television so I can keep my mind busy."

That seemed fair. Gabrielle walked over and turned on the TV. When the screen cleared, she and Mahmoud saw what appeared to be a major protest in Paris. It soon became clear that the protest was over a recent French decision to ban the wear of hijab in schools. There were at least two German states, or *Länder*, that were considering similar measures.

"That's just so wrong," Gabrielle said.

Mahmoud disagreed. Shaking his head firmly, he said, "It's not wrong, though it might be pointless and it might turn out to be a mistake. Trust me; I know my people. Any toe in the door you give them they will exploit ruthlessly. Any concession you make will convince them you are weak and lead only to demands for ever greater concessions. Which you'll give because making the concession in the first place showed that you *were* weak; that, or stupid, which amounts to the same thing.

"That said, the only thing worse than making a concession is first making a show of strength and defiance and *then* backing down. That will convince my people that you are both stupid *and* weak. And I'm not sure the French will understand that . . . or understand that, once having taken their stand, they can't ever back off from it. You're making some of the same mistakes here, with your publicly funded mosques."

"Oh, hell, Mahmoud, that's ridiculous!" Gabrielle exclaimed. "To think that a few little headscarves are going to bring about the collapse of the Republic of France. To think that treating Turks here with some decency is going to ruin Germany."

"It's not the symbols, Gabi, it's what the symbols do to the minds of men, how they affect the cost-benefit calculus, and where they indicate the direction of movement is."

"I still think it's ridiculous to think that a minority population— what is it in France? Five percent? Ten?—is going to overthrow the country."

"Probably closer to ten percent," Mahmoud said, "Eight, at least. But it's a population that's young and growing." He stopped for a moment and asked, "Gabrielle, how many brothers and sisters do you have?"

"None, as you well know."

"First cousins?"

"Two."

"And the typical French artiste has but few more. The same for the Italians, the Spanish, the Portuguese, the Belgians, the Dutch, the Scandinavians, the—"

"What's your point? The world can't support more."

Mahmoud gestured with his chin at the television, the screen of which showed thousands upon thousands of young women and girls, each wearing at least hijab, and many in burkas. "Tell *them* that. Those girls will be married by the time they're eighteen, sixteen or seventeen for some of them. They will pump out four or even five children each. The half of those children who are girls will do the same. In a hundred years, if things don't change, one Moslem women will have increased her gene pool—more importantly, her religious and cultural pool—at least thirty-two times over. Still more girls come in illegally from overseas and are entered into arranged, often polygamous marriages. Maybe they'll have fewer children, sharing a husband; maybe they won't, either. But from the point of view of the imams, it's all good, all free increase in the numbers of the faithful, here, on the battlefield they believe matters."

"You can't *know* that that will happen," she countered.

Mahmoud shook his head, sadly. "No, I can't know. But that's the way to bet it."

He thought about it for a minute and then announced, "Tell you what, Gabi. This Friday, we're going to drape you in a burka—don't worry, I'll buy it; they're already very easy to find here now. Then you and I are going to a mosque, one that preaches in German. I want you to hear what the people you're defending say about you."

# CHAPTER FOUR

"These Germans, these atheists, these Europeans don't shave under their arms and their sweat collects under their hair with a revolting smell and they stink. Hell lives for the infidels! Down with all democracies and all democrats!"

—Imam Sheikh Mohammed Abdullah Al-Amari, Preaching the Friday sermon in a Berlin Mosque, 2006

## Kitznen, Province of Affrankon, 25 Jumahdi I, 1531 AH (18 May, 2107)

It wasn't all, nor even mostly, fun and games and learning to read and shopping. Petra was still a slave, and as such, she had work to do.

The work was easy, not least because Besma, though not at all a slave, was required to do as much or, because she was older, more. Indeed, much of Besma's work involved teaching Petra how to perform domestic duties.

Often, even the work was fun and games. Two girls, who truly care for each other, can turn a broom and dustbin into tools for a game of an odd kind of catch.

"Enough silliness!" Petra felt the switch of Abdul Mohsem's current wife, Al Khalifa, across her back as she lined up the dustbin for Besma to slide a pile of dirt towards. "You're a slave, *Nazrani* slut; act like it."

"Bitch!" Besma whispered after her stepmother had left the room. She had to whisper it. While she was pretty sure the *mutaween* would not molest the daughter of Abdul Mohsem, she knew for a fact that al Khalifa could punish her slave with impunity. She ran and knelt by Petra, who was crying with her face in the dirt. Besma lifted the slave girl's head, pressing it in to the juncture of her own neck and shoulder. "Bitch!" she repeated. "If she's cut you, I swear I'll kill her."

"She . . . didn't," Petra sniffled. "I'm all right."

"Her father had a *Nazrani* slave girl he preferred to her mother," Besma said. "That's why she hates the *Nazrani*. But I think she hates almost everyone. She surely hates me but can't do anything about it."

Besma had a horrible thought. *Except she can get to me through you.* She kept the thought to herself for now.

"What happened to your mother?" Petra asked.

Besma sighed. "She died, giving birth to me. My father said she didn't have to, that if the American devils weren't so cheap with their medicine she could have lived. It's why I hate them; because I never knew my mother. And instead got stuck with that *bitch*—already with a son from a prior marriage to a man who divorced her and wanted nothing to do with their rotter of a child—because my father wanted me to have a mother."

USAF TCA (Troop Carrier Airship) *Retaliation*,
over the ruins of central Kansas City, Missouri,
19 May, 2107

In a world where *energy* is fairly abundant, but easily
packaged and transportable fuel much rarer, airships can
begin to assume an ascendancy over faster, more convenient, but more fuel-guzzling winged aircraft. This
becomes even more true when, as in the case of the
*Retaliation* and her several score USAF sisters, the airship itself can become a wing, allowing it to be slightly
heavier than air, and thus much more controllable. Add
in a pebble bed modular reactor for power and, cost-
benefit-wise, the airplane can't even come close.

As important, airships were about seven times faster
than wet water ships. This meant that they could make
the flight, Fort Stewart to Manila, nearly nine thousand
miles, in about two and a half days. Taking the slight
detour to show the departing troops the remains of Kansas City didn't add appreciably to that.

Five such—and indeed, *Retaliation* was the lead of
the five ships in the lift—are capable of picking up and
moving halfway around the globe an entire mixed brigade of Light Infantry, Mechanized Infantry and Suited
Heavy Infantry, plus support, and enough in the way of
supply to operate for at least a month without further
resupply. And why not? The ships were nearly two kilometers long, half that in beam, and about four hundred
meters from AAA Deck down to the landing apparatus.

This five-ship lift consisted of the First Brigade of the
24th Infantry Division, the Victory Division, sharing Fort
Stewart, Georgia as a home base with the 3rd Infantry

Division and the Constabulary Infantry School. The brigade consisted of 2nd Battalion, 21st Infantry (Light); 2nd Battalion, 34th Infantry (Mechanized); 2nd Battalion, 19th Infantry (SHI); 1st Battalion, 52nd Field Artillery (LRB), along with batteries, troops and companies of engineers, operational reconnaissance, aerial reconnaissance, aerial interdiction artillery, heavy-armor direct fire support, tactical airlift (Chinook W), and a whopping headquarters and service support battalion. In all, and even counting some individual replacement for units already committed to the Philippine campaign, it was just over five thousand men and women.

Two of those, one man, one woman, fairly recently assigned as lieutenants to Company B, 2nd Battalion, 19th Infantry, sat in the officers' lounge looking out over the no longer radioactive ruins of one of America's heartland cities.

Everyone staring at the skeletal remains was quiet, eyes jerking back and forth over what was once a vibrant city filled with their countrymen and women. Indeed, the airship itself had grown quiet after the captain made the announcement over the PA system.

Laurie Hodge thought and said, "That's the saddest thing I've ever seen."

Over the PA, the captain countered, "You ain't seen nothing yet, folks. We'll be passing over Los Angeles in a few hours. That's worse."

## Kitznen, Province of Affrankon, 26 Jumahdi I, 1531 AH (19 May, 2107)

"But why won't the Americans share their medicine with you, Besma?"

The older girl sighed, "Because we're at war, and it's a war we don't know how to end and they won't until we're all extinct." She thought about it for a minute and then walked to her trunk. From this she removed a textbook which she brought to the other girl.

She opened the book to a map of the globe. "This is what the world looks like. Here's where we are," she said, pointing to a green patch at one end of the largest land mass. That piece, Petra read, was labeled "Caliphate of Europe and Western North Africa." One small section, surrounded by green, was in red and labeled "Switzerland."

Besma's finger traced east, to a large red swatch extending down into the Balkans. "This is the Socialist Empire of the Tsar, Vladimir the Fifth. He's an enemy, too, but he isn't trying to extinguish us." The finger moved down to another section, colored in paler green, that stretched all the way from the upper part of the area labeled "Africa" over to some islands far to the right. "This is the Caliphate of Islam, Triumphant. I understand it's a mess."

Petra noticed that right in the middle of the Caliphate of Islam, Triumphant, on the eastern shore of the middle sea, there was a bare patch unmarked and unnamed. "And this?"

"I don't know," Besma said. "My teachers wouldn't talk about it."

Still farther down, the finger pointed to, "The Boer Free State, which owns most of Africa below the Sahara. A lot of the black slaves come from there. The Boers sell us their surplus population. The only good things about them are that they distrust America, too, and they provide us with a lot of technology we can't make for ourselves."

Moving her finger to the right, Besma marked, "This is the Celestial Kingdom of the Han. They also sell us some things we can't make for ourselves. They are at war with Nihon," the finger touched a large group of islands in the ocean marked "Peaceful." "Nihon is an ally of the American devils."

From there the finger moved southwest to a multicolored patchwork of little states, all crowded into a triangular peninsula. "This used to be a big country, but split into two, then three, then dozens. I don't know why."

"What's all this black?" Petra asked, her own little hand sweeping the two continents of the west, various islands in the sea called "Peaceful," the area south of the Kingdom of the Han, and two large islands off the coast of the Caliphate.

"That's the American devils, places they rule and places so closely allied to them they may as well rule them."

## Diosdado Macapagal International Airport, Philippine Sovereign Allied Territory, 22 May, 2107

Imperialism not only can come in light-handed and heavy-handed varieties, just how light or heavy those hands feel can depend on whether or not the subject peoples feel the need to have the imperialists around.

The imperial hand laid upon the Philippines was so light that there was talk of statehood, full membership in the Union. Moreover, the need was great, what with the Moros of Mindanao and Cebu. Indeed, it was the remaining presence of so many Moslems in the PSAT that had kept it from statehood, so far.

That's why the 24th Infantry Division had been sent for the *second* time to the islands. The first time had been to help liberate them from the Japanese.

(The Japanese had actually volunteered troops to the ongoing campaign in the Philippines but the Filipinos, with memories that a mere hundred and sixty-odd years could not erase, had said, in effect, "Been there; done that. It wasn't all that much fun the first time. So, thanks, but no thanks.")

Thus, the faces on the troops of the 43rd, 45th and 57th Infantry Regiments of the Army of the Philippines, standing in ranks to welcome the newly arrived 24th Infantry Division, were brightly lit with smiles as the first of the Suited Heavy Infantry debarked from the *Retaliation*. Those Filipinos were all already United States citizens and only looked forward to full joinder in the Empire. Their band, the 12th Infantry Division band, played the song the Filipinos still sometimes thought of as "Caissons." And why not? The song, under that title, had been born at this very base, then known as Fort Stotsenberg, in the Philippines, one hundred and ninety-nine years before.

Though it was tied down and partly sunk into an artificial depression, the airship still shuddered with the impact of hundreds of pairs of armored, powered feet, running in place and in cadence, as the twin side ramps hummed down to the tarmac of the airship port to the east of the airfield.

In their communications system, Hamilton and Hodge heard the voice of their not-too-terribly beloved company commander, Carl Thompson, a medium-sized, overly large brained, relentless and vicious mustang with a bad attitude towards graduates of the Imperial Military Academy. There was something about Thompson that was just plain uncomfortable.

"Bravo Company!"

"Platoon!" echoed the lieutenants Laurie Hodge, John Hamilton, Kennedy Parker and Jerome Miles. Parker's supplemental command was late and hesitant.

"Double time—"

"Double time—"

"March!"

At first, since the only troopers really able to run were right at the loading ramp, the pounding and the shuddering of the airship's deck decreased. Then, as the forward ranks thinned and more and more of the troops were able to actually run, the deck could be seen to visibly vibrate.

Far above, on the bridge of the airship, the ship's captain, Lieutenant Colonel Mike (the) Pike, shuddered, grimaced and cursed through gritted teeth, "I friggin' *hate* when they do that."

The captain—"that asshole Thompson"—was already posted on the tarmac when Hamilton and his platoon emerged from the airship. Hodge, leading her platoon, had slowed to allow the troops to form into a solid mass in four files behind her. Thompson was pointing with his left, armored, hand at the precise spot he wanted her to take. For whatever reason—and rumor control said he'd had a bad experience as a lieutenant in the northern territories when some rebels had compromised the radio net—he was much more inclined to point, where that would do, than to use the radio.

Hamilton likewise slowed down and his boys and girls, quick on the uptake as pretty much all SHI troopers were, began forming from the column of twos they'd been in on the airship into a column of fours to mirror Hodge's 1st Platoon.

Thompson wasn't as precise in signaling to Hamilton as he had been with Hodge; Hamilton should have gotten the general idea of where he belonged from where Hodge was. In fact, he did. Leading his platoon to form up next to Hodge's, as soon as he was aligned with her he raised one arm and changed from a double time to running in place.

Third Platoon and Weapons likewise formed to the left. Only when they were properly lined up did Thompson order, "Company . . . halt. Parade . . . rest," then snap to attention, turn about (which took *practice* in a suit), and come to parade rest himself.

The rest, the welcoming speech by General Miguel Maglalang of the Philippine Army, the pass in review, and the march off to the barracks, was anticlimactic.

## Al Harv Kaserne, Province of Affrankon, 30 Jumahdi I, 1531 AH (23 May, 2107)

"There shall be no compulsion in religion!" thundered the muscled, graying drill instructor, Abdul Rahman von Seydlitz, to the one hundred and nineteen newly gathered boys in the Hall of Arms. One of those boys was Hans Ibn Minden. "None whatsoever!"

The boys, none of them over twelve years of age, were positioned in what the Imperial Army would have called "the front leaning rest." Most of the world would have recognized it as the pushup position. They'd been that way so long that tears ran down faces even as arms, quivering, threatened to collapse.

In fact, some did collapse until the heavily booted feet of their overseers brought them back up to the pushup position. From those, the tears flowed without ceasc.

"No compulsion in religion," the senior drill instructor repeated. "Yet there is bounty, under the mercy of Allah, for those who forswear their false religion."

One of the boys, apparently no dummy, raised his head and gasped, "Bounty?"

"Indeed. It is our custom to fete those who join the faithful. It is very hard to do so with someone in the position you are in and so we relieve them of it."

Hans gritted his teeth. His mother's parting whispers echoed in his ears. *My son, whatever they may take from you, do not let them have your soul as well. Keep true to our faith. God will not forget you.*

Yet it was hard, *hard*. The work of a rural *fellahin* should have built good muscle in Hans' arms. And so it would have, if food had not been perennially scarce. As it was, he was not so strong as he might have been, either in body or in soul. With the rising agony in his arms, his mother's parting words grew fainter and fainter. When one by one the other boys took the drill instructor up on his offer, repeating the words, *"La illaha illa Allah: Mohamedan rasulu Allah,"* There is no God but God; Mohamed is the prophet of God; Hans' will weakened and finally broke.

*And this*, thought Abdul Rahman, himself a *Nazrani* weaned from the faith of his fathers, *this is why we take them so young.*

## Kitznen, Province of Affrankon, 2 Jumahdi II, 1531 AH (25 May, 2107)

Even as Hans and his newfound barracks mates underwent conversion in the Al Harv Kaserne, Petra, too was learning new things. Her instruction was even less pleasant than his was.

Besma, held fast by Fudail's, her stepbrother's, strong arms, struggled and wept and pleaded for her father's wife to lay off the beating. Petra, the object of that beating, wept and begged and chewed with her teeth upon the table over which she was bent. Petra's long skirt was lifted over her back, exposing her buttocks. Al Khalifa, the stepmother, held her neck to the table with one hand while she lashed those buttocks mercilessly, raising welts and occasional bright red drops of blood.

Al Khalifa stopped the beating just long enough to turn to Besma and say, "Didn't you ever wonder why I let your father waste money on this *Nazrani* slut? He might not let me punish *you* as you deserve, but he'll not say a word over punishing a slave."

She turned back to Petra and laid on four more strokes. "Think about that the next time you think you can talk back to me, or disobey me, or fail in any way to show me the respect I am due."

"Please," Besma begged. "I'm sorry; I'm so, so sorry. I promise I'll be good but *please* don't hit her anymore."

"PLEASE!" Besma shrieked as al Khalifa turned back to the slave's bare buttocks and began to thrash her even more viciously than before. *"Please!"*

Only when the *Nazrani* girl fainted did al Khalifa leave off. "It will be like this, only worse, every time you fail to please me," the woman said. To her son she said, "Let Besma go," before she, and he, left.

"I didn't do anything; I didn't do anything; I didn't do anything," Petra repeated, over and over, hysterically, without there being anything Besma could say or do to make her stop. Instead, she just held the younger girl and rocked her back and forth, stroking her hair and whispering how sorry she was.

Though it took much time, hours, little by little Petra's shuddering lessened, then finally stopped. Her sobbing, too, let off. Still Besma held her until, certain Petra had fallen asleep, the Moslem girl was able to lay her down on her own bed. She was very careful to lay Petra on her side, lest the pressure on her bruised and bleeding buttocks might awaken her again in agony.

Besma's face was a study in pure hatred. *She waited, that bitch, until I loved you like a sister to use you to get to me. And now what can I do? Have father sell you somewhere else? I couldn't bear it and you couldn't bear being where you would end up. And so now I am a slave, because I cannot bear for you to be hurt. Because of that . . . that . . . that . . . stinking-vile-foul-slimy-filthy woman owns me.*

Her face softened, looking down at the sleeping doll-like figure on her bed. Besma bent and kissed the slave girl's cheek. *But if I must be owned, at least I have the satisfaction of knowing that the price is fair.*

Orderly Room, Co-B, 2nd Battalion, 19th Infantry, Camp Stotsenberg, Philippine Islands, 30 May, 2107

"There's a price for everything in life, Lieutenant Hamilton, and the price is always fair when it isn't exorbitant."

Thus spoke "that asshole, Captain Thompson." Hamilton hadn't the first clue what the captain was talking about. The Old Man had ordered him to his office without explanation. "Sit," he'd said, once Hamilton had reported. "We need to have a chat."

Having said that, though, Thompson just stared at Hamilton, studying him, with his left eyebrow lifted and head cocked to the right. The captain's studying made the lieutenant distinctly uncomfortable and did so very quickly. He had a scary look about him anyway and the extended silence only made it worse.

After several long minutes, and having made his lieutenant nervous enough to climb walls, Thompson spoke again. His voice was something between conversational and prosecutorial as he said, "There are no secrets in an infantry company. Have you ever asked yourself, Lieutenant, what the effect on your troops will be if you ever have to order them into a bad situation to save Hodge's ass? If you weren't fucking her, it would be no problem. But since you *are* fucking her, *that* will be the reason they think you're risking their lives, to save your little honey-buns. The same holds true for her."

"Sir, I—"

"Shut up."

"Yes, sir."

"In a country," Thompson continued, "where many civil rights once thought normal and above infringement have slipped away, *you* are in the least privileged class of all, Lieutenant Hamilton. You're an infantry officer. You have no rights. You have no personal interests that cannot be classified as trivial. You exist for the sole purpose of supporting the interests of the Empire through violence. Anything you do that undermines your ability to support the Empire through violence is ethically and morally wrong. Do you understand me?"

"Sir, I have the right to have sex with anyone I want not in my chain of command," Hamilton objected.

Thompson, for once, smiled. "Lieutenant, wherever did you hear that?"

"The bastard said he'd transfer me to 3rd of the 19th in Second Brigade, John. I don't want to give up my platoon. I don't want to be in a different unit from you."

Hodge lay naked with her head on Hamilton's chest and one arm draped over his torso. His chest was wet with the tears she'd shed when she'd told him they had to revert to just being friends.

"He was pretty specific, too, John, the foul-mouthed, tactless son of a bitch. 'No fucking, no sucking, no kissing, no cuddling, no anything, Lieutenant Hodge, that so much as suggests he is anything to you but a brother officer.' I had to give my word or he'd have shipped me out—well, one of us out, anyway—without even the chance to say goodbye. I was lucky I was able to talk him into turning a blind eye for one last night."

Hamilton nodded. "Hard-assed bastard isn't he?" Sighing, he continued, "Well . . . if he had shipped one of us out, we'd never have seen each other at all, not with the way they're going to rotate us and Second Brigade in and out of the field in sequence. At least this way we can be close, if not as close as we'd like. I'd never get a moment's sleep if I had to worry about you all the time without being able to watch out for you."

"Why, John, I'd almost think you cared."

"Silly bitch. I love you. Didn't you know?"

In answer, she gasped, hugged him tightly, and threw one leg over both of his. She then began moving downwards along his chest. While she still could, she whispered, just loudly enough for him to hear, "I love you, too, you bastard. I have since we were plebs."

◇   ◇   ◇

Jungle insects swarmed, buzzing in ears and feasting on the exposed faces of three very uncomfortable lieutenants.

"Moose cock," Captain Thompson said, to his three line platoon leaders. "You all suck moose cock. Where the fuck did you people learn that drills were a substitute for brains?"

The line lieutenants stood at attention, suit helmets off and held under their left arms. The weapons platoon leader and the exec were both old Thompson hands, *first* lieutenants. Thus they hadn't fucked up; *they* weren't at attention; and they both wore amused smirks at the other lieutenants' discomfiture. Miles' smile, in particular, shone against his black skin.

"Hodge, what the fuck did you think you were doing leading my boys and girls into a goddamned minefield? Didn't anyone ever tell you mines are *deadly* to us?"

The captain's evil eyes swiveled to Hamilton. "Dipshit," he sneered, "when the terrain doesn't suit bounding overwatch then don't do bounding overwatch. I don't give a flying fuck what the book says; you're paid to use your mind. Use it."

At third platoon leader Thompson didn't swear, nor even sneer. Instead he said, "Even very large directional mines can be fired from quite close to the troop line provided you sandbag behind them. Failure to so use them is an indicator of cowardice. *That* is something beyond my power to fix. You're relieved. Get out of my sight and send your platoon sergeant up. Then turn in your suit to the company armorer and report to battalion headquarters. Maybe Woody can find a use for you that fits your lack of talent."

◇　◇　◇

"Where did he ever learn to be such a bastard?" Hodge asked, over a cold meal from a pouch. She, all fastidious, was trying very hard to eat the meal without at the same time eating the bugs that swarmed it.

Both Miles and the XO, Fitzgerald, laughed. Miles added, "A bastard? You think so? You ain't seen nothin' yet."

"Look, Laurie," Fitzgerald added. "He's got another three weeks to prep us for combat. It wouldn't be so bad if we'd kept our old platoons, Miles with First and me in Third, with the adjutant leading Second. But the personnel shuffle before we deployed wrecked all that. In point of fact the Army might need you someday, but the company doesn't. It would do as well or better with the platoon sergeants running the show and *no* lieutenants rather than still wet-behind-the-ears ones.

"But Thompson's stuck with you and making the best of it in the time he has."

"Is that why he dumped Ken Parker?" Hamilton asked. "Is he going to try to get rid of Laurie and me, too?"

"No," Miles said. "Or at least I don't think so. Parker was incompetent, an embarrassment to me as an American, and a worse one because we're both black. If the CO had wanted to get rid of you, he would have, but Parker *had* to go."

"But he's just so *mean* about it," Hodge said.

Fitzgerald shrugged. "The man's short on tact, I'll grant you. Hell, the last battalion commander was actually *afraid* of him, he's such a tactless bastard. But he's long on tactics and that matters more."

"Pretty good loggie, too," Miles added.

# Al Harv Kaserne, Province of Affrankon, 8 Jumahdi II, 1531 AH (31 May, 2107)

Hans was heartily sick of the religious instruction. Sure, they provided some snacks to supplement the otherwise bland diet. Sure, the bearded imam—a Sunni—in charge was an interesting, at least an enthusiastic, speaker and teacher. Sure, and best of all, no one was torturing his body to prepare it for future use as a janissary.

None of that made up for the consistent, and concerted attacks on Hans' most cherished beliefs, learned from earliest age at his mother's knee, and in school.

"To say that man is born into a state of original sin," said the imam scornfully, "means that the very handiwork of Allah Himself must be flawed. Yet this cannot be; Allah is perfect, in all he does. We do not worship mere power, boys, but perfection. Indeed, every child born is born into a state without sin, a state of purity."

Hans was pretty certain, based on his dealings with other children, that they were no such thing.

"Thus, there cannot have been a need for Jesus, Peace be upon Him, who was a prophet and no son of Allah except in the sense that all of mankind are His sons and daughters . . . there was no need for him to die on the cross to redeem that which Allah had—in His infinite mercy—already long since forgiven. This is perhaps the greatest of lies the *Nazrani* tell."

It was tempting to think and yet . . .

*If Christ suffered and died for our sins, it is greater proof of His love for us than if he merely forgave us those sins.*

"Now there are some who think," the imam—no slouch as either a theologian or a teacher of young boys—continued, "that this alleged crucifixion of Christ is greater proof of Allah's love for man. Nothing could be further from the truth; for Allah's forgiveness alone is perfect and sufficient. The alleged crucifixion is superfluous."

The imam must have noticed Hans' facial expression.

"Yes, young eagle," he said, with a warm and friendly smile, "I *can* read your thoughts." The imam laughed. "No, I can't. But I've seen young reverted boys like you balk at that statement so many times I've come to expect it, and to note the signs of it. You have a question; I can see."

Hans bowed his head respectfully. "Yes, sir. How do we know Allah did not have a son, as the *Nazrani* teach? He can, after all, do whatever he wishes."

"Ah, but why would He want to?" the imam answered. "We have sons to carry on after us, because we all must grow old and die. But Allah is eternal and unchanging. He needs no son and His having one would be, again, superfluous. Worse, it is a form of polytheism, no different, in principle, from the beliefs of the old pagans. Even the accursed Jews never fell into this trap, though they fell into or created many others."

"But Jesus, in both texts, performed miracles," Hans objected.

The imam nodded, his face serious. "In both texts, indeed. Note, though, that even the *Nazrani* texts tend to agree that Jesus made few or no miracles on his own word, but always invoked the name of Allah. A son, one who was begotten by a father and thus like unto the father, would have needed no help."

Hans nodded, not as if he agreed but as if he had no counter-argument. The imam saw this.

"I know it is hard to give up the beliefs in which you were raised," he said, still smiling. The smile, if anything, grew self-deprecating. "Instant miracles are Allah's purview, not mine. There is time for you to come to the truth, boy. And the longer and harder the road, the more forcefully will you hold on to the truth once you reach it."

# Interlude

Gabrielle shook all the way home from the mosque. She'd torn her burka off and thrown it in the gutter scant steps after passing the mosque door. "They hate us that much? I can't believe it," she said, over and over.

"Believe it, Gabi," Mahmoud said. "They despise everything about you . . . and about me, since I love you."

She missed that admission. Hands waving widely, she said, "But surely those . . . those . . . *lunatics* are a tiny minority. Mahmoud, I *know* Muslim people who are nothing like that."

"You *think* you know them," he corrected. "But you do not *know* that you know them. We have no problem

91

lying to or hiding our beliefs from the 'infidels' when necessary . . . or just useful."

Gabi shook her head. "But most of our Moslems come from Turkey, which is secular. A lot of them, too, come from the Balkans which didn't take religion seriously anyway."

"And why do you suppose they *left*, then, some of them? Maybe because secularism and indifference to religion were not very comfortable to them, hmmm?"

"But we're even more secular than Turkey and more indifferent than Bosnians."

"That's true," he admitted, slowly shaking his head in quasi-agreement. "For now, it's true. Yet the Turkish army stands as a bulwark against mixing church and state, if only to preserve its own power. Does your army? As for the Bosnians . . . well, being Moslem there was a decidedly dangerous thing. Little wonder some of them left. And then, too, several thousand Germans convert to Islam annually."

Gabrielle stopped walking and turned to face him. "You keep speaking as if religion mattered. I don't understand that. It doesn't matter to *you*."

"Just because I'm not devout doesn't mean I'm an atheist, Gabi." He held his hands up defensively. "Yes, yes, I know you *claim* to be—something I hope to talk you out of, someday, by the way. Yet I've seen you clasp your hands sometimes in what looks to the casual outside observer to be much like prayer. You say things like, 'God help us,' and 'God damn them'—usually with regards to the Americans, of course."

"Childhood conditioning with no faith behind it," she insisted.

"Of course," Mahmoud said dryly.

Ignoring the sarcasm, Gabi turned and began walking again, quietly at first. When she resumed speaking, she said, "It's all because we treat them as second class people here. No wonder they hate us when they see the fat and idle rich drive by in their Benzes. No wonder they *hate* us when we relegate them to jobs we think are beneath us. They have a right to hate us when we deprive them of the vote, even though they pay taxes, and refuse to let them become full citizens."

"Well," Mahmoud said, in a deliberately neutral voice, "you've changed the law to do that."

"Yes," she hissed, "but with such unfair restrictions that only a few can qualify. What? Fifty-six thousand Turks allowed to join our blessed *Reich* last year? Fewer, so they say, this year. Out of almost three million?"

"Ah, so you *would* prefer to be more like the Americans," he chided.

She started to answer and then stopped, mouth half open. When she did speak it was only to say, "Fuck you, Mahmoud."

At that he nodded vigorously. "Excellent idea. Your apartment or mine? And while we're on the subject, why are we still paying for two apartments?"

It was only at that point that she realized what he had said earlier: "since I love you."

# CHAPTER FIVE

I was never so enthusiastically proud of the flag till now!
—Mark Twain, *Incident in the Philippines*

## Mindanao, Philippine Islands, 29 June, 2107

The mosque burned with a greasy, sooty smoke. No wonder in that; there were bodies still inside. Around the mosque, likewise burned houses, stores, government buildings. From many of those, too, the smoke carried the savor of long pig.

Hamilton watched Captain Thompson with interest. The captain himself watched several attached Filipino Military Police sweeping the clothing of the prisoners with chemical-sensitive wands. Those who failed the test were pushed off by Suited Heavy Infantry troopers to where others like them were engaged in digging a great ditch with hands and hand tools. Thompson raised a hand as the troopers began herding off a group of children, aged perhaps eight through eleven.

"Put them with the other group, the monks' group," the captain ordered, causing Hamilton to breathe a sigh of relief.

"But, Captain—" one of the MPs began to protest, a protest cut short by a snarl and a flash of eye.

"They are just children, not responsible for being used as they were. Put them in the other group."

"I don't see the frigging point," one of the MPs muttered under his breath. "What will the kids do with their parents dead? Besides, nits make lice."

Hodge escorted a film group from IDI, the Imperial Department of Information, as they recorded scenes of the village. The group was arranging corpses. Rather, Hodge's platoon did the arranging, under IDI direction.

IDI had, of course, closely monitored the approach to and fighting for the place, all recorded by satellite and lower-flying recon drones. They had some pretty good shots, she knew, of the few casualties taken in the assault: one man's suit utterly destroyed by a large, command-detonated mine, two more killed by shaped-charge grenades carried on rockets, one man whose suit was disabled and whom the Moros had de-suited and then hacked to bits. There had also been several each killed and wounded by large caliber rifle fire.

Where the heavy caliber rifles had come from was a matter of some conjecture. The likeliest possibility, likely enough to call it a "probability," was that they had been smuggled across the sea by sympathizers in Moslem

Malaysia and Indonesia. Already, airships were being
loaded with massive quantities of aerial ordnance to level
the coastal Malaysian and Indonesian cities from which
the rifles had probably come. At other fields, fighter
escorts and electronic warfare planes were likewise being
readied to support and protect the airships. For that
matter, given their size and carrying capacity, the airships
packed an impressive defensive suite of their own, to
include four fighters each.

In a way, it was a waste. The ruins of the cities of the
Caliphate of Islam, Triumphant, produced no technology
able to stand up to the Empire's aerial juggernaut. What
little they had was purchased, at ruinous expense, from
the Chinese of the Celestial Kingdom of the Han.

And if the Malaysians and Indonesians hadn't shipped
the arms? Well, so what? It wasn't as if the Malaysians
and Indonesians weren't numbered among the enemy,
after all.

Imperial casualties the locals would never be permit-
ted to see, lest it give them hope, in the case of the
Moros, or doubt in the case of the Christian Filipinos.
Instead, they would see the results of the assault on the
Moros themselves, a one-sided slaughter.

Folks back home, on the other hand, would see the
full story. It would just be highly edited to show the
iniquity of the enemy; that, and the dire punishment
meted out to him. IDI had had decades to perfect the
art of the propaganda film, the masterful skill of the
consummate liar. Michael Moore (despite his having
been hanged in 2020) and Leni Riefenstahl were the
unofficial heroes of the department.

Around a fire a group of the troops were singing a
song they'd rediscovered from a happier and simpler day
and then modified to suit:

"Damn, damn, damn the stinking Mor-or-ros,
Cross-eyed, kakiak *ladrones.*
Underneath the starry flag
Christianize 'em with a Slag
Then return us to our own beloved homes . . . "

"You're a bona fide hero now, Hamilton," Thompson kidded, once the sorting had begun and the war crimes trials had commenced.

The captain was joking, obviously enough, and so Hamilton didn't respond directly. Instead, he asked, "Why did you save those kids, sir?"

"Softhearted, I guess," Thompson shrugged. "Besides, it was within my discretion. You object?"

Actually, that was the first remotely human response Hamilton had ever seen from his commander. He answered, "No, sir, it just surprised me. It's a . . . weakness. I didn't think you had any."

"I'm human enough, I assure you," Thompson said with a grim smile. "Those kids will be sent to a Christian orphanage," he explained. "There, they'll have the religion knocked out of them. Rather, they'll have *their* religion knocked out of them and ours, one of ours, substituted. In time, they'll become assets."

Hamilton raised one eyebrow doubtfully. "That's not why you saved them."

Thompson shook his head. "No . . . no, I saved them to sleep better at night. If you stay with the Army, young lieutenant, I suggest you find ways to help yourself sleep better at night, too."

"I haven't done anything yet that bothers my conscience," Hamilton said.

"No? You will."

The captain directed his gaze out to sea where a dozen large amphibious craft were bringing in new, Christian, settlers to occupy the area just cleared of Moslems. The landing craft, under escort, of course, would be used to cart off the remaining original inhabitants—even now moving under guard to the shoreline—and dump them on the Malaysian or Indonesian coasts. The villagers hadn't been driven off with nothing; they still had their eyes to weep with.

"All this would have been unthinkable, you know," the captain said, gesturing with one armored hand at the surrounding destruction, and not neglecting the long lines of Moros being ushered into tents where courts-martial were being held by the Army of the Philippines. "Even a century ago it would have been unthinkable, though a century and a half ago it was all too common.

"The old law of war, you see, was a fragile thing, easily broken. And when the enemy ignored it and some of our own people tried to mold it to do too much, it broke. Now there's no law except for who is fastest, who is best armed and trained, who is most ruthless. And when the enemy demonstrated that the planet wasn't big enough for both of us and we demonstrated that it didn't necessarily have to *contain* both of us? That's when—"

The captain's words were interrupted by a massive burst of weapons fire as the Filipino troops working with the company shot the first dozen of those villagers convicted of war crimes into the ditch they had themselves been forced to dig.

By the fire, unbothered by the shootings, the troopers sang:

"In that land of dopey dreams
Happy peaceful Philippines . . ."

## Al Harv Barracks, Province of Affrankon, 10 Rajab, 1531 AH (1 July, 2107)

They started the boys off with light rifles, .22 caliber repeaters. *Nazrani* were barred from owning or holding arms by law. Yet the boys were no longer *Nazrani* and so they all—being, after all, *boys*—were simply thrilled. *Here* was power. *Here* was delight in destruction.

The paper targets being destroyed would not have been thrilled, had they been anything other than paper targets. The one hare who bumbled onto the rifle range was definitely not thrilled. That hare had had too many close calls with death already in the last few years.

Fortunately for the hare, the boys had not learned yet to be nearly as proficient with the rifles as falcons are born to be with their talons. Though little devils of dust burst all around the hare wherever the bullets struck, none of them struck the hare. A few hops and it was lost in the grass, trembling.

The tent shuddered as its flap billowed in the midsummer's evening breeze. Within the tent, by the flaring light of a gas lantern, the instructors for the new recruits gathered to discuss their charges over coffee and tea. The senior drill instructor of the company, Abdul Rahman, held forth a number of names, Hans' among them, of recruits for whom it might be well to give advanced training in marksmanship, in time, and perhaps even in leadership.

The boys slept out in the open under the stars.

"Minden missed the hare, just like all the rest of them did," objected Abdul Rahman's senior assistant, Rustam. Where Abdul Rahman was tall and beefy, Rustam was shorter and much more slender. Both had the blue eyes that were typical among the janissaries of the Caliphate.

"Buck fever," Abdul Rahman answered. "He still is proving a better shot than all but a few of the others."

"He was among the very last to accept the faith."

"That's true," Abdul Rahman conceded, "and it speaks well of the boy. He doesn't give up easily." He raised one sardonic eyebrow. "And I seem to recall another ex-*Nazrani* revert who likewise didn't give up his religion lightly or easily."

"I was just stupid, mule headed," answered Rustam. "It signifies nothing."

Abdul Rahman, who had been a junior drill instructor when Rustam had first been gathered to the janissaries, barely suppressed a snort. "You were the most mule headed, if not the most stupid. As you are among the most faithful now, if not the most clever. I think we'll give this boy the same chance I gave you."

Rocking his head from side to side, making the crescent decoration on his neck swing, Rustam reluctantly and doubtfully agreed. "Oh, all *right*. Have it your own way. And I suppose it isn't as if we had a better candidate."

"No, and with the American Empire almost done tidying up their perimeter, I have no doubt it will be our turn soon enough, certainly within the lifetime of the boys."

"Is the *ordu* scheduled to move to the Atlantic Wall when the boys are ready in six years?"

"I don't know," Abdul Rahman answered. "And who really plans anyway? Who even *can* plan. We'll go wherever the will of the Almighty sends us, east or west or south."

"South? Greeks? Serbs? I *hate* the Greeks and Serbs," Rustam said with a noticeable shudder. He'd been on the Balkans Front for some years and found too many comrades staked out, castrated and with their eyes gouged out. War was endemic around the borders of the *Dar al Islam* and the *Dar al Harb*, the House of Submission and the House of War. But in the Balkans it wasn't just endemic, it was virulent.

"Not a lot of quarter given or received with either of them," Abdul Rahman agreed, a little sadly. "Not a lot of quarter given or received by anybody anymore."

## Kitznen, Province of Affrankon, 13 Rajab, 1531 AH (4 July, 2107)

There was little in the way of fun and games anymore, not with Besma living in terror of the beatings al Khalifa would administer to Petra for the slightest failings of either of them. It was all Besma could do to keep her promise to Hans to teach Petra to read. And she couldn't let her stepmother see that, either, lest she decide that was a sufficient excuse to beat Petra again.

There was something deeply sick, Besma thought, about the look on al Khalifa's face when she took her whip or a switch or a belt to Petra's back and rear. She was enjoying it, yes, that much was clear. But there was something more, too, something Besma didn't understand and perhaps didn't want to. She found the slack lips, the glassy eyes, and the heavy breathing sufficiently frightening in themselves without delving into whatever thoughts and feelings lay behind those external symptoms.

"School will start for me soon," Besma announced, as she and Petra practiced Petra's reading by a flashlight hidden under the covers of Besma's bed. "I'll be gone most of every day. I'm frightened of leaving you alone with al Khalifa."

Petra didn't say anything but began to chew her lip nervously. "Please don't," she begged. "I'll do anything . . . carry your books for you . . . anything. But that woman will *hurt* me every day; I know she will."

"I know. I'm terrified of it, too. But I don't know what to do about it."

Petra began to rock and softly to cry. "I'm just a poor slave girl," she whimpered. "Why does she hate me?"

Besma shook her head. "I don't even think you exist for her," she said. "It's *me* the bitch hates. She'd much rather have me stretched over the table with my skirt up, but she doesn't dare."

"Your father's a good man," Petra said, still crying. "Can't he help? He helped me before."

"My father *is* a good man," Besma agreed, putting one arm around Petra and using the hand on the other to gather the slave girl's head into her shoulder. She rested her own cheek on the top of Petra's head. "But he is also a pious one and the law gives the management of the household to the woman. He would never interfere. Oh, he might beat al Khalifa himself if she ever gave him cause, but she never does. If he calls for her she will come even if she's in the kitchen making bread. And she lets him plow her as he will; I've heard them."

"Plow her?"

"I'll explain when you're older. Now stop crying and get back to your reading."

## Mindanao, Philippine Islands, 4 July, 2107

The Philippine Scout, in this case a genuine tracker and not a mere infantryman, read the signs by the charred corpse. The scout—he went by Aguinaldo—was perhaps forty, though the years, the sun and the rain had aged him beyond those years. He had probably been an Imperial retainer since youth. His English was, in any case, quite good though he still had some of his native accent.

Some of what there was to see was obvious: the single bullets in the power packs that had rendered two suits helpless, the scraps of armor chiseled apart . . . the tripod under which one soldier had apparently been roasted with his belly down towards the coals.

Hodge had taken one look and run off, vomit pouring into her helmet and down the flexible neck guard to gather on her breasts.

Well, it had been her man, after all. Originally she had dispatched two soldiers on a patrol. One of them was still missing.

Hamilton refrained from following her, in both senses, but just barely.

"Over there," the Filipino said, pointing towards some vine-shrouded rocks. "They fired from over there." The finger rotated to a cave in the side of the jungle-clad hill to the east. "Some ran in there from the west. Your men followed. They were ambushed. Then the Moros in the cave came out and dismembered their armor. They want you to think they roasted this man alive but he was already dead when they strung him up over the fire. The other they dragged off, I think . . . alive. Initially they went south. I can't tell from here if they kept going that way."

Thompson nodded. He'd had opportunity enough these last few weeks to have learned to trust the scout's eyes and senses. "Can you track them?" he asked.

Aguinaldo said he could but, "Captain . . . they want you to follow. They didn't have to leave the trail so well marked and they usually don't. Then, too—" the scout hesitated.

"Yes, go on," Thompson commanded.

"You're the least suitable type of unit to track them."

"I know," the captain sighed. "But we're here . . . and nobody else is."

Thompson had already radioed for a light infantry unit to insert and track down the Moros. None had been available. He'd had high altitude aerial recon check out the area for twenty miles around. They'd seen nothing.

*And yet,* Thompson thought, *we know they're out there. If they can't be seen that means they're ready, waiting and, just as Aguinaldo said, they want us to follow.*

Hodge returned, a little unsteady in her armored feet. "I'm sorry, sir. I—"

"Never mind, Laurie," Thompson cut her off. "No shame."

*It's not like I have all that much choice,* the captain continued with his musing. *If I owe the men nothing else, I owe them that they won't be abandoned while we can still try to help. Is this going to cost me more? Yes, probably. But the soldiers can be replaced. What can't be replaced if it's lost is the faith that we—this company—won't give up on them.*

*Then, too, assume the worst, that there's a company or two of unusually well armed, well trained, and well led Moros out there. So we follow and they get in the first licks . . . maybe hurt us, maybe even badly. After they get in their first licks, we get in the last ones. How many lives do I save if that group of Moros can be destroyed?*

*Man,* all *my choices* suck; *not a good one to be had. Hell, I don't even* have *a choice. I'm not going to leave one of my boys out there to be skinned or roasted alive.*

*So the question is, do I have everybody strip down to just Exos and follow or only enough to catch the Moros and pin them in position. The latter, I think. One platoon should do.*

Thompson looked directly at Hodge. "Lieutenant, you want to get your own back?"

No hesitation: "Yes, *sir*!"

"Fine. Have your children strip down to just Exos, helmets, chest plates and small arms. That will give you the speed and the endurance to follow and catch them. The rest of the company will follow you as fast as we can, carrying your extra armor. I'll arrange for aerial recon and fire support . . . that, and an on-call power pack drop. I'll *try* again to get some light infantry inserted to block their escape but I can't promise it.

"Sergeant Aguinaldo, you go with them."

"Yes, sir," the scout answered.

"Be careful with my boys and girls, Laurie," Thompson cautioned. "Now *go*!"

Hodge was just as glad that the captain had ordered her platoon out of their suits. She wasn't sure she'd have been able to stand the stench of her own puke fermenting in the jungle heat.

That wasn't all that dumping full armor had done for her. Thus lightened, the suits were quieter, faster, and had a *lot* greater endurance. Since all the processing power was located in the back and all the sensing was in the helmets, she and her platoon lost nothing in those departments.

Unfortunately, the suits still weren't going through any major trees. These, the platoon had to snake around. Even as they did, though, branches and leaves and long, sharp grasses lashed at them, tearing at uniforms and sometimes slashing the skin beneath. No matter; one of theirs was somewhere ahead, facing a grisly death unless rescued. What was a little blood and pain not to have to face that failure?

Hodge stopped as Aguinaldo stiffened. The scout gestured with one hand, the other holding his rifle, for the platoon to move to the left. They did.

While they were doing so, Aguinaldo took a small remotely piloted vehicle, a miniature helicopter, from his pack and prepared to send it aloft.

"What is it, Sergeant?" Hodge asked, once she and the platoon were off the trail and hidden amongst the jungle's fronds.

Aguinaldo started the small RPV and lofted it before answering, "I can't say, ma'am. Something's not right up ahead. It's—"

The air was suddenly split by half a dozen large explosions, the homicidal shriek of the jagged metal those explosions threw forth, and by heavy fire from more rifles and machine guns than Hodge had devoutly hoped would ever be aimed in her direction.

## Al Harv Barracks, Province of Affrankon, 13 Rajab, 1531 AH (4 July, 2107)

"Listen carefully to the sounds, boys," said Rustam. "That's fire going high."

Down in the pit, prepared to bring down a target, mark it, and hoist the target back up, Hans listened.

He also watched as new holes appeared in the target. Sometimes he could catch them as they were created and match the distance and direction to the quality of the bullets' crack.

*This is what it will sound like when I am under fire. This is what I will hear after I pass training and am accepted as a full janissary.*

Once the boys had been trained on the .22s, they'd moved up almost immediately to thirty caliber rifles, about the most they could handle with thirteen-year-old bodies just now beginning to fill out properly (because only recently given enough to eat reliably). It was with the .30s that they were taking turns firing on the known distance range, one half firing while the other half worked the targets. It was a low tech solution, one that would have been sneered at in any of the armed forces of the Empire (excepting only the Imperial Marine Corps, a regressive lot, to be sure). And yet it not only worked, it had the double benefit of accustoming the troops to the variable sounds of fire directed their way.

This was also one of the benefits of using janissary troops. With boys raised in Islam, not only the religion but the culture behind it—or most of the cultures behind it; there were some exceptions—it was almost impossible, and at best, with the best candidates, very difficult to train them to shoot properly. Hits, after all, came through the grace of Allah as did everything else. This, for mainstream Sunni boys (Moros and Afghans being among those exceptions), was so much a given that no amount of lecturing and no amount of punishment could break them of it.

Christian boys, however, raised in the belief that God helps those who help themselves, would retain that attitude—it was too inchoate to call it a philosophy —even after they reverted to Islam. For one generation, they would, anyway; which was one reason why janissaries, after release from service, were never permitted to send their own sons to the corps. Abdul Rahman's, for example, were, in one case, a cobbler, in another a fireman, while a third was still apprenticed to a shopkeeper. But janissaries they would never be.

What the Corps of Janissaries would do after the last Christian in western Europe reverted neither Abdul Rahman, nor Rustam, nor even the caliph, knew.

## Mindanao, Philippine Islands, 4 July, 2107

Hodge never knew what hit her. One moment Aguinaldo was telling her something, the next his body had practically disintegrated in a blizzard of hot metal shards while Hodge herself was knocked almost senseless by the blast and spun head over heels by something striking her right thigh.

When she recovered enough to rise to her hands and knees, she saw and smelled the blood, not hers she hoped, dripping from her helmet and Exo. Hodge shook her head to try to clear and felt a wave of nausea wash over her. That she'd emptied her stomach earlier didn't help her as she'd eaten again, hurriedly from a pouch, while on the track of her lost soldier. She re-emptied her stomach, the puke mixing with the scout sergeant's ghastly remains. Then she looked at the bloody, torn meat of her right thigh and wanted to puke again.

*When the shock wears off, that's really going to hurt.*

Already, Hodge's Exo had analyzed the damage and applied a nondisorienting general pain killer. It wouldn't make the damaged leg any better, but it would help Hodge make full use of what was left.

There was firing all around; that much she could hear even if her vision was blurry with concussion. An indistinct shape appeared over some rocks hard by. It was shouting something unintelligible and waving something that looked shiny. Automatically Hodge pointed her left hand at the shape, formed a fist and dropped it. A burst of fire from her Slag leapt out, ripping the bolo-wielding *Moro* to shreds. His ruined body tumbled back over the rocks.

"Charlie Niner-Six, Bravo Two-Three," Hodge gasped out. "Ambush. We're fucked."

"Hang on, Two-Three," answered Thompson's calm voice. "I've got a drone inbound, ETA three minutes. Air support is coming."

"No go on the air support," Hodge answered. "I think they're all mixed in among us. Wait, out."

Even as Hodge said that, her left arm was once again pointing at a *Moro*, this one carrying a rifle rather than a bolo. The stream of fire that lanced out practically sliced the man in two.

"Report," she managed to get out.

"One: Sergeant Caudillo's dead. . . . three others down. Pinned. Returning fire."

"Two: Six left unhurt, two wounded. Holding on. They're between us and first. I think third's out of it. What we gonna to do, El Tee?"

She waited in vain for a report from her third squad leader. "Sergeant Ryan," she ordered, "report. Anybody in third squad, report. Anybody?"

There was no answer from third. She'd had to force herself to keep the sound of desperate pleading out of her voice when she asked that last, "Anybody?"

"Ma'am, Sergeant Pierantoni here. I'm with second . . . close enough, anyway. The rest of the company's better than half an hour behind us. Maybe more; if they hit us here they might have something waiting back there. I don't think we're going to hold on that long."

Hodge had been up near the point, near Aguinaldo. One could argue she'd been too near the point, but that was for the future if, indeed, that argument was ever to be made. Third squad, which had been nearest to her, was destroyed, insofar as she could tell. Sure, it was possible there was a man out there wounded and alive, or one with broken communications. But the way to bet it was that they were dead or soon would be.

"Recommendations, Sergeant?" The drug in her system was all that allowed her to keep her voice human.

"You pull back to first. We'll cover you and first. Then we can take turns, bounding back."

"No go, Sergeant, I can't move far."

"I'll come for you."

Hodge's voice was both sad and determined. "No. Here's what I want. First squad?"

"Ma'am?"

"I'll cover as best I can from here. Get yourself back to second and the platoon sergeant. Sergeant P, carry out your plan once you and second and first link up. I'll . . . "

"No, ma'am, we'll wait."

Hodge wanted to cry, not just from the pain that was ebbing from her ruined thigh, but also from the knowledge that the life she'd hoped to have with Hamilton after she left the army was just not going to happen. She wanted to cry; what she didn't want was to argue.

"No. I've only got a little left in me. I need to use that to cover first squad."

"Ma'am . . . "

"Don't argue with me. First squad?"

"Ma'am?"

"If I can't get the order out; when you hear me fire, go."


Thompson and Hamilton could hear Hodge through the command circuit.

"Laurie, hold on. I'm coming," Hamilton cried into the radio, as he started tearing the jungle apart in an attempt to move farther, faster—

"Lieutenant Hamilton, hold fast," ordered Thompson in the same calm voice as usual. The captain had the good grace not to say, *I warned you about this.*

"Captain, that's—"

Hamilton couldn't quite bring himself to say it, that Hodge was the woman he loved. It would have been worse than Thompson saying, "I told you so." Instead, after a pause, he said, "That's one of ours. We can't just—"

"I'm aware, Lieutenant, of who she is."

Another voice, the forward observer sergeant's, piped up, "Captain, airship Pershing on station with a heavy load of ordnance. They're carrying whatever we might want to ask for. Well, short of nukes, they are."

The company was still pushing on through the jungle. In his head, and aided by a map painted onto his eye with a low-powered laser,

Thompson calculated the time it would take to get to Hodge against her very short life expectancy. No matter how he tried to calculate it, he kept coming up short. There was no way he and the troops would reach her in time.

"Private circuit, Lieutenant Hodge," he said into the radio. "Laurie, your plan is approved. We won't make it to you in time. I can deal you aces and eights to prevent capture. Your call."

"Give what's left of my platoon a chance to break contact, Captain," she answered. "And . . ."

"Yes?"

"Don't make John call in the dead man's hand . . . It wouldn't be fair."

"I understand. Let me know when."

"Yes, sir. . . . Sir, if you don't hear from me . . . if I'm not able—"

"I'll call it in myself, Laurie."

"Thank you, Captain. Hodge out . . . break, break . . . First squad; prepare to move."

Dragging her ruined right leg behind her, Hodge slithered to the blood-flecked rocks nearby. She extended a monofilament microviewer from her right glove and looked over the area first squad had been in. Already some of the Moros were out, rifles slung across backs and wavy swords in hand, chopping their way through the tough battledress and inner coolsuits of the dead and wounded troopers.

"Bastards," she whispered, before retracting the miniviewer and taking her rifle in hand.

The rifle, a Model-2098, had its own viewer, which was connected by radio to Hodge's helmet. In theory, and especially when augmented by the Exo to absorb recoil, one could fire the thing effectively from behind cover with only the armored hands exposed. Practice was better than theory, though, and practice said that the natural shooting position of rifle against shoulder and eye aligned with barrel was more effective.

Hodge had counted seven of the Moros out in the open, finishing off the wounded and making sure the dead were dead. Her firing position had her to the right side of the base of the rock gathering. Sensibly, she opted to take out the rightmost Moros first, thus keeping the rock between her and those she had not yet engaged. With a whisper, she instructed the rifle, "Activate. Fire on center of thermal signatures as you bear."

With that, she swept the rifle steadily from right to left. When the first thermal image was center of mass, it opened fire with a five round in a sixth-of-a-second burst, then repeated as its operator aligned it with the next target. Hodge was quick and four of the seven went down before the remaining three realized what was happening and dove for cover.

In seconds, Hodge's rock was deluged with fire, driving her back to shelter behind it.

"Go, first squad, GO!"

"Sir, Sergeant Pierantoni here. We're out of immediate danger . . . maybe half a klick from where we were ambushed. The El Tee's stopped firing right as we heard a pretty big blast. I think it's time. We can be seven- or eight hundred meters away before anything can hit."

"Concur, Sergeant P . . . break . . . Lieutenant Hodge? Lieutenant Hodge? . . . negative contact . . . break . . . FO? Does Pershing have an FAE pod ready?"

"Yes, Captain."

"Release on Lieutenant Hodge's position."

Much as one could only rarely train someone raised in Moslem culture to be a decent shot, so too the Moros expected that if Allah did not want them to rape their captives, He would say so or otherwise prevent it. If He allowed it, as He invariably did, it was because He wanted it to happen. If there was a different price to be paid for it, then that, too, was merely in accordance with the will of the Almighty.

Thus, by the time Hodge awakened from the blast that had propelled her into unconsciousness, the Moros had stripped her from her Exo and, apparently noticing she had tits, begun to strip her of her battledress. A line of them were forming up even as eight of them began staking her arms out and her legs spread. A ninth and tenth cut away her clothing, taking some care not to cut her so as not to damage the merchandise any further. A blond infidel with tits? She'd bring a high price from one of the *datus*, the Moro chieftains. Or maybe she could be presented as a gift to the sultan.

Hodge's vision swam in and out of focus. She raised her head and saw one of the Moros pulling out what she couldn't help thinking was a laughably small penis. In fact, she did laugh and was rewarded with a light kick to the head. That made her see stars and wretch yet again.

"Goodbye, John; I loved you," she whispered. "Anytime now, Captain. Anyti—"

She barely caught the flash as a huge thermobaric bomb detonated a few hundred meters overhead.

They found Hodge's lost soldier in among a group of Moros. That much satisfaction the men and women of her platoon had; at least their comrade hadn't been roasted alive. They found Hodge, herself, *apparently* raped, with her skin—where it had been exposed—dried and scorched and her body blue where it wasn't scorched black. (In fact, there had not been time for rape but the soldiers couldn't know that.) Her luxurious strawberry blonde hair was gone, except for a blackened, crispy residue next to her scalp. Her eyes . . . well, the less said about those, the better; Fuel Air Explosive did bad things to soft eyes.

The company set up a wide perimeter around the site. Within that perimeter, military police gathered DNA samples of every *Moro* body found. Those samples would be used in every village they cleared out. Adults who matched as being family of the ambushers would be killed, in every case.

It had long since become that kind of war.

Hamilton, suited but with his helmet off, grieved beside Hodge's body, arms wrapped around shins and rocking erratically. Yes, the lieutenant had responsibilities that he was neglecting but Thompson gave him a pass on those for a while.

Thompson still didn't say, "*I told you so.*"

He did say, however, "I'm sending you back with the body. I'm allowed to send someone back and your platoon sergeant can handle things well enough for a week or ten days." That was being tactful; the platoon sergeant needed no lieutenant and would do better without having one whose nose he had to wipe.

Hamilton stopped his rocking and shook his head, "No. Being gone for a week or ten days would be a week or ten days I wouldn't be killing the people who did this. All in all, I'd rather be killing Moros than drinking in a bar in Iowa. She was from Iowa, you know."

"I knew." Thompson didn't bother to mention that "the people who did this" were already dead. He knew Hamilton knew that and he knew Hamilton meant the People, the entire People, ranged against them in the field. "You're still going. Her parents deserve to hear what happened from someone who loved their daughter, too."

Sergeant Pierantoni came up, with three other troopers, one of them with a stretcher over one shoulder. "We've got a landing zone hacked out, Captain. All the other bodies have been brought to it. She's the last one."

"Give Lieutenant Hamilton a minute alone with her," Thompson said. "And come on." With that, the captain led the party a few score meters away.

Hamilton, once he'd been left alone, started to reach over to brush the burnt stubble from Hodge's scalp. His hand stopped of its own accord millimeters from her. He couldn't bring himself to touch her, not the obscene ruin she'd become. No more could he stroke her face. Instead, he just spoke to the corpse.

"I'm sorry; I can't touch you because *this* isn't you. I'll punish them for this, Laurie. I promise I will."

He knew the pain he felt was as nothing to the pain he would feel once he really, deep down, came to understand she was gone and was never coming back. *And how will I feel when I realize I wasn't man enough to kiss her goodbye?*

Then, however hard it was to do, Hamilton leaned over and kissed Hodge's forehead. As he backed away, tears fell.

"God, what a shitty world."

## Camp Stotsenberg, Philippine Islands, 18 July, 2107

"Sit. Drink. That's not a request."

The O' Club for the camp was in a large plastic foam building, set off away from the troop billets lest the soldiers see their officers drunk and silly. Local hires did the maintenance, keeping the grass trimmed and the

jungle at bay. The building itself was formed by blowing
up a large, Quonset hut shaped balloon and then spraying
it with the foam. Once the foam hardened, the balloon
was removed and sections were cut away for doors, windows, and air conditioning units, which were installed as
kits. Furniture came disassembled in shipping containers, it being the job of the troops to assemble it. The
foam came pre-tinted for the natural environment. In
some cases, of course, no tint was necessary as white,
snow-white, was the dominant color.

The method had many advantages—cheap to heat and
cool, more durable than canvas, and bugs loathed the
taste of the foam.

"Sit, I said."

Hamilton, just returned from Iowa, looked at the table
around which sat Thompson, Miles and Fitzgerald. An
amber bottle graced the center, standing out against the
starched white tablecloth. Hamilton couldn't see how
much was left in the bottle. It didn't matter anyway; the
club had plenty more where that came from.

"Yes, sir," Hamilton answered Thompson's command,
pulling out a chair and taking a seat.

Miles reached over and took the glass from in front
of Hamilton, while Fitzgerald uncorked the bottle. Into
the glass Miles plunked several cubes of perforated ice.
He then held the glass out for Fitzgerald to fill before
setting it down in front of the company's junior lieutenant.

"How was the funeral?" Thompson asked.

"Bad," Hamilton answered, ignoring the glass. "I had
to lie to her parents, and her brothers and sisters, her
aunts, uncles, cousins, high school friends. 'I'm sure she
went quickly, without pain.' 'No, no . . . she wasn't

raped.' Do you have any idea how hard it is to explain to parents why the coffin has to stay closed?"

"I do, actually," Thompson said. "And, as it turns out, she wasn't raped. I got the forensic report while you were gone."

"That's something anyway," Hamilton said, wanting to believe but not at all sure his commander wouldn't lie to him to spare his feelings.

Thompson, no dummy, caught the doubting tone in Hamilton's voice. "I'll let you read it, if you think you're up to it."

"Maybe later, sir."

"Drink up, Lieutenant," Thompson said.

"Drink to forget?" he asked.

"No, son. We don't drink to forget. We drink to *remember*."

# Interlude

Erfurt, Federal Republic of Germany, 1
February, 2005

The sounds of the concert still echoed in their ears
even as Gabi's and Mahmoud's eyes were etched with
the pyrotechnic display.

Rammstein was in town.

"I'm not so sure I liked what you've shown me of the
inner soul of modern Germany any more than you liked
the sermon at the mosque," Mahmoud said, as they
walked to his small car parked not far away.

"Surely you're not one of those who see neo-Nazism
in a harmless concert." Gabi gave his hand a half-mock-
ing squeeze.

Mahmoud shook his head. His face looked . . .
confused. "No, no . . . not neo-Nazis. This . . . *that*, goes

back much further than the Nazis. I didn't see *Triumph of the Will* in there; for one thing it wasn't orderly enough. For another it was too . . . primitive."

"Then what did you see, lover?"

Mahmoud hesitated, still thinking and still trying to frame his thoughts in words. "Did you study your own history in school, Gabi?"

"Yes, of course."

"Hermann? The Teutoberger Wald?"

"That, yes," she admitted.

*"That's* what that music makes me see. I saw Roman legionaries sacrificed over flat rocks. I saw them nailed to trees. In the fires of the concert I saw them being burned alive . . . in the Teutoberger Wald." He chewed his lower lip for a few moments, then said, "Maybe the Nazis, themselves, were just a symptom—sure, an *extreme* symptom—of something deeper in the soul, something very primitive, very dark, very real . . . and very scary. Also something very envious; *Amerika* was not, after all, a love song."

They both went silent then, still walking and holding hands. They heard the chant before they recognized it. When they recognized it, the two were almost at Mahmoud's auto. And by then it was too late.

*"Kanaken raus! Kanaken raus! Kanaken raus! Kanaken . . . "*

There were nine of them, standing around Mahmoud's car, pounding on it with their fists in time with the chant: *"Kanaken raus!"* They wore leather and chains, or bomber jackets, and high, American-style, jump boots. Some were pierced; still others tattooed, though with only one exception the tattoos could only be seen where the neck met the chest and the shirts and jackets failed to cover them. The one exception had the numbers "88" tattooed on his forehead.

"There are *nine* of them, Mahmoud," Gabi cautioned.

"Yes," he agreed, sadly, "but I only have the one car."

Gabi screamed as a booted foot came down on Mahmoud's head for the dozenth time. In the near distance, a siren wailed with the peculiar soul-searing screech of the *Polizei*. It was a sound that conveyed images of burning buildings pouring off bricks as they crumbled, amidst ruined, blasted city blocks, with bombers droning overhead.

After a final flurry of kicks, the thugs turned as one and took off into the darkness. Perhaps they would be caught and perhaps not.

By the time the police car stopped, Gabi was on her knees, bent over Mahmoud's prostrate body, weeping. He was unconscious, his scalp split, blood seeping onto the asphalt of the pavement, and his face covered with it.

While one policeman trotted over to investigate, the other called for an ambulance.

"Animals!" Gabi screeched. "Animals!"

"Yes," the policeman agreed. "But at least the assholes haven't learned how to march in step." He saw that Mahmoud was breathing, then felt at his neck for a pulse. Satisfied with that, the policeman touched lightly around the bloody hair and scalp.

"I think he'll be all right, eventually," the officer said in an attempt to calm the woman. "I don't envy him the headache he'll have, though. Can you tell me what happened?"

Between gasps and bouts of tears, Gabi explained as best she could. As she did, the policeman, still listening, walked around the car, illuminating outside and in with his flashlight. As he did, the other policeman, call to the ambulance service completed, came to see to Mahmoud.

"Nothing on the outside to indicate the driver wasn't German," he observed, "but . . . oh, oh . . . " The light settled on a text laying on the back seat. The cover was in Arabic. "This must have caught their eye."

"That?" Gabi said, incredulously. "That's the *Rubiyat of Omar Khayyam*. It's a book of poetry."

"It's in a foreign, non-Latin or Gothic alphabet," the policeman said. "That's often enough. With easterners especially is that often enough, particularly if they're unemployed."

"You're his wife?" the policeman asked.

"He's ask . . . we live together," Gabi answered.

"I don't envy you either then, the task of cleaning up his vomit when he returns home from the hospital."

# CHAPTER SIX

The Europeans were once our slaves; today it is the Muslims. This must change. We must drive the unbelievers into deepest hell. We must stick together and hold our peace until the time comes. You can't see anything yet, but everything is being prepared in secret. You must hold yourself in readiness for the right moment. We must exploit democracy for our cause. We must cover Europe with mosques and schools.

—Sermon recorded in a Bavarian mosque, Early 21st Century

Kitznen, Province of Affrankon, 12 Jumadah II, 1533 AH (13 May, 2109)

"I don't understand why we work so hard after we do the housework," Petra said, despairingly. "I mean . . . you go to school while I work all day. Then you come home and Ishmael escorts us so we can do outside work for pay. Then we spend most every night while you try to drum some education through my dense skull into my stupid brain. It's too much."

"Your skull isn't dense and you're *not* stupid," Besma corrected.

Besma bit her lower lip, uncertain whether she should tell Petra the reasons. Finally, she decided that, yes, the slave girl who was also her best friend was old enough to know.

"I'm fourteen now," she began. "Within a year, two years at the most, my father will arrange a marriage for me. Ordinarily, I'd ask for you to be part of my dowry so I could free you. But I *know* my stepmother won't permit that so she can keep a hold over me even after I'm married."

Petra suddenly looked sick at the thought of her only real friend going away. Indeed, she felt sick, so much so that she almost missed the next sentence.

"We're working so we can make enough money to buy you from my father or, if he won't sell to me, to let you buy your own freedom which, as a pious man, he is certain to permit. Either way, you'll be free."

"Free," Petra echoed, wistfully. "I can't even imagine . . ."

Besma smiled, ruefully. While she was not, technically, a slave, she would never be free and she knew it.

## USAF Airship *Prince Eugene*, 15 May, 2109

The airship moved nearly silently over the shoreline. From the officers' lounge in the lower stern, Hamilton could see the white-capped waves buffeting that shore-line and the vague outline of the once magnificent mansions which had stood guard over equally ostentatious yachts. As the airship progressed, the shore fell away and the ruins of Los Angeles began to come into view.

Los Angeles had never been rebuilt. With each forward mile more and more ruins came into view. It was *much* worse than Kansas City had been. Most of the dead in L.A. had never been found.

Hollywood had never recovered, either. What the blast hadn't done the purges had. This was so much true that Australia (an allied state, neither a protectorate nor an imperially ruled province) provided the bulk of films shown in the contiguous fifty-seven states plus the imperial provinces of Ontario and Quebec. What didn't come from Australia, feature-length film-wise, tended to be Indian in origin, that, or Japanese.

IDI exercised very tight control over which films were permitted to be shown in public theaters.

Hamilton hadn't been home since Hodge's funeral. That had been miserable enough—virtually her entire hometown grieving as one—that for a time he'd doubted he'd ever go home again. Instead, he'd taken his leaves and R&Rs (Rest and Recreation periods, also called I&I, Intercourse and Intoxication) around the Pacific, drinking heavily and screwing whatever was available. That is, he'd screwed whatever was available for a while, right up until he'd realized that none of them—Anglo girls from Australia, delicate and graceful Japanese, superbly-legged and almond-eyed Thais, or smoky-dark Hindus—made him miss Laurie a jot less. With that realization his on-leave drinking had gone up even as his sexual escapades dropped to nothing.

He sipped at a scotch now, a product of the Province of Scotland imported through the allied Kingdom of England, even as the crumbling ruins of Los Angeles passed below.

Thompson was gone, not killed but promoted out of command over his vociferous and bitter objections. Fitzgerald, on the other hand, *had* been killed, victim of a five hundred pound bomb buried in a village square and command detonated by a *Moro* who was likewise killed.

The company was Miles' now and Hamilton was Miles' exec. After two years of combat and forcible resettlement operations, Miles had gone from beefy to thin and Hamilton—despite the calories from the drinking—from thin to almost skeletal.

The tall, now thin, newly promoted black captain signaled the bartender in the lounge for a beer and sat beside Hamilton.

"Pretty awful, isn't it?" Miles said, gesturing towards the destruction spreading out below.

"Worse than any village or town we cleared out for Christian settlement," Hamilton agreed, taking another sip at his scotch. "Though those were bad enough."

Miles nodded agreement. After a time—once they'd realized that they weren't going to win; they weren't going to hold; and the combined Imperial and Philippine forces *were* going to drive them completely out of their homeland—the Moros' fighting had grown desperate, even suicidal. And, in the long run, it had made no difference to the outcome. They were gone from the Philippines, their fields and homes now the property of the settlers who came after.

"I had relatives down there, so say the family legends," Miles sighed. "Must have been awful."

"Yeah . . . at least we left alive those Moros who wanted to live . . . most of them anyway." Hamilton sounded perhaps a bit bitter.

"It did get old after a while," Miles agreed.

"Where are we going next, do you think?" Hamilton asked. "I mean after refit and retraining at Stewart."

"Nobody knows," Miles said. "The PI campaign is over. Class Two statehood for them within two years." Class Two Statehood was like normal statehood excepting only that the state had but one senator, and representation in the House operated under the new three-fifths rule. In was one way of centering control of the empire in the original fifty states. "The Canadian rebels—"

" 'There are no 'Canadian' rebels," Hamilton parroted. "There are Americans. Then there are imperial subjects. There are also rebels, allies—' "

" '—and enemies. *No* Canadians, however.' " Miles shrugged. "Yes, John, I know the Pravda. In any case, the rebels in the frozen north have been quiet for a while now. And with the Latin provinces being admitted to Class Two, slowly but surely, troubles down that way are dropping, too. Basically, we've got the world pretty much the way we want it."

*Not entirely,* Hamilton thought. *Not entirely the way I want it. If it were, I'd still have Laurie.*

"I hear Charlie Company is opening up and the colonel's thinking of putting you in command," Miles said.

"I heard the same rumors," Hamilton agreed. He shook his head in negation, "I'm really not interested. I've had it with burned villages and resettlement and feeling like some kind of monster. Thompson had it right; you've got to find a reason to sleep at night and I never did. What's worse, I deliberately never looked for one. After Laurie was killed . . . "

There was, after all, a reason the colonel was considering putting Hamilton in command of Company C. For the last two years he'd been the most unflagging butcher of Moros in the battalion. There was also a reason the colonel hadn't yet put Hamilton in command. In those two years he'd lost something of his soul, or "whatever it is that keeps a man on two legs instead of four."

Miles shrugged again. "I know. You still thinking of punching out? You've got two years to go, you know."

"There's a way around that. The Office of Strategic Intelligence"—this was the successor to the old Central Intelligence Agency which had been renamed following the purges—"can get two years waived—even three, actually, though I don't need three—for people who sign up with them. As to whether I want to or not . . . I'll listen to them. I've an appointment with their recruiter at Kevin Barry's in Savannah when we get back."

"I have a hard time seeing you as a spook, even if you're thinner than a corpse."

"Just something I've been thinking about. I don't know myself. I know something though."

"What's that?"

"If I keep up at this *Einsatzgruppen* shit, I'll go crazier than I am."

"They do dirty shit, too," Miles said.

"Dirtier than us? Not possible."

"Never know what the future holds," Miles observed.

## Kitznen, Province of Affrankon, 17 Jumadah II, 1533 AH (18 May, 2109)

Al Khalifa was thinking about the future. *My first husband wants nothing to do with our son, preferring to lavish his substance on his Christian slave girl's bastard. If I am to secure my son's position for the future, it can only be by having Abdul Mohsem make him his heir. But he fawns on his bitch of a daughter so, spoiling the little tramp rotten.*

She glanced up, to where twelve-year-old Petra scrubbed a hallway floor on her hands and knees. Al Khalifa snarled, thinking, *Nazrani bitch! And soon enough Besma will be married off and I'll lose control of her unless I can keep this little twat under my control. I know they've been plotting to get the Christian girl her freedom. Bah! As if a Christian is worthy of freedom.*

*Then again, if I can't keep control of the Nazrani, and lose my power over Besma, perhaps I can make it so that Besma infuriates her father enough that he cuts her off from her inheritance? She's hot tempered; that will help. Maybe if . . .*

*I must consult the law,* was al Khalifa's thought. *And then, if the law supports what I have in mind, I must consult with my son . . . and he with his friends.*

## Savannah, Georgia, 25 May, 2109

The strains of ancient music wafted up the stairs, seeping under the door of a small, green-painted room. Hamilton and another man—he'd given his name as "Caruthers"—sat at a wooden table covered by a checked tablecloth. Between them sat a bottle of Irish whiskey, two glasses, and a small metallic box the size and shape of a pack of cigarettes.

"All clear," announced a metallic voice, emanating from the small box.

Caruthers, a deliberately nondescript, middle-aged black man, with a receding hairline and clothed lightly against the city's oppressive late spring; He said, "It had best be all clear, Atkinson, or you will be canned. By that I mean—"

"—that I will be ground up, melted down, and stamped out into cat food cans. Yes, sir, I know. The room *is* clear."

Hamilton raised one eyebrow. "I've never before met a machine with personality. Atkinson?"

Caruthers chuckled slightly and said, "Atkinson was an intelligence warrant and the stupidest human being I've ever met, so I named the machine for him. It doesn't have a personality, but then neither did the real Atkinson. I programmed a certain number of smart-ass answers into the thing because, frankly, my job permits me minimal human interaction. And since the original Atkinson was barely human, and a smart ass, it sort of fits."

*How does a recruiter have "minimal human interaction"?* Hamilton wondered.

"Even recruiting," Caruthers continued, "isn't really human interaction. To me you're just a file, Lieutenant Hamilton, a block to check. Don't take that personally; if I allowed myself to think of my recruits as human it might bother me when they fail to return from a job."

*Ah, wise, very wise. If we can avoid thinking of our losses as people then the pain is much less.*

Caruthers said, "Atkinson, you moron, pull up Lieutenant Hamilton's file." Immediately a hologram mimicking a brown file appeared above the table. Caruthers didn't pretend to study it, nor even order the machine to open it.

"You were well regarded in your battalion, I see," the recruiter said.

Hamilton pursed his lips and shook his head slightly. "I think they felt sorry for me."

"Yes, perhaps," Caruthers agreed. "A pity about young Lieutenant Hodge; we always have openings for husband-wife teams. They draw much less suspicion and are about three times more effective— synergy, don't you know; that and teamwork—than two single operatives or artificial couples. Never mind that; we see you as more the lone operative at this point.

"Atkinson, you dolt: linguistic scores."

The holographic file opened to an equally insubstantial sheet documenting, among other things, Hamilton's Defense Language Aptitude Test, or DLAT, which was used not only by the military, but by State and OSI as well.

"We could teach you any language or combination of languages," Caruthers said, admiringly. "This would make you useful anywhere. Do you already speak any languages beyond English, Spanish, and French?"

"A little German, and I picked up fairly decent Tagalog in the PI campaign."

"Not much use for that anymore, *except* in the Philippine Scouts as the Philippine Army is absorbed into the Imperial Army and expanded. Certainly, *we* don't have a great need for the language. You *didn't* want to be a sepoy general, after all, did you?"

"I don't want to be any kind of general," Hamilton answered. "I don't think I ever did."

Caruthers shrugged. "If you join us, of course, you won't be."

"What *will* I be?"

"That I am not sure of, though the way we do business now I will be your handler, if you join and are accepted for field work. Several of my colleagues have looked over your file and suggested you might be best used for direct action, 'wet work,' as we sometimes say. That, however, is all speculation. Your exact training track will not be determined until you are well into the BIOC, the Basic Intelligence Operatives Course."

"I get to be a shavetail again, do I?" Hamilton asked, noticing the similarity between the letters BIOC and IOBC.

"Not exactly," Caruthers said. "For one thing, *we* won't get you up at two in the morning for a nine AM movement." Seeing the look on Hamilton's face, Caruthers added, "Yes, Lieutenant Hamilton, I was a grunt, too. That's where I met that buffoon, Atkinson."

## Kitznen, Affrankon, 24 Jumadah II, 1533 AH (25 May, 2109)

It was still early morning, though the sun was full up. Besma was at school, Ishmael having escorted her. Most of the other servants were off at their various tasks. Inside the house of Abdul Mohsem were only Petra, al Khalifa, her son, and two of her son's friends.

With a grunt, Fudail, al Khalifa's son, closed the kitchen door firmly, tripping the latch. Two of his friends, Hanif and Ghalib, stood leaning against adjacent walls with their arms folded. The three formed a U, trapping Petra against the last wall. Not liking the looks in the boys' eyes, liking even less the obscene wagging of Hanif's tongue, the slave girl backed away.

Her back pressed against the broad oak table, the same one upon which al Khalifa flogged her approximately weekly. She remembered that there was a knife on the table and turned to grab it.

Too late. Like a cat, Fudail sprang forward, grabbing the slave's arms in a firm grip. He pulled her from the table. "Move that knife, Ghalib," Fudail ordered. "We'll have use for the table."

"Let me *go!*" Petra demanded, trying to kick backwards, a blow Fudail easily avoided. In answer to the demand, Fudail released one arm, the hand of which found new purchase in her long blond hair. The other hand spun her around, causing her hair to twist and pull. He released the other arm and slapped her across the face, twice, hard. Petra would wear the bruises for many days.

"In France they call this '*le tournante*,' " Fudail explained.

Taking advantage of the girl's shock, Fudail, still grasping her by the hair, reached up and tore open her bodice. Her breasts, still growing, were too small to actually need a bra. The ripped cloth exposed them to the boys. Ghalib and Hanif clapped their approval. Fudail's fingers grasped the right nipple, squeezed as hard as he could, and then twisted, raising a cry of pain and despair from Petra.

"I think the *Nazrani* whore liked that," Hanif said.

"Then she'll like the rest of the program even more," said Fudail. He twisted Petra's hair harder, forcing her to her knees. "Open your mouth, slut," he ordered, using his free hand to lift his *kurta*, the long Islamic shirt, above his privates.

When Petra failed to obey immediately, Fudail twisted her hair still more viciously until her mouth opened in a pained, horrified moan, The moan was cut off as he stuffed her mouth with his penis.

"Don't even think about biting," he hissed, "or I'll cut your throat with a dull, rusty knife. Now suck it, whore."

Terrified, Petra did. Fudail kept his grip on her hair, moving her head back and forth even as he thrust with his hips. That the repeated pressure of his penis on the back of her throat caused her to gag, and tears to pour from her eyes, bothered him not a whit.

Fudail was young, no more than fifteen himself, and had no great experience. In scant minutes he'd groaned and thrashed and filled the girl's mouth with his seed. "Swallow it, slut!" he commanded.

Finished for the moment, he hurled Petra to Hanif's feet. "It's your turn," Fudail said. "Use her the same way. We'll fuck her after she's sucked each of us."

Hanif repeated Fudail's performance, hauling the girl up to her knees by her hair and forcing himself into her mouth. Petra barely resisted. When Ghalib's turn came she resisted not at all.

Then they took the last of her clothing and tied her, face down, to the oaken table.

*It isn't me; it isn't me; it isn't me,* Petra repeated in her mind, over and over, as the boys took turns with her. Her arms and legs were tied to the table legs with crude rope. Her belly and young breasts pressed to the smooth surface of the table. A thin trickle of blood ran from between her legs and onto that surface at one end; tears gathered in a puddle at the other. The forced rubbing of her nipples on the oak was beginning to hurt almost as much as her nether regions did.

*It isn't me; it isn't me; it isn't me.*

She'd lost count of how many times she'd been violated, though she could remember the ways. The times had been many; the ways only three. Of those, one had hurt and still did, while the other had been so agonizing the boys had gagged her first to keep her from screaming. The gag remained, even after the last of them had pulled out of her anus.

*It isn't me; it isn't me; it isn't me.*

And then, with a final gasp and groan from Fudail, it was over and the boys were untying her from the table.

"Cover yourself, bitch," Fudail demanded, tossing her torn clothing across her back. "And if you think you can do any good by telling anyone, I assure you it will be far worse on you than it will on us."

In a daze, Petra arose and pulled her garments over herself. In a daze she staggered back to the room she shared with Besma. It was only when she'd collapsed into a corner that she finally screamed.

Not far from the door to Besma's room, al Khalifa smiled wickedly. *Perfect*, she thought.

Besma found Petra there, later that afternoon, no longer screaming but quietly rocking and weeping, her head in her hands and self-inflicted scratches across her face and upper torso. When Besma knelt before her friend she saw bruises that had turned ugly—black and blue and swollen.

"What happened? My God, what happened?"

Petra didn't answer. She lifted her head from her hands but stared off into the distance blankly. At this distance, Besma saw the scratches, little lines of blood welling up, clearly. She looked down at the ones lower, those across Petra's chest and breasts. Around them, the material of the slave girl's garment was plainly torn. Two rounded red spots marked where Petra's abraded nipples had touched the cloth. Looking down still further, Besma saw the blood stain where the garment touched between Petra's legs.

"Who *DID* this!" Besma demanded. When Petra didn't answer she shook the girl violently, repeating, "Who *DID* this?"

Petra's lower jaw shook as more tears welled up. "Fudail . . ." She gasped out. "Fudail . . . and his friends."

Besma's hands were curled into claws. Her long red nails—her father indulged her in the vanity—ached for the eyes of Fudail. Her teeth longed to rip out her stepbrother's throat. She walked with purposeful steps to the house's main room. Ishmael, standing at the inner door, backed away when he saw her face.

Her father sat on a cushion on the floor, reading an expensive, leather-bound copy of the Koran. al Khalifa, wearing a satisfied smile, sat demurely in a corner opposite Abdul Mohsem, busying herself with knitting. Fudail sat near his mother, eating some nuts from a bowl. If anything, his smile was even more satisfied than his mother's.

"Monster," Besma whispered, as she closed the distance between her and her stepbrother. "Monster," she said aloud as she neared his sitting form. "Monster!" she screamed as she launched herself, claws outstretched, for his eyes.

Fudail barely managed to get his arms over his eyes in time. That didn't stop Besma. Though normally he was much stronger than she was, sheer hate and rage had given her a strength beyond her age, size, and sex. Blocked from his eyes she still managed to bowl him over onto the floor. While one of her claws raked his throat, the other sought his penis, intending, if at all possible, to rip the thing off. At the same time her teeth chewed one of his arms, causing blood to squirt out over her face.

She got a good grip on his penis, but discovered it wouldn't tear out so easily. Instead, she let it go and grabbed his testicles. Those she grasped and *squeezed*, bringing forth from the rapist a gagging shriek: "Mother! Help me!"

Al Khalifa was the first to try to drag the little she-demon off of her prized son. Besma managed to get one kick to her stepmother's face, sending the woman sprawling.

"Abdul Mohsem, *do* something!" al Khalifa screamed from the floor. "Stop her!"

As shocked as anyone present by the attack, Abdul Mohsem called, "Ishmael! Help me!" Between them they managed to draw Besma's head away from Fudail's throat (the boy had been losing the battle to keep her teeth away). Her father and his slave also managed to pull her off of Fudail, but the last thing she held onto was the boy's scrotum. He screamed again as his testes were nearly forced out of their sack by Besma's fanatical iron grip.

"Hold her, Ishmael," the father ordered. "And just what in the ninety and nine beautiful names of Allah is going on here?"

"That filthy bastard raped Petra," Besma cursed, still showing her now bloody claws and struggling to get out from Ishmael's control. "He and two of his pig friends.

I'll *kill* the swine, I *swear* I will." Her struggle to get away from Ishmael intensified. "Let me go! Let me at the piece of pig filth!"

Abdul Mohsem took a deep breath. He looked over at Fudail, still gasping and now beginning to vomit onto the rug on the floor, the yellowish, chunky stain spreading even as it sank into the carpet. Al Khalifa had recovered and had positioned herself protectively in front of her son.

"What happened?" Abdul Mohsem demanded, quite despite Fudail's obvious distress. "Tell me what *happened*!"

"Hanif . . . and  Ghalid . . . and  I . . . were  in  the kitchen. The little . . . *Nazrani* slut . . . threw herself . . . at us."

"Liar!" Besma shrieked, twisting like a python and redoubling her efforts to get out from Ishmael's grasp. "Filthy pig *liar*!"

"My son is a good boy," al Khalifa insisted. "He would never do such a thing. And I've seen the little slave wench wriggling her ass in front of the boys whenever she had the chance. It's obvious what happened; that he's telling the truth."

"You fucking cunt! You liar! You bitch-whore-slut-twat! You cocksucking, manipulative, vicious *tramp!*"

Abdul Mohsem's eyes widened in shock. He'd never imagined his dear Besma even *knew* such words.

"Father," Besma nearly wept, "she beats Petra all the time for no reason, beats her like an animal and for *no* reason. She put her stinking bastard of a son up to this; I know she did."

"Nonsense," al Khalifa insisted, her chin rising haughtily. "I maintain discipline in the household, as the hadiths insist I must."

"There must be a trial," Abdul Mohsem announced. In truth, he simply didn't want to get in the middle of a domestic dispute if he could dump the responsibility elsewhere. "Let the judges decide where the truth lies."

Besma wept alone, seated in the back of the courtroom. In the front, fully draped and in chains, Petra was even more alone. Even so, she did not weep. Tears were, for the nonce, beyond her.

"The law is very clear," the turbaned judge explained patiently, and even perhaps a little sadly. "We have one *Nazrani* female, not even a woman yet by their reckoning but still we will give her testimony the full weight of a woman, under ours, and even of a woman of the faithful. That is to say, we have one half of a story claiming rape without provocation.

"On the other hand, we have three males, all of whom agree that there was no rape, that the slave threw herself upon them. Each of these witnesses counts fully. Thus, by a weight of six to one, the testimony is that the rape, if it was a rape, is the fault of the slave girl. This is corroborated by the testimony of the woman, al Khalifa, that the slave girl did not even cry out until the supposed rape was over. Not even the slave's own words refute that."

The judge opened a heavy volume and began to read, verbatim: "If I came across a rape crime, I would discipline the man and order that the woman be jailed for life . . . because if she had not left the meat uncovered, the cat wouldn't have snatched it.

"If you get a kilo of meat, and you don't put it in the fridge or in the pot or in the kitchen but you leave it on a plate in the backyard, and then you have a fight with the neighbor because his cats eat the meat, you're crazy. Isn't this true?" The judge looked up for confirmation. All the men present nodded their heads with the wisdom.

Continuing, the judge said, "If you take uncovered meat and put it on the street, on the pavement, in a garden, in a park, or in the backyard, without a cover and the cats eat it, then whose fault will it be, the cats', or the uncovered meat's? The uncovered meat is the disaster. If the meat was covered the cats wouldn't roam around it. If the meat is inside the fridge, they won't get it."

The judge cleared his throat, then looked left and right for agreement from his two co-judges.

"It is the judgment of this court that the slave girl, Petra bint Minden, shall be taken from this court to the pens reserved for slaves for sale, that she be auctioned next Friday to the highest bidder. That the proceeds from that sale shall go first to the court's fees, then to her current owner, Abdul Mohsem. As for the boy, Fudail, who suffered injury in the attack by Abdul Mohsem's daughter Besma, we judge that no recompense is due him and further adjudge that he and his two friends, Hanif and Ghalid, shall each receive thirty lashes on the soles of their feet—"

At this patent injustice al Khalifa gasped with indignation.

The judge sneered. "And if you interrupt this court again, woman, you shall be next in line for lashes after your son and his friends."

"They won't even let me see her," Besma wailed to her father.

"I gave those orders," Abdul Mohsem said. "It would do neither of you any good to be together again."

The Moslem girl's eyes flashed with anger. "We will be together again, father. I love her like my own child and I will not be separated from her."

"You will never see her again."

"Let me tell you something, father," Besma said, her voice very firm and sure. "If you do not go and buy her back, bidding against yourself if necessary, you will never have a moment's peace out of me." Besma turned away, went to the bookshelf, and withdrew Abdul Mohsem's prized Koran. This she held flat in her left hand, placing her right above it. "This I swear, father. If Petra is not returned here and *freed*—Do you hear me? Freed!—I shall become the greatest whore in the province, a greater whore even than that vicious slut you wed. I will bring shame to our clan that will last until the final generation. There will be no cave deep enough to—"

Of its own accord Abdul Mohsem's hand lashed out, slapping his daughter across the mouth with a force hard enough to spin her to the floor. "I am your father and you will be silent."

Besma smiled through her pain. "You can silence me now, father. Do you not think my voice will carry when I writhe in heat under slaves and stable boys? Bring me back my friend!"

*"It will not happen!"*

Again, listening from around a corner, al Khalifa thought, *Perfect*.

There was really nothing in Islam to prevent a slave from owning a slave. Shamsuddin Iltutmish, for example, a sultan, had been the slave of a slave. Thus, Ishmael, armed with the money Besma and Petra had saved towards Petra's freedom, went to the slave barracks not far from the crooked tower.

"Please buy her, Ishmael," Besma had begged, pressing the coins into his hands. "Buy her so that we can free her. Don't let what is planned for her happen. She's too pretty. You *know* what they'll sell her to be."

He'd agreed, of course. He'd never really been able to deny Besma anything. And when she'd said, "I would give you my body for your enjoyment, if you thought you could make use of it," his heart had melted.

"I will try," he'd promised, then added, with a very sad smile, "I wish I could take you up on your offer."

At the slave barracks, Ishmael walked from cell to cell, looking for Petra. Though the cells were full of wretched, hungry, dirty and miserable slaves, and even though some of them were women, Petra was not among them. Ishmael looked for the barracks master or the chief slave dealer to ask about her.

"The reddish-blond *Nazrani*?" the slave dealer shrugged. "She's too choice to let rot down here. Or she will be, once her bruises and scratches heal. In any event, I'll get a much better price for her all dolled up and in proper clothing. Still, if you want to inspect her, she's upstairs." He pointed as a flight of stone steps. "Remember," the dealer cautioned, "look but don't touch."

Bowing his head and thanking the dealer, Ishmael made his way up the stone steps to a corridor. There were perhaps a half dozen doorways, each of them barred. He called out, "Petra?"

A pair of small, delicate hands appeared at one of the barred doors. "Ishmael, is that you?" a desperate voice called out.

He ran to it . . . and stopped dead once he saw. Suddenly, the purse at his belt seemed very light indeed. Clothes, hair, face . . . despite the bruises, Petra had been transformed from a skinny twelve-year-old into something—

"Beautiful," Ishmael said, despairingly. "They've made you *beautiful*. Allah have pity; I'll never be able to buy you for Miss Besma now."

# Interlude

Kitzingen, Federal Republic of Germany,
13 February, 2005

They hadn't moved Mahmoud from the hospital at Erfurt to the *Kreisskrankenhaus* Kitzingen until he'd come out of the coma and shown some fair progress towards recovery. This had taken six days. On the seventh he was moved. By the ninth, he was spending almost as much time awake as unconscious, though a fair amount of that awake time was spent in pain and nausea. Three days after that the hospital pronounced him well enough to go home with Gabrielle. The next day, she'd picked him up.

"I can't stay here anymore, Gabi," he said, on the drive home.

"In Kitzingen, you mean? Why? There's no trouble here."

147

"No . . . I mean in Germany. I mean in Europe."

"But where would you go? Where would *we* go?"

"I am thinking . . . America, if we could get in there."

"America," she sneered, not at her lover but at the thought. "Why ever would anyone want to go to America? I couldn't, I mean I just *couldn't* abide it. I think you're still distraught and not thinking clearly. Just because some thugs attacked you—"

Mahmoud sighed. *How to explain?*

"It's not because they attacked me personally," he began. "It's that they attacked me as a Moslem, not even caring that I am not much of one. Now you think it's an isolated incident, I am sure. But it's not. How long do you think it will be before they, or people like them, attack another?"

Before she could even begin to form an answer he said, "I would be surprised if it hasn't happened already, a half dozen times. And even that isn't the main problem."

"Then what *is* 'the main problem'?"

"My people will begin to strike back. You've heard the sermons; you've read the papers I've shown you. Troubles are coming here, troubles are coming to all of Europe. *Bad* troubles. People like me, reasonable people, are going to run. And who will be left? The lunatics. And don't tell me about self-fulfilling prophecies; some prophecies are self-fulfilling *because they're destined to come true*."

"I can't go to America," she said definitively. "Canada, maybe."

"Canada's as badly off as Europe," he said. "Lunacy is coming there, too. Australia?"

"Too militaristic," she answered, "too much in the Americans' camp. Too much a willing tool for American imperialism. Why, anyway? Why are you so certain everything's going down the tubes."

"Because my people could fuck up a wet dream," he answered, putting his head down in his hands. "And I'm beginning to think that yours can, too."

## Church of St. Vinzenz, Kitzingen, Federal Republic of Georgia, 5 March, 2005

It didn't appear to Mahmoud to be a very old church, certainly nothing like the age of the town. Stuccoed off-white, with three inset crosses framing a niched statue of its namesake, the church's roof was red tiled. A blocky square tower jutted out from the left. Mahmoud entered the church by passing under a small overhang, likewise with tiled roof, the whole being held up by twin columns. His footsteps were still a little unsteady, the legacy of his beating.

It was a decidedly odd feeling, entering a Catholic church. There were some in Mahmoud's native Egypt, of course, and rather more Coptic churches. Yet he'd never been in one.

In the dim shadows toward the front, by the ornate altar, Mahmoud saw a priest going about some inexplicable business. He cleared his throat, nervously, causing the priest to turn.

"Can I help you, my son?" the priest asked.

"Possibly . . . sir,"—for Mahmoud didn't yet know to address the priest as "Father"—"just possibly."

# CHAPTER SEVEN

"We must be open and tolerant towards Islam and Muslims because when we become a minority, they will be so towards us."
>—Jens Orback, Swedish Minister for Democracy,
>Metropolitan Affairs, Integration and
>Gender Equality, 2004

Kitznen, Province of Affrankon, 8 Rajab, 1533 AH (7 June, 2109)

"Twenty-three dinar, seven dirhem is the bid. Do I hear twenty-three, eight?"

Petra stood, ashamed, her face down. The auctioneer reached out to lift her chin with his whip, but when he saw the tears he let her face fall again.

She was not naked, precisely, but the auctioneer had disrobed her sufficiently to permit the bidders to see the budding promise of her body. In effect, she was down to what passed for an inadequate bra and with a thin wrap around her hips. This was not exactly in the best spirit of Islam, but, on the other hand, she wasn't Moslem.

"Twenty-four dinar," shouted a bearded, robed factor whom Ishmael didn't recognize.

"Twenty-four, five," answered Ishmael, and that was as much as Besma had been able to scrape up. In other circumstances, Abdul Mohsem would have freed the girl for less. It was beyond his power now.

"Twenty-seven," shouted the factor, obviously tired of the game and sensing that Ishmael was at the end of the resources he had to spare. *What does an obvious eunuch care for owning a girl like that?* the factor wondered. *Perhaps he, too, intends to whore her out. No matter, she'll make a better whore when she's trained by my staff.*

Ishmael shuddered. That was the last of the money Besma had given. He had his own, the scrapings of years intended to purchase his own liberty. Where would he ever come up with . . .

"I have twenty-seven. Do I have twenty-eight? Twenty-seven . . . twenty seven . . . going for . . . "

"Thirty!"

Petra looked up from the platform on which her wares were being paraded. She knew how much Besma had had to spare, down to the last thin *fil.* If Ishmael was bidding more . . . ? Petra looked directly at Ishmael. Through her tears of shame she smiled warmly at him, in thanks.

"Thirty-five," said the factor. His glance at Ishmael showed that he was plainly annoyed that this tiresome game continued.

Ishmael gulped. "Forty."

Without the slightest hesitation, the factor said, "Fifty," sneering at the presumptuous slave as he did so.

"Sixty." Ishmael's face looked stricken. He could not go much higher.

A man, his face covered, stepped up beside Ishmael. The slave felt a nudge. A heavy purse was pressed into his hand. Abdul Mohsem's voice said, "This is what I could come up with on short notice. Two hundred and twenty dinar. If the bloody bank had been open, I'd have gotten more. You can raise your bids up to that amount. All I'll lose by it is the auctioneer's fee."

"I never before realized that my master is also a saint," Ishmael said.

Abdul Mohsem said nothing, but, shaking his head, he turned away and left the auction house. He thought, *I'm no saint. I'm weak. If I'd been a saint I'd have disciplined that little bastard, Fudail, myself. Instead I let someone else do it and look what I've done. Allah forgive a stupid man.*

Face suddenly flushed with hope, Ishmael bid, "Eighty."

The factor dabbed at the sweat running across his face and neck. Who would have imagined that obtaining this skinny infidel wench would be such a bother? He'd wear her out, all three holes, making his money back.

"Enough is enough," he whispered. "Three hundred!"

That was a bid Ishmael could not match, even if he were able to throw his own value into the bargain, which—not owning himself—he was not.

Defeated, Ishmael turned away. The auctioneer covered Petra with a robe—if she were to catch pneumonia and die his fee would be lost as well—and turned her over to an assistant. Petra, now stone faced, followed the assistant back to her cell.

"I'm sorry, Petra," Ishmael said, early the next morning. "I tried."

The girl nodded sadly, sitting on the floor of her cell. "I know. Where did you ever get the money to bid so high? I never expected . . . " her voice trailed off.

"My own savings," Ishmael admitted. "And then Abdul Mohsem gave me more, all he could come up with in a hurry. It wasn't enough. I'm sorry," he repeated.

"So am I," the girl said, her voice so low and so hopelessly sad that it was all Ishmael could do not to weep.

"At least you'll be away from al Khalifa," he offered.

"That's something, I suppose. I'll try to remember that when they turn me over to a gang of men." The girl shuddered at the memory.

"Oh, I almost forgot," Ishmael said. He drew out his purse and counted out from it all the money he'd been given by Besma. To this he added ten gold dinar of his own. These he pressed into Petra's small hands.

"Besma wants you to have the money you both earned," he said.

"It's too much."

"A little, maybe. Call it a gift from me. An apology for all men, everywhere."

She nodded, thankfully.

"And one other thing." From underneath his robe Ishmael drew out the heavy journal of Petra's great-grandmother. "Besma said this belongs to you. If I failed to win the auction, I was to give it to you."

Petra clasped the journal to her small breasts. To her, its value wasn't so much in the words her great-grandmother had written, but in the fact that it had been the primary text used by Besma to teach her to read.

Tears formed. "I will miss my Besma *so*," the slave girl wailed.

"Don't be so hard on your father, Besma," Ishmael had said. "He really tried. The man bidding on Petra wanted her so badly I don't think any amount of money the entire family could raise would have been enough."

"Sure," she said, doubtfully, then cried out "What's going to happen to my Petra? What will they do to her?"

"Nothing worse than what's already been done to her, I imagine," Ishmael answered, shaking his head sadly. "Just . . . more of it." *A lot more of it.*

"I'll get her back someday," Besma said. "I don't know how yet but this *atrocity* will not stand."

They took Petra away early the next day, even before the sun rose. She'd expected a horse-drawn wagon, at best. In fact, the factor had come for her in a genuine automobile. She'd only ever ridden in one once before and was, despite herself, excited at the prospect.

"I paid far too much for you, little *Nazrani*, to risk you catching a cold or, worse still, pneumonia," the fat factor had explained.

She'd more than half expected him to use her on the way and was surprised when he didn't. In years to come she would understand why he'd not forced her to do anything; the factor far preferred fat little boys and pre-pubescent girls.

The car stank far worse than any shit wagon Petra had ever smelled fertilizing the fields around Grolanhei. She wrinkled her nose at the stench, something that caused the fat factor to laugh.

"It runs off oil made from coal, little *Nazrani*. Naturally, it stinks. I, by the way, am Latif. You may call me, 'master.' "

Latif tapped the lowered window between himself and his indentured driver. "Bring us to the castle," he ordered.

While most new production automobiles in the Empire, Australia, and Japan had robotic auxiliary drivers, slaves were cheaper in the two Caliphates and could polish the exterior to boot. Besides, the roads were simply not up to robotic drivers.

The driver obediently started the car and began heading northwest to pick up the A7 south.

"Wait!" Petra shouted then said, more quietly, "I'll never see my home, Grolanhei, again. Would it be possible to drive through it? Once? Please?"

"I know where it is, sir," the driver said. "Opposite direction, not far, maybe six kilometers. I can keep going, pick up the A3, then come west to the A7." The driver shrugged. "Fifteen minutes out of our way, no more, sir."

Robotic drivers rarely showed such judgment.

Latif considered. "Allah smiles upon those who are kind even to slaves. Very well, little one, we'll show you your town one last time." His face turned stern. "But I'll expect even more dedication to your lessons once we reach the castle. I paid a great deal for you and I expect a good return."

By the time they'd passed through Grolanhei, Petra wished they had not. Where it had been a bright and happy memory, in her mind, after several years in the larger, busier, and above all cleaner Kitznen, the town seemed to her very small and dirty, the people very downtrodden and unhappy.

Briefly she considered asking for the boon of seeing her family. That thought lasted until she realized her mother and father would have questions, questions about her current status. She didn't want to blight their lives any further by having to say, *They've sold me to be a whore.* Nor did she want to bring any shame to her brother Hans. What the other janissaries would say to him, how they would torment him with the shame of having a whore for a sister, she didn't even want to think about.

She was just as happy when the car passed through the town, passed through its neighbor, Kleilanhei, and moved onto the highway to the north.

Even the five men being crucified by the on ramp to the A3 didn't upset her, so happy was she to be heading away from her home.


The on ramp looked old and broken down. It was, in fact, considerably newer than either of the roads, A3 and KT11. Nobody really built well anymore.

There were nine crosses already erected, four more than needed. These were permanent, made of steel, no more than eight feet high and with crosspieces four feet wide affixed about a foot and a half below the very summit of each upright. They might once have been taken for Christian symbols. No more.

Trying to ignore the crosses, Hans sighed at the shiny car whizzing by on its way west. Those were not for such as he, though he might hope, after his discharge, that his son might rise high enough to be able to afford one.

*Never mind, business to attend to.*

Rashid was in charge of the detail. Janissaries were often used to enforce civil law, even as Roman centurions once supervised their men in executing punishment. It was to harden the boys as much as for any other reason.

The boys were strong now, after several years of both good eating and diligent training. Though their background may have been Christian, they bore little resemblance to the half-starved, recently flogged wretches under sentence of death for plotting against the Caliphate.

Hans had no clue about the details of the case. It really wasn't any of his business. Even so, he felt decidedly odd about putting to death a priest, as one of the condemned was.

With the *Nazrani* traitors arranged in a line surrounded by the young janissaries, Rashid read from an execution order. "In accordance with Sura Five, for fighting against God and his prophet, for bringing disorder to the world, you are condemned to death by crucifixion." Lifting his head to the janissaries, he said, "Take them."

Hans and three comrades immediately grabbed the priest. While Hans and another held the priest fast, a third bound his hands together in front of him. The fourth stood idle, holding two large nails in one hand and a heavy sledgehammer in the other.

"Up he goes," said Müller, one of Hans' comrades, once the priest's hands were firmly tied together. With a grunt, the three lifted him up, hooking his bound hands over the upright.

"And . . . drop." As one they let the man go. He hung there for a moment, in shock, as the drop had nearly dislocated his shoulders. The priest made no sound.

*Tough infidel,* Hans thought. *That had to have hurt some.*

"His feet now, boys," Müller said.

There were blocks of wood affixed to each side of the upright. The boys formed a loop of rope around both the upright and the priest's ankles. This they tightened by twisting a piece of wood within the loop, drawing the victim's heels up to the blocks of wood. The block was marked with the proper places to align those heels. By the time this was done, two others among the condemned had begun to scream.

"Be brave, my brothers," the priest shouted out.

The boy who had been holding the nails and hammer handed one of the nails to Hans and the other to Müller. "You first, Hans," the hammer wielder said.

Obediently, Hans stepped out of the arc of the hammer and held the six inch spike point first to the priest's heel. Above, unseen by Hans, the man turned his head and eyes away and began to sing:

*"Christus der is mein leben*
*Sterben ist mein Ge . . . "*

The hammer swung, the nail bit into the heel, and the hymn turned into a scream. Another swing and the bones in the heel began to separate and shatter. Still a third and the point was at the wood. A fourth and fifth ringing of hammer on steel and that part of the job was done.

Hans felt dirtied by the blood pouring out over his hand. He was glad to let the spike go after the third strike.

"Now your turn, Müller."

Again the priest screamed, like a girl, or a hare caught in a falcon's talons. He screamed, but he did not cry. He screamed, but no more, Hans thought, than absolutely necessary.

The other four, on the other hand, did cry, and sob, and beg, and plead. The young janissaries ignored them as they went to set up their tents. Death would be a long and miserable time in coming and there was no reason to sleep in the rain while it did.

Hans was not alone in walking to the water cans to wash the *Nazrani* blood from his hands. *What would my sister think, if she could see me now?* he wondered.

## Honsvang, Province of Baya, 8 Rajab, 1533 AH (7 June, 2109)

It was a long time driving over half-broken roads before the factor's auto pulled into the town of Honswang and up to a hotel. The building was, in some sense, grand, yet its walls were discolored and there was an air of incipient decay about it. Petra, used to the residue of decay all her young life, barely noticed.

"We'll wait here overnight," Latif said to Petra. "Tomorrow we can take a horse carriage to the top and your new home.

"Take care of the bags," he said to his driver.

"Yes, sir."

The hotel provided a suite: living room, bedroom and bath. Latif pointed to a couch and said, "That's for you." He looked her up and down and *tsked* wistfully. "Pity you've already begun to sprout. I'd have enjoyed you three or four years ago. Oh, well," he shrugged, "no matter. I can always send for something if I feel the need."

Sitting on the couch of the suite's living room, Petra felt so alone and so very, very lonely. Strange room, strange building . . . and Latif was a very strange man. And the future? She was afraid even to let herself think about a future.

"And my past is lost," she whispered to herself. "Or maybe not, not entirely."

She reached into the little bag she'd been allowed and withdrew her great-grandmother's journal. She didn't intend to read it but just to hold it to feel some of the connection with Besma and the life she'd grown used to. Whatever her intent, though, she opened the journal and discovered therein a letter. Recognizing Besma's handwriting, Petra laid her own head down on the letter for a moment before raising up again and taking it in hand to read:

My Beloved Petra:

I'd hoped you would never read this. If you are reading it, it can only be that I've failed to free you. For that, I am sorrier than I can say. I miss you already as if half my heart were torn out. I will not be whole until we are together again.

Fudail and Hanif and Ghalib were beaten a couple of days ago. Ishmael took me to the shop where we bought your clothes and I watched from an upstairs window. They suffered, but not enough. I will make them suffer more, if I can.

Fudail fears to be alone in the house with me. He should. Whether I can get at Hanif and Ghalib I cannot promise you. I *do* promise you Fudail's eyes and his manhood, whatever it may cost me to get them.

I have already begun to punish al Khalifa, whom I am certain was responsible for all this. My father, I am sure, senses this. He has moved to another room in the house and will not share his bed with her. I can only hope that she turns to some other so that I can denounce her and watch her be stoned to Hell. I am waiting for that day.

My father tried to buy you back. For this reason alone have I forgiven him.

Do not lose hope. I will never forget you. I will come for you, or send for you, when I can . . . though it take me all my life.

All my love, your *sister*,

Besma

By the time Petra had read the letter for the fourth time, many of the letters and words had been smudged with what poured from her eyes.

## Intersection, A3 and KT11, Province of Affrankon, 10 Rajab, 1533 AH (9 June, 2109)

It was early morning and, despite the season, quite chilly. The wind blew sometimes from the east, sometimes from the north. Wrapped in his janissary's field cloak, Hans shivered.

*God, what a shitty world,* he thought, as the five condemned writhed and struggled for breath on their crosses. They moaned now but seldom cried out. For this Hans gave full credit to the priest who spoke up, encouraging his charges to rejoice at their martyrdom and to bear up under their pain. They sang hymns, sometimes, when their strength allowed.

*I should do as well, under the circumstances.*

The boy, for he was still a boy, sat on a grassy slope, chewing his lip and watching the priest slowly expire. *I'd help if I could,* Hans thought.

"Boy? You . . . boy? What's your name?" the priest asked. His head lolled to one side with weakness. His steel-gray hair moved with the breeze.

"Hans, Father." He'd not forgotten how to address a priest, despite three years of indoctrination.

"You were . . . Catholic . . . Hans?"

"Yes, Father."

"Tell me how they convinced you to change?"

Hans opened his mouth to answer and then realized, *I don't really know how. We were just all in pain and . . .*

The boy poured out the story to the priest.

The priest laughed and, though the laugh was strained, it was still an amazing thing from a man dying on the cross. "Didn't you find it a little odd that they claim 'no compulsion in religion' and then compelled you and your friends?"

"I—" Hans changed the subject. "How did you end up here, Father?"

The priest laughed, then went into a fit of violent coughing. "I was sold out by another priest."

When he saw Hans' eyes go wide at that, the priest explained, "Many of the clergy *like* having the masters in charge, Hans. How else, after all, could they enforce support for the church among Catholics and Protestants? How else could they have the religious laws *they* believe in enforced, except by the will of the masters?

"What of your mother and father, Hans?" the priest asked, changing the subject. "Are they still Catholic?"

"Yes, Father."

"Does the Koran teach to honor them?"

"Yes, Father, in Sura 17, 23 and 24."

"As does the Christian Bible?"

"The words are different but, I think, the intent is the same."

"Do you honor them by casting off their faith? Don't answer, Hans. It's just something for you to think about."

The priest stood upon the spikes passing through his heels and moaned with the effort and the pain. After breathing heavily several times, and coughing forth great quantities of phlegm, he let his body down again.

"Not too much longer now, I think," the priest said. "And that's the truth. Tell me Hans, what does the Koran say about lying to unbelievers?"

"That it's permissible, when necessary, Father."

"Then let me leave you with this thought, Hans: Turn-about is fair play. Oh, and one other thought. If you ever have the chance: Look up 'Skanderbeg.' Go now, before they punish you. I will pray for you, my son."

## Castle Noisvastei, Province of Baya, 10 Rajab, 1533 AH (9 June, 2109)

The word "houri" meant, among other things, "having lovely eyes." It did not necessarily mean, nor was it related to, the English word "whore" or its Teutonic antecedents. Notwithstanding, the girls at the castle were all called "houris" by the staff and the management, even though they were just whores.

After Latif had turned Petra over to a member of the staff, the first day had been taken up with inoculations and other medical treatment. The houris had value, it was explained to her and a dozen other new girls, most of them of about her age, and so it was worth while taking better care of them than it was with the usual filthy *Nazrani*.

Fortunately, Petra had had little opportunity to experience candy in her life and so she was spared more than the most cursory dental treatment. Some girls were not so lucky.

Each of the new girls was then assigned to an experienced, older houri for training. There was something about the idea of a line of a bakers' dozen kneeling twelve-year-olds, practicing fellatio in cadence, under the supervision of a washed-up whore, that offended even Latif's atrophied sensibilities.

Petra's teacher was called Zheng Ling and Petra thought she had the most beautiful, exotic eyes she'd ever seen, almond shaped but very large.

"I've never seen anyone like you," Petra said, in wonder, as Ling showed her around the castle.

"I'm an import," Ling said. "Bred in a brothel in Shanghai and sold here when I was four."

"*Four!*"

"I was a maid for five years before they ever put me to 'work,' " Ling said. "Even that pederast, Latif, has some scruples. He was my first.

"What did he pay for you, by the way?" Ling asked.

"About three hundred dinar," Petra answered.

"That's a *lot!*" Ling said admiringly. "No wonder they assigned you to me; they always give me the best girls to train."

"Train me, *how*, exactly?" Petra asked.

"There are many things to learn," Ling answered. "To clothe yourself, to wear make up to make yourself beautiful, to use your mind and your body to please men—"

"My body was already used to please men," Petra said, her face wrinkling and her eyes lowering. She shivered with the vile memory.

Ling chewed at her lower lip. The way this new girl had said it she assumed her first experience with men had been a bitter one. Should she ask about it? *Perhaps not, but* . . . "You can talk to me about it if it will help. Now or later."

Petra just shook her head, rapidly. She definitely did *not* want to talk about it.

"Okay," Ling answered. "Let me tell you up front, though, that whatever happened to you will not save you from having to use your mind and body to please men now. It is your only reason for existence, from now until you grow too old to earn a fee. At that point, if you've saved any money they may let you buy your freedom. You may be able to get work here, on the staff. But if you're frivolous, if you fail to please your clients so that they do not tip you, you can expect to be tossed out in the cold without so much as a blanket.

"I'll teach you what to do to make men want to tip you and to keep yourself up so you can earn the highest fees."

"But the very idea of it makes me want to throw up," Petra said.

Ling smiled, mostly sadly. "It isn't necessary to *like* it, only to be good at it. For enjoyment, we houris have each other."

## Intersection, A3 and KT11, Province of Affrankon, 11 Rajab, 1533 AH (10 June, 2109)

The wind had slackened and the rain had come. Hans shivered under his field cloak, still looking up at the priest hanging high on his cross. The others were dead, now, though their bodies would remain for most of another day. The priest, though he was older than his charges, appeared to Hans to have hung on this long through a sheer act of will, through the sheer determination to comfort the others with words, song and prayer until such time as they no longer needed him.

Weakly, the priest's teeth sought the chain of the crucifix about his neck. They found that chain eventually, and the old man's teeth nipped the chain in two, allowing it to fall to the base of the cross. If the hard metal of the chain broke his teeth, the priest gave no sign. Then the priest gave Hans a glare that said, more strongly than any words, *Take up the cross.*

The priest then whispered, *"Deus vult . . . Deus vult."*

Hans could not imagine the pain the priest had endured. He felt deeply ashamed. *I gave up my faith over a few minutes in the pushup position. He held onto his through all this.*

*And perhaps* that *is why God might demand that his prophet endure crucifixion*, Hans thought. *And perhaps that is why it had to be his son that was crucified.*

*And perhaps I and my comrades have been lied to.*

When no one was looking, and with the priest's breathing reduced to an intermittent and unconscious labor, Hans went to the base of the cross, and took the crucifix by its bitten-through chain.

# Interlude

Kitzingen, Federal Republic of Germany,
7 April, 2005

Mahmoud sat, cross-legged, on a couch in the apartment
he shared with Gabrielle. On one thigh sat a copy of the
Koran, on the other a Bible, containing both the New
Testament and the Old, loaned to him by the priest of
St. Vinzenz's. Furiously he flipped pages in each, from
one subject to the next, matching, comparing, above all
*thinking*.

Gabi sketched Mahmoud as he read and thought, paying particular attention to the varying looks—agreement,
doubt, satisfaction, consternation—that crossed his face
as he read. Most especially was she trying to capture that
rare and fleeting look of intellectual triumph.

She almost wished she could, herself, believe whenever Mahmoud's face assumed that look. Wish as she might though, she was raised with morals and ethics; she was not raised with faith. Leaps of faith were beyond her, she thought.

*There's no doubt about it,* Mahmoud thought. *The Old Testament God is a petty, petulant, vindictive, homicidal maniac. Allah, early on, is little different. The destruction of Sodom; the swallowing of Ubar by the Earth and the desert sands . . . what's to choose from? They are* clearly *the same God, even if the message and the law may differ in details.*

*Yet is the Koran an improvement over the Old Testament? Just as clearly, yes it is, in many ways. In the Old Testament God is for the Jews and the Jews alone. In the Koran, He is for all mankind. This alone would be reason enough to prefer the Koran.*

*And yet, in the New Testament, God—whether Jesus is a prophet or his son makes no difference to this; he* still *speaks* for *God—is not only for all mankind, he's* not *a maniac.*

Gabi hurried her hand and pencil to catch it—the slight curving smile, the eyes lifted up, even while they squinted slightly—that gave her lover's face an almost beatific look. Quickly she drew in slight lines of compression around the eyes. She could polish those lines later; for now it was important to catch their *feel.*

*And then, too, there's the whole question of* people. *If I am a Christian, and I become a Moslem, what happens? Nothing. People yawn, even devout Christians. If I am a*

*Moslem and become a Christian, what happens? Devout
Moslems want my head. Even reasonable, responsible,
kind and sane Moslems want me dead. It speaks well of
no religion that it is so weak and fragile it must kill to
keep people from making individual choices.*

*Freedom? That's an interesting question, too. Under
the Koran, and even in the Old Testament, there is little
freedom. And yet God permits great evil, evil He could
easily prevent. Why should this be so except that He
wants his creations free, that even great evil is preferable
to the destruction of personal freedom?*

*God, he's so beautiful when he looks like that,* Gabi
thought. *But what if he's serious? What if he becomes a
devout Christian? How do I deal with that?*

*As a "bad" Moslem, Mahmoud could accept me as a
"bad" Christian, which is the way he thinks of me. And
I suppose I do drop expressions like "God," "My God,"
or "God damn it" into conversations. But that's just an
unconscious reflex. I don't believe. I can't believe. It just
isn't in me. But I'm a good person, a kind and caring
person, despite that . . . or maybe because of it.*

*What does a "bad" Christian do living with a "good"
one? And I have no doubt that, if he converts, he will
be a good one.*

Mahmoud turned his face back to the books. He
wasn't reading, though; he was thinking. Moreover, his
thoughts closely paralleled those of Gabi, seated
opposite.

*What if I do convert? Life with Gabi will be harder.*

*Never mind that,* he decided suddenly. *"Render unto
Caesar." She will still be my woman and queen of my
heart. If she does not believe, I will make up for it.*

# CHAPTER EIGHT

Any realistic assessment of any possible scenario will
inevitably conclude that nothing that al Qaeda can do
can cause the collapse of America and the capitalist system. The worse eventuality in the long run would be
that America would be forced to break its hallowed ideal
of universal tolerance, in order to make an exception of
those who fit the racial profiling of an al Qaeda terrorist.
It is ridiculous to think that if al Qaeda continued to
attack us such measures would not be taken. They would
be forced upon the government by the people (and anyone who thinks that the supposed cultural hegemony of
the left might stop this populist fury is deluded).

—Lee Harris,
"The Intellectual Origins of America Bashing"

## HQ, Office of Strategic Intelligence, 25 May, 2112

A hologram of a castle hovered above the table at which sat Caruthers and the deputy director of OSI for Direct Action. The picture was fuzzy, out of focus, as if the taker either had a very poor lens or was moving rapidly at the time the picture was taken.

"I think we should nuke the place right now," said Caruthers.

"The President has said no," answered the deputy director, shaking his head, "not until we've tried everything else. I asked. I insisted. He still said no. The secretary is still trying to convince him otherwise."

"Fuck. Send a battalion of Rangers?"

Again the DDDA said, "No. And you yourself know better. The preparations for any such operation will only guarantee that, instead of a company of security troops being around the place, there would be a division. That; and that if they haven't dispersed their research, they would quickly."

"I don't know that that's true," Caruthers said, "but even accepting that it is—"

"We might get them in, but we'd never get them out. Moreover, the Han insist on being in on this. They don't trust us with having what's in that castle any more than we would trust them. And we *need* their assistance, since they're the only ones with anyone on site."

"A small special ops team?" Caruthers asked. "Maybe one of the private outfits?"

"We thought about those," the DDDA answered. "And they might be doable. But a spec ops team would be too big to infiltrate through any of the ingresses we have. And a private contractor simply can't be trusted with something of this magnitude. The Swiss have already told us to fuck off: Neutrality *über alles*. We think we'd have a better chance with a two- or three-man team of our own."

"Well," Caruthers admitted with a shrug, "Old Bongo is about due to be pulled out of South Africa. And I've got another kid with the right background for the mission."

"Your baby, then," the deputy director said. "I'll see if I can't get the Han to get us some better pictures."

## Castle Noisvastei, Province of Baya, 28 Rajab, 1536 AH (25 May, 2112)

Ling and Petra sat on the walkway around a tower on the side of the castle facing the other one, far below. There was a chainlink fence around the walkway, as there was for all the other towers and battlements of the castle. Girls in fits of depression, and houris were endemically depressed, had been known to throw themselves off in the past, before the fencing had gone up. This was, of course, bad for business.

The lower castle was a bustle of activity. Not only was a new wall and fence being put around it, but concrete was being poured around the outside for additional rooms, workmen—all apparently *Nazrani*—were installing cameras, and the place swarmed with black- clad janissaries. Above, a new chimney arose.

"A better whorehouse to compete with us, do you think?" Petra asked.

Ling didn't take her gaze from the place even when she answered, "No."

Ling seemed strangely uncommunicative. Since she was Petra's only real friend among the houris, this bothered the younger girl. Still trying to make conversation, she said, "They're doing an amazing amount of work."

"Yes," Ling agreed, "and apparently doing it well."

## Montreal, Imperial Province of Quebec, 9 June, 2112

"That was very well done, John," Caruthers said, as the rebels were herded out of the apartment on Papineau Avenue not far from where it intersected with St. Catherine Street. Once, those routes had borne French names or been listed in the French style: Avenue Papineau and Rue Ste. Catharine. The United States, however, had never once since the beginning of the occupation shown any sympathy whatsoever for Quebec's distaste for cultural assimilation. French was not taught in the schools. Neither was in permitted to be on display in shops. Street names were right out. And if people spoke it at home, if that caused their children to be less than fluent in the imperial tongue, English? For that there were the knocks on the door and arrests in the night.

Habeas corpus did not apply to imperial provinces.

"It was a waste of a year of my life," Hamilton said. "Those people weren't rebels; they were poseurs, Marxist idiots caught up in the drivel of a century ago." Hamilton stopped speaking as one of the "rebels"—a lovely, tall, dark-blond girl named Hélène—stopped to glare at him, resisting the shove of the escorting officer. She looked terribly disappointed and terribly hurt. They'd been bedmates for the last six months and she had never suspected he was working for the other side. Hamilton looked ashamed.

*Ah, she was such a sweetheart. Maybe if . . .*

Caruthers noticed. "What is it with you and tall blondes, anyway? Oh, never mind."

"John, we've been tolerant before and we suffered for it, badly. This is what 'zero tolerance' means."

Hamilton sighed as the police pushed the girl onward. "Can we get her some . . . consideration? 'Services to the Empire,' if nothing else?"

"I'll see what I can do," Caruthers said. "You cared for that one?"

"As much as I *can* care anymore, I suppose. She was very sweet and she's very young. I'd rather not have to think that I sent her to a freezing labor camp in Nunavut."

"All right," Caruthers agreed. "We owe you one and getting her sent to a re-education camp in Puerto Rico probably about covers that. Besides, she's young enough that re-education just might take."

"Thank you." Hamilton breathed a small sigh of relief. "What's next?"

"You can't operate here anymore," Caruthers said. "While this group may have been ineffectual, there are others that are considerably more capable." He paused to think for a bit before continuing, "School again, I think, language school."

"Fuck!"

"Trust me; you'll like the reason why, once it's explained."


Castle Noisvastei, Province of Baya, 21 Sha'ban, 1536 AH (17 June, 2112)

Her head moved rhythmically, the object of her attentions pulsing in her mouth. A crucifix swung back and forth in time with her bobbing head, hanging from a chain about her neck. "The men like the idea of fucking Christian women," Ling had explained once, when she'd given Petra the cross. "It asserts their superiority. It's also good for tips."

Petra was a full-fledged houri now; Ling had taught her well and patiently. She no longer knew how many men she had serviced since coming to the castle. It was over a thousand, certainly, even subtracting for repeat customers. She actually tried *not* to remember the numbers, or the acts. Though, of course, if she wanted to keep repeat customers, she did have to remember preferences. It was a difficult game of mental gymnastics.

For the first few months, Ling had been content merely to have Petra sit or kneel nearby and watch her perform. Well, not *quite* content; the almond-eyed girl had also taken Petra to her own bed and shown her how to enjoy a woman and how to please one.

"It's how we keep our sanity," Ling had explained.

After that first few months of observation, Ling had had Petra begin to take part, whenever she had a cooperative and suitable man in her quarters. Under Ling's patient coaching, Petra had learned the use of her lips and tongue, Ling's words explaining and encouraging,

Ling's hand firmly but gently guiding Petra's head, Ling scolding at first until Petra learned to accept whatever gift the customer might deposit in her mouth or on her face or lips. Only once had Ling beaten her, and that was because Petra had rudely thrown up after such a "gift."

Before her thirteenth birthday, Petra was a past master in the use of her mouth.

From there, Ling had moved on to more advanced courses. Always she was careful though, selecting, for example, very small men to open and stretch Petra's anus until she could handle larger. One day, Petra had balked, complaining, "It *hurts* and I hate the pain."

Thereupon Ling had taken Petra down to a lower level of quarters. There, blank faced women sat staring at walls. Others sucked frantically on men. Still others rode customers with seeming wanton abandon. Those last two categories were as blank-faced as the first.

"These are women who complained," Ling explained. "Women who complained once too often."

"What happened to them?" a horrified Petra had asked.

Ling had unconsciously rubbed the crown of her own head, above the hairline. "Oh . . . they were sent to doctors and little things were implanted in their brains. Some other things, parts of their brains, were removed. All their fucking and sucking is controlled by a computer brought from China that sits in the lowest levels of the castle. So far as I know, they feel nothing. So far as I know, they aren't even there. Maybe if the computer didn't make them eat they'd starve to death. But what if they *are* still there?

"Yes," Ling had answered the unspoken question, "it *is* a shitty world."

Petra never complained about the pain of anal sex after that. Nor did she complain this time when the customer pushed her head away and placed her on all fours, not even when lined his penis up on her anus, nor even when he thrust forward roughly. All she did was bite the inside of her cheeks and force out a false grunt of pleasure.

In her own room—she was entitled to her own room now that she was a full houri—Petra kept the letters she received from Besma. All of them spoke of how much the Moslem girl missed her sister and friend. None of them asked about Petra's life. Petra had been very clear in the first letter she'd been able to send, "Please, please, please never ask me what I do here." The letters had to go through Ishmael because Besma's father would have gone ballistic if she'd been caught receiving mail from or sending it to a famous brothel.

She reread the letters, sometimes. One in particular, she reread often.

> "Fudail is dead. I could not take his manhood, but I did scratch out his eyes when he tried to do to me what he did to you. And, perhaps because I am small, he thought he didn't need his friends to help. I scratched out his eyes and then stabbed the pig through the heart.
>
> "His mother, the lying bitch, said that her son did no such thing. My father, shortly before divorcing her, swore that it could only have been self defense. It was my word against al Khalifa's, with my father's testimony weighing heavily in the balance. The judges let me go.
>
> "Al Khalifa, so I understand, has taken residence in the brothel here in Kitznen. Father won't discuss it, but Ishmael says it is so.
>
> "Of course, you *know* I would never *plan* on doing such a thing to my poor, demented stepbrother."

It was that last line, coupled with the letter Besma had left in her great-grandmother's journal, that convinced Petra that Fudail had never tried to commit any crime against Besma, but that she had ruthlessly blinded and murdered him.

"Good for you, Besma," Petra said every time she reread the letter.

Petra thought upon that very letter, even as the grotesquely fat customer behind her ground his passion into her anus and squeezed the flesh over her hips hard enough to bruise. It helped . . . a little.

The fat man straining her anus was a frequent customer. She knew his name and preferences and shouted out in feigned passion, and in English, "Fuck me, Claude, fuck me!" while slamming herself backwards against him. He stank, but then they all stank. What matter; slaves had no right to object to stench. They could, however, at least think, *Fuck you, you clod, fuck you.*

When the customer was finished, while the filthy drool from his slack mouth dripped onto her back, Petra stayed still, remaining on all fours, his penis inside her upraised rear end. Eventually the customer pulled out, wiping his penis off on the cheeks of her ass. He stood, adjusted his robe and began to walk to the shower. Apparently rethinking it, he turned back and patted her posterior gently. "Good girl," he said, before leaving the bedroom. "Nice fuck." On his waddling way, he dropped two silver dirhem in a plate on a small table by the bathroom door.

Sex was cheap in the Caliphate, as cheap as female *Nazrani* slaves.

# OSI Headquarters, Langley, Virginia, 17 June, 2112

"All rested up, John?"

Hamilton just snarled. Eight days, including travel time, did not amount to much of a rest.

The meeting was small, just Caruthers, Hamilton, and an unfamiliar woman who, despite wearing more or less fashionable female business garb, had something of the medical look about her, somehow. Caruthers didn't introduce her and she didn't introduce herself except as "Mary."

Hamilton was reasonably sure her name was neither "Mary" nor anything close to it. Mary was older, perhaps forty, tall, blond and . . .

*Stop it! She's not Laurie and she doesn't even look much like Laurie.*

Caruthers snapped his fingers in front of Hamilton's face. "Knock it off, John. Pay attention. This is important."

"Oh. Sorry."

Mary touched a button and three holographic images appeared above the table in front of Hamilton. Each was a more or less natural photo, not mug shots, of three men in white jackets of the type Hamilton associated with science and research.

Mary's right index finger pointed at the leftmost of the men Hamilton was already thinking of as "scientists."

"This is Dr. Claude Oliver Meara," she said. "Ph.D., Microbiology. He disappeared from his home near Atlanta six months ago. He was under suspicion of committing statutory rape when he fled. A search of his house after his disappearance indicates a strong predilection for pederasty."

"We tracked him to Montreal, actually, before losing him," Caruthers added, raising a single eyebrow. *You thought your little group of Frenchie separatists was so innocent and harmless,* his mocking glance seemed to say.

Mary's finger moved to the next photo. That one was tall and slender, but bald, and almost unbelievably ugly. "Dr. Guillaume Sands. Ph.D. Biochemistry. Also disappeared. Also from Atlanta."

"Also via Montreal," Caruthers added, "which he was from, as a matter of fact. Just goes to show we still can't trust the Frogs."

Her finger lingered over the last picture for a moment, an especially nerdy looking character, before she said, "Dr. John Johnston IV. Epidemiology. Same story. I actually know this one, personally. Rude, arrogant bastard."

"Microbiology, biochemistry, and epidemiology? Why don't I like the sound of that?"

"Nobody likes the sound of that, John," Caruthers said.

"Okay . . . they disappeared. Where to?"

It was Caruthers' turn to show a picture, this one a high-definition satellite photo. "Here, we think." The three scientists disappeared to be replaced by a much larger view of two mountain-girt, snow-covered castles. One of these had a prominent, golden dome apparently grafted on as an afterthought. Certainly it didn't fit the architecture of the whole.

"The Caliphate? You want me to go inside the Caliphate? That's suicidal."

"For you or for them? Oh, never mind, we'll get to 'suicidal' later. Let me assure you, though, that the move has not been suicidal for them; quite the opposite."

"Let me understand," Hamilton said, "we are talking about some kind of biological warfare agent being developed by the Caliphate to attack us?"

"More to counterattack us, we think," offered Mary.

Hamilton cocked his head to one side, quizzically. "Counter-attack?"

"It should be obvious to you, John," Caruthers said, "that we've pretty much cleaned up our Moslem problems around the periphery. There are effectively none *openly* left in North or South America. The last of the Pacific islands that are of interest to us were cleared in the campaign you participated in, in the Philippines. Africa south of the Sahara has few that are not enslaved and none that are not oppressed. Japan and China—Australia, too—exterminated or drove out theirs long ago. Except for infiltrators coming across from the European Caliphate, and the odd group of raiders from the other Caliphate, those left in the Russian Empire are illiterate serfs, bound to the land. The traditional Moslem lands . . . the grandly named Caliphate of Islam, Triumphant, is a virtual wasteland. And Israel finally learned the lessons Himmler and Eichmann sought to teach, as well.

"All that's left is Europe. It's only a matter of time before we undertake *Reconquista* there, too."

Hamilton gestured with a hand, palm up, and a one-shouldered shrug. "Yes, all that's obvious enough. Tell me something new."

"They're not going to take the loss of their last worthwhile homeland lightly. If necessary, they'll destroy the world before turning it all over to us. We would do the same."

"I still don't—"

"They can build nukes and, more or less, maintain them. They've still got a huge, if decreasing, number of *dhimmis* to keep some poor semblance of a modern society going. They have never—so far as we can tell, and our intel on this is *good*—been able to develop a delivery system capable of getting through our defenses. Since we don't permit them travel, and we don't permit them freedom of the seas, and we do sink any ships or subs they launch on sight, they've got no effective way to bomb us."

"Introducing diseases, however," Mary interrupted, "they could probably do. They're much lighter, much more easily transported, and potentially much deadlier."

"We think, John," Caruthers said, "that they've enticed those three men over precisely to develop for them a superbug."

"And I'm supposed to find out if they are?"

"No. We can't take any chances on this. Your job will be to kill or capture them before they can. Actually, that's not strong enough. John, you need to kill or capture them and destroy their facility no matter what it takes or what it costs."

"Why me? I'm new . . . barely wet behind the ears as you've never ceased to tell me."

"Language aptitude, military background, biochemistry degree," answered Caruthers, simply enough.

"John," Mary added, "let me tell you about something that makes this so important that no level of violence is too much. No . . . first, let me ask you how much you know about disease?"

"What any biochemistry major would, I suppose," Hamilton answered.

"That may not be enough," Mary said, unconsciously wringing her hands. "I'll give you the quick version. There are several reasons why the human race has survived epidemics and pandemics, but the biggest are these: The strongest strains of any given disease kill quickest and do not spread so readily. The weakest do spread, and the weaker they are the more and the faster, overall, they can spread. Therefore, diseases tend to

spread immunity before them because once you've survived the weaker strain, you are very likely to be highly
resistant to the stronger. Secondly, the human body is
capable of dealing with a very wide range of diseases.
But it has to know that it is under attack. A truly new
disease is very difficult for the immune system to deal
with because it doesn't recognize it as a disease. Thirdly,
and related to the other two, the ideal disease, from a
weapons point of view, is spread via air, has a very long
time it can be communicated between initial infection
and onset of serious symptoms, enters a stage where it
could not be communicated, and then kills more or less
quickly, dying out itself. Fourthly, an ideal disease would
not mutate and would exempt one's own population. We
think that such a disease can be created from scratch.
We know that if any group of three men can do it, these
three can."

"These men are working on such a disease?" Hamilton asked.

"We think so . . . for a number of reasons."

Hamilton looked at Caruthers and sighed. "All right;
sign me up."

"You have a long and intense training program ahead
of you, then."

"I have one question: *Why* would someone be willing
to do this? Money?"

"No," Mary said, "not money."

## Castle Noisvastei, Province of Baya, 22 Sha'ban, 1536 AH (18 June, 2112)

Ling waited until the fat man had left before easing
into Petra's room and crawling into bed next to her,

conforming her own body to Petra's like one spoon to another. When Ling put her arm around her, Petra was stiff and unresponsive. Then again, she always was whenever that grotesquery in vaguely human form came to visit her.

"Bad, honey?" Ling asked.

Petra sniffled, "He didn't even grease my ass first . . . and I had to pretend I liked it. Oh, God, Ling . . . I *hate* my life."

"There are worse things," Ling said, thinking of the computer-controlled creatures down below.

"That's the worst part," Petra wailed. "I *know* there are worse things and I'm *terrified* of them." She spun within Ling's arms and buried her head in the Chinese slave's neck and hair.

Under the circumstances, Ling didn't even try to make love to Petra. Instead she just held her tightly and softly kissed her hair while the sixteen-year old houri cried herself to sleep.

*When the Ministry of State Security recalls me*, Ling thought, *I will take this girl with me.*

For while Ling had told the truth about having been sold when she was four, she'd neglected to mention that she had a chip in her head as well, one planted there when she was purchased by MSS and just before she was "sold west." In her case, however, nothing had been removed from her brain. Instead, she'd had a whole suite of things implanted—little things, mostly: loyalty, duty . . . code words and phrases . . . field craft.

Not even the Hindus did better human programming than did the Celestial Kingdom of the Han, once known as the People's Republic of China.

*If possible*, said a small voice in Ling's head.

## OSI Headquarters, Langley, Virginia, 19 June, 2112

"My local contact is a *what*?"

Caruthers sighed. "She's a slave girl, a prostitute. More specifically, she's an implanted agent. She has a chip in her head. The Chinese have been doing this kind of thing for thirty years. It's the major reason we stopped allowing immigration from China."

"That's abominable."

Caruthers gave a characteristic shrug. "We do the same things with convicted criminals. So they don't *bother* with convictions? Not our problem."

"But we're at war with them."

Caruthers put out one hand, palm down and fingers spread. He wagged it, saying, "Not by declaration. Almost everybody is at war with almost everybody, these days, and all the time, too. What that means in practice though is that nobody's at war—not emotionally, anyway—unless bullets are actually flying. So, yeah, we're at war with them but, also yeah, we can cooperate."

"Do we know anything else about this woman?"

"We have a picture, sort of," Caruthers answered, then produced a hologram of that. The hologram was . . . decidedly odd, out of focus, as if taken through a bad lens.

"Awfully white, for a Chinese. Unusually large breasts, too. Why is the picture so fuzzy?"

"She's also relatively tall. The chinks were coy. We think she was specially bred, maybe even genengineered, for exoticism. As for the picture . . . our best guess is that the camera was her own eye, tapped by the chip in her head."

Hamilton had a sudden thought and as suddenly looked ill. "Jesus, that's vile. This poor girl was chipped, then sold as a hooker, and everything she does is recorded for anyone to see. And she *knows* this? Knows she's performing for a camera?"

"Look, I didn't make the world," Carruthers said testily. "I don't even approve. I just observe and report. They sell us—we buy from them—redundant human organs and we should balk over a little incidental voyeurism?"

Rocking his head from side to side, Hamilton grudgingly agreed. "Okay. Sure. Go on. What's her name, by the way?"

"Zheng Ling."

## Castle Noisvastei, Province of Baya, 22 Sha'ban, 1536 AH (18 June, 2112)

"Petra, Honey, wake up," Ling said, while gently shaking the girl awake.

"What is it, Ling?" Petra asked sleepily.

"I just got the word. There's a big group of new-minted janissaries coming to the castle for their graduation party. We have to prepare. It's going to be a busy few nights."

Petra groaned. After all, she was still sore.

"Oh, stop it, you. At least they'll be young, strong and virile, with normal urges, and not grotesque, smelly, perverted old men. Now get up, lazy bones, and start making yourself *gorgeous*. There's money to be made and *fun* to be had."

"I don't want to have any 'fun.' The money, on the other hand . . . "

*"Exactly!"* Ling said. "Now pull on a robe and let's get down to Costuming and Jewelry before all the nice things are taken."

Sometimes Petra thought she could see elaborate paintings under the plain, off-white of the walls. Certainly the gilt, the blue and purple columns of what some of the staff still called "the Throne Room," suggested that the original builder—of whom Petra knew precisely nothing—had intended something very elaborate. Yet the masters insisted on "no graven images," and took this to include paintings of living creatures. She understood that if there ever had been paintings on the walls, these would have been covered up or destroyed.

Hurrying with Ling along one covered and arched walkway, framed by blue columns on one side and walls covered with erratic geometric shapes on the other, Petra stopped for a moment to gaze down at the "Throne Room."

*It's makes no sense . . . it was not part of the builder's design . . . that this room should be only color. It calls out for something . . . more . . . something alive.*

"Hurry, silly!" Ling demanded, impatiently.

Most of the girls were still asleep from the night's revelries. Of those who were awake, not all had heard of the arrival of a large party of janissaries. Of those who had heard, not all cared. Of those who cared, none had quite the fire of Ling.

She raced through Costuming and Jewelry, pulling this dress from that rack, that dress from this. Some she held up to herself. Still others, *more* others, actually, she sized and colored to Petra. For herself, Ling settled on a simple but painstakingly embroidered black silk, thigh-length tunic, the embroidery being of golden dragons and silvery phoenixes. Ling had learned over the years to accentuate her exoticism. The little voice in her head, the one she never told anyone about, pushed her in that direction as well. Ling sometimes wondered about the double standard the masters showed regularly: paintings on walls of real things were right out for them; embroideries of mythical beings for infidels were just fine.

Petra though . . . she was classic and only classic, in Ling's opinion, would do. For the *Nazrani* slave, Ling selected an ankle-length gown of white, crumply material, mostly silk as well, cut in the Empire fashion (the *French* Empire, not the American). The gown was high-waisted, with a golden belt just under the breasts. Those the gown left half-exposed, covering only the nipples and—were a girl a bit daring—not necessarily all of them.

"Try it on! Try it on!" Ling urged. "I've wanted to see you in this for *ages*."

Once satisfied with the fit of Petra's gown, Ling dragged her to Jewelry. There she selected pearls—earrings and necklace both—for herself, and golden pendants for Petra. Unsatisfied with just the pendants, however, Ling insisted that the slave managing the Jewelry department also produce a pair of gold torques for Petra's upper arms. For her necklace Petra could continue to wear the crucifix she always did.

"Classic," Ling said when Petra had donned both gown and gold. "Now take it all off and change back. We have time to make love before everything is ready and before we have to report to Cosmetics and Hairdressing —yes, I've already made us appointments. And you're too beautiful for me not to show my appreciation for it."

## Honsvang, Province of Baya, 22 Sha'ban, 1536 AH (18 June, 2112)

"Really, Abdul Rahman," Rustam said, "this is just too much. Sure, it's beautiful but when I think of the cost—"

"Oh, be still," the senior janissary trainer said. "The boys have done well. They deserve this bounty. Soon enough they'll be going off to different schools . . . or to face the infidels across the English Channel, or the Russian border or the Balkan Front. There'll be little enough beauty there. Let them enjoy."

"But the *expense* . . ."

"Twenty score gold dinar for three days of carousing? Seems fair to me."

"But . . ."

"You didn't bitch when Captain Masood brought *you* and *your* mates here, Rustam."

The junior sniffed. "That was *different*."

Abdul Rahman laughed aloud, the sound echoing off the rocky steeps surrounding. "Oh, yes, of *course*. Then it was *your* dick getting wet. I see it all clearly now. That makes all the difference in the world. You are absolutely right, Rustam. Go fetch the busses. We're heading back to the barracks . . ."

"Well . . . let's not be hasty," Rustam said, setting his face and his feet upon the steep upward path.


"Quick, boys," Müller said. "Paradise is on the top of this hill."

"Or if not Paradise," answered another, "a reasonably close facsimile. I hear the houris up there put those of Heaven to shame."

"I doubt that," Hans said, even while thinking, *I doubt there are any houris at all in the real Heaven.*

Even so, Hans trudged up with his pack—light marching order only—on his back. He made an effort to seem as enthusiastic about losing his virginity as any of the rest of the boys. Indeed, he seemed quite a bit more enthusiastic than some. Those? Well, put any couple of hundred young boys together and some of them are going to discover that they prefer the company, in all senses, of boys. Still, even those five or six put on a fair show of interest.

The janissaries made rather less of such things than the Caliphate for which they worked though, of course, they would hang any boys actually caught in any of a number of forbidden acts. They simply refused to infer such acts from extraneous behavior. In any case, such hangings were, in practice, rare. Only two of Hans' original company, for example, had been put to death for homosexuality and that had been years ago. Far more boys had been killed in training.

Within half an hour the point of the column, led by Rustam, reached a magnificent brick gate, framed by graceful minarets. From the right of the gatehouse, where Rustam formed up the company, Hans could see the upper third of a large golden dome, glittering in the sunset's light. Despite the minarets, the dome seemed out of place, as if it had been grafted onto a non-Islamic or a pre-Islamic building.

While Rustam formed the company and made sure nobody had drifted off, Adbul Rahman met by the main gate with a very fat man with two young children in tow.

"*Can* your establishment handle all one hundred and fifty-seven of my men, plus thirteen cadre?" Abdul Rahman asked. "I understood that you could."

Latif answered, "No problem, Abdul Rahman von Seydlitz. I've pulled in another thirty-two houris from some of my outlying establishments and had several servant's quarters done up as boudoirs. I've got a girl for each of you. That said, the girls are of varying qualities. Would you like to make assignments or would you prefer a lottery? Or would you prefer to let the boys pick their own?"

"They've had little enough choice in their lives," Abdul Rahman answered, "and will get little more in the future. Let us let them select their own temporary wives, but by rank in the corps and the class."

"As you wish, so shall it be," answered Latif. "I have on hand enough mullahs for the required services. And now the little matter of payment?"

Wordlessly, Abdul Rahman passed over a bank draft. "Four hundred gold dinar," he said, "as agreed."

"Riiighghght . . . FACE!" Rustam ordered. "Column of files from the left . . . "

"Follow me," said one of the section leaders, the leftmost one, while the others, including Hans, shouted, "Stand fast!"

"March!"

As the boys marched forward from the left, Hans kept his head and eyes fixed over his left shoulder. When he saw the third from the last man of the section to his left come up parallel, he gave the order, "Forward . . . March," and stepped off. Rather than giving commands for minor movements, Hans simply followed the last man of the previous section even as his men followed him. In a short time, he had led them through the massive gate and into a courtyard dominated by a huge mosque with an outsized golden onion dome perched above. This was the same dome he had glimpsed from outside.

Ahead was a broad stone staircase, hunched up against one wing of the castle. Up this the janissaries marched, then through a magnificent doorway, before entering a great hall.

None of the janissaries had eyes for the hall or for its decorations. Instead, they only had eyes for the girls lining each side.

Müller spoke for nearly all when he said, aloud, "I have died and gone to Heaven."

Ling nudged Petra discreetly. "Didn't I tell you this would be better than nasty old men?"

Petra didn't answer. Instead, she looked with shock upon one, in particular, of the boys filling the great hall. After a few moments' shock she managed to whisper, "I've got to get out of here."

"I don't understand," Ling said. "After hundreds of filthy perverts I thought—"

"One of them is my *brother*!"

"Oh . . . " The almond eyes widened. "Oh! Oh, *shit*!"

# Interlude

Kitzingen, Federal Republic of Germany, 1
October, 2005

Gabi wrote in her journal:

*My life has turned to absolute shit.*

*Mahmoud was serious about going to America. I
thought it was just a passing fad but I was wrong. He
didn't tell me until yesterday. I think he was in doubt
until then.*

*It was the bombings in London. He expected the Brit-
ish to crack down on Muslims, to start rounding them
up. When it didn't happen he still said, "We'll see. The
people who once ruled a quarter of the world are not
going to bend over for this. Give them two months to get
the machinery in place."*

*Yesterday he said, "Even they lack the will to defend themselves."*

*That's when he told me that he'd gone to Frankfurt late last year, to the American consulate, not on orders from his company, but to apply for a work visa. And apparently his company decided better to send him overseas, and let him take a job from an American, than to keep him here and keep a "good German" out of work. I'm sure that's what they were thinking.*

*Since Mahmoud is a Christian now, it seems the Americans are a little more willing to let him in than they otherwise might be. Racist bastards! I told Mahmoud they were, too, and he said, "No. It has nothing to do with race. They just have a proper sense of caution . . . and the will to defend their homeland."*

*Why can't I make him see? What's missing in him that he can't see that "homelands" are not worth defending; that only people are?*

*He says that I'm blind.*

*Ooo, he makes me so angry sometimes!*

*I tell him that if he leaves, he's helping bring about a self-fulfilling prophecy; that if all the most reasonable Moslems or ex-Moslems leave then only the lunatics will remain. He tells me that some prophecies are destined to be fulfilled, and that those who don't heed them suffer for it. He tells me to look to the number of Germans who are leaving Germany, the number of French who are leaving France, the number of English that are leaving England, and then to deny that this prophecy will be fulfilled. He says to look to the birthrates and tell him that this prophecy won't be fulfilled.*

*As if there weren't already too many people in the world for the world to support. Why should we make even more of them?*

*Not that we haven't done our own little part. I haven't told him yet but the doctor told me last week that I'm going to have a baby. His baby, of course. If I tell him, he'll start nagging me for us to get married. If I tell him, too, he'll think it's to try to hold him here with me. If I tell him, he'll call it blackmail. And then he'll want all three of us to go to America.*

*As if I'd let my child be raised as an American! Never! Never! Never! Let my child be imbued with atavistic, virulent nationalism? Raised in a place so violent and lawless people keep guns? Never!*

*It's in everything they do. Six weeks ago Mahmoud made me go to an NFL Europe American football game, the Cologne Centurions playing the Frankfurt Galaxy. Our football allows for ties, it even prefers them. Not American football, though. They insist on fighting it out to the finish, with nothing but winners and losers. It's so wrong. And so typical.*

*Well, I have to run now. There's a demonstration scheduled by the Falterturm to remind the British that decent minded people will not tolerate them discriminating against their Moslems merely because some of those Moslems, prompted—I have no doubt—by racism, fought back.*

*I hope Mahmoud begins to see sense soon. My life would be blighted without him. I hope he knows that.*

# CHAPTER NINE

The open society is not threatened, it is in a state of dissolution. The date on which the unconditional surrender was announced can be exactly identified: It was the day that the fatwa was issued against Salman Rushdie and the European institutions and governments did NOT react with an immediate break in ALL ties to the Mullah-Regime. Instead those multi-culturally oriented knowers came out and explained to us why Rushdie would have done better not to provoke the mullahs. Europe—Your Last Name is Appeasement!

—Henryk Broder,
*Welt am Sonntag*, 14 November, 2004

# Castle Noisvastei, Province of Baya, 22 Sha'ban, 1536 AH (18 June, 2112)

"Choose me, master," the exotic girl said, her eyes demurely downcast. "I will make it worth your while in more ways than the poets tell of."

"I don't know much about poetry, girl," Hans answered. "They give us little of it. And it seems—"

"Please choose me, master," the girl repeated. She looked up at Hans and said it again, but with a slightly different emphasis of tone. When Hans still didn't agree, the almond-eyed houri bit her lower lip and added, "In the name of God, choose me."

"All right, girl, since you're so insistent. But I can't promise much from me."

"It's not for you to promise, master, it is for me to."

The stop by the mullah for him to pronounce a properly contractual temporary marriage was brief. The only question was, "For how long?"

"Two days," the exotic girl had said, explaining to Hans, "You may tire of me after that, though I guarantee you will not before then."

Hans had agreed. What, after all, did he know about the heavenly delights of the houris?

Hans let the girl lead him upstairs, through several ornate halls, down a corridor and into a room furnished in ways he'd never imagined before, all hanging silks and rich wood. Once in the room she'd removed the diaphanous veil she'd worn across the lower half of her face. She was very beautiful, Hans thought. No . . . that wasn't strong enough. He had to admit to himself that he'd never seen anything more beautiful in his life.

The girl had sat him in a chair, then knelt to untie and remove his boots. The carpet on the floor felt amazingly plush and soft to Hans' march-hardened feet.

"Wait here," the girl had said. "I have a small surprise for you."

Impatiently, and with some small amount of bad grace, Hans had agreed. The girl slipped out silently through a side door.

A few minutes passed before Hans heard someone, not his *exotique*, saying, "No . . . I won't go . . . this is wrong . . . I said . . . "

A woman, tall and blond and, if anything, more beautiful than his temporary wife was pushed into the bedroom. She turned around and tried to push her way back but the door was blocked by the slender almond-eyed one. "Zheng Ling," she'd given her name as.

"Master," she said. "Meet your sister."

At that, the blond girl wailed and crumpled to the floor.

"In the name of God, what's wrong with her?" Hans asked frantically, while helping Ling move Petra's inert form to the bed.

"Mostly, she's ashamed," Ling answered.

"Of . . . oh."

"Oh."

"But it isn't like she did this to herself," Hans objected.

"Does that matter in our world?" Ling asked, rhetorically.

They laid Petra out on Ling's wide bed. Ling tactfully neglected to mention how frequent an occupant of that bed Petra was.

While busying themselves with silly, ineffectual things like rubbing Petra's wrists, Hans asked, "Why did you show her to me when she didn't want to be seen?"

"She *said* she didn't want to, but there are two people about whom she can never talk without love creeping into her voice. You're one of them. She didn't want to see you because she was afraid of what you would think and say . . . that, and that she didn't want you to have to endure the shame among your friends of having a houri for a sister."

"I knew she was a slave," Hans said. "All else follows from that. And what does she think *I* am, but a slave soldier. As for which of the professions chosen for us by others is the more obscene? That I leave for God to decide."

Ling stopped rubbing for a moment and, smiling warmly, said, "You know, master, I think I *am* going to make good on the promise I made you."

Far up in one of the towers, the one where Latif made his personal quarters, the brothel owner poured three large vodkas for himself and his two guests.

"I get it from across the border," Latif said. "You can get anything for a little *baksheesh*."

"The Holy Koran forbids the drinking of fermented grain or grape," Rustam objected.

Latif nodded piously. "Very true," he agreed. "But vodka is made from *potatoes*; Allah will be none the wiser."

"And neither will the caliph," said Abdul Rahman.

"Well . . . as for the caliph," Latif said, "he prefers scotch; or so my contacts tell me. And are your boys settling in well?"

"They seem to be," said Abdul Rahman, sipping at the frosty glass. "They seem to be settling in very happily, indeed."

It was a time for tears. By the time Petra was awake, and Ling left for Petra's room to leave the siblings some privacy in her own, the two were weeping onto each other's shoulders, hugging, and each trying—and failing—to get a word in edgewise.

*I never knew any family of my own,* Ling had thought, glancing over her shoulder as she'd left. *The idea of having actual blood relatives is . . . fascinating. And strangely . . .*

Ling cut off the dangerous thought, closing the door between the rooms. For her there never would be, never could be, such a thing as family.

*What wouldn't I do to have a family?*

A little voice in her head told her, *Don't even think about it. You have your duty to your people. That should be enough.*

*But what if it* isn't?

## OSI Headquarters, Langley, Virginia, 20 June, 2112

"No, I won't do it," Hamilton snarled. "That goes way past any duty I owe to you or the company or the country. Two hundred and fifty years ago my people *fought* against this monstrosity. Nothing you can say can make me. It's *evil.*"

"Yes, you will," Caruthers said with great assurance. "It's the only ingress to the place we have. You can't pass for Chinese. The Japanese are too close to us to be permitted in and you couldn't pass for one of them either. The only way we can get you in there is as a South African and just about the only ones of those who are allowed in are slave traders. Which is why the only cover we've been able to prepare for you is as a slave dealer. So you *will* do it."

"Couldn't I be a *buyer*, instead? Then we could free the slaves after the mission, rather than leaving them behind in mines and workshops and whorehouses."

"South Africa doesn't buy much. Mostly, they *sell*. It just wouldn't wash. Even if it would, your target area is the kind of place that buys slaves, not one that sells them."

Hamilton turned away, looking sick. "Please don't ask me to do this."

"No other way." To drive home the point, Caruthers asked, "You did read that paper Claude O. Meara was working on, didn't you, John?"

When Hamilton didn't answer, Caruthers said, "Atkinson, you shithead: read back the introduction to Meara's research paper on artificial smallpox variant VA5H."

The little box answered, "Yes, sir. Proposed artificial smallpox, variant VA5H, is a completely genengineered pathogen which very nearly approximates the ideal biological weapon. VA5H is not actually smallpox at all but has very similar symptoms at one stage of its development. It can be expected to produce ninety-seven percent fatalities in the affected population if left untreated and fifty to sixty percent if full medical care is available. Because of the society-wide spread of the disease, most victims could not be given full treatment. Due to the artificial virus' ability to use any conceivable mode of transmission—contact, air, or vector—coupled with the long delay between infection and the onset of symptoms, defense is highly problematic.

"The cleverest part of the disease is in its pattern of morphing, which follows five stages. In stage one, which is the stage at which it is released from deepfreeze, the disease is asymptomatic and is spread mostly by air and, more rarely, bodily fluids or insect vector. This stage lasts thirteen days, after which it mutates into something which closely mimics the symptoms of the common cold. The coughing and sneezing act as an aid to transmission and, because colds are, in fact, common, can be expected to create no great interest. This stage, stage two, lasts twenty days. It then mutates into something harmless again, and lies dormant for a period of five days. In stage four, the disease turns deadly, killing virtually all who are infected within seven days, and more usually within four. This stage lasts nine days. In stage five the disease once again turns harmless and becomes incapable of reproduction.

"Moreover, every offspring of the virus begins life at the same stage of morphing as the original parent. This is achieved by the genengineering of excess segments on the virus' DNA, which decay or slough off at the times given, leaving a DNA strand with the pathogenic characteristics listed. Subsequent generations breed true to the stage the parent was at, *at conception*.

"Computer simulations show that nearly one hundred percent of a given population will encounter VA5H and be infected by it sometime in the forty-seven days prior to it mutating into stage five. Of the three percent who survive exposure, approximately one third can be expected to go blind, while another third will become sterile. Casualties among the very young and very old will closely approach one hundred percent. It is a civilization destroying disease.

"There is no known cure and no known vaccine. Natural immunity can be expected to be quite limited. Creation of a vaccine would be highly problematic without a sample of the original. In effect, VA5H would operate against a target population as a virgin field epidemic.

"As the virus will be very large, physical defense in the form of air filtration and isolation is possible but dependent upon warning. The major transmission stage, the long stage two, should aid in defeating any such attempts.

"The symptoms of the disease in its fourth stage are similar to Hemorrhagic Smallpox rather than to its less deadly cousins, Malignant Smallpox and Variola Major and Minor. In essence, VA5H causes the victim to fall apart, beginning with the mucous—"

"Stop!" Hamilton shouted, causing the machine to go suddenly silent. "It doesn't make me feel any better about committing one obscenity by hearing about another."

Caruthers set his face into a mask of anger. "Look at me, John," he said. "*Look* at me!" Caruthers held out one hand and pinched a fold of skin with the fingers of the other. "See that? What's that color? John, I'm *black*! How do you think *I* feel about it? Do you think those lily white bastards below the Sahara are selling off any of their precious *white volk*? Hmmm? Do you think *I'm* not going to see the faces of the people you sell to my last day? There is no good choice, none that works well enough. Not for something this serious."

"God," Hamilton sighed, "how did the world ever get to be like this?"

"I think they used to call it 'progress.'"

"Yeah . . . I guess the decay of a corpse is progress, too . . . from the point of view of the bacteria."

## Castle Noisvastei, Province of Baya, 24 Sha'ban, 1536 AH (20 June, 2112)

Graduation holiday was over. From a high window overlooking the courtyard Petra watched her brother's company of janissaries forming in the courtyard next to the great, golden-domed mosque. She wondered if she'd ever see him again. She doubted it. Even so, she thanked a God she was not at all sure even existed (and, to be fair, Petra had reasons for doubt, if anyone did) that she'd had at least this one last chance to be together.

Ling wasn't taking it particularly well. She'd grown genuinely fond of Hans in the few days together. Petra thought that "fond" might be something of an under-statement, yet that was all Ling would admit to.

*Her eyes say something else though,* Petra thought. *Who would ever have thought it; little Ling-ling in love? And* Brüder *Hans as much so?*

Petra asked directly, "Are you in love with my brother? You *told* me, when I first came here, never to get attached to the clients."

Ling sighed. "I don't know what love is. I know this, though: Of the thousands of men who've had me only one ever treated me like a princess, rather than a piece of meat."

She didn't say, but thought, *And I might not be a real girl . . . but I have a real girl's feelings. The breeders couldn't breed that out of me. And when I look down there and see your brother marching away, I feel like a part of me is leaving, too.*

Ling stood up and left. On the outside she seemed calm enough. What she was feeling inside Petra could only guess at.

Petra watched as the boys turned right and began filing away down the mountain path. She saw Hans turn around several times and look up at the windows. Whether he was seeking her or Ling, Petra didn't know. It was probably both, she decided.

When the last of the boys had disappeared, Petra turned away from her perch and began searching the castle for Ling.

She found Ling sitting alone on a wooden bench in what some of the staff called, "The Singer's Hall." The janissaries had banqueted there, each night of their stay.

Ling didn't notice her at first, or didn't seem to. That the Chinese slave was fully aware of Petra's presence became obvious once Petra was within a dozen feet.

Though Ling didn't turn her eyes from the painted wall upon which she had been gazing, she said, "There's a picture under there, you know."

Petra didn't know. As far as she could see the wall was blank.

"I can't see anything but white. What do you see?" Truthfully, Petra thought Ling was simply seeing things that weren't there. This would have been troublesome if their lives weren't already so miserably blighted.

"It's a man on a horse, an armed and armored man. He's dressed in silvered armor. His horse is roan and draped in red. Over the armor the man is wearing red as well. There's a castle in the background. Not this one, some other. The red clothed, armored man is fighting someone in brown."

"I can't see anything," Petra repeated.

Ling said nothing. A little voice in her head, however, said to her, *Shut up about it. Now.*

"Hans promised me he'd write to us," Petra offered.

"They often say that," Ling answered. "And sometimes, for a little while, they do. It never lasts. After all, we're just houris, polluted and polluting. Not real people, just slaves. Not someone real people care about."

"Hans is a slave, too."

Ling sighed. "I know. That's why I'll allow myself a little hope that he really cares."

"Both of us do."

Ling's brown, almond eyes looked up into Petra's rounder, blue ones. "Did I ever mention how much you two look alike?"

"A couple of dozen times, yes. It's the other reason I hid all the time my brother's company was here. If they'd seen me they'd have known his shame."

Ling stood and yawned. Taking Petra by the hand she said, "Well . . . if I can't have the boy I want, I'll just have to take the girl. Come on; it's bedtime."

Hand in hand the two houris walked toward their quarters.

## OSI Headquarters, Langley, Virginia, 27 November, 2112

There was snow on the breeze. Hamilton and Caruthers walked under a covered walkway between one of the academic buildings and the nearest cafeteria.

"Man, I *hate* Afrikaans," Hamilton said to Caruthers, following a language lesson. He could have been implanted, or "chipped," and learned the language quickly and perfectly. No free man ever gladly submitted to being "chipped," though it had uses for the disabled.

"Cheer up," Caruthers answered. "You don't have to learn it perfectly; just well enough to pass as a Cape English type who learned it as a second language. You *do*, on the other hand, have to get the Cape English accent down perfectly."

Hamilton nodded. "Working on it."

"I know. You had best concentrate, though, because there's not a lot of time before you have to go to D-D-S," —Demolition, Destruction and Sabotage—"refresher, then the Mission Course"—special courses of instruction designed for particularly high value operations—"then into LCA"—local cultural assimilation—"followed by insertion."

"To say nothing about the knife," Hamilton said, his distaste palpable. Yet there was no choice but to send him to plastic surgery to alter his features and change the color of his eyes. It was altogether too possible that the Quebecers had managed to send off a picture of him before their ring was broken.

Caruthers shrugged. "There are worse things. At least you get to keep your mind and your thoughts to yourself. Even though I think that's a mistake."

Early on, when the chips had first been developed, OSI had made it a requirement that all foreign service operatives had to be implanted. The Han had been the ones to figure out how to hack into those chips. OSI was still not recovered from that particular disaster. And while the chips were infinitely more secure now, the prejudice remained. It remained so strongly that OSI couldn't force its operatives to be chipped; they'd resign first and in droves.

"No one is going to chip me," Hamilton answered. "Even before I knew about that poor Chinese slave, I thought the idea was disgusting. Since then . . ." He let the thought trail off.

"Well, . . . as to the Chinese girl . . . the Ministry of State Security is now telling us she's become somewhat unstable."

"Oh, great. Now what?"

"Nothing important. We still think we can make use of her. And she has been able to confirm the presence of Meara, Sands and Johnston in the castle we had thought them in."

"Any word on their 'progress' to date."

"No, and we don't think we can make any good guesses. I mean, how much can you read into it when one of them beats a slave girl half to death? When he normally beats the slaves?"

"Not much, I suppose."

"No," Caruthers said. "Not much."

"I really don't understand why we just don't nuke the castle out of existence."

"Couple of reasons. One of them is a good one, the other is even better. The good one is that England is a hostage. The Caliphate doesn't have much in the way of delivery systems, but they can range the British Isles. There are seventy million of our allies, citizens and subjects there. If we nuke the castle, they probably die."

"Better seventy million than five billion or more."

"True," Caruthers agreed. "That's where the better reason comes in. We have to know *where* research is being conducted, where backups might be, where strains of VA5H might be stored."

"It used to be easier, I understand," Caruthers continued, "to keep track of goings on in the Caliphate. But then their cell phone system deteriorated to the point that they had to fall back on landlines, most of them underground. Those we can't track for beans."

Caruthers' face grew contemplative. "You know," he said, "it would be worth it to let them use our satellite system just so we could listen in on the bastards . . . not that they'd be stupid enough to take us up on the offer if we made it."

The range bench held an assortment of weapons, all of types typically found in the Caliphate. Some of those types were imported there from other places, typically South Africa and China; still others were locally manufactured. How OSI came upon them the instructor didn't offer and Hamilton didn't ask. Nor did it matter; if he were going to be armed—something almost expected for fully free men within the Caliphate—it would have to be with something that would excite no comment.

Arranged from left to right on the bench were seven pistols, four submachine guns, three shotguns, six assault rifles, and two versions of the basic janissary armor piercing rifle.

"We've got five days," the instructor said, "five days to teach you to shoot and maintain all of these."

"Why so many versions?" Hamilton asked.

"Because we've not a clue what you'll actually be able to get. We can't even guarantee you *will* be able to get one of these; there are other types to be found within the enemy's country."

"Now wait a minute," Hamilton objected. "I'm going in as a slave dealer. The slaves will surely object to being slaves. It's only reasonable I'd carry arms with me from South Africa."

The instructor hesitated for a moment before speaking. When he did speak it was to ask, "Didn't they tell you the typical ages of the cargo?"

"You son of a bitch! You didn't tell me I was going to be transporting *children!*"

"Calm down, John," Caruthers said. The controller looked even more bone weary than usual. "There was no need for you to know."

*And I'm going to have a few words with one large-mouthed instructor for telling you prematurely.*

"Kids?"

"That's the usual cargo, yes."

"Sweet Jesus. Kids?"

"They don't take up as much space. They don't eat much. They're cheap. They're docile. They're easily converted to Islam once they're sold. Besides, the guy who runs the brothel in the larger castle prefers kids. That gives you an in to our Chinese chippie." *Although when you find out the real destination of the kids you are going to puke.*

"This is it," Hamilton said. "I'll do this mission because I said I would. But after this, I'm putting in my papers. My obligation will be over by the time this is and after that I am *out of here.*"

There wasn't a building big enough, or expendable enough, to simulate actually blowing up the castle. Instead, demolitions refresher training concentrated more on the theoretical: dust initiators, expedient timing devices, local manufacture of high explosives, and such.

"What good does it do to know how to make triacetone triperoxide, when there isn't going to be any in the castle?" Hamilton asked. "What is the logic of using low explosives—or even high explosives—when they might do no more than release the agent?"

"Mr. Caruthers insisted on a full refresher course, Mr. Hamilton," the explosives instructor, a Dr. Richter, said. "We follow orders. How you come up with the material, is up to you."

"It's box of rocks, stupid. And this shit"—Hamilton's finger pointed at a small cone of what looked to be a very damp white powder— "doesn't release any heat. It couldn't destroy the virus if I used two hundred tons of it."

"I need a nuke," Hamilton said. "Nothing else will work."

"No nukes. I've explained why."

"C'mon, Caruthers, you . . . or your bosses, are being ridiculous. Any attempt at destroying the VA5H without a nuke is just as likely to release it."

"Any attempt at nuking it, if there is another supply somewhere, is just as likely to get it released as simply cracking the castle would."

"Fuck."

"Fuck," Caruthers agreed.

"We need to talk to Mary."

"Talk to me about transportation," Hamilton said. "*Safe* transportation. Talk to me about how long it would take to make a vaccine if we had a sample of the virus."

"We could give you a general purpose containment unit, small enough to carry, cold enough to keep the virus inactive, and large enough to hold any likely container you might find the virus in," Mary answered. "But the risks . . ."

"John," Caruthers said, "if you got caught and engaged . . . if the containment unit were breached . . . we're talking end of the world here."

"We're talking end of the world anyway. This way we might have a chance of preventing that." Hamilton turned his attention back to Mary. "How long to manufacture a vaccine?"

"Full court press? Even assuming it can be done . . . maybe six weeks. Maybe a little less. But what difference would that make? Meara, Sanders and Johnston could simply—well, not 'simply'; but still they *could*—modify the virus to some other configuration."

Caruthers smiled cynically. "Mary, it isn't like John is going to leave them there alive. He'll either bring them back or . . ."

Her eyes grew wide. After all, she *knew* one of them. But . . . "Oh. Yes, I suppose that makes sense."

"No, Mr. Hamilton, not like that. Didn't you learn anything when you were among the heathen in the Philippines? You must remember to sit without pointing the soles of your feet at anyone more important than a servant."

Wearily, Hamilton stood in front of the large tray of *kibsa*, a rice- and, in this case, lamb-based dish, and sat again, this time tucking his legs under him in such a way—and a damned uncomfortable way it was, too—without pointing the soles of his feet anywhere but behind him.

"Much better. We'll practice that more later but for now let's try the *kibsa* while it's still hot."

The instructor reached out one hand, saying, "There are a number of ways to do this, all more or less correct. We'll begin with the classic method, the one that prevails over most of the Arabian Peninsula." Palm down, using his right hand, the instructor bent his fingers and dug them into the mass of steaming rice. He then closed his fist, causing a wash of gooey, yogurt-based sauce to run through his fingers and out each side of the cup of his hand. He continued to press until the mass of rice and lamb was compressed into a small ball about and inch and a quarter in diameter. This he then popped into his mouth.

"Your turn," he said to Hamilton, once he'd swallowed the ball.

The instructor saw Hamilton reaching out with his left hand and, quick as a snake, grabbed a long pointer and used it to rap Hamilton's knuckles. "Never," he said, "*never*, reach for or take anything with your left hand."

"Motherfucker!" Hamilton exclaimed, alternately rubbing and flopping his hand with a loosed wrist. "What the fuck was that for?"

"You learned *nothing* in the Philippines?"

Hamilton shrugged. "Look, we killed them when they fought and rounded them up and deported them when they didn't, or couldn't anymore. We did *not* socialize."

"I see," said the instructor. He sighed. "Where to begin? Mr. Hamilton, the Arabian Peninsula is not a place much given to trees or any crops from which paper could be made. Leather was, in olden times—and again, today—too valuable to use wastefully. Even rocks were rare in most places."

"So?"

"What are you going to do after we eat this meal, oh, sometime over the next day or two?"

"Sleep?"

"Besides that?"

"Ohhh."

"Yes, Mr. Hamilton. The culture our enemies sprang from never really got used to the idea of toilet paper. They used their hands. Given that they ate with their hands, it only made sense—you'll agree—for them to use one for one thing, and one for the other."

"Got it. Right hand only or you're shitting in the pot."

"Not just shitting in the pot, Mr. Hamilton. Use your left hand for anything involving another person and you are sending him the mortal insult of shitting on *him*."

"*Shokran*," Hamilton said.

"Very good. *Afwan*."


Hamilton ran doubting hands over another man's face. Not that the face wasn't attached to the front of his skull; it was. But that face was not *his*. The cheekbones were higher; the eyes had been reshaped; the nose was broadened and the ears subtly reoriented to stick out ever so slightly more. His eyes were green now—"The enemy has a thing for green eyes," Caruthers had said—and his chin more substantial.

"Who the fuck *am* I?" Hamilton asked.

"No one important," Caruthers answered, chuckling. Hamilton didn't look amused. "Oh, all *right*! You are Johann De Wet, scion of a not-very-important family from Cape Town. Though your name is Boer, and though you had a distant Boer ancestor of some importance, your ancestry is almost entirely English. You speak Afrikaans well enough, but with an accent. You elected to do military service, as all white South Africans must, prior to going to college. You rose to the rank of sergeant in the Logistics Corps, which sparked your interest in the transportation side of business. You are a graduate of the University of Cape Town where you majored in business administration, with a minor in international shipping."

Hamilton raised one eyebrow. "It's probably a stupid question, but . . . uh . . . I assume there is documentation? An electronic and paper trail to back this up?"

"All the important things, yes. The actual Johann De Wet died as a baby of pneumonia. Parents subsequently divorced and there were no other children." Caruthers laughed. "I imagine they'd both be very surprised to discover that their baby boy has returned from the grave."

Caruthers continued, "Upon graduation, you were hired by Koop Human Resources, based in Natal, but immediately sent to be an assistant administrator of a slave breeding camp in the Congo which has since been closed. Thereafter, you were resident in a hospital for two years while recovering from the outbreak of Ebola III that closed the camp.

"KHR, by the way, is a wholly owned subsidiary of OSI, though nobody knows that but us and South African Intelligence. And neither of us is saying. As I told you once, we can cooperate."

"You mean the company has been in the slave trading business for *years* now?" Hamilton asked.

"Leave off, *Mister* Hamilton!" After he said it, the man seemed almost to shrink. "It's a shitty world, John . . . and neither of us made it; we just have to live in it. Now if you'll allow me to continue, you will be working for one of our senior people over there. You don't need to know his real name but he goes by a local one . . ."

# Excursus

**Introduction**

The United States finds itself now with an empire it does not want, that costs more than it brings in, and that requires the perversion of our values and the suppression of civil liberties we had enjoyed since the late eighteenth century and in some cases the early seventeenth, to the early twenty-first.

How did we get this way? Why is it that only now that we are *beginning* to be able to discuss it openly? Can we ever get rid of it? Can we keep some parts and dispense with others?

Can we even remain a nation . . .

221

◇   ◇   ◇

## Chapter II

We have seen in the previous chapter how various security measures, some sensible and others silly, some intrusive and others not, had never really sat well with the American psyche. It is open to debate whether those measures, even if maintained, could have stopped the attacks that followed their dismantling. What is not open to debate is that the security measures adopted at the beginning of the century *were* dismantled, and that attacks followed.

Seven bombs had been introduced into the then United States, and one into the United Kingdom. A further bomb was stopped by Israeli security forces as terrorists attempted to bring it in over the shore. Sadly, because it was stopped at sea, and the yacht carrying it sunk, the Israelis were unable to warn us, because they were ignorant themselves, for some days, of the nature of the yacht's cargo.

Of the American bombs, three came through Mexico and three through what was then Canada. A seventh, and the largest, came by sea. The targeted cities were Los Angeles, Kansas City, Chicago, Boston, New York, Houston, and Washington, plus London in the United Kingdom. The Chicago, New York, Houston and Washington bombs failed to create a nuclear detonation. In two of these, Houston and Washington, it was determined that the bombs were simply defective in manufacture. They exploded, spread a fair amount of radioactive material about the targeted cities, but killed very few and did little lasting damage. Two others, Chicago and

New York, had degraded over time due to poor maintenance, failing to explode at all. Notwithstanding, on September 11th, 2015, three American cities and approximately four million American citizens and residents ceased to exist, along with just under one million of the king's subjects, including King William, himself.

Initially, no one took credit for the attacks. Then again, given the date, no one really had to. Both sides had taken to injuring each other on any given year's September 11th. It was almost a tradition.

The provenance of the bombs was mixed. The two that had failed to detonate fully were found to be of North Korean origin. One that had detonated was proven to be Pakistani. Two that failed were of very old Russian manufacture. For two others that exploded, we do not and likely never shall know. It is possible that they were of Iranian manufacture.

Only Russia, which had a much clearer idea of American retaliatory capabilities than most others, came forth and provided evidence of how their bombs had ended up in terrorist hands. Several dozen scientists, security personnel, and their families were subsequently shot as an act of good faith *cum* human sacrifice. In addition, Russia promised and gave substantial aid, especially in the form of oil and natural gas. Volunteers from there for clean up and recovery came by the thousands. Many times the numbers that came volunteered to, though no place could be found for them.

Pakistan professed ignorance while North Korea simply glared defiance and threatened ever more severe attacks should we retaliate. China, allied to both of those, kept its own counsel.

The entire world held its breath for weeks. Meanwhile, the United States did nothing but weep and dig in the rubble. Indeed, not all wept. There was a strong feeling in certain quarters that the bombings had been just. Professor Montgomery Chamberlain, of the University of Michigan at Ann Arbor summed up these views nicely when he pronounced the dead, "So many little Himmlers" and called for "one hundred more attacks, until the blood-sucking, Jew-controlled United States is humbled and brought to its knees."

Neither of the major political parties in the United States lined up behind any program of major retaliation, though the President increased security along both the Canadian and Mexican borders . . .

## Chapter IV

Within weeks of the attacks, and with no sign of significant retaliation in the offing, a new and highly populist party arose. Officially, it was known as the "Wake Up, America Party." Unofficially, it was often called "the Armageddon Party." It began small, with a speech by its founder, Pat Buckman, in Central Park in New York City. Half a million New Yorkers heard Buckman in person, and perhaps twice that on the TV. Tens of millions heard him across the country. Where the money came from for advanced advertising for the speech is not known. Why the people came is obvious; but for a few defects and decays, they, too, would have been numbered among the dead.

Buckman's message was simple and he wasn't shy about it. He began with the simple line, "Those motherfuckers are going to pay." Buckman didn't specify which group of motherfuckers he meant. As subsequent events were to show he had some very expansive ideas on the subject.

Within months, sixty million people had signed on to the WUA program. Moreover, substantial numbers of Democrats and Republicans in the House and Senate likewise defected to Buckman's cause.

In the United Kingdom, the new-crowned king, and king in more than name now, launched a very similar program on his own. Moreover, the new king unilaterally seceded from the European Union when that body attempted to interfere. The king's subjects met the news joyfully. They *were* Britons, after all, and had had just about enough . . .

◇ ◇ ◇

## Chapter VII

The election of 2016 was a foregone conclusion months before the polls opened, though both of the traditional parties, and the mainstream media, denied it until the last. Though both Democrats and Republicans attempted to mount the populist bandwagon, the people weren't listening anymore. Buckman carried every state, even—since Boston and its hard core of liberal voters had been destroyed—Massachusetts, and had unprecedented majorities in both houses of Congress.

Despite predictions, the missiles did not fly within an hour of Buckman's inauguration. He explained why: "We must put our own house in order first. We must . . . "

◇ ◇ ◇

## Chapter VIII

No one thought it particularly odd when President Buckman, with the overwhelming support of his party's members in Congress, pushed through a bill making a very large number of crimes, most notably politically motivated homicide, purely federal in jurisdiction. Even many of the remaining Democratic and Republican members of Congress joined in supporting this "Federal Supremacy over Politically Motivated Crimes Act of 2017." Some, to include we must suppose, Montgomery Chamberlain, must have breathed a heavy sigh of relief when political speech was not criminalized.

If so, such sighs of relief were soon proven to be premature. Chamberlain was found in his Ann Arbor apartment, wounded by gunfire and then strangled to death by the sole surviving member of a family lost in the Kansas City attack. The killer, former liberal Democrat and former husband and father of four, Mark Moulas, called the police after the murder to inform them of it, and calmly awaited arrest while contemplating Chamberlain's cooling corpse. He confessed immediately, and never showed a trace of remorse. At the subsequent bench trial, Moulas was found guilty and sentenced to a term of ninety-nine years by the judge.

Though there is not the slightest bit of evidence that either Buckman, or any member of WUA, was complicit in the Chamberlain murder, Moulas was immediately pardoned and released.

This murder was followed by the private killing of two left-leaning Supreme Court justices, half a dozen congressmen, forty-seven newspaper editors, and an amazingly large number of academicians. All the murderers except one was pardoned, and that one was not pardoned only, so it would seem, because his motivation for the killing had been that the academician concerned had been sleeping with the killer's wife.

This was perhaps the only truly original and brilliant bit of domestic statesmanship ever engaged in by Pat Buckman. No one previously had ever suspected that the power of pardon, of executive clemency, was also a power of summary execution . . .

◇　◇　◇

## Chapter XII

By early 2018, President Buckman had his "house in order." Similarly, across the Atlantic, the king, too, was ruling with an iron fist. Whether there was collaboration between the two may be doubted. What cannot be doubted was that, under similar threats even rather dissimilar men may act similarly. Unlike Buckman, of course, the king was sane.

The first Muslim containment camps opened near Dearborn, Michigan, in the spring of 2018. Citing the case of *Korematsu v. United States*, as well as the related cases, *Yasui* and *Hirabayashi*, and the *Alien and Sedition Act of 1798*, the President, by executive order, directed the internment of all male Moslems, to include Black Muslims, over the age of twelve, whatever their citizenship. The Supreme Court, now with two more justices firmly in the WUA camp, endorsed the order, eight to one.

Another pardon from the president was required, when that one dissenting member of the court was killed.

The next major political act of the Buckman administration, the "Redefinition of Religion Act of 2018," defined Islam as "primarily a hostile and dangerous political movement, and only incidentally and dishonestly a religion," and expressly placed it "squarely outside the protections of the First Amendment." This the Supreme Court approved unanimously.

◇ ◇ ◇

While the order originally purported to intern only males, a subsequent order also directed the internment of females who were related to males implicated in "terrorist or anti-American activities, whatever the degree of relation, and whatever the degree of complicity."

Separate camps were established for women, in order to avoid future pregnancies and, hence, future Moslems. Moreover, any who could produce permission from an Islamic country for asylum, and were not suspected of complicity in terrorism, were permitted to go, under guard, and at their own expense.

The United Kingdom did not establish camps; the prison system was adequate to hold those Muslims believed to pose a threat. For the rest, in a sort of reverse Dunkirk, the Royal Navy dumped them unceremoniously on the shores of France. After all, the EU thought them citizens of the EU and so could hardly object.

It must be said that the British were fairly civilized about the operation, more so than the United States, in any case.

In addition to the camps for males and females, President Buckman also opened camps for the political opposition, such as it was, though these were integrated. No particular effort was made to fill these camps. Instead, the administration published lengthy lists of people it considered enemies of the state. The camps were declared to be "safe zones," where those same people would be protected from the anger of the masses.

Implicitly, of course, Buckman was saying, "Outside of these camps, you will be murdered and we both know you will because I will pardon your killers. Inside, we will keep you alive. Or, of course, you can leave the country. And good riddance."

Many chose to leave, rather than be interned. Many of those leaving left for Canada, which was convenient, prosperous, civilized, highly humanitarian in outlook, and always a willing home for true political refugees.

Even so, the total numbers, exclusive of Moslems, who left for other climes in the years 2018–2020 were only about one million, about eighty-five percent of those going north . . .

◇　　◇　　◇

## Chapter XV

Whatever his sanity, or lack thereof, no one could accuse President Buckman of not thinking ahead, of not planning for the future. Even while the social order was being altered, his administration and its allies in Congress were busy making the country approximately energy self-sufficient.

This program was unprecedentedly huge. Not only did nuclear plants begin to spring up like mushrooms, every major city was scheduled for a thermal depolymerization plant, solar chimneys began to rise in the deserts of the southwest, all barriers to drilling for oil in northern Alaska were swept away, Colorado and adjoining states were gifted, if that's quite the word, with further plants to begin to convert the huge shale deposits of the Green

River Basin, holding enough recoverable oil to meet the needs of the United States for several centuries.

With this level of government sponsored planning and employment, to which must be added the rough quadrupling of the size of the Army, from five hundred thousand to just over two million, the United States experienced a more or less severe labor shortage. This was partially made up by a guest worker program that allowed in millions of Indians and other East Asians. Many of these later achieved citizenship, enough so that "Dinesh" and "Aishwarya" began to compete with "John" and "Jennifer" among most popular baby names.

It should perhaps be noted that Hindus, Sikhs, Buddhists, and even Christian-Animists have never once, as of this writing, set off a bomb or engaged in any other act of terrorism on mainland American soil.

Mexicans and other Latins were generally not allowed in, as much of that newly huge Army was deployed along the Mexican border with orders to shoot crossers without warning. Much of the Army not deployed on the borders was devoted to massive roundups of illegal immigrants, generally. Most of these were, of course, Latin.

The Supreme Court decided that that was not a violation of *Posse Comitatus* as the illegal immigration had arisen to the level of an invasion and invasion was a military rather than a legal matter.

The resultant loss of revenue experienced by Mexico, in particular, as millions of Mexican citizens were unceremoniously dumped back across the border was to create a massive and rising level of instability within that country. Nor was the loss of revenue the sole factor in the later outbreak of civil war within Mexico, for those same illegal immigrants to the United States—even though cut

off from the mainstream of American society—had also
seen a society that worked far, far better than Mexico
ever had. These returnees saw no insuperable reason
why Mexico could not work as well . . .

◇    ◇    ◇

## Chapter XXI

A Marine amphibious force, of roughly corps size, was
dispatched to the Indian Ocean weeks before President
Buckman went to Congress to ask for a declaration of
war. This was duly granted by substantial majorities in
Congress. The form of that declaration was unique in
that no specific national enemy was identified. Rather,
the declaration of war of 2019 merely stated that a state
of war shall exist between the United States of America
and "any nation which supports, or has supported, or
defends, or has defended, or permits, or has permitted,
its soil to be used as a haven for terrorism inspired by
the pernicious pseudo-religion known as Islam."

In theory this would have placed the United States at
war with most of the world. In practice, Buckman
defined the enemy unilaterally, on 1 September, 2019,
by insisting in a public broadcast that each of thirty-two
Muslim majority nations which had had one or more of
their citizens implicated in the "three cities attacks," plus
North Korea, surrender unconditionally.

They failed to do so. While the initial demand had
resulted in widespread panic and flight from Islamic
cities, within a week calm had returned and most people
in those cities returned to their normal occupations
and lives.

On September 11, 2019, the missiles flew . . .

◇ ◇ ◇

## Chapter XXII

It seems likely that few, if any, of the people voting Buckman into office had quite envisioned the terrible vengeance he would wreak upon the Islamic world.

A dozen Trident missile-carrying submarines were used for the attacks, six firing from the Atlantic, four from the Pacific, and two from the Indian Ocean. Only about half of each submarine's load of missiles was fired, a total of one hundred and forty-six missiles and seven hundred and thirty warheads, each in the four hundred and seventy-five kiloton range.

Fifty-five major Islamic cities, and many minor ones were on the targeting list. No major city was hit by fewer than two warheads nor more than four, except Cairo, which received five. Riyadh, Medina and Mecca were each hit by three, spaced some hours apart. In addition to those cities, the entire Nile River Valley saw nuclear weapons essentially *walked* along its length, a tribute of sorts to the significant Egyptian participation in the Three Cities Attacks, courtesy of the Muslim Brotherhood.

Nine missiles and forty-five warheads were sufficient to scour North Korea free of substantial concentrations of human life. The fourteen largest North Korean cities were attacked, and Pyongyang obliterated.

Marines began landing to either side of the city of Dhahran, headquarters of ARAMCO, within twenty-four hours of the nuclear attacks. It fell with little fighting as did its neighbors, Dammam and Khobar. The local populations, excepting only those critical to the oil industry and their families, were driven into the desert to die.

As those remaining locals were replaced with Americans, they too were driven off.

The American presence in Arabia was to end only when the last drop of economically recoverable oil had been taken. By that time, the United States had become energy self-sufficient, once the energy assets of the former Canada were taken into account and a full rationing regime imposed. The triple cities of Dammam, Dhahran and Khobar were destroyed by nuclear weapons once the last Americans had been withdrawn.

It is believed that President Buckman's guiding principles governing the attacks were that every Islamic nation which had had a national involved in the Three Cities attacks was to be struck, that major Islamic cities were to be destroyed at a rate of not less than ten for one, that Mecca and Medina were to be reduced to the point that no landmark should remain, and that deaths were to be inflicted at a rate of not less than one hundred for one.

It known that the second and third goals were met. Indeed, no single trace remains of the Kabaa or the Grand Mosque. It is believed that the first and fourth were met as well. Indeed, counting not merely the direct victims of the attacks, but adding to that those who subsequently died of starvation, disease, lack of potable water, lack of medical care for injuries, and the complete breakdown of anything approaching civilization in the Islamic world, it is very likely that total deaths approached eight hundred million, or roughly two hundred to one.

It was the greatest mass murder in history.

Nor should it have surprised anyone. It was not only predictable; it had been predicted. As one Lee Harris, a sophont of the day had put it:

> In other words, the only effect on America of a continuation of September 11–style attacks would be an increasingly repressive state apparatus domestically and a populist home front demand for increasingly severe retaliation against those nations supporting or hiding terrorists. But neither one of these reactions would seriously undermine the strength of the United States—indeed, it is quite evident that further attacks would continue to unite the overwhelming majority of the American population, creating an irresistible "general will" to eradicate terrorism by any means necessary, including the most brutal and ruthless.

◊ ◊ ◊

## Chapter XXIX

The first imperial acquisition, outside of the lodgment on the Arabian peninsula, was Canada. It was that former state's misfortune that, while the United States had been her last line of defense, Canada had been America's first line.

Buckman had hinted all along that Canada must move to eliminate the threat its Moslems presented to the United States. These tacit warnings were ignored, for the most part, though some Canadians living in the United States or who had lived there, tried desperately to warn their countrymen that America was in utter earnest, that it was no longer in a mood to accept the threat Canada's insistence on diversity presented. It had taken fewer than forty terrorists to introduce the nuclear weap ons used in the Three Cities Attacks. It was believe that Canada contained more than four thousand more.

Even so, it took a combination of three miscalculations to make the United States move. The core states of the European Union broke diplomatic relations with America within hours of the launch of the retaliatory attacks. Canada, always one with the EU in spirit if not in fact or law, did likewise. Cooperation in terms of border control ceased. The effect of this, though, in the case of Canada, was to rob the United States of any sense of security on its northern border.

The second miscalculation was to admit into Canada some two millions of mainly Moslem refugees from the irradiated ruins of Islamic civilization. A few of these attempted cross-border operations against the United States. Most of these Canada put down. It only took one failure, however, to give the United States all the excuse it needed to invade.

The final miscalculation, on Canada's part, was the assumption that the United Kingdom could somehow dissuade the United States from taking action. The UK, under the new monarchy, busily rounding up its own Moslems and fearful of terrorists entering the Kingdom from Canada, was simply not interested.

Nineteen Regular Army divisions, one dozen divisions of the Army National Guard, plus the Second and Fourth Marine Divisions, rolled across the border just before dawn on 11 May, 2020.

Despite the gallant resistance put up by the main elements of the Canadian Forces, notably the Royal 22nd and Twelfth Armored, which died in defense of Quebec City, the Royal Canadian Regiment and Royal Canadian

Dragoons, shattered in the forlorn defense of Ottawa, and the Princess Patricia's Canadian Light Infantry and Lord Strathcona's Horse, butchered in detail in a hopeless defense of the long western border, Canada—rather the thin strip of well-populated area that roughly paralleled the border with the United States—fell quickly.

It is both interesting and sad to note that it was only those most despised by the government of Canada, and its ruling party, who actually proved willing to defend that government. Those who had most despised their own forces, and who had themselves signally failed to fight, soon found themselves the center of attention of a country-wide sweep. Almost as quickly they found themselves in various well-guarded logging and mining camps in the cold, cold lands of Nunavut and the Northwest Territories . . .

◇   ◇   ◇

## Chapter XXXII

Mexico had been a vital trading partner for the United States for many decades. This trade continued, even after the completion of the wall between the two countries, until the Revolution broke out and grew beyond the ability of the government of Mexico to handle.

Even then, President (now, as a practical matter, given the repeal of the 22nd Amendment and the control he exercised over every aspect of American life, "for life") Buckman did not intervene. Canada, with its thirty-five-odd-million people, not all of them averse to American occupation and *Anschluss*, had been comparatively easy. Mexico, with one hundred and thirty million people—

almost to a man and woman loathing the United States, and not without reason—was a patently tougher case.

Nonetheless, following a series of attacks on the wall between the countries, Buckman ordered the armed forces to intervene. It was to be fifteen years and as many as ten million lives, before anyone could, with a straight face, call Mexico pacified . . .

◊    ◊    ◊

## Chapter XXXIV

The precedent of Mexico established, Buckman felt very comfortable invading Cuba, not because there were any numbers of Moslems there and not because it represented a threat, but merely because he was a child of the Cold War and could hold a grudge.

It was only that the United States armed forces were so tied down in Cuba, Mexico, Canada, and the Arabian peninsula that allowed the Latin and Caribbean states to retain that measure of independence they enjoy today. The price of retaining that independence was, however, high. Each remaining independent nation (except for Brazil which was frankly too large and powerful to be all that easily intimidated) was required to sign on to a heavily amended update of the Rio Pact. This Protocol, as it was called, required each to expel or intern any Moslems found within its borders, to provide either military formations for the use of the United States, or their equivalent value in money or goods and, in the latter case, to permit free recruiting by the United States. The Latin states were also required to submit all questions of foreign policy to the United States for approval, and to suppress within their borders any movement founded upon disloyalty or opposition to the United States.

As Buckman said, at the convention, "I can't take you all on at once. We all know this. But I can knock you off one or two at a time. Choose wisely."

In the end, only Venezuela chose unwisely. It was transformed from a sovereign state to an imperial province in 2023. Most of the troops for the expedition were other Latins, acting under American command pursuant to the 2022 Protocol to the Rio Pact . . .

◊   ◊   ◊

## Afterword

It would have been pleasant to report, had it come to pass, that President Buckman had somehow been overthrown, and that he had been tried for his many crimes and hanged. Sadly, this was not to be. Rather, he passed away quietly one night in 2036, leaving us his legacy: an empire we don't want yet can't get rid of, the enmity of most of the world, a crushing military burden, and damage to our traditional civil liberties that has yet to be fully undone and may never be.

As pleasant as it might have been, however, and as pleasant at it may be to contemplate, in all probability it would not have mattered. Once the United States let down its guard while at the same time not removing—even assuming it was possible to remove—the causes and reasons that caused us to be hated throughout the Moslem world, the Three Cities attacks became inevitable. Once those attacks took place, Buckman, or someone just like him by another name, became equally inevitable.

# PART II

# CHAPTER TEN

Then the Lord passed by in front of him and proclaimed, "The Lord, the Lord God, compassionate and gracious, slow to anger, and abounding in loving kindness and truth; who keeps loving kindness for thousands, who forgives iniquity, transgression and sin; yet He will by no means leave the guilty unpunished, visiting the iniquity of fathers on the children and on the grandchildren to the third and fourth generations."

—Exodus 34: 6–7

## Cape Town, South Africa, 14 October, 2113

Curiously enough, paper books had never gone out of style. Perhaps this was because there was something comforting about the solidity of a book. Perhaps it was because, as many said, books made attractive wall coverings. Perhaps it was merely that books suited the human mind and body in a way that screen images and holographic projections simply could not. Whatever the case, books were still commonly printed in dead-tree format.

Caruthers had made a present of such a book to Hamilton, just as the latter had boarded the airship at Reagan National.

"I know you think we're dirty, John," Caruthers had said. "And you're right; we are. But the difference between us and the people we are fighting is that we have a chance to get better on our own . . . and they don't and never will. Here's proof that we might get better."

It was a huge book, *Empire Rising*, more than twelve hundred pages, exclusive of appendices, end notes, tables, bibliography and photographs. Hamilton had spent most of the three-day trip to Cape Town engrossed in it.

Hamilton closed the book just as the airship slid over the coastline on its way to the aerodrome northeast of Cape Town. From this altitude, the entire scene looked very neat, almost antiseptic. He knew, from both his readings and his instruction at OSI headquarters, that the core of the place was anything but antiseptic. Moslems might hate the American Empire, a feeling that was fully reciprocated, but the every day, present tense loathing of most African blacks and whites for each other put those American-Moslem antipathies in the shade for sheer intensity, if not necessarily for destructiveness.

Looking down at the book before sliding it into his carryall, Hamilton thought, *Well . . . it's got to be a good step that things like this can be published again. After ninety years of censorship, perhaps we've gotten over the Three Cities.*

In his heart though, however much he wanted to, he didn't believe it.

"*Meneer* De Wet?" the black driver from Koop Human Resources asked, as Hamilton stepped out of the underground corridor that connected the airship landing pit with the main terminal. The driver was medium height, balding, with a neatly trimmed beard and an expansive gut. Hamilton suspected the fat concealed an impressive amount of muscle.

"Yes," Hamilton answered. He'd been expecting to be picked up. Almost he offered his hand to the driver before the endless hours of drill in South African customs reasserted itself. "I'm De Wet."

"Caruthers told me to say, 'Hi,' " the driver said, in Bronx-accented English. Hamilton immediately felt a profound sense of relief. "You'll be working for me. My name here is Bonginkosi Mathebula . . . and if I see you almost offer me your hand again, I will break it. Control yourself, *baas*. My friends call me 'Bongo.' That's good enough.

"Officially," Bongo continued, "I am your indentured manservant. Unofficially, I'm in charge. Don't forget it. If we didn't need a reliable white front man, you wouldn't even be here."

The drive to the company guesthouse on the outskirts of Cape Town was long. Bongo drove while Hamilton sat in back. The black used the opportunity to lecture.

"A century and a half ago, the whites were on top. You should already have known that but one can never tell what the idiots at Langley may forget to pass on.

"They'd have stayed there, too," Bongo continued, "through a combination of pigheaded determination and bloody-minded ruthlessness. Ultimately, they were pretty sure that as long as the black opposition was supported by and in turn supported the communists, the west would never let white South Africa go under. That was true, too, until the collapse of the Soviet Union in the late twentieth century. This made the value of the white regime to the anti-Soviet coalition drop like a lead weight.

"The Boers and the Cape English saw the writing on the walls then and, facing a desperate race war with no possibility of help from their racial kin, they made the best deal they could.

"Unfortunately for South Africa, while not all the whites' fears came to pass, enough of them did. After majority rule was instituted, whites fled the country in droves. Some of them left because of the crime. Other got sick of nepotism and corruption masquerading as affirmative action. I'm sure still others left in sheer funk at not being the local master race anymore.

"Whatever the cause, the white portion of the South African population dropped substantially, about in half, even while the black and mixed populations grew. Even worse, it was the most technically skilled and capable whites who left, while those who stayed tended to be government flunkies and corporate bureaucrats."

Bongo slammed on the brakes and cursed at a black couple crossing the street in front of the company car. The couple just smiled at him and waved.

"Two factors changed that rough demographic stability. One was the roughly one third of the black female population of child bearing age that was infected with

HIV, the virus that caused AIDS, the Acquired Immune Deficiency Syndrome. This not only killed them in disproportionate numbers, generally in their most fertile years, it caused a very serious social breakdown because of the number of orphans produced. Still worse, it put financial strain on a government that had difficulty enough eking out tax dollars from the many sticky fingers, white and black, those tax dollars passed through. The government, hoping for yet more money in foreign aid to pilfer, even denied that HIV caused AIDS, which of course let the problem rage out of control.

"Still, with low white birthrates and white flight from the country, one could have expected roughly similar proportions to be maintained.

"And so they would have been, had there not been a different wave of white flight in the world, commencing in the 2020s. That wave emanated from Europe. Some of it washed up in Australia and New Zealand. Some small part was allowed into the United States and its possessions. But only South Africa found itself in really desperate need for immigrants. Thirteen million Europeans found their way here."

Bongo's voice grew contemplative. "I have often wondered if the barbarian migrations that wrecked the Western Roman Empire didn't start just that way, one group in Mongolia raiding Chinese living north of the Great Wall, thereby causing the Chinese to push the first offending group right off its lands, starting a chain reaction. Whether it did or not, it sure worked that way here. First the Moslems nudged us, then we made their lands uninhabitable, they in turn went to Europe, which drove the Europeans here, which further fucked the blacks here, in the ass and without grease.

"It might not have been so bad, except for two other factors. Those Europeans who fled were typically highly fertile and more than a little bitter about being driven—whatever the truth of the matter, that's how *they* felt about it—from their original homes. They were, moreover, the most highly conservative of Europeans. They were not remotely interested in nepotism masquerading as affirmative action. Nor did they see why affirmative action should disadvantage them, since their ancestors had had nothing to do with *apartheid*. This is all a fair point of view, you'll agree," Bongo said, smiling over his shoulder at Hamilton.

"The civil war that broke out in 2038 lasted for nine years and cost millions of lives. At the end of it, disciplined fire, the old European military tradition, and a critical alliance with the Zulu people ended black majority rule in South Africa. By 2065, virtually all of sub-Saharan Africa was under white sway once again. They've learned a lot, though. That controlling hand is often felt only lightly. They prefer to rule through locals, much as the French did for more than half a century after notionally giving up their empire.

"Still, give the Boers . . . oh, yes, they're all Boers now, even the Cape English . . . give them their due. They pay their bills. The only exception to effective white rule in sub-Saharan Africa is Zululand, a hefty chunk carved out of Natal and points north for the Zulu in full payment for their services. And this time they weren't idiot cheapskates about it; this time they gave the Zulu a real country."

"What the fuck?" Hamilton's eyes could not believe what they were seeing, one man, two women in *hijab*, half a dozen kids with the oldest girl in *hijab* as well. "A *Moslem* family? Running around free?"

Bongo raised his eyes heavenward and shook his head with disgust. "I *knew* those assholes at Langley would miss important details." His hand left the steering wheel to point a finger generally off to the right front. "We've got maybe three hundred thousand Moslems here in Cape Town, something like three-quarters of a million in the country as a whole, exclusive of possessions and protectorates. There's a mosque over there," he said. "Pretty large one, actually. They call it the 'Red Mosque.' No, it isn't painted red and never has been. About forty years ago, a wild-eyed imam used to preach the *jihad* from its pulpit. Then one Friday, the Boers sent in ten thousand assegai-wielding Zulu. They killed every man, woman, and child in the place, then went on to kill every imam in Cape Town and their families, except for a very few the government took under its protection. After that, about fifty-thousand more of them were sold, some locally and some to the Caliphate, as slaves.

"Since then? Never a problem with the Moslems here. Never a peep, as a matter of fact. And some thousands of them drop Islam and become Christians every year. See, *Baas* De Wet, terror *works*."

## KHR House, Swartland, Western Cape Province, Boer Republic of South Africa, 14 October, 2113

"Well, it beats the fuck out of Olson Hall," Hamilton whispered very softly to himself when shown to his temporary quarters. The woman guiding him was extraordinarily tall, being just over six feet. If Hamilton had been more familiar with South Africa he might have identified her as being a mix of Dutch, Irish, English, French, Arab, Malay, Swede, Bantu, and Hindi. The percentages would have defied even a native to guess. He thought her very pretty as, indeed, any man would have. The woman, not much more than a girl, really, whatever her height, introduced herself as "Alice."

She directed Bongo to place Hamilton's bags on the bed, then dismissed him, peremptorily. Hamilton thought it a fine commentary of the senior agent's fieldcraft that he bowed and scraped his way out on the suite with a more servile expression on his face than any Hamilton had seen on the liberated slaves of the Moros, during the Philippines campaign.

Alice then proceeded to empty out Hamilton's two suitcases, leaving alone only the contents of the locked carryall. The suits were hung in a large armoire, one of a pair to one side of the queen-sized bed. Underwear and socks went into drawers inside the armoire, while Alice carried his toiletries to the suite's expansive bath. Shoes she placed on a tree, without comment.

It was always a pleasure to watch an expert at work. Deciding that Alice knew what she was doing better than he did, Hamilton sat down in a comfortable stuffed chair and watched her work. She spoke very little.

*It doesn't matter; a girl with an ass like that doesn't need to talk to be entertaining. Not that she's beautiful, but she's at least very pretty and her body is . . . amazing. If I weren't on mission I'd be a fool not to at least think about asking her out.*

Some of Hamilton's clothing she found faulty upon examination. These she separated out for the maids to take care of.

And then she was done, standing there in the middle of the room. "Why don't you take a shower, *baas*," Alice suggested.

Hamilton's hair was full of shampoo and his eyes burning with soap when he heard a small click and felt a cool draft on his wet body. There was somebody inside the shower with him. He immediately backed into one corner, putting out one hand to guard while trying desperately to get the soap from his eyes.

He stopped himself, feeling inexpressibly silly, when he heard Alice laugh. "Didn't you understand?" she asked. "I come with the room . . . like a piece of furniture. I'm here for your enjoyment."

"How did you end up here?" Hamilton asked, later, as the two lay in bed, half-exhausted.

"I was born," Alice answered, cryptically. "I'm sorry," she amended. "That wasn't fair. I wanted to go to school. I couldn't afford it. KIIR made me an offer. I get room and board—and it's a very *nice* room, don't you think?"

"Very nice," Hamilton agreed.

"Yes. The company gave me a budget to decorate and I did it myself. I was even able to save a little.

"Anyway . . . well, I get room and board, a small stipend, and can go to class when I don't have duties here. It may take me six years to get a degree, instead of four, but six years is better than never."

"And for that?"

"For that I signed a contract of indenture . . . I have to be nice to men assigned to this suite." She smiled warmly. "I was happy when you were assigned, *baas*. Usually the men are a lot older and I don't care for them much.

"Someday, if I graduate well, I'd like to put in papers to emigrate to America . . . or maybe some of its possessions where the rules for immigration are a little easier."

Hamilton said nothing but thought, *You should try and I wish you luck, Alice. We may suck . . . but the rest of the world is just one giant vacuum that pulls away hopes and dreams and runs them through filth on the way to the garbage can.*

Hamilton's last thought, as he drifted off to sleep, was, *Amend will. Give ten thousand? No, that wouldn't be enough. Give twenty-thousand Imperial New Dollars to Alice Mbatha, of KHR House, Cape Town, with hopes that it helps her make her way . . .*

## Slave Pen Number Five, KHR House Holding Facility, Cape Town, South Africa, 17 October, 2113

"If you wince," Bongo said, on the elevator ride down to the pens, "if you give any indication that those kids are anything more than cattle, you are out of here." It was an idle threat, after spending so much time training Hamilton for this one mission, he was not going to be replaced. Still, Bongo thought, perhaps he didn't understand that.

"I won't," Hamilton assured his ostensible servant and genuine boss. "But I've got to ask: How the hell do you stand it, day after day, year after year?"

"You can get used to anything," Bongo replied. The subterranean elevator doors opened to the sound of wailing and moaning and utter human misery. "Some things are just a lot harder than others.

"This is one of the hardest," Bongo whispered, before taking the lead and saying aloud, "This way, *baas*, your lot is right over this way."

There were six pits below the elevator walkway. Separated by some kind of tough, clear plastic, they allowed the staff of the complex to walk between them to distribute food and water. The oddest thing, to Hamilton's eye, was that to one or two sides of each of five of the six pits women, some black, some brown, a few obviously with some white in their ancestry, stood staring at the sixth, their hands seeming desperate to push through the clear barriers that held them.

"Why—"

Bongo answered before the question was fully formed. "Those are mothers, pining for their children. The children —our cargo—are in the sixth pen."

Unbidden, Hamilton walked to stand above the sixth pen, the one obviously holding nothing but wide-eyed, mostly silent in shock or weeping with terror and despair, black and colored children aged from about six to nine or ten.

*God is never going to forgive me for this,* he thought. *For that matter, I am never going to forgive me for this.*


"You seem upset, *baas*," Alice said, standing in front of a seated Hamilton and wearing little but a short silk robe. "Can I help?" Before Hamilton could answer she dropped to her knees and began to undo his trousers.

"Later, Alice," he said. "Please. Later tonight I'd be very happy to have you again. For now, I just need to think."

"As you wish, *baas*," she answered, rising to her feet gracefully. "If you change your mind, just call. I'll be at the desk working on my studies."

◇    ◇    ◇

South Africa had produced high quality wines and beers for centuries. Wine or beer, however, just wouldn't do. And the local whiskey was . . . charitably . . . not good.

The brandy, however, was superb. Hamilton poured his own drink from a net-wrapped, amber bottle labeled "Klipdrift."

*Damned shame,* he thought, *that I can't allow myself to get drunk. Crimes like the ones I'm engaged in cry out for sweet oblivion.*

*Is there a way out of this? Caruthers was right; better two hundred should be enslaved than that four or five billion, and civilization itself, should die. But it would be better still if nobody were enslaved and all those billions, plus civilization, lived.*

*Is that possible, though? Is there any way I can save these kids? Save their mothers down in the slave pens? Do that while still stopping VA5H? I doubt it.*

*And what if I do? I mean, just imagine I had the money to buy every one of them down there and free them. What does that do? It improves the market so that more people get sold off. I could save those kids . . . but I can't do a damned thing about the two hundred that will be enslaved to make up for them. The demand will still be there . . . and that demand will be filled. And there is precisely nothing I can do about it.*

*Fuck.*


As it turned out, Hamilton couldn't make love to Alice. She tried her very fine best to make it happen, of course, but under the circumstances her very fine best was not up to the task. No woman's would have been.

Even after he told her to give it up, and waited until she began softly to snore beside him, he still lay awake thinking of the problem of the slave children . . . and of slavery in general.

*It has always existed, John,* he told himself. *Wars have been fought to end it, and it survived those. Alliances were formed to crush it; still it endured. Almost the whole world united against it, and still it survived.*

*It makes no legal sense, in that it puts an undue burden on everyone to protect the intelligent, self-willed, and dangerous property of a few. It makes no economic sense; you can get more profit paying a free man well than you will ever get from a slave that you pay nothing. Morally, it is not better than killing them; slavery is just death drawn out, the absence of liberty which is the absence of everything life is about, of everything that makes it worthwhile to live.*

*And then, too, what values does a slave learn? Looking out for number one, if they have any sense. And still they get manumitted, regularly. Hell, some Moslems buy slaves expressly to manumit to earn a few brownie points with God. But those slaves enter civil society with the "looking out for myself" attitude they learned as slaves. And they never lose it . . . but pass it on to the next generation . . . and the next.*

*And I'm going to deliver two hundred children to that? Fuck, fuck, fuck!*

*Okay, so it's an unutterable evil; what the fuck can I do about it? Anything? Am I lying here sleepless from guilt or from impotence.*

He laughed at himself as that last thought. Surely Alice thought he must have a problem in that department.

*No matter,* he thought, suddenly, and the thought made Hamilton feel much, much better about himself.

*Yes, it looks impossible to do both, stop the VA5H and save those kids. But perhaps the horse will learn to sing; perhaps I can teach it to. I'm sure Laurie would have wanted me to try, at least. And . . . if I am too impotent to succeed, I am still not too impotent to try. Speaking of which . . .*

"Alice . . . how asleep are you?"

### Slave Pen Number Five, KHR House Holding Facility, Cape Town, South Africa, 19 October, 2113

One wall of the children's pen opened up with an echoing clatter of wheels, chains and gears. Black and colored security personnel in KHR House livery immediately entered the pen and began prodding the children out, forcing them through the newly opened wall and into two waiting cattle cars. Though the children were quiet enough, the mothers set up an awful wail as their babies were herded away. Their hands scraped helplessly at the clear plastic barriers holding them. Some cursed; others fainted; not a few wept to God for deliverance. Most of the children kept turning around, until forced onward, for a last glimpse of mothers they never expected to see again.

Hamilton's face was a cold stone mask, a fact that pleased Bongo. *Perhaps the boy's learning.*

Hamilton was reasonably certain he could not have maintained the stone mask if he hadn't determined that he was not going to let these kids be sold. *Of course, even if I can save the kids, the mothers left behind I will not be able to save. I will not be able to reunite the*

*families. Still, I must and will do what I can, save what
I can. Now if I could only figure out how.*

The cattle trucks backed up to the looming bulk of
the airship scheduled for the northern flight to am-
Munch, in the Caliphate's province of Baya. Liveried
guards formed up to either side, with two more guards
between the pair of cattle trucks. The drivers dismounted
and unlocked the back gates, turning cranks to allow the
gates to descend from lower pivots to form ramps. Some
of the children, most of them, really, came out willingly
enough when the drivers beckoned them. Not all did,
however, until the drivers set off shrieking alarms inside
the cargo sections. These drove the remaining boys and
girls out, most of them wailing in terror.

Cargo slaves assigned to the airship stood inside to
guide the children to their pen on the cargo deck. Whatever the cargo crew's feelings on the subject, their faces
remained stone masks.

Hamilton's face mirrored those of the cargo slaves. He
wondered, *Okay, let's assume I can somehow free them.
How do I then get them out of the Caliphate without
returning them to South Africa? Little kids are not going
to be doing any forced marching. And there are too many
to put in one truck, even if I could drive them out through
every checkpoint between am-Munch and the Channel
or the Adriatic. How then? An airship? I can't fly an
airship.*

*Fuck.*

The Great Rift Valley spread below as Hamilton
knocked on the cockpit of the airship. A small closed
circuit camera emerged from the wall and proceeded to

look him over, head to shoes. A door opened and one of the flight crew emerged asking, "Can I help you, *Mineer* De Wet?"

"I've never been in the cockpit of an airship," Hamilton said. "I was wondering if you good *volk* might be willing to give me a little tour, show me the ropes. Never know when it might be useful in my business."

The crewman shrugged and called out over one shoulder to his captain.

"Sure," the captain said. "Always glad to show hospitality to a member of KHR. C'mon in, *mineer*. Klaas, get up and give *Mineer* De Wet your seat."

*No, way,* Hamilton thought, after two hours of instruction and the captain of the ship even allowing him to take the controls. *No way I can fly this thing except on autopilot and then only to one of the programmed airship ports. Which would mean predictability which would mean the kids and I would be shot down within minutes. No way to land the thing either, except under the same circumstances. Fuck.*

*The captain says he or his copilot, or any experienced pilot, could do all that alone in a pinch . . . but I am not, nor will I be, an experienced pilot. Again,* fuck.

*Take a crew hostage and force them to fly me? That's a thought. But then, how do I arrange to have the crew waiting? And even if I do, what keeps the caliph's Air Force from shooting us down anyway?*

"They do build them pretty, no?" said the flight engineer to Hamilton, pointing as he spoke out a porthole towards another airship heading in the opposite direction. Hamilton read the name, "Retief," on the engineer's uniform.

"Who builds them pretty?" Hamilton asked. To him, all airships looked pretty much alike, differing only in size and, at unknown distances, not even in that.

"The Chinks," the flight engineer answered. "That's one of theirs, an *Admiral Cheng Ho* class, if I'm not mistaken . . . that, or a *Long March*. They differ only in size, not in shape. The *Long March* class carries about five- or six hundred tons more."

"Well," Hamilton said, "all airships are pretty. What makes that so special?"

"The lines of the thing." Retief shook his head, saying, "You don't see it, do you?"

"I confess not."

"Oh, well." The engineer sighed. "I suppose the Parthenon wouldn't have been pretty to the Maya, either. Just trust me, though, that is one beautiful ship."

"If you say so," Hamilton half-agreed.

"The other thing is," Retief added, "the Chinks don't use theirs much to carry slaves."

"You don't approve of the slave trade?" Hamilton asked, stone mask descending once again.

"No insult intended," the engineer answered, "but no, I don't. But I've got a family back in Pretoria and they have to eat, so I do my job and mind my own business. It's still disgusting."

*You give me a little hope for humanity, friend,* Hamilton thought, even as he made himself turn on his heels and walk away as if angry. He had to walk away; the temptation to ask the flight engineer for help in freeing the children was too great to trust himself had he stayed.

The Austrian Alps, rugged, forbidding and ice-capped, showed out the side windows. Switzerland was somewhere off to the west. The airships never crossed Swiss airspace unless they were planning on landing in Switzerland or had authorized passage through. Unauthorized crossings would invite the immediate attention of the Swiss Air Force, at which point the choices were landing or being shot down. Since slavery was illegal in Switzerland, the only western European state *not* subsumed in the Caliphate, ships like this one were well advised to avoid the country's airspace entirely.

"How do you live with yourself, Bongo?" Hamilton asked, in the privacy of their shared quarters. "How do you deal with the things you do?"

"You might as well know," Bongo said, "my real name is Bernard Matheson. And, yes, I'm from the Bronx. As for how I live with it, with myself . . . well . . . about a century ago four million of our countrymen were murdered because there was a mindset that wouldn't do bad things even to prevent worse ones. That allowed another mindset to arise, the kind that would do horrible things to prevent bad ones. For me, I'm content to take the middle road, and do bad things to prevent horrible ones. Yeah, it bothers me. Yeah, sometimes I sleep badly. But the fact remains, because of the bad things I do, a lot of much worse things are prevented."

Hamilton sighed, thinking of the PI campaign. And there, the evil—he thought there was no other word for the ethnic cleansing campaign he'd been a part of—was justified only by the prospect that, once the Moros were moved out, there would be a modicum of peace and an end to the endemic mutual massacre that had plagued the islands for centuries.

"Yeah . . . I understand. Been there; done that."

"You've done well, by the way, hiding how you feel about this," Bongo said. "I overheard the flight engineer worrying about his job because he might have offended you. You *know* they never pay any attention to us *kaffirs*, so they speak freely in front of us. Even the good ones do that."

Bongo frowned. "I almost forgot." He reached into a pocket and drew out a small computer memory card. "This message came in last night. I took the liberty of looking it over. At least you're not going to have to watch the kids auctioned off. Someone bought the whole lot, sight unseen. We have to deliver them to the town of Honsvang after we land. I've already arranged ground transportation from am-Munch."

# Interlude

Kitzingen, Federal Republic of Germany,
11 November, 2005

It was late night and the town was quiet. Gabrielle and Mahmoud's apartment, however, was anything but. Nor had it been peaceful for months, ever since Mahmoud had revealed his intention of emigrating to America.

"There," said Mahmoud, pointing at the television screen as he stormed from one side of the small living room to the other, "*there* is the face of Europe's future! *That* is what you insist on staying to see."

The screen showed the face of a young Belgian woman, one Muriel Degauque, who had blown herself up in a fairly unsuccessful suicide attack on American forces in Iraq. She was a convert to Islam or, as Moslems preferred to think of it, a "revert."

"Nonsense," Gabi countered. While Mahmoud was enraged, she remained very calm. It was one of the things he loved about her . . . and that infuriated him at the same time. "She is, she *was*, just one poor disillusioned girl, hardly the wave of a flood of conversion."

"Indeed?" said Mahmoud, sneering. "Well then, how do you categorize Cat Stevens? Idris Tawfik? Yvonne Ridley?"

"If any of them were suicide bombers, surely I'd have heard of their names. Well . . . except for Cat Stevens, of course. Him I know about. And they're all harmless." Gabi shrugged eloquently.

"Susanne Osthof? Have you heard of her? Do you think for a minute she didn't participate in her own kidnapping in Iraq? They even found money on her that was paid for her ransom!"

"There was a perfectly reasonable explanation for that, Mahmoud. The kidnappers simply reimbursed her for property she lost when they took her." Gabi looked upon Mahmoud with suspicion. "It's that Catholic priest who's filling you with this nonsense, isn't it?"

"You really believe both those things, don't you?" Mahmoud seemed to wilt. Before her calm, he felt his rage melt away.

"What I believe is that since you took up this Christian nonsense you've gone from a very reasonable and very bad Moslem to a very unreasonable and altogether too 'good' Christian. Relax, Mahmoud; there are several hundred millions of us. It will be a very long time before the nuts take over here."

"There are several hundred million of you that are spiritually empty vessels that Islam is eager to fill," Mahmoud said. "It's your lack of faith that makes you, and Europe, vulnerable."

Gabi shook her head. She was quite comfortable without religion, indeed, to the extent she retained some trappings of it, *those* made her uncomfortable. She couldn't imagine converting, and especially not to such an austere and anti-female faith as Islam. (As she saw it, Islam was anti-female; there were many who would have disputed that.) Since she could not imagine it for herself, imagining it for any substantial numbers of other people was simply inconceivable.

Mahmoud sat heavily on the couch next to Gabi and reached out to take her hand. "Please come with me?" he asked, for the hundredth time.

"To America? Mahmoud, I can't, I just *can't*. Anyplace but there."

"It is the only safe place for us, Gabi. It's the only place in the world with the will, the faith, the heart, and the strength of culture to remain free."

Gabi snorted. "Culture? America *has* no culture."

"This culture they don't have? It seems to dominate the world pretty well for something nonexistent."

Undeterred, Gabi marched on. "It's a place where the poor are free to sleep under bridges in the winter, yes? It's a place where the rich are free to exploit the workers, no? It's a place with race riots and lynchings . . . a place where the garbage is piled a meter deep to either side of their ramshackle highways."

"You really believe that? Racism? What does racism mean when blacks in America have higher per capita incomes than whites in Europe."

"That's not true anymore," Gabi answered huffily, pulling away her hand. "I just saw the figures and—"

"Don't think just about some exchange rates," Mahmoud interrupted. "Think purchasing power parity. And there, Sweden is beneath Mississippi. Why do you have ten percent unemployment when America's is under five percent? It's not even supposed to be possible to *get* under five percent, but they've done it. And most of the Americans are out of work only for a very short time. Most of Europe's unemployed are going to stay unemployed. Ah . . . never mind that. Just answer: How are you going to make jobs for all the Moslems if you've got ten percent unemployment? Coolie jobs? Do you think they'll settle, in the long run, for coolie jobs? In the last sixty years Europe has created maybe five million jobs, almost all of them in government, which produces nothing. America has created more than ten times as many, almost all of them productive."

"I still can't go with you, Mahmoud. I just can't."

# CHAPTER ELEVEN

The weakness of the Arab nations stems from the fact that they buy weapons instead of choosing to do their own research. If it chose the latter course, an Arab state could pull off two miracles at one stroke: invest in an army of researchers and engineers, thus contributing to full employment, and free itself from military dependence on the West.

> —Fatima Mernissi, modern, enlightened, liberal, Moslem feminist, *Islam and Democracy*

## Castle Noisvastei, Province of Baya, 8 Muharram, 1538 AH (19 October, 2113)

Petra watched as thick, greasy looking smoke poured up from a chimney—a new one, not one of the old—at

Castle Honsvang, far down the slopes. She'd seen such smoke dozens of times before and never thought much of it unless the wind came from that direction. On those days, she generally closed the window of her perch and retired down to her quarters. Her mother had been a decent cook and had never made pork smell quite so burnt and quite so bad.

Fortunately, today the wind blew from some other quarter, leaving Petra free to enjoy the fresh fall air and to peruse her great-grandmother's journal. She'd read it all many times before; between Besma and Ling she'd become quite well lettered. Still she found herself drawn back to certain passages over and over. With a sigh she closed the journal after reading once more great-grandmother Gabi's *cri-de-coeur* for her lost Mahmoud.

"Silly woman, grandma," she whispered. "You should have gone . . . as you yourself realized eventually. God knows, *I* wish you had. I wish—"

The words were interrupted as Ling danced in, waving a sheet of paper and exalting, "He's coming here again, Petra! And he's going to be here for a long time he says!"

"He?"

"Your *brother*, silly. Hans arranged to be assigned to local security at Honsvang, down the hill. He's finished all his training and is being assigned as an officer in the security company."

"Oh . . . oh, shit!"

"What? What 'Oh, shit'?"

"How often are we called down to Honsvang to service the men there, Ling, rather than them coming here? Every other month? Three times in four months? How do you think Hans will take it having you fucked in a different room in the castle? How will he take it when I am?"

"Oh." The Han girl bit her lip. "Hadn't thought about that. But . . . I mean it isn't like it's anything more than a job for me, and not one I like, either. Surely Hans would . . . no, I guess not. But he knows *we* sleep together and it doesn't bother him."

" 'We' are a different matter entirely. What we do never seems to bother men, and that's not even counting when we're hired to put on a show."

"Crap. We'll have to think of something then . . . that, or explain it to Hans in . . . right, forget I said that. Stupid idea to explain things rationally to stupid men."

## Castle Honsvang, Province of Baya, 8 Muharram, 1538 AH (19 October, 2113)

Sands, Johnston, and Meara watched through a high temperature glass window as flames raised the internal heat of the furnace to over two thousand degrees. The two bodies inside quickly burst into flames as their own fat caught fire, then burned down to ash. Even then, the residue was not released until that temperature had been maintained for some time. They were playing gods with world-destroying organisms here, and there was no room for chance.

"Damn" said Sands sadly, in a French accent, as he watched the last bits of bone from two human bodies turn to ash, "I thought we really had something there."

Meara shook his jowly head. "Bitch mutates too rapidly. Just when we think we've got a counter-virus to render it sterile in some phase, it changes to something we can't sterilize."

"Sometimes I wonder if we might not have been better off going with the discarding strands theory we left behind to throw the Empire off the track," added Johnston.

"No . . . no, I don't think so," Sands said. "The form we have would be better *if* we can find a way to control it."

And this was something of which the American Empire had no clue. The trio had been working on a virus such as described by Mary to Hamilton . . . officially. This virus did indeed change from harmless to deadly to sterile in five generations, being transmissible in all but the last stage. Yet they had never managed to time the thing just right. The extra strands simply would not slough off as planned.

On their own, though, and without leaving any computer record for the Empire to dissect, they had tried a very different approach, one which caused the virus to change by attacking different types of organs in turn. It was the theory and the work on this they had brought through Montreal to the Caliphate, for a very substantial set of fees and regular free access to highly desirable female slaves (except for Meara whose preferences switched between teenaged girls and very young boys).

This virus, the true VA5H, began by going after endothelial cells, those lining the throat and mouth. There, in those cells, the virus inserted various introns (DNA sections added), removed various exons (DNA sections removed), and produced a substantially different set of progeny because of the specific DNA of the cells invaded. These then went on to infect the nasal mucosa, and only the nasal mucosa, mimicking a cold and allowing the virus at that stage to spread by sneeze.

Within the nasal mucosa, a codon, coming from the DNA of the mucosa itself, inserted into the strand, changing its target to the lymph cells. There, it was spread by bodily fluid. This is to say, it didn't spread much.

It didn't have to. At the lymph cells, new modifications occurred, caused, once again, by the DNA of the lymphocytes themselves. This modification turned into full blown disease highly analogous to hemorrhagic smallpox. Moreover, it did so so quickly and so—literally, without pun—*virulently*, that infection of close family, co-workers, and medical staff was highly likely . . . for whichever of those co-workers, family and medicos had not already contracted the virus during its sneezing stage.

It was during this stage that the virus began sloughing off sections of that codon which controlled lethality, becoming more deadly with each new transmission. Within five such generations, the last bit of that codon had disappeared, leaving a virus that was no longer deadly and incapable of reproduction, in theory.

It was that "in theory" part that had Sands, Meara, and Johnston up late, infecting and then incinerating the bodies of superfluous slaves, because the virus did *not* always lose the last, deadly section of that particular codon and those that did not went on replicating at the deadliest level.

Thus, they were working on two other projects. The first of these was to mimic the exterior polyglyceride coat of the virus to rapidly spread immunity through the Caliphate without giving warning to the Empire. The other, and more promising, project was a virus that would attack the ability of the human cells that produced the deadly form to do so.

Promising, however, was neither promised nor certain.

"And we're running out of test subjects," said Johnston.

"No matter," wheezed Meara, "the Caliph is sending us another two hundred."

## Province of Baya, 19 October, 2113

Customs had been surprisingly thorough. Hamilton had assumed that the Caliphate would be as sloppy and susceptible to bribes there as it was reputed to be everywhere else. It hadn't worked that way. Oh, yes, the customs agent had taken the bribe and pocketed it. He'd then proceeded to go through Hamilton's and Bongo's bags with a fine toothed comb.

"The bribe," Bongo had explained, "is only good to keep them from taking the things you have legally. It does absolutely nothing as far as getting them to let you bring in something illegal unless you're already well connected."

"Glad we came in clean," Hamilton had agreed.

The city of am-Munch was . . . well, to call it a "disappointment" was far too mild. It was, in Hamilton's words, "Run down, unsightly, with garbage piled a meter deep to either side of the roads, creepy, depressing, dirty-rotten-filthy, and I can't believe any of my people ever lived in such a dump." He'd been more than happy to leave, despite the quality—or lack, thereof—of the road that lay ahead.

That road was a crumbling highway running through sheer-sided mountain passes. Along that highway, a half dozen small cargo trucks bearing two hundred children trudged behind an auto bearing Hamilton and his black chief toward their destination. Bongo drove. Provided one wasn't a female, the Caliphate was pretty easy as far as licensing went. In other words, no license was required for males and none were possible for females. Rental cars and trucks were somewhat pricey.

Besides driving, Bongo had surreptitiously swept the auto for listening devices. By and large the Caliphate was less than sophisticated about such things. Still, it was always wise to make sure.

"Okay," Hamilton said, "this is too much. We need an 'in' to the castle and we get a purchase order for the entire group *going* to the castle. That shit just doesn't happen. Anything too good—"

"—to be true, isn't," Bongo interrupted. "I really don't understand your confusion. How do you suppose we knew where the three renegades were? How do you suppose we manage to operate here at all?"

Hamilton thought about that for a while before saying, "We own somebody at the highest levels in the Caliphate, don't we?"

"That's always been my guess, *baas*." It was a measure of Bongo's sheer professionalism that he'd never yet said that "*baas*" with the verbal sneer he felt. "There'd be a lot more of them, too, I think, if most of them weren't terrified of extermination."

"It's not like we haven't given them reason for that," said Hamilton.

"Nor like they didn't give us reason to give them reason. 'Sins of the fathers . . . to the third and fourth generations.' Sucks, don't it?"

Bongo downshifted to get over a particularly vile section of the road. He echoed his own words, answered his own question. "Yeah, *baas*, it sucks. But there's not a lot you or I can do about it."

"But how do we get control of someone in the Caliphate?" Hamilton asked. "We don't have the infrastructure there, so far as I can tell, to do much under the table recruiting."

Bongo kept silent for a moment before answering, "This isn't classified, though it probably should be. Even so, keep it close hold." He looked at Hamilton to make sure he understood before continuing, "I've got a cousin who works with the Bureau of Engraving. They don't do all that much engraving anymore, of course; that's all done by machines now. But they do make the coins. One of the coins they make, so my cousin told me, is the gold dinar. Another is the silver dirhem. Actually, they make the dirhem in about five denominations and the dinar in four."

"So we just bought somebody? Somebody would trade their cause for some gold and silver? That's pathetic."

"Yesss, *baas*," Bongo nodded, seriously, "And none of *us* would *ever* sell out for money."

"I take your point," Hamilton agreed.

## Castle Honsvang, Province of Baya, 9 Muharram, 1538 AH (20 October, 2113)

Hans took a small pride in his rank of *odabasi*. It meant "janitor" but was, in practice, the equivalent of a first lieutenant in the Imperial Army or Marines. He'd worked long and hard for the rank, graduating near the top of his class in what the Imperials would have called "OCS." That he was still a secret Christian, such as he remembered of Christianity, added yet more spice to the achievement. Indeed, in his five daily prayers, Hans always adjusted his compass to point ever-so-slightly nearer to Jerusalem the Lost than to Mecca the Obliterated. When he was alone, he pointed towards Rome. What his thoughts were as those prayers were held was much closer to "*Pater Noster*" and "*Ave Maria*" than to "*Alahu Akbar.*"

None of this had been suspected by his superiors and leaders, trainers and evaluators, for one of the things the crucified priest had told him was that if it was permissible for Moslems to lie to Christians then it was no less permissible for Christians to lie to Moslems. To all appearances he was a model of submission to the will of Allah even as he prepared himself to do the maximum possible damage someday—*God give me the chance!*—to the Caliphate.

Hans was actually a bit irritated at being dispatched as second in command of this out of the way, little, castellated station in the mountains of Baya. This was completely illogical, on his part, as he'd *asked* for the assignment in order to be closer to his sister and Ling.

He reported to the sentry at the main gate and received that sentry's salute. Hans announced himself and his rank, and said, "Send someone for me and my bags," before entering the compound and waiting for an escort. While he waited he looked over the sentry's uniform and found no cause for complaint. It was while he was doing that that Hans first noticed the vile smell of burnt meat. He wrinkled his nose with distaste.

"What's that stench?" he asked the sentry on duty.

"We don't know, sir," the sentry answered, "not exactly. We're not allowed in the lab area, generally. But it happens a couple of times a month and has for as long as I've been here, and I've been here longer than most." The sentry pointed upward at a chimney from which emanated the heavy, sooty smoke. The smoke trail at the top of the chimney was a thin wisp, leading to a much heavier cloud far above. "It's that crap. You should be happy you weren't here ten minutes ago, sir. Then it was *really* vile. And be thankful it's cold. The stench is much worse in the summer months."

Hans nodded absently. A vile stench a couple of times a month was a small price to pay for being surrounded by all the natural and man-made splendor of the area. That his sister and Ling were nearby didn't hurt any, either.

*Not that there's not going to be a problem with both of them,* he thought. *Where Ling's concerned I'm just going to have to accept that she's property, owned and used by others, until I can buy her and free her. For Petra . . . it won't matter as long as no one in the security company notices the similarity. And if she's ever escorted here I'm sure she wears the veil. Except . . . shit. She told me that one of the men who is in charge of this place makes use of her regularly. He'll recognize that we look alike. How do I deal with that?*

*Ah . . . that's easy.* "I am a member of the corps of janissaries. I have no family but my corps. Certainly I have no family that are filthy, stinking, worthless, infidel Christians and, just as certainly, if I did I would approve of them being enslaved and fucked silly on a regular basis. That I have an infidel last name is just a way for the corps to keep track of me and to remind me to be grateful for being brought out of the darkness and into the light." *That's it; my defense is in apparent fanaticism.*

Hans felt rather than saw the approach of three janissaries. A quick glance confirmed them as two rankers and one junior noncom.

"Sir, I'm Corporal Mashouf ad-Din, corporal of the watch. I am here to take you to the commander. These men will bring your bags to your new quarters in the castle."

"Very good, Corporal. Lead on."

Hans hadn't known, from anything his written orders had said, the rank of his new commander. Thus, he was a little surprised to see a full-fledged *corbasi*, or colonel, in charge of this one company. He said so.

"In fact," the colonel explained, "I am not just in charge of this one company. It's just the most important thing we do in this area. Over and above that, there are four more companies stationed at af-Fridhav who fall under my command and are responsible for border security. They, however, have nothing to do with this facility. We don't rotate personnel.

"I'm actually very pleased to see you, ibn Minden," the colonel said. "I've had no competent commander for this company and have had to give it most of my attention. As you might imagine, the wretches down at af-Fridhav have taken advantage of that and become sloppy. The *bayraktar*"—ensign or second lieutenant—"here is not very good. Enthusiastic? Yes. Dedicated? Yes. Faithful? Yes. Stupid? Also yes. On the plus side, your *baseski*"—senior noncom, or first sergeant—"is quite competent.

"Come, I'll show you around and introduce you to the company and the infidels whose project we are guarding. Be prepared for frightening things, ibn Minden."

"Infidels?" Hans asked.

"The right number of dinar; the right slave girls, and we can buy infidels like beans," the colonel explained.

"These ones, however, cost a lot of dinar and go through slave girls—other slaves, too; you'll find out about that—at an amazing rate. Frankly, ibn Minden, without these infidels we would be facing the extinction of our faith here."

*Now isn't that an intriguing idea*, thought Hans. *I must learn all there is to learn about this place . . . and these renegades.*

## Honsvang, Province of Baya, 20 October, 2113

Despite the cold, Hamilton was relieved beyond measure to finally get out from the auto, stretch his legs and relieve the pain in his ass. The pounding of the road—*Road? What road? I saw and felt only a linear arrangement of asphalt and rock chunks interspersed with potholes, and lined with garbage to either side*—he'd had more than his fill of.

From the town square where Bongo pulled the auto up to park Hamilton could see one crenellated gothic castle not too far away. Turning his gaze in another direction he saw an altogether more impressive structure. For all that, though, both castles, and the town, as well, showed significant signs of poor maintenance and general decay.

Still looking at the more impressive of the pair of castles, Hamilton said, "I've seen that before . . . in pictures. It looks different though."

"Used to be called 'Neuschwanstein,' before the creation of the Caliphate," Bongo said. "They modified it some . . . but haven't really kept it up. That golden dome is new, for example, where 'new' is defined as less than seventy years old. It's a high-end bordello now. You can visit it if you like. Later."

"How do the Moslems get away with having bor dellos?" Hamilton asked.

"Sheer moral ingenuity," Bongo answered. "They temporarily marry the girls to customers . . . for an hour . . . a day . . . a weekend." The agent laughed. "You can marry up to four at a time, if your tastes run to the kinky," he added.

"What's the going rate?" Hamilton asked but, before Bongo could answer, laughed and said, "No, I'm really not interested."

"Actually," Bongo said, "you *need* to visit the place and make use of the . . . facilities. For one thing, in case you've forgotten, our chippie contact is in there. For another, it will give me a chance to nose around the castle that we really *are* interested in."

"Oh, the sacrifices I make for the Empire."

"Speaking of sacrifices for the Empire," Bongo said, "we'd best deliver these human sacrifices. And that's not something to laugh about."

## Castle Honsvang, Province of Baya, 10 Muharram, 1538 AH (21 October, 2113)

"There are, of course, a few side benefits of being stationed here," the colonel told Hans, as they walked through the stone corridors of the castle. "One is that we get a substantial discount at the whorehouse. At least, the officers do. And the manager, Latif, prides himself on providing only the best. You can even get a decent vodka there."

"Vodka? But—"

"The holy Koran forbids the drinking of fermented grain and grape. Vodka is made from potatoes . . . "

"Ah," Hans said.

"After what I have to show you," the colonel added, "you're going to need a drink. If it makes you feel any better about it, I'll have the regimental surgeon prescribe it for you."

"Maybe," Hans half agreed. "And I've been there, actually, though I didn't drink. It's a very nice place."

The colonel cocked his head. "Really? When were you there?"

"My senior instructor at al-Harv Barracks, Abdul Rahman von Seydlitz, brought the entire company there for our graduation party," Hans explained.

The colonel smiled warmly. "I know Abdul Rahman. A fine old janissary, if a little too softhearted."

"His softheartedness was tolerably hard to see, for a new recruit," Hans said. "And I think it's mostly that he's just a man filled with the love of Allah and for his fellow man . . . and perhaps for women, as well."

"That would be Abdul Rahman. Turn right here," the colonel said. "Down those stone stairs and I'll introduce you to the renegades. And remember what I told you about awful things."

A heavy clattering coming from outside stopped the two janissary officers in their tracks.

"What the Hell is that?" Hans asked.

"Delivery of the new batch of experimental subjects, I suspect," the colonel answered. He walked to the window and beckoned Hans over. Hans saw several trucks, what looked to be a couple of hundred children, a black man in livery and a well-dressed white he took to be a slave dealer.

The colonel said, "You'll see where they're going down below."

◊   ◊   ◊

*It was a small mercy*, Hamilton thought, standing in the chill air, his breath frosting before his face, *that we packed the kids in like sardines. They'd have frozen to death otherwise.*

The children, all of them drained and numb, and numb with more than cold alone, shuffled stiffly out of the cargo trucks and began forming up in a mass as they'd learned to do. In this strange, cold and forbidding place, none even tried to make an escape, though guards were watching just in case.

A janissary noncom—*Funny that I never saw a janissary before this trip*—emerged from the main gate and politely introduced himself. Once Hamilton had made his business clear, the janissary sent for another man, this one responsible for logistics. The logistician counted the children, carefully, twice, and signed for them. His signature on the inventory sheet was all that was required for payment to be completed.

The noncom, he'd given his name as "Mashouf," looked Hamilton over with something between contempt and pity. Whether that was because Hamilton's assumed persona was that of a Boer infidel, or because he was in the distasteful business of selling children, Hamilton couldn't have guessed.

*But it couldn't be worse than I feel about myself.*

Hamilton felt no better as he and Bongo checked into one of the town's better hotels. The manager was all obsequious politeness as he showed the two to the "deluxe" suite. It had a living room and two bedrooms, was more or less reasonably furnished, although the furniture tended to the tacky in Hamilton's opinion.

"The maid will clean daily," the manager had said, "and if you need, she can perform other services as well."

"No . . . no, we won't need her for either," Hamilton answered. "My man here will keep the place up and if I need a woman, I'll probably go up to the other castle."

"Very good, sir. If you do, ask for Latif and tell him you're a guest of this hotel. We have an agreement for a discount."

"Thank you, I will."

## Castle Noisvastei, Province of Baya, 10 Muharram, 1538 AH (21 October, 2113)

The sun was long down, and Hans had repaired to the brothel with almost frantic haste. Ling hadn't been expecting him so soon, less still had Petra. If Ling was expecting anyone it was the agent from the American Empire, whose image had been electronically transferred via her chip directly to her memory.

Nonetheless, Ling cleared her slate while Petra rescheduled to give herself an hour's free time before the customers began rolling in heavily. The two had then taken charge of Hans.

In fact, they took very close charge of the man. Ling, with one look at his stricken face, had settled him in an alcove in the common room and then raced off to Latif to beg for him a bottle of forbidden alcohol.

"Sure, why not?" the whoremaster had shrugged. "You're one of my best girls . . . I can spare you a bottle in a worthy cause . . . for, let us say, five dinar?"

"Don't be a pirate, Latif," Ling had answered. "The stuff's worth no more than a few dirhem."

"For you," Latif countered, "four dinar."

"Twelve dirhem."

They'd finally settled on "one dinar, five dirhem" —objectively outrageous, but Ling had had little alternative —to be added to Ling's freedom price. Since she was not just a slave, but a chippie and hence could never be truly free, that seemed a small matter to her.

Now, Ling and Petra poured the stuff into Hans while he poured forth his story.

"It's monstrous," he said, not merely visibly shaken but visibly *shaking*, despite the copious amount of unfamiliar alcohol he'd taken on. "What goes on down in that castle is just . . . beyond belief . . . they're *infecting* people with a disease just to see if it works and to see if they can turn it off on command. Mostly old slaves but today they brought in a shipment of *children*. Can you imagine? Children?"

A little voice in Ling's head told her, *Get him to shut up. At least get him out of there. What he's talking about so freely could get you all put to death.*

"Come on, Petra," Ling said, as naturally as if there were no voice. "We'll take him to my quarters. This is too public."

Expertly, the girls got Hans to his feet and maneuvered their way under his arms. This was not so unfamiliar a sight in the common room that any of the other clients really paid any attention, though Ling, of course, immediately alerted on her contact.

At least, none of the customers paid attention until Hans screamed, "Monster" and launched himself at a newly arrived customer, a tall, slender white type in clothing that screamed, "Infidel."

Hamilton had remembered a picture book from his childhood, showing a fairy castle then lost behind the

"Iron Veil" of the Caliphate. As a boy, the romance of the thing, the beauty in the pictures, hadn't moved him nearly so much as the crenellated battlements and towers. The differences he saw in the exterior of the castle were substantial enough that he had doubts the two images were even of the same structure. And, of course, the thing hadn't been painted in a very long time. White had changed to a dirty gray. Even the golden dome didn't really shine. It was all rather sordid and disappointing.

The inside of the place was still pretty splendid, Hamilton had to admit. *Better than the thatched roofs and dirt floors of* Moroland, *in any case. And that's even before counting the hookers in.*

A doorman, elegantly dressed and of medium build, took Hamilton's heavy coat and asked, "How shall I sign you in, sir?"

"Johann De Wet, Boer Republic of South Africa," Hamilton answered. By now the use of the false name came easily.

"Very good, *Mineer* De Wet. And may I ask, is there a particular kind of girl you're looking for or would you prefer to look around?"

Being in no particular hurry, not wanting to make himself obvious by asking for the uniquely exotic Chinese chippie by type, and knowing Bongo could use the time to scout out the castle, Hamilton answered, "They all look so nice. Why don't I just look around?"

The doorman bobbed his head appreciatively and said, "Then, sir, I recommend that you take a table in the common room. The girls are trained not to be aggressive— this isn't that kind of place—but if you see one you like just call her over. They *are* trained to be accommodating."

"Thank you. I think I'll do that."

There were signs, written in three languages, pointing the way. Hamilton followed those. With no art, neither statuary nor paintings, to adorn the walls, Hamilton had no reason or excuse to draw the passage out. He went directly up the broad staircase and then proceeded on to what he would have known, from the noise, to be the common room even if the signs hadn't indicated it.

Walking through the main door, Hamilton was unsurprised to see two girls carting off an obviously drunken soldier. He recognized the uniform as being very similar to those worn by the guards at the other castle. He also noticed that his contact was one of the two girls.

Notwithstanding, he was immediately very taken by the other, the one on the left, a tall and svelte blonde much to his taste. The closer she came the more intrigued he became. She wasn't Laurie Hodge, if anything this girl was prettier, but she could have been a close cousin, or even a sister.

Thus it was that Hamilton was taken completely off guard when the uniformed soldier screamed "Monster!" and launched himself at him.

Both girls were bowled over by Hans' mad charge. By the time they managed to get to their feet Hans and the stranger were grappling on the floor, trading ineffectual punches and kicks. A couple of patrons grabbed their drinks and their girls and backed away from a table just in time to avoid Hans and Hamilton's knocking it over on them.

Latif was at the scene in an instant, accompanied by two amazingly beefy guards. These latter pulled Hans and Hamilton apart effortlessly even as Latif bellowed,

"What in the one hundredth name of Allah is going on here?"

Ling glided over to stand in front of Hans. "He must have been fed something bad to drink," she said, lifting her head defiantly. *And you don't want to get in trouble for feeding alcohol to a janissary, do you?*

The whoremaster nodded. *No, as a matter of fact I don't. Yet this will come out of your hide before it comes out of mine.* "Take him to your quarters," he commanded Ling. "And don't let him out until he's sober." To one of the guards he said, "Assist her."

Petra made as if to follow Ling until Latif held up one hand to block her. Latif glanced from the now bedraggled-looking new customer to Petra and back again. *Yes, he's interested in her.*

To Hamilton he said, "Would it be considered adequate recompense, sir, for the insult you have suffered in my house if this woman is turned over to your use for . . . say . . . a week?"

*Pity it isn't the chippie that he offered. Still, the two look like they work together so this may be useful. But be a Boer,* Hamilton thought. *Bargain.*

"A week is hardly—"

"Two then. Surely that will assuage your honor."

"Two," Hamilton agreed, with a solemn nod.

"And the hospitality of the house," Latif said, loudly enough for the staff to hear.

"Must be something serious for Latif to give out free booze," said one of the nonhooking staff to a currently unattached girl.

"No shit," the houri answered.

# Interlude

Kitzingen, Federal Republic of Germany,
30 June, 2006

"Push," the doctor said, gently but firmly and encouragingly. "Puuushshsh!"

Gabi heard him dimly, all her senses concentrated in the white light of sheer agony with its source somewhere around her stretched and tortured vagina.

"Ohgodohgodohgooo . . . aiaiaiai! Mahmoud, you SON OF A BIIITCH!" she screamed, head thrashing wildly from side to side on the thin hospital pillow. Of course, Mahmoud wasn't there. He was in Boston from which place he still wrote regularly, all glowing reports designed—she was sure—to lure her into the embrace of the enemy.

She missed him pretty badly. Ordinarily. When she wasn't passing a baby.

Mahmoud, and how much she missed him, however, were all quite forgotten as the next wave of wracking pain, this one worse than the previous, overtook her. Once again Gabi began her "Ohgodohgod . . . you motherFUCKER, Mahmouououd!" refrain.

"Funny how few genuine atheists there are in birthing beds," muttered the doctor in attendance. Even as Gabi gasped, his skilled hands were working to catch and lift the baby, while cutting and binding the umbilical.

Her breasts were still heaving when she heard a slap and an outraged cry. And then the doctor laid her new daughter to her breast and it was all much, much better.

In many ways, art was an ideal occupation for a single mother in the Federal Republic of Germany, for not only was there a substantial social safety net, but art was, as often as not, sold "under the table" and much of the income derived from its sale was never reported. Of course, some of it was reported because Germany's social safety net benefits went up, up to a certain point, based on the normal income and contributions of the worker. It was going to be a high tight-rope walk for Gabi to eke out the most benefit for herself and the baby, reporting some income and keeping the rest to herself.

The baby was not, of course—and never would be, as far as Gabrielle was concerned—christened. For that matter, she didn't opt for a traditional name, Germanic or Christian. Instead, mindful of the baby's father and wanting her to be a part of Mahmoud, as well, Gabi chose "Amal." In Arabic, this meant "Hope."

One of the reasons, and perhaps the major one, that Gabi had always been ambivalent about motherhood was, as she frankly admitted to herself, a mix of fear of inadequacy and fear of responsibility. She was pleased to discover that both fears were groundless, that she already had everything important required to be a mother. That was one surprise, but not the biggest. The biggest was that she *loved* being a mother.

"Not that I want to do the whole thing over again, mind you," she said to Amal while changing the baby's diaper. *And isn't it funny how your own baby's poop doesn't really stink?* "You are quite enough for me and if your father will only come to his senses, I'll have everything I want."

Gabi was just finished taping the diaper in place when the phone rang, setting her to running for it even as it set Amal to crying.

"Hello?"

"Gabi, it's Mahmoud. What's that crying in the background?"

*I suppose there's no sense in trying to hide it now,* she thought.

"Ummm . . . the baby. Your baby . . . errr . . . our baby."

"And you didn't fucking *tell* me?"

"I didn't want to trap you," she said, softly, less certain at the moment that she'd done the right thing. "Or to seem like I was trying to trap you."

Mahmoud, on the other end of the line, sighed heavily. Gabi could almost see him nodding in his fatalistic and accepting way.

"Okay," he said. "What now?"

"I don't know," she answered. "I still won't go to the United States."

"And I won't live in Europe."

# CHAPTER TWELVE

Certain persons have been begging me for the past five years to write about war against the Turks, and encourage our people and stir them up to it, and now that the Turk is actually approaching, my friends are compelling me to do this duty, especially since there are some stupid preachers among us Germans (as I am sorry to hear) who are making the people believe that we ought not and must not fight against the Turks. Some are even so crazy as to say that it is not proper for Christians to bear the temporal sword or to be rulers; also because our German people are such a wild and uncivilized folk that there are some who want the Turk to come and rule.

—Martin Luther, "On War Against the Turks," 1528 AD

## Castle Noisvastei, Province of Baya, 10 Muharram, 1538 AH (21 October, 2113)

"You'd never been drunk before, had you?" Ling asked.

Hans, a study in misery, just shook his head and said, "That's the second kind of virginity I gave to you. I much preferred giving you the other kind. Much."

"I'm sure," Ling said, grinning widely. She hadn't known she'd been his first and that was . . . warming. That he remembered and appreciated was much more so.

*Find out, if possible, why he attacked your contact,* said the little voice in Ling's head.

She asked.

She asked and was surprised as such a torrent of hate and loathing poured out of Hans as she had never heard before. Not just hate for Hamilton, whom Ling only knew of as "De Wet," but Hans also felt deep hatred for the Corps of Janissaries, for Moslems, for all slave dealers, and for the Caliphate. He hated the boys who'd raped Petra, the dealer who had auctioned her, and the bastard tax gatherer who had taken both the siblings away from their home. Hans hated the laws that had made him crucify a priest. He hated everything.

"Everything?"

"Okay, not everything. Not you. Not Petra. But I hate everything else about this land."

*I wish we could be sure it's not an act,* said the little voice. *He would be a great asset.*

*Is there a way to test him?* she thought back.

*We are considering this.*

◇   ◇   ◇

Hamilton lay on his side, head propped up on one elbow, considering the face and form of the sleeping girl next to him. *Seventeen,* he thought. *Maybe eighteen. So much skillful wickedness in so young a girl. Almost . . . almost, I can see the attraction of Islam if it enables a man to own such beauty. Better, she makes it seem as if she's a lover, not just a whore playing a part. Perhaps that's only because she's a natural whore, though, if she is. It's possible, too, that she's just been very well trained. Or both.*

*Only things I can be sure of are that she's both beautiful and an amazing fuck.*

*Christ, what kind of pervert am I, fucking a seventeen-year-old?*

A little contrary voice said, *Hey, look at the bright side; maybe she's eighteen.*

*Oh, that helps a lot.*

*Could have been worse. She could have been thirteen and you would still have had to fuck her to keep up your cover.*

Unable to stand it anymore, Hamilton reached out one hand, shook the girl awake and asked, "How old are you?"

"Seventeen," Petra answered groggily. "Why?"

*Pervert.*

*Our best consensus, for the moment, is to ask him for proof,* the little voice in Ling's head said. *It is not perfect but, if he turns out to be an agent provocateur, you can claim you asked for proof in order to denounce him. In the interim, it moves us a bit along toward confirming his true thoughts.*

*Did you know they made a whore of his sister and that she's my best friend and lover here?* Ling asked back.

*We watch your every move. Of course we knew. That is still not proof. The Caliphate produces only one thing of genuine excellence, and that product is fanaticism.*

*True,* she agreed.

*If you had access to a laboratory, we could teleoperate you to create a first grade truth serum. Sadly—*

*—I don't. And the still where Latif makes the poor stuff won't do.* In truth, Ling hated the very *idea* of being teleoperated, which involved surrendering complete control over her own body to another. It was bad enough sucking and fucking people she didn't want to. Teleoperation was, in its way, even more degrading.

*Still,* in vino veritas. *What he said last night while drunk is a good indicator of his true feelings. We're still reviewing the tapes. We'll get back to you. In the interim, ask for proof. And try to be clever about it, won't you?*

"*Reviewing the tapes*"? Ling sent back. *I'm sure you voyeuristic bastards are.*

*Be nice, Ling. We can teleoperate you without permission, you know.*

Breakfast for the two was delivered to Petra's quarters by a eunuch. It didn't have any bacon, or pork sausage, of course, but was otherwise decent.

Hamilton already had the name of the girl sitting opposite: Petra. Moreover, she was already, technically, his wife for the next thirteen days.

"I've never had a wife before," Hamilton said.

"You don't really have one now," Petra answered, perhaps a little sadly. Clothed in a nightgown, still her young, firm breasts showed through the front opening.

Her nipples were pink, Hamilton saw. "It's just something they do to get around the law. Doesn't mean anything."

*I will* not *ask, "how did a nice girl like you end up in a place like this,"* Hamilton thought. *I will not ask . . .*

"How did you ever end up here?" he asked.

"You don't want to know."

"Yes, sure I do."

"It's a sad story," Petra said. *Saddest of all for me.*

"Even so."

She sighed, cast her eyes upward and then down to the floor. "I was a pretty little girl—"

"I can believe *that*."

"The tax gatherer picked me and my brother. First he set the jizya—"

"Jizya?" Hamilton asked.

"A tax non-Moslems pay here as part of their surrender," she explained. "Anyway, he set it so high my father couldn't pay . . . and when he couldn't the taxman took me instead. I was nine. My brother, Hans—he's the one who attacked you last night—they took later."

"They sold you to this place when you were *nine*?" *And how are they any worse than Bongo and I? We've just sold some six year olds.*

"No . . . no. That came later. Though my friend, Ling, was sold even younger. At first I was sold to a wonderful family . . . I thought they were wonderful anyway. Their daughter, Besma, really was. We still write. She's married—*really* married, I mean . . . not the travesty we have here—and has two children now. She named the girl for me. She's says she will come for me, and not to lose faith. Faith! Like I have any reason for *faith*."

"It's okay," Hamilton said, disconcerted at the pain growing in Petra's voice. "You don't have to talk about it if you don't want."

"You are my Lord and Master, for the next two weeks," Petra said, a trifle bitterly. She sensed, somehow, that with this client she could get away with a lot more than with most. "You asked; it is my duty to tell you."

"Anyway," she continued, "life with Besma was pretty good. If you don't count her stepmother who used me to control her. And then her stepbrother and two friends decided I was just the thing for a dull afternoon—"

And then the tears came forth. The force with which they gushed took Hamilton completely by surprise.

"I never talk about it," Petra sobbed, "I never talk about—"

After which she couldn't say anything, as Hamilton was kneeling beside her chair, holding her in his arms, and pressing her head into his shoulder. "Shhh," he said soothingly. "It's all right. You don't have to talk about it and I am a complete ass for even asking. I'm really sorry."


"Hans, I need you to listen carefully to me," Ling said. "This is important and the answer means everything. Why did you attack that man last night?"

Hans drew in a deep breath and then exhaled forcefully. "He's a slave trader, and I saw his cargo. They were just children, Ling, even younger than Petra was when they took her away. He's a stinking slave trader."

Ling chewed on her lower lip, wracked with indecision. Finally, she asked, "What if he wasn't?"

Hans just shook his head in confusion. "What if he wasn't what?"

"What if he wasn't a slave trader, but was something else?"

"Something else? Like what?"

"I can't tell you. Not won't; *can't*. Someday you'll understand, maybe someday soon. But what if he really wasn't a slave trader?"

"I saw what I saw," Hans insisted.

"Yes . . . but you didn't necessarily *understand* what you saw." Ling started chewing her lip again. She continued at that for several confused minutes—confused for both her and Hans—before saying, "I need you to *prove* to me you're not with the Caliphate."

"I'm a dead man," he said, "dead before I can do any good, if I can't trust you. Everything I've told you so far would get me nailed up to a wooden cross. How much more can I do?"

She insisted, "I need more, Hans."

He thought about that for a minute. Then he went to his overnight bag, dropped off in her quarters by a servant the previous night. From the bag he pulled out a Koran. He opened in to a random page and spit on it. "That's one," he said. "Now follow me."

There were, after all, reasons why Abdul Rahman had thought Hans had a future. If he had flaws, lack of decisiveness wasn't among them.

Ling followed Hans to her bathroom. There he thumbed through the book, apparently looking for a choice passage. When he'd found it, he tore that page from the Koran, bent over, and wiped his rear end with it. "That's two." He dropped the page in the toilet, spit again, and flushed.

Hans walked back to the bedroom and picked up his bag again, feeling inside for a small box. This he withdrew from the bag and opened. From the box he pulled out a crucifix, kissed it and said, "This was given to me by a man, a priest, I helped murder . . ."

◇   ◇   ◇

"These mountains are murder, I know," Hamilton said in sympathy, as he helped Petra over a rock lying across their path.

Feeling like an absolute rat, Hamilton had offered anything to make up to her his—"stupid, insensitive, moronic, unfeeling, idiotic"—question.

Shyly, she'd asked, "I don't get to go out much. If I dress properly, could you, maybe . . . take me for a walk?"

He'd had to leave a six hundred dinar deposit, but that was within his means. (Why six hundred when her purchase price had been three? The cost of her training had been added to her value.) Other than that, the management had had no objections whatsoever. Since Hamilton had "hospitality of the house," they'd sent for a picnic lunch for the two from the kitchen. The two had left by the main gate to the castle, before the mosque and between the minarets.

From the castle they walked down to the town, and then to the lakeshore.

"I have a place," she confessed, still full of shyness, "up in a tower where I can see this. I dream sometimes of being free to walk the lake. Sometimes—yes, I know it sounds foolish—but sometimes I dream I'm a princess up there and a hero will cross the lake and take me away. Silly, no?"

"Maybe not so silly. Anything's possible."

"Not in the Caliphate," she said. "Not in the Caliphate for a woman . . . or a Christian . . . or a slave . . . or a whore."

"Stop it," he said. "What you have to do is not the same thing as what you are."

"Thank you, Johann," she said, quietly. "But even if that's true there are many things that I can never do that also define what I am." She stood facing the lake, wind blowing through the few loose strands of her hair, and continued, "I don't know how to cook. I can't sew or weave. Unless they decide to breed me they'll keep me from ever getting pregnant until it's too late for me to be a mother. If they did breed me it would be to produce a slave. I'd strangle the baby with my own hands, before I let that happen. No respectable man would ever marry me, not now. Independence for a woman is simply not possible here, except as a freelance whore.

"At least I can read and write. Well," she admitted, "I can read. My writing is not . . . good."

"That's okay," he said. "You could learn."

"Like you learned German?" she asked. "Yours is so much better than mine, so much more formal and correct. I was just a country girl, you see and . . .

"And this isn't even my country anymore."

Hamilton shook his head in agreement. No, it wasn't her country anymore.

"I've read of back when it was," Petra said. "My great-grandmother kept a journal. It's the only thing I really own for myself. I'd like to have lived back then. I wouldn't have done what she did. I'd either have fought, back when we could still fight, or I'd have left. She knew she should have done one or the other, too. By the time she knew that, though, it was too late."

"All right. Enough!" Ling said. "I believe you."

*Yes, we do,* said the voice in her head.

Hans stopped his gleeful dancing atop the Koran and said, "Okay. Now what was this all about?"

*Tell him. Bring him to our side.*

Ling exhaled heavily. "Where to begin?"

*At the beginning is usually a good spot.*

She nodded.

*Stop nodding. You* know *how annoying that is to watch on a viewing screen back here. Now tell him.*

"Your sister doesn't know any of this, but I'm not human," Ling said. She laughed at the expression on Hans' face, an even mix of disbelief and horror. "I mean I'm not human the way you are. Not born of woman. No father. I'm a genetically engineered being."

Hans' horrified look was like a dagger to her heart. She hastened to add, "I am one hundred percent human genes. But surely you noticed my skin and my breasts. Those are not normally found where I came from . . . where I was sold from. But Hans, I am all human inside. I can have children, provided that my pregnancy blocker is removed or allowed to run down. I feel. I think." She shrugged and let her head fall to one side. "What more do you want?"

"I'm sorry," he apologized, forcing his face to something less objectionable. "It was just a shock. You're wonderful. Please go on."

"Okay. I'm also a chippie. I have a thing planted in my brain."

*My, this is a day for shocks,* thought Hans.

"The reason I have a chip in my brain, and the reason I was genengineered, and the reason I was sold here, is that I am an enemy agent."

"Here to work against the Caliphate?" he asked. "Be still my heart."

"Yes," she admitted. "And that man you attacked . . . "

◇    ◇    ◇

Hamilton spread out the thin blanket he'd found in the picnic basket, then walked to the lakeshore to look for some rocks to tack down the corners with. He was lucky to find two and an old brick; it just wasn't that kind of lake. He returned with these, adjusted the sheet slightly, then tacked down the three corners that were most into the wind. He invited Petra to sit.

She kicked off her shoes—more slippers than shoes, really; that was part of what had made the walk down "murder"—and stepped lightly onto the blanket. Moreover, she sat with a sheer grace he found utterly delightful, like a film of a growing tulip shown in faster than real time but in reverse.

Hamilton looked at the girl, sighed and said, "You really are incredibly lovely, you know."

"They tell me that sometimes. For myself, I don't know. Ling says I am."

"Ling?" He really didn't need to ask but it would have been odd not to have.

"The girl who was with me when my brother attacked you."

"That was your *brother*?" Hamilton suddenly had an altogether too kinky hint of something. It must have showed on his face.

Petra laughed. "No, no, no. It's nothing like that. He and Ling are . . . special to each other. It happens sometimes, even with houris. I, on the other hand, am going to have to go to some pains to make sure no one from my brother's new command ever sees my face. It would be a great shame to him."

*This girl's brother and my contact have the hots for each other. Is this a good or a bad thing?*

◇ ◇ ◇

"He's *not* a slave trader?"

"No," Ling said. "Yes, he's had to put on a show and yes, those children really were sold, but no—and my control tells me this De Wet person was up in arms over the whole thing—he's not really a slave trader."

"Do you know what those children were sold for?" Hans asked. "Does he?"

"We've got a pretty good idea, Hans, yes. But if they're the price to pay for saving a world?"

"No one asked *them* if they were willing to pay it, did they?"

"No one asked me either, Hans, when they sold me to this place."

He nodded and said, "What a perfect Hell of a world. What now?"

"I'm not sure," she answered. "How far are you willing to go to hurt the Caliphate?"

Hans started to laugh. The laugh grew and grew until it filled Ling's entire room. It grew deep and belly splitting. It had to grow, for it held twenty or more years of hate in it.

"I love it here," Petra said. "Here by the lake, I mean, not up there in the castle. I wish it never had to end, that I could turn into one of the rocks, a tall one so I could see out, and just see the seasons pass, watch the birds and the bees fly, and never, ever, have to feel anything again. Thank you for taking me." She put her head down, shyly.

Hamilton wasn't sure quite what he felt at that moment. There was still some shame from being a boor earlier, surely. And he felt a great pity for the girl, too.

But there was something else he hadn't felt in a very long time, something he absolutely didn't want to put to words or even admit to feeling.

*Later*, he thought. *Later on, I'll take that out and examine it. For now, there's a job to do. Several, actually. And for God's sake don't give this girl a hope you won't be able to deliver on.*

"It's getting late," he said, "and it's a longish walk. Let's head back to the castle."

"You mean you're not going to . . . " She didn't sound disappointed so much as surprised. Then again, it was a romantic setting and she was sure he'd want to. In fact, she'd been sure he'd taken her to the lake only to fuck her.

"No," he smiled. "Not here and maybe not there either. We need to have a long talk first. And I need to have a talk with my . . . ummm . . . servant."

## Honsvang, Province of Baya, 10 Muharran, 1538 AH (21 October, 2113

"You're out of your fucking mind," Bongo said. "No way. No effing way! Not gonna happen."

Bongo and Hamilton were walking not far from where Petra and he had had their picnic earlier in the day. He'd walked her home, seen her to her room, kissed her chastely, picked up his deposit and gone immediately back to town to the hotel room. From there he and Bongo had left for the lake because, as Bongo had said, "I can sweep this room for bugs; I can't sweep it for ears."

"Let's let that go, for now," Hamilton suggested. "What have you found out?"

Reluctantly, despite the security of the open field by the lake, Bongo continued, "I did a recon of the castle—the one we're interested in—last night. It's pretty tightly sewn up. There's never less than forty guards on duty, on a one-in-three watch schedule. They're all well armed and apparently well disciplined. They're in layers, too. Some more high tech security also, sensors, lasers, CCTV . . . the kind of shit the Caliphate produces little of. They've got dogs . . . one of the furry bastards got my scent, too. I had a helluva time getting away unseen. Those guys will alert on anything. We're not getting in on the sly."

"I know," Hamilton agreed, "which is why—"

"Like I said, no fucking way. We are not taking into our confidence a fucking *janissary* for Christ's Holy Sake! Better to kill the bastard."

Hamilton looked up, intending to continue the argument, when he spotted a black-uniformed man leading a woman shrouded in a burka by the hand. The woman was not Petra; that much he could see by her walk. So he assumed . . .

"Why don't you kill him now?" Hamilton asked conversationally. "Me, personally, I think he looks kind of tough. You're on your own."


"Ibn Minden, Hans, *Odabasi*, Corps of Janissaries," Hans introduced himself, with a polite bow of his head. "And I understand I owe you a serious apology . . . which you have."

Hans inclined that head toward Ling. "She's told me everything—"

"Everything I know," Ling corrected. "Which may not be everything."

*Don't be a bitch,* said the little voice.

In response, Ling nodded her head vigorously, half a dozen times.

*Stop that!*

For the first time since Hamilton had known him, Bongo laughed uproariously. Everyone, Ling included, looked at him strangely. That only made him laugh harder.

"I'm a chippie, too," Bongo finally explained. "She was punishing her control . . . weren't you, dear?"

"You never told me," Hamilton said.

" 'Need to know,' " Bongo quoted. "I needed to have the chip put in to control some of my voluntary and involuntary muscles after I was medically discharged. It's not pleasant to have."

"*I* know your mission," Hans said. "And I will help. But I have conditions. You will be thinking of killing me now," he added. "This will not only be harder to do than you suspect, but my disappearance will alert the local forces. This you cannot afford."

Bongo began to tense, as if for a killing fight, then just as suddenly relaxed. "*What* conditions?" he asked.

"First, the children slaves in the lower castle must be freed and delivered to a safe place. You can do this."

"We've no way to get them across Lake Constance," Bongo objected.

"That is merely a detail to be worked out," Hans said. "Second, you must free my sister and get her out as well."

"Done," said Hamilton, drawing an angry look from Bongo.

"Third," continued Hans, "you must get Ling—"

"—I'm not allowed to leave, Hans," Ling interjected.

"We'll talk about that later," he insisted. "For now I want these gentlemen to agree in principle."

"I can agree in principle to anything," Bongo said. "Doesn't mean I can follow through."

"Ling?" Hans asked.

She shut her eyes for a moment, then answered, in a voice that was not quite her own, "His name is Bernard Matheson. Bronx, New York, American Empire. He is a veteran of the Imperial Army's Special Forces. He holds their Distinguished Service Cross for gallantry above and beyond the call of duty in the Fourth Colombian Pacification Campaign. Married three times. No current wife. No children. Entered Imperial Intelligence after being invalided out of—no, medically retired from—the Army as a result of wounds received in the action for which he received the Distinguished Service Cross. Terminal rank: Lieutenant Colonel. He's been working the Boer Republic for the last—"

"That's about enough!" said Bongo.

"Bongo, Caruthers never told me—" Hamilton began.

"Need to know," Bongo repeated. "Besides, did I never mention how fucking much I *hate* the nickname Bongo? Just because my friends call me that doesn't mean I like it."

"I think you can follow through," said Hans, which drew from Bongo a shrug.

Beside them, Ling shuddered, gasped and said, "I *hate* being teleoperated."

"I sympathize," answered Bongo. "Now give me a minute while I consult with higher." He turned away and walked closer to the lake.

While Bongo was consulting, Hamilton asked Ling, "How did your people know about him? I mean, *me* I can understand. I assumed my file was downloaded to you just as I was briefed on you. But him?"

*If you answer, you will be punished.*

She just shook her head. Hans, instead, answered, "It should be pretty obvious they keep close tabs on you people. As obvious as that you are infiltrated."

"I suppose. And it must be easier for them, with Chinese unremarkably common in our Empire, while whites in theirs are pretty rare." Hamilton laughed. "I wonder who *isn't* infiltrated."

Ling said, "The Swiss."

"Yesss," Hamilton agreed, slowly. "The *Swiss*."

"Ahhh," said Hans. "Indeed. The Swiss."

All three looked generally southwestward, and said, almost together, "The Swiss."


"We agree," Bongo said. "But, there are a couple of things you should know. One is that the Empire will not provide any external assistance. They have asked the Swiss to allow the temporary basing of a single battalion of Rangers and that has been denied. They've asked for permission to base a single airship. That, too, has been denied. For reasons I'll explain later, we're not going to get any air support. No nuclear strike unless we fail . . . in which case the strike will be general in the hope of utterly destroying any trace of the virus or, failing that, to so disorganize the Caliphate that it cannot deliver the virus to our shores, allies, or possessions."

"But I thought . . . I mean Caruthers said . . . "

"*Baas*," and this time Bongo *did* let the contempt he felt for the title show through, "the President has changed his mind. Rather, it seems the secretaries of Defense, State and Intelligence have gotten together and browbeaten him into changing his mind. To paraphrase, 'fuck the Christians in the Caliphate and fuck England, too; we have to watch out for our own.' "

"Oh, and folks . . . one other thing: The President said if we haven't solved his problem in two weeks he's launching anyway. The subs are already moving into position."

"Holy shit," said Hamilton.

"Nothing holy about it."

# Interlude

Grosslangheim, Federal Republic of Germany,
4 July, 2006

There wouldn't be any more fireworks exploding over
Harvey Barracks in the future, Gabi knew. The Americans were pulling out towards the end of the year and,
so it was assumed, never coming back. For this year
though, from the side of a hill by the nearby town of
Grosslangheim, she and Mahmoud and little Amal
watched the display. Gabi thought the Americans had
put some extra effort into the show, perhaps as a way of
saying, "You're going to miss us."

*No we won't,* she thought.

Mahmoud was here only for a couple of weeks' vacation. He was an American now, as perhaps he'd been

born to be, and worked like a slave. Not for him five or six weeks' annual vacation; American workers usually didn't even use the paltry couple of weeks their oppressors granted them. But also not for him taxes that took more than half his income. He worked more and harder; he earned more, and he got to keep a *lot* more of what he made.

"You would like Boston, Gabi," he said, "really you would. It's like here, most ways. You want multiculturalism? They've got it and it works . . . better, anyway. You want culture? They've got the greatest collection, per capita, of art, public works, parks, restaurants, amusements . . . sheer things-to-do . . . in the world. Nothing else I've seen or read of comes close." He smiled, a little ruefully. "Gabi, there's more of Egypt in their Museum of Fine Arts than there is in Egypt at *al Mataf*. Well, almost more and certainly better. And theater . . . ballet . . . symphonies . . . whatever you want. Massachusetts is a densely populated state, and it's still seventy percent forest."

Gabi was about to object, "Looted," when she realized two things. Most if not all Egyptian antiquities in Europe were looted, and the Americans, being latecomers to the game, had probably actually paid for theirs.

"Tell me about the Museum, Mahmoud," she said instead.

"I go there about every month, in part because it's grand in itself, and in part because it reminds me of you. I imagine you and the baby are there with me. It makes it better . . . a little."

Her heart, a part of it anyway, ached to go. That would never do.

"And where do they hold their lynchings in Boston?" she asked. "And by restaurants I assume you mean your choice of fast food. And how do you get to your museum, or the fast food places, with garbage piled up a meter deep in the roadways? And how many times a day do you have to duck gunfire?"

Mahmoud sighed and shook his head. He could see where this was going. He put one elbow on his knee and rested his chin upon the hand. For a while, he simply fumed in silence. Yet he'd chosen to be American, chosen to become a part of that team, just as Gabi had chosen to remain a part of her team. If Gabi could defend hers, unreasonably in his view, why should he not defend *his*?

He answered, "You know, it's funny. Europeans look down their noses at Americans, sneering at their ignorance and lack of culture. Yet the Euros are themselves more ignorant of America than Americans are of Europe. And but for American culture, what would Europe have that wasn't old and dead or dying? That, or a poor imitation of what the Americans have? And I'll be sure to note it for you, the next time I lack for something different to eat in Boston. Arab? They've got it. French? They've got it. German, Thai, Korean, Ethiopian, Italian, Vietnamese . . . what*ever*. They've got it. And a lot more than you do here."

Mahmoud pointed with his chin at the fireworks. He, too, was sure that, because the post of Harvey Barracks was closing, the Americans had put on more of a display than usual. "They're giving up on you, you know. They're leaving because Europe doesn't matter anymore. They don't need to control you. They don't need to fear you. They don't even have to worry about you dragging them into another war, as you've done twice. You know what those fireworks are saying, Gabi? They're saying, 'We're independent of you, as we have been since 1776 . . . and you don't matter anymore. We are the future. You are only the past.' "

"Arrogant bastards," Gabi sneered.

"No," Mahmoud disagreed. "Not arrogant. Arrogance exists when someone thinks they are better, more capable, or more important than they really are. Europe is like that. Europe really *is* arrogant. America is capable, is important, and is, frankly, better. It's the indispensable nation. No arrogance there, or at least not much."

And *that* set off the fight.

## Kitzingen, Federal Republic of Germany, 6 September, 2007

"American Bases Targeted for Attack."

The TV screens were full of the news: Three men arrested, two of them German reverts to Islam, deep in a conspiracy to produce bombs that dwarfed those used in Madrid and London in previous years. Were the bombs intended for the American bases still on German soil? Were they intended to strike at the German civilian populace?

Gabi didn't know. It would be wrong to say that she didn't care. Rather, she rejected the existence of the news entirely. It called into question her own most cherished beliefs about the fundamental decency of mankind, the ability of people to get along if only they would talk and tolerate, the total irrelevance of religion to modern life.

Faced with this, Gabi simply turned off the television and went back to her drawing.

# CHAPTER THIRTEEN

Islam is a revolutionary ideology and program which seeks to alter the social order of the whole world and rebuild it in conformity with its own tenets and ideals. Islam wishes to destroy all States and Governments anywhere on the face of the Earth which are opposed to the ideology and program of Islam, regardless of the country or the Nation which rules it.

—Sayyed Abul Ala Maududi, founder of Pakistan's Jamaat-e-Islami, April, *1939*

## Honsvang, Province of Baya, 12 Muharram, 1538 AH (23 October, 2113)

They met in Hamilton's bug-swept suite: Hans, Ling, Hamilton, Bongo, and Petra. Petra was not present in the sitting room. Indeed, she was sleeping in Hamilton's bed. The others agreed; the less she knew the better for everyone. She had no useful skills that anyone could see. Neither did Ling, of course, but she—however much it disgusted her—could be teleoperated.

"We can't fight them heads up," said Hans. "Not even with me to sabotage the defense."

"I agree," said Bongo—no, "Bernie," now that he'd mentioned how much he hated his nickname. "Besides, if we even started, we'd have two companies from af-Fridhav on us in no time."

"One company," Hans corrected. "The others would be split up watching the Swiss. It would take them hours to collect themselves and move."

"Still," Bernie said. "The four of us against two companies of janissaries is . . . well, just not possible."

"Three of us," said Hamilton. "Neither Hans nor I can fly an airship to get the slaves out. I know neither you nor Ling can, on your own, but you can be teleoperated by a qualified pilot."

"We don't even know how we're going to get an airship," said Ling.

"Rent one? Steal one?" asked Hamilton.

"Easier to rent, I think," said Bernie. "But then we have the problem with the crew. Not many are likely to risk getting shot down just to free some slaves. And while our expense account is effectively unlimited, there is probably no amount of money that would get someone to fly on those odds.

"Ah . . . then again, there might be," Matheson added. "That crew that brought us and the kids? They seemed pretty disaffected to me, at least one of them. It *might* be something. Maybe." the Black agent shrugged.

"Maybe, if we rent the same ship that brought us here and then seize it, that one might help us. But we're not bringing any of them in on this in advance. There are already too many people involved."

"All right then," said Hans. "Let's suppose that we can rent an airship and seize it. That takes . . . two people, one of them either Ling or myself?"

"Can't be you," Hamilton said. "We need you to get into the castle."

"The best choice would be Ling *and* myself," offered Bernie. "That way, if one of us is taken out the other can still pilot."

*And besides,* Bernie thought, *it's not like I trust the Chinks not to have their own agenda. I'll feel a lot better if our escape is at least partially in my hands, not theirs.*

"Which leaves only John and myself for both the castle and scaling off the road from af-Fridhav," Hans observed. "Can't be done. We'd need one more."

"That would be me," said Petra, whom everyone had thought to be asleep.

The fight over that one went on for quite a while.

"My little black ass," said Bernie. "She's only seventeen and she knows precisely *nothing.*"

"On the contrary," Hans argued. "At this point she knows altogether too much. Everything, except the reason, as a matter of fact."

"Freeing the slave children and getting us out of here is all the reason I need," said Petra. "Striking out against the masters?" She laughed. "That's all *gravy.*"

Hamilton found that he rather liked her laugh.

"She *could* control a line of command-detonated mines along the road from af-Fridhav," he said. "Not a lot of skill needed there."

"Provided we emplace them," said Bernie.

"We'd have to do that anyway," said Hans, "and some days in advance, too."

"Where would we get the mines?" asked Hamilton. "There's not enough time to gather the materials and make them."

Hans laughed aloud. "I'm sure you people have intricate forms and procedures for control of munitions. *We* don't. As long as the Christians don't get them there's little control, little organization for that matter. It's just a question of signing some out and having some reason for it."

Bernie thought about that for a while before saying, "One company from af-Fridhav. Call it . . . what? Five trucks? Six to be safe?"

"That sounds right," agreed Hans.

"So . . . a dozen directional antivehicular mines. With det cord, wire and detonators. Can you get that many?"

Hans just nodded and said, "I'll start by complaining about security around the castle and insist we put out some mines. I'll just take out extra. Say . . . mmm . . . half of those I'll use to refresh the security company's training in mines before we lay them around the castle. The rest we'll leave at the training location, intending to collect them later."

"No," Bernie said. "A little too pat. Too likely someone will notice when they don't show up. Try something else."

"If I had the dinar, I could bribe the men at the ammunition dump at Garmsch to give me extra, beyond what my colonel authorizes. It wouldn't be too suspicious, really. We have to bribe to get much of anything done in the Caliphate. I'll claim I need them for training and

ask for an extra two dozen. Halfway between here and
Garmsch we transfer over one dozen. Have you a vehicle
that can hold a dozen?"

"Yes," Bernie agreed. "Barely. But what about the
driver of the truck?"

"What driver? Driving is a manly thing here and I
would drive. Loading would be done by the slaves at the
ammunition dump and unloading by the soldiers here at
the castle. I only need security if I claim I need security."

"That would work," Bernie agreed. "We can meet you
halfway and transfer the mines to the sedan. How do we
get them set up?"

"A couple of days before, John and I will go to the
road and find an ambush position, set it up, camouflage
them, and bury the detonator nearby. Then we bring
Petra there, hook everything up and leave her to set
them off if she sees a column of trucks coming. Or I can
drop them off myself and hide them."

"I don't like that," Bernie said. "How's she to know
it's really the right column, when she's out of communications?"

"I should have had myself chipped, after all," Hamilton said.

"That wouldn't fix the problem," Matheson disagreed,
"because one of us two *has* to go into the castle and the
other has to grab the airship. No, the girl's going to be
on her own anyway."

"I could get us five tactical communications systems,"
Hans offered. "They're probably as good as what you are
used to, since both the Empire and the Caliphate buy
from China. Since I'm getting the weapons those would
be little more trouble."

"That might help," Bernie conceded. "But we'll have to modify the frequency so that Caliphate forces don't pick it up."

*You can do that,* said the small voice in Ling's head. She said as much, aloud.

"Okay," agreed Bernie. "Now what I wouldn't give for a holocaust cloak."

"A what?"

"Never mind. It's an inside joke, an *old* inside joke. And we *still* haven't figured out what to do at the castle. *Or* how to pick up and extract Petra, since she's going to be separate."

## af-Fridhav, Province of Baya, 13 Muharram, 1538 AH (24 October, 2113)

The amazing thing to Hamilton was that there were pleasure boats to rent, right there on the tightly guarded, watery border between Switzerland and the Caliphate. Military boats he'd expected. Fishing boats he'd expected. He'd come there, Petra in tow, looking for a way to steal one or the other.

But *pleasure* boats?

"Still," he said to Petra, as the two of them put-putted across the water on the Caliphate side, "they're awfully slow. And it isn't just a governor; they've got tiny little underpowered engines. We'd be out on the water for . . . " —he did some quick calculations—"ummm . . . nearly an hour. I could almost swim the lake as fast."

"I can't swim," Petra gulped. "There were streams and lakes near home but . . . well, you can't swim in a burka."

Hamilton nodded. "It's not too late for you to learn but it *is* too late to learn to do it well enough to make it across this lake. It's got to be a boat. But these are just too slow. We'd never make it, not once the janissaries were alerted."

He reached down to feel the water. "Brrrr. Cold. We couldn't swim this without wet suits."

"What are those?" she asked.

"Never mind. I'll show you once we're back home." He said that last with more confidence than he felt.

That was the first time he'd so much as suggested he'd want to have anything to do with Petra—*miserable houri that I am*—since they'd met. She held onto that thought, that hope, very tightly. *Maybe I might mean something more to him than just a body to use.*

Hamilton didn't notice any flash of emotion or expression on Petra's face. Instead, he was looking to the south, generally. There, two patrol boats passed within a few hundred meters of each other. One was Swiss, he gathered, the other from the Caliphate. The two boats trained guns on each other as they passed. Though it was too far— about a kilometer away—for Hamilton to make out the faces, every line in the pose of the bodies exuded menace, hate, and outright eagerness to open fire.

Life was hard in Switzerland, Hamilton had heard more than once, and food was always rationed. But the million men and women of the Swiss Army took their turns on the border and rebuffed any threat from the Caliphate, usually with much fall of blood and with few or no prisoners taken on either side. In a sense, the country was in a continuous low-level war that for level of sacrifice per capita matched the endless war to maintain and expand the Empire.

"I'm an idiot," he announced.

"Why? How?"

"Because we don't have to cross the lake. We only have to get to the Swiss side of it. And that's *much* closer."

"Won't the Swiss shoot at us?" Petra asked.

"That's always a possibility, yes. But 'the enemy of my enemy is my friend.' As long as the janissaries are trying to kill us, the odds are on our side that the Swiss will help us."

"Oh. I'm not sure I like that word: Odds."

Hamilton laughed. "Honey," he said, "all of life is nothing but playing the odds."

Petra really didn't want to think about her perforated body sinking to the bottom of the cold deep lake. Instead, she changed the subject to life on the outside.

"Well, for one thing, you're going to like learning to swim and going scuba diving in a wet suit," Hamilton answered, as he turned the little rental boat to shore. *And I am so going to like teaching you.*

Petra leaned over and kissed him on the cheek. She had to raise her veil to do it.

## Castle Honsvang, Province of Baya, 13 Muharram, 1538 AH (24 October, 2113)

Hans stood at attention in front of his *corbasi*. "Sir, the security around the castle could be much improved," he said.

As an initial matter, the colonel was inclined to be unpleasant over someone telling him that his own arrangements were inadequate. On the other hand, he *had* been somewhat distracted. He decided to hear the young *odabasi* out.

"Speak."

"There are two things, sir, that I think we can do. One is that the boys have become stale, doing nothing but standing guard. I think we should take . . . *I* should take, one to three platoons at a time out and train them in janissary skills that have become . . . slack."

"And?"

"There is no reason that the space between the wire obstacles cannot be mined," Hans said. "That's the second thing."

The colonel thought about that. He agreed wholeheartedly about the training suggestion. It was *so* refreshing to have a young officer with some initiative. He was less enthusiastic about the mines, given how often the American renegades staggered back to the castle drunk. He said as much.

"Command armed and optionally command detonated," said Hans. "We can ordinarily leave them disarmed and harmless, and only arm them if there is ever an attack on the facility."

"Well . . . " the colonel agreed, "we *do* have a fairly liberal ammunition budget that we've hardly ever touched. I approve, young *odabasi*. Start your training program and start improving the defenses."

## Honsvang, Province of Baya, 13 Muharram, 1538 AH (24 October, 2113)

There were two ways that control, back at Langley, suggested to Matheson that he could proceed. One involved Andrussov oxidation. This was comparatively difficult and dangerous. On the other hand, the materials were certain. He began with that.

The materials *weren't* much of a problem. Methane was easy; the sedan ran on it and getting a spare tank was no problem. Pure oxygen was available, Matheson discovered, from the local pharmacy. Better, no prescription was required. He bought three tanks and two masks. Ammonia? That was available everywhere.

Platinum was a little more difficult. There was no jeweler's shop in Honsvang that had any. Nor had those of any of the other towns nearby had anything like the quantity he needed. And it would have been very suspicious for a *kaffir*, as he obviously was, to buy several hundred thousand rand or dinar worth of gold and diamond jewelry just to extract the little bit of platinum that held the stones in place.

He'd had to go all the way to am-Munch to find any substantial quantity of platinum, and then it came in coin form rather than in jewelry. The drive over country roads and along the decrepit remains of E533 had taken the better part of the day.

Still, there was an easier and safer method, if he could get the materials for that. Bernie hadn't been sure until he actually tried.

There was a print shop in am-Munch, one with a sign proclaiming it had been there for centuries. This provided a dye, Prussian blue, for no more than cost plus a moderate bribe to one of the workers. A bakery, of all places, had lye in sufficient quantities. Sulfuric acid he didn't bother getting, as Hans had said he could get it in any reasonable quantity from the motor pool.

Having the materials for the easier and safer method in hand, Bernie went after the lab gear required. In am-Munch, he also picked up the makings of a burner, beakers and tubing, plumbing supplies, a double walled stainless steel pressure cooker, a *lot* of epoxy, and some glass jars in large and small sizes, the smaller being able to fit inside the larger. That had taken most of the rest of the day. Almost as an afterthought, he picked up a bag of charcoal.

He drove back to Honsvang, then moved all of his little treasures into the suite. There he discovered that Hans had left him several liters of sulfuric acid, rather more than he needed. When it was all present and accounted for he thought, *Okay, you bastards. Teleoperate me. Let's make us some* cyanide.

*Oh, and be really fucking careful, huh?*

The thought came back, *Mr. Matheson, this is Doctor Richter. I'll be operating you. I'll do my best.*


## Castle Noisvastei, Province of Baya, 13 Muharram, 1538 AH (24 October, 2113

It wouldn't do to have Petra in the suite while Bernie Matheson cooked up his devil's brew. For that matter, Hamilton had no desire to be there either. *Mom didn't raise no fools.*

Hans and Ling were in the next room. The castle's original walls were, of course, very thick and utterly soundproof. Not so the dividing walls that had been put in to make more cubicles for the houris. Thus, between the gasps, the moans, the thump-thump-thumping of bed against wall . . .

"Does that bother you?" Hamilton asked Petra, lying beside him wearing nothing but a smile.

She shrugged, then rolled over on one side to face him, her head resting on one hand. "You really get to where you don't even hear it."

"I suppose," he conceded. "That is, *you* don't. *I* do."

"Does it bother *you*?" she asked, then glanced down and, giggling, said, "I see that it does."

Her face grew serious. "You own me for the next week or more. I am your field. You know you can have me, if you want me."

He sighed and rolled his eyes. "I know. And I know it wouldn't mean very much to you. Or maybe it would be nothing. And . . . I'd rather not have you if it doesn't mean anything. Call me old fashioned."

"You're 'old fashioned,' " she echoed, and then laughed.

"I like the sound of your laughter," Hamilton said. "Truly, I do."

"No one's ever said that to me," she admitted. "Tell me more of what it's like where you live."

"It's a long way from perfect," Hamilton said. "And it used to be better, so I'm told . . . so I've read. It's more free for individuals, especially for women." He reached over and fingered the small crucifix that rested against the inside of her right breast. "Christians are in charge, though they're not all all *that* Christian. Some are though.

"We're a lot richer than in the Caliphate. Poor people there are generally better off than rich ones here."

She thought about that for a minute before asking, "Autos? My great-grandmother wrote that back then almost everyone had a car. Not that she approved of that, mind you."

"No," he shook his head. "Those are kind of rare. I own one, and have since I was twenty-one. But that was because I was in a position where I needed to be able to get around without relying on public transport. Now, of course, I still have one and for much the same reason."

"Could I have one? If I lived there, I mean."

"Probably, if you had the need and could pay the tax and pay for the fuel. Portable fuel is rare, expensive, and rationed. Most of it goes to the government. Most regular people get around by public transportation.

"You could drive mine," he offered. "Once you learned how to drive, anyway. Or at least how to tell the car where to take you."

That was a nice dream. But it was also, possibly, a suggestion of some future relationship together. *He's not really thinking about what I am, what I have been. I think I owe it to him not to let him forget, not to let him be taken in by a false picture.*

"I had a client who used to take me for drives," she said, "back when I was fourteen and fifteen. But I never saw anything. From the moment he started his car until the moment he stopped it I had to have my head bent over him. He was older than you . . . maybe forty."

*Got no words for that one,* Hamilton thought, *except . . .* "Well . . . if I drive you somewhere you won't have to unless you want to."

Her eyes narrowed slightly. She chewed for a few moments on her lower lip. Then she said, "You know . . . for *you* I might just want to. Especially because I won't *have* to."

"You don't have to do anything now, either," he said.

"I know," she answered, bending her head while reaching down with one hand. "Maybe that's why I *want* to."

"*When* do you turn eighteen?" he asked, just before she engulfed him. She didn't answer and he, for a while, lost the ability to think.

## Honsvang, Province of Baya, 13 Muharram, 1538 AH (24 October, 2113)

While Hamilton groaned under Petra's ministrations, Matheson's body worked under the guidance of Doctor Richter. The entire apparatus looked something less than professional. Above, on a small table, rested a drip bottle containing ferric ferrocyanide, or Prussian blue dye. This was nontoxic. From the bottle a tube led into the stainless steel pressure cooker, through a hole Bernie had hand cut and then sealed. Exactly beneath the hole, a burner projected, located so that the drip from the tube would drop Prussian blue right onto the flame. The burner had its own oxygen supply, fed in before combustion took place, from a medical bottle.

Another tube led from the top of the stainless steel vessel to a stoppered glass beaker. The tube extended nearly to the bottom of the beaker. Above the level of the end of that tube was the lye he'd obtained at the bakery. A tube above the level of the lye led out through the stopper and to another beaker containing a slurry of charcoal and water. A further tube from that last beaker led to a just-slightly-opened window.

Matheson lit the burner and started the Prussian blue drip.

## Castle Noisvastei, Province of Baya, 13 Muharram, 1538 AH (24 October, 2113)

Petra lifted her head away. *I don't have anything to offer*, she thought, *except for this. Maybe it will be enough to make him really want to take me away. Or maybe it will just remind him that I'm a filthy whore. I wish I had more to give. Might as well wish to turn back the clock and change history.*

She looked up into Hamilton's eyes, hoping to find that she'd pleased him. Instead she saw a look she had never seen before on any man's face. She really didn't know what it meant.

Nor did Hamilton explain. He just pulled her up along the bed, toward the pillow. Then he spread her legs, and took a position very similar to the one she had held until a few moments before.

This wasn't exactly new to Petra, after all, she and Ling had been lovers for years now. But none of her clients had ever shown any interest.

*He's not as good as Ling,* she thought, dreamily, *but he's better than any man who's ever had me. And . . . he smells more . . . right than Ling does.*

## Honsvang, Province of Baya, 14 Muharram, 1538 AH (25 October, 2113)

Bernie was a mere observer as Richter stopped the drip and then turned off the burner. Almost immediately, gaseous bubbles that had been rising in both of the beakers stopped. In one beaker, bathed in lye, was a layer of whitish crystals. He shared minds, to a degree, with Richter and knew that these were hydrogen cyanide, harmless in the current form. The crystals Richter separated out, storing them in one of the larger glass jars. The used lye was thrown away and replaced. The charcoal-water slurry likewise went down the toilet and a new batch was added to the second beaker.

*I can smell almonds,* Bernie thought.

*Good,* answered Richter. *That means you're not one of those people who can't smell cyanide. Don't worry, this is not a dangerous concentration.*

*If you say so, but that's my body you're exposing.*

*I'd feel your death,* said Richter, in defense.

*Sure, but you'd still wake up back in Langley, safe and sound, while my corpse cooled here.*

*Relax.*

Bernie tried. Nonetheless, the potentially deadly bubbles arising on the second batch reminded him continuously that this chemist operating his body from thousands of miles away held his life in his hands.

And they were going to be at this all night.

*I said, "Relax,"* Richter thought. *I can do this without you. Why don't you let your mind go to sleep?*

*Because I might wake up dead. How much of this shit do we need?*

*By your plan? To put a sufficient concentration into four barracks rooms of thirty-two thousand cubic feet each to kill everyone in them in a couple of minutes? More, a lot more.*

*Fuck.*

*Relax. It's a piece of cake.*

## Castle Noisvastei, Province of Baya, 14 Muharram, 1538 AH (25 October, 2113)

"Can't you tell them to knock it off?" Ling's mouth asked as her torso bent over the tuning set attached to the first of the five communications systems Hans had lifted from unit supply. She gave a dirty look toward the room in which Petra and the American, Hamilton, were staying. "It's unnerving."

"Jealous?" Hans asked with a smile.

"Since I am not Ling, how can I be jealous?"

"Oh. Sorry, I forgot."

"I understand. Now go tell them to shut up and you do the same."

Hans arose and started to go but then stopped.

"I can't," he said.

"Why?"

"She's my sister. It would be too . . . embarrassing. For both of us."

With Ling's head shaking with annoyance, the teleoperator went to the door and knocked. When there was no answer—indeed, the couple in the other room seemed not even to notice—she opened the door, walked to the bed, grabbed Hamilton by the hair and pulled him away from Petra's body. In a voice that was only half Ling's, the body said, "Stop it. You're ruining my concentration. Fuck; if you *must* fuck. But do so *quietly*."

Ling's body turned around brusquely and marched out of Petra's room, slamming the door behind her.

"Jealous, you think?" asked Hamilton.

"No . . . no, that wasn't my Ling."

"Still, the suggestion was a good one," Hamilton said

"Suggestion. Ooohhh . . . her 'suggestion.' But I don't think I can do it quietly . . . not with you," Petra said.

"Let's try."

"Yes," she said with a wanton smile. "*Let's*!"

# Honsvang, Province of Baya, 14 Muharram, 1538 AH (25 October, 2113)

The sun was already over the horizon and streaming in through the suite's windows.

*Is that enough?* Bernie asked, looking at four large glass jars, partly filled and sealed with the hydrogen cyanide crystals, standing against the wall. There were other jars, smaller ones, containing an oily liquid. Those were all in the sink. In addition, several more small jars were better than half full with the crystals. Of the lye and Prussian blue dye, almost none remained.

*I think so. You've enough for the four barracks, plus some more for just in case. If you need to change the distribution around, the crystals are safe enough. Just don't get any acid on them.*

*I won't. Time for you to go?*

*Yes.*

*Well . . . not to be rude or anything but . . . get the fuck out.*

*You'll still need me for the thermobaric bomb you may need to sterilize the laboratory,* Dr. Richter pointed out.

*Later. If we need it. For now . . . just go away. This shit is worse than rape.*

## Castle Noisvastei, Province of Baya, 14 Muharram, 1538 AH (25 October, 2113)

*Finally they've quieted down,* thought the Chinese communications specialist controlling Ling's body.

*What's your problem, asshole? I'm the one who's losing a lover; I'm the one who has to give up my own body.*

*I am not used to working in these kinds of circumstances,* thought the specialist.

*I don't see what's so difficult about it,* Ling thought back.

*It's reading the proper settings here and then transferring them through your body to the set. And it isn't difficult; it's* tedious. *Worse, distractions mean I might set it wrong, input the wrong codes, so that either you won't be able to talk to each other or, worse still, the Caliphate's people will hear you. Now shut up and quit pestering me.*

## Castle Honsvang, Province of Baya, 15 Muharram, 1538 AH (26 October, 2113)

The colonel was gone, trying to bring some order and discipline back to the border troops at af-Fridhav. This left Hans alone with the company. He spent the time usefully, inspecting weapons in the arms room. The weapons were not common issue; the janissaries in the security force slept with theirs. Rather, these were extras and special purpose arms, along with some of the pricey electronics purchased from China or the tsar that made the Corps of Janissaries near equals of Imperial Infantry.

*Not bad shape,* Hans conceded, while looking down the stubby barrel of a submachine gun. The weapon was disassembled into its components on the same crude wooden table the unit armorer used for his own inspections and repairs. Hans sat at the table on a backless, slightly padded, rotating stool.

"How many of these do we have?" he asked of the armorer. "Unissued, I mean."

"A dozen, sir," the armorer answered. He was an older type, wearing glasses, with a short, neatly trimmed, gray beard, and a ginger step that told of knees beginning to decay from arthritis.

*He was probably a janissary cadet when my parents were in diapers,* Hans thought. "You must be coming up on retirement soon," Hans said.

"Yes, sir," the armorer answered. "I'll have my thirty years in next year, about this time."

*Okay, not quite that old. I guess the service really does wear.*

"Not going to stay past that?" Hans asked.

In answer the armorer smiled and raised one hand, palm down facing the floor. The hand was raised above neck level: *I've had this shit up to here.*

Hamilton would have recognized the gesture instantly from a statue back at Fort Benning. Hans did as well, though not from the statue. He laughed.

"What are you planning to do after that, then?"

The armorer shrugged. "Not sure, sir. Settle down with a wife, start a business . . . grocer, I was thinking . . . raise a few kids. I've still got a year to think about it."

Hans felt a sudden lump form in his chest. *No you don't. You've less than two weeks before I have to kill you. And for what? Because some asshole grabbed you, as with me, and took you as a child to make you into a soldier for a bunch of fucking aliens. What a shitty fucking world.*

Hans did not, of course, say any of that but, rather, contented himself with, "That's as good a plan as I've heard. Still, the unit will miss you when you go."

The older man smiled. "I'll miss the boys, too. And maybe the life . . . I've gotten used to it, after all. Thirty-two years since I was gathered? They're not easy to let go of, sir, all those years. Still, when it's time; it's time. And I *am* getting old."

The armorer was such a likeable old soldier. Hans found that he did, in fact, like him. He sighed with regret. *Not for much longer.*

"Going back to your old town?" Hans asked.

The armorer shook his head. "How could I, sir? My parents are long dead. My brother and sisters are *Nazrani*. The boys I played with, as a boy, too. It would be . . . too . . . ."

"Awkward?" Hans supplied.

"Exactly that, sir. It would be too awkward."

"I understand. Have you picked a wife yet?"

"Yes, sir. Nice girl. A widow who lost her husband down in the Balks facing the infidel Greeks."

"Ah. Yes. 'A troop sergeant's widow's the nicest, I'm told.' How old is she?"

"Half my age plus seven years," the armorer answered. "Just as the Prophet, peace be upon him, recommended. She already has a kid. I've been helping out a little with money."

"Sounds perfect," agreed Hans.

He went silent then, as he reassembled the submachine gun he'd been inspecting. When finished, he handed it back to the armorer, saying, "It all looks good. Tell me, is there a good place to buy personal arms in town?"

"A *good* place, sir? No, not here. There's one north of here past Svang in Walnhov, though. What were you looking for?"

Hans pointed at the submachine gun with his chin. "Maybe one or two of those and a couple of pistols. Just for practice, you understand. Well . . . that and the sheer joy of owning my own, now that I'm an *odabasi* and can afford them."

"Oh, yes, sir. I understand perfectly. Walnhov's your place. Tell the owner, Achmed's his name, that Sig will rip his balls off if he cheats you." Sig, the armorer, hastily amended, "Not that he would. He's one of us, too."

# Interlude

Nuremberg, Federal Republic of Germany,
1 December, 2011

The city had seen much beauty in its centuries as it had, too, much ugliness, from party rallies to war crimes trials and hangings, with bomb and fire and ruin in between. As with every city in Germany, its history was an eloquent witness to the horrors of war, a demanding call for a better way. Though there had been peace for sixty-six years, yet the stones and the tortured bricks remembered . . . yet children still learned from adults.

In the *Christkindlmarkt*—a once a year for four weeks, open air city of wood and canvas—Amal clapped her hands with childish glee at the brightly lit, colorfully costumed pageant being put on for her, among some thousands of others. The baby was at an age when her favorite colors were "oo" and "shiny." Those criteria the show met well.

She sat on her mother's lap; Gabrielle enduring the thing for the baby's sake and not from any religious devotion of her own. Still, despite the religious theme, Gabi found herself drawn into the pageant. Perhaps it was only because of the reminder of her own innocent and trouble-free babyhood. That, and that Amal was certainly enjoying it.

*Children don't learn Christmas from us,* Gabi thought, ruefully. *We learn it from them.*

As the lovely blond girl with the curls and the golden crown had said, at the opening, from the gallery of the Church of Our Lady, "You gentlemen and ladies, who were once children, too . . . "

The air was cold but still, still enough that their coats held warmth enough for comfort. A children's choir was forming up as Gabi rose with Amal in her arms. She didn't have to stay for that; the singing would reach to every little corner and stall of the Markt. And, in a way, it would be all the better for being background.

"Mommy," Amal asked, "Will Daddy be here this Christmas?"

"He says he can't, Honey," Gabi answered. "He's still working over there and that he can't take vacation for Christmas this year. He promised to be here for your birthday, though."

*Yet another reason to hate America,* Gabi thought. *They take no rest and leave none for others, either. Why are they like that? It must be something in the blood, or a disease that infects all who go there to stay.*

"He *did* send you several presents, though," Gabi added, as Amal's face sank. *Sure he can send presents. He earns enough there. And gives next to nothing in tax.*

Tax in Germany was becoming a problem, even in *German* terms, and they'd grown used to being nearly as heavily taxed as the French. The country was graying fast. Worse, because there were places where young people could earn more and keep more, places like America, Canada, Australia and, increasingly under the assault of AIDS, South Africa—young Germans were leaving. This left more tax to be paid by fewer workers, which drove even more to think about leaving. Nor was there much sign of improvement. There were not so many children in the *Christkindlmarkt* as Gabi remembered from her own youth and those had been few enough.

*And still Mahmoud pesters me to go there and marry him. Sometimes it's tempting. But then he'll say something like, "I'm an American citizen now; Amal should have the same chance when she's older . . . if she wants."* He knows *how that pisses me off.*

Gabi watched Amal's eyes as they passed a stand with spicy Nuremberg gingerbread on display. She made as if to keep going, watching the baby's eyes stay fixed on the treats. Then she turned, abruptly, scooped up a piece and passed it to the girl. Gabi took a silver and gold colored two Euro coin and gave it to the stall keeper.

While she awaited her change, the baby leaned over and kissed her cheek.

"Thank you, Mommy."

And *that* just *made* Gabrielle's Christmas.

# CHAPTER FOURTEEN

> We hope that we can either return to the policies of that imagined past or approximate some imagined ideal to recapture our innocence. It is easier than facing the hard truth: America's expansiveness, intrusiveness, and tendency toward political, economic, and strategic dominance are not some aberration from our true nature. That *is* our nature.
>
> Robert Kagan, "Cowboy Nation"

## Honsvang, Province of Baya, 16 Muharram, 1538 AH (27 October, 2113)

"Merry fucking Christmas!" Hamilton exclaimed at the display of chemical and metal deadliness laid out in the sitting room of his suite. Hans hadn't stopped with the single submachine gun and two pistols he'd mentioned to Sig, the armorer. "If we hadn't arranged for maid service to be cancelled, we'd be fucked."

"Not really," Bernie corrected. "All this will fit in the lockable armoires. I just wanted to do an inventory."

"Oh."

"Nerve agent antidote?" Bernie asked.

"Two containers of three each," Hans answered, pointing to a bed.

"What do you need NAA for?" Hamilton.

"Incapacitate people we don't want to kill," Hans answered.

"Fair enough," Hamilton agreed. "What about the mines?"

"Rather than wait, I buried a dozen of them near the road to af-Fridhav, last night," Hans answered. "Along with five hundred meters of det cord, two detonators, wire, etc. All we have to do is dig them up and emplace them. Well, and arm them, too, of course."

"Night vision goggles?" Bernie asked.

"Four pair," Hans answered.

"Where the hell did you get this much firepower?" Hamilton asked. "How the hell did you get suppressors, for God's sake?"

Hans explained, "We don't have much in the way of gun control for Moslems within Islamic lands. You go in, show an ID, give the man money and he gives you the weapons. It's not hard."

Hamilton, coming from a country where the Second Amendment was pretty much a dead letter, was surprised.

"You never can tell what they'll leave out of an intelligence briefing," Bernie said. "Body armor?" he asked of Hans.

"I was only able to get one other set besides my own," the janissary apologized. "Sorry."

"No problem; we'll make do."

Petra was there, though Ling was back at the brothel. There were two busloads of tourists from the province of al-Andalus so she'd be busy for a couple of days. Hans tried, not always with success, not to let it bother him.

"When are you going to teach me about the mines?" Petra asked.

"Nothing to teach, really," Hans said with a shrug. "We'll set them up and mark off when you should detonate, if you have to. For the rest . . . well . . . hold up your hand."

Petra did. Hans then put up one hand with two fingers, index and middle, forming a V.

"Squeeze those together." When she did, easily, he said, "Release them and do it again." She did. "There's no more to it than that," he finished.

"That's it? I squeeze something and a couple of hundred men who've never, so far as I know, done me any harm just die?"

"They probably won't all die," Hans answered. "A lot of them will just be really badly hurt. You're going to hear some awful things. Can you deal with that, sister?"

Petra sighed, thought about it for long silent minutes, then answered. "In the basement of Castle Noisvastei there are several dozen women without brains, or at least without full brains. They're chippies like Ling and Bernard . . . but not like them either. These women have chips that make them simple fuck-machines.

"In the other castle are two hundred children, no worse than . . . as innocent as . . . I was, who are going to be infected with a disease to see if it works to kill them.

"Back home . . . near home, rather, there's a Moslem girl who's my best friend in life . . . and she's nearly as much a slave as I am.

"So yes; if I have to kill a couple of hundred men who've never done me any harm to help bring this rotten society down . . . I can do it."

"That's my girl," said Hans. "Tomorrow, we go to teach you how to use a submachine gun . . . and to familiarize Bernie and John with the ones we use here."

*Actually,* thought Hamilton, *if I can arrange it and we succeed in getting her out of here, that's my girl.*

Both Bernie and Petra were asleep as Hans and Hamilton made plans for the assault.

Hans explained the security arrangements. "There are five barracks rooms, one per guard platoon and one for the headquarters. Each is maybe twelve hundred cubic meters . . . here, here, here, here, and here." His finger pointed in turn to five large spaces, apparently added on to the castle's exterior, on the diagram of the ground floor of the castle he'd drawn up earlier. "One platoon of about forty-five is assigned to each. One of those rooms will be empty on any given day. In addition, on the second floor are rooms for some of the senior noncoms."

His finger touched down lightly at various spots around the perimeter drawn on the diagram. He said, "There are usually fourteen or fifteen guards on duty around the perimeter at any given time. In addition, the platoon headquarters and the two squads from that platoon not on the perimeter will be down in the command post, what we call the 'ready room,' in the basement. That's also where the security cameras feed to. The ready room is capable of alerting the perimeter guards, the barracks rooms, and the noncom rooms with the push of a button. The perimeter can likewise alert the ready room."

"The children?" Hamilton asked.

Hans flipped a page in the notebook and pointed again. "Here, just off the laboratory and the crematorium."

"I don't see any way to do it," said Hamilton. "We take out the perimeter guards and the ready room alerts as soon as one of them fails to answer . . . assuming we even *could* take out the perimeter guards. We take out the ready room and the perimeter guards alert as soon as one of them reports in and no one answers. We take out the barracks that are full first and the noncoms and headquarters alert the ready room."

"I was thinking timers on the cyanide but—"

"—but that means they have to be emplaced early. Can't you just imagine it: every room gets its own suspicious looking jar within a jar with a sign on it saying 'Warning: don't jostle. Cyanide within.' Hmmm . . . maybe we're going about it all wrong. Maybe the trick isn't to kill them inside the castle. Maybe the trick is to get them to go outside the castle and . . . oh, that won't work, will it?"

"No," Hans shook his head. "We still have to get the children out. Even if Ling under her controller can hold the thing steady against the wind, with a ramp from the ship to the battlements, she can't do it while two hundred men are shooting at her unarmored airship."

"I had another idea I've been considering . . . it's not a war-winner but it might help."

Hamilton raised one quizzical eyebrow.

"It depends on the fact that I'm new, fresh out of school, an honor graduate and therefore an unknown quantity but quite possibly a fanatic," Hans began. "I can get away with a lot of simple weirdness and harsh or unusually kind behavior for a while without exciting any more commentary than troops usually have for the new boss."

"What's that get you?"

"Well . . . suppose I start tiring the janissaries out so they sleep like rocks. That makes it easier to get the cyanide into their rooms without causing a fuss, right?"

"It would," Hamilton agreed.

"And suppose that within the overall program of tiring them out, there's a reward for the platoon that does the best . . . a reward of, say, a night at our favorite local brothel. That cuts out one guard platoon of four."

"Helps . . . but what about the noncoms?"

"Can't send troops to have fun without supervision," Hans said. "Got to be a regulation against it . . . somewhere."

Hamilton chuckled.

"What's so funny?"

"You remind me of my first commander when I was in the Army. He was a dick, too, but he usually had reasons for what he did, reasons he would almost never let you in on unless you *had* to know."

"Oh. Okay . . . so how does it work out if we do this?"

Hamilton thought about that. "All right . . . assume that two barracks and the noncom's rooms are empty, one from the duty platoon in the ready room and one at the brothel. One of us takes two rooms, the other takes one. We go in, open the jars, pour the acid and get the hell out, quick, closing the doors behind us. Then the one who took out only one room—you, I think—goes to the ready room. I go outside. Then . . . ah, vug." Hamilton paused. "We're still stuck. In communication or not, there's no good way for you to kill twenty-eight men single-handed, while I try to off another fourteen or fifteen one or two at a time. Someone, somewhere in there, is going to notice. Is there anyway to cut off communications between the perimeter guards and the ready room?"

"No . . . it's wireless. Even the cameras are wireless," Hans said.

"Shit. This is a job for a company, better still a battalion, of Rangers in Exo suits . . . not for two men."

"That's not true," Hans said. "Your Ranger company, or battalion, would be so noticeable that there would be a division here guarding the place."

"Yeah," Hamilton conceded. "Maybe so. Shit. Oh, well, it's not like we could get that company or battalion if we asked. And we're still fucked."

"Hard. No grease," agreed Hans. "I'm out of ideas."

There was something Hans had said earlier nagging at Hamilton's mind. Something about . . .

"I know how, maybe. It's a long shot but it might work. It's not going to be subtle, mind you. And it will still require some timing . . . *and* that you send a platoon plus to the brothel."

"Now didn't you say that the perimeter mines are command armed and optionally command detonated?"

The next day Hans directed Bernie in how to drive the other three conspirators to a secluded valley he'd found, about three miles to the east of Honsvang and slightly to the south. Hans met them there in a janissary issue truck. He'd brought along the weapons and enough ammunition for a fair degree of familiarization practice. The valley was too close to civilization, still, to fire without the silencers.

Looking at the pistol Hans had bought for her, Ling demurred. "My controller will know how to use the weapon," she said. "And far better than you could teach me. After all, China made it."

"It still needs to be test-fired," Bernie said.

"Not really," said Hans. "I did that at the weapons house where I bought them. It was funny, too, the way the owner's assistant looked at me when I insisted."

"Why funny?" asked Hamilton.

"People here . . . most Moslems, anyway, don't test much. Or maintain much. Or train much. If Allah wants something to work, it will. If he doesn't, it won't. And nothing any human being does or fails to do will make the slightest difference."

"That's bizarre," Hamilton said.

"Yes," Hans agreed, nodding seriously. "Most of the people aren't even aware that they think like that, they just act that way naturally. It's one reason why the janissaries are so important to the Caliphate. We weren't brought up to think that way and by the time they gather us it's too late for us to change. So we *do* test and we *do* maintain and we *do* act as if God helps those who help themselves, impious though the thought may be.

"Anyway, Ling, if you don't want to shoot you can load magazines."

Matheson and Hamilton loaded their own, while Hamilton and Hans loaded half a dozen submachine gun magazines for Petra. She was not a natural, a half dozen magazines were not enough.

After Matheson was satisfied that he had the measure of his pistol, he moved off to one side and broke it down to clean and oil it. Meanwhile, Hans and Hamilton took turns working with Petra while Ling kept reloading. After perhaps a thousand rounds, they'd gotten Petra to the point where she could hit a man-sized target at twenty-five meters, with at least one round of a three-round burst, about six times in ten. At that level she stuck, though, so much so that neither thought there would be much benefit in keeping at it.

"And besides," said Hans, "the sun is going down soon. It may be that no one can hear us shooting; but they may still see the muzzle flash if we keep it up."

"Right," Bernie agreed.


"He's . . . going to . . . fucking . . . kill . . . us," grunted one janissary to another as Hans led all but one platoon of the company through the ninth mile of a twelve-mile run. The troops' feet and knees shrieked in protest. Air heated by exertion formed little frosted cones in front of their faces. It was too dark to see that, of course.

The run had led over hill and dale, which is to say up sheer-sided mountain and down again, for over an hour so far. From the open area in front of Castle Honsvang, he'd led them down to and around the town, then up to Castle Noisvastei and back down again, over the bridge to the town of af-Füss, to Walnhov, and with many a twist and turn thrown in for good measure. And the young commander showed no signs of flagging, still.

Behind the formation, cursing the fate that had delivered him into the hands of an outright lunatic of an *odabasi*, the *baseski*, or first sergeant, pushed from behind to ensure that none of the older or weaker men fell out. Hans had left the idiot *bayraktar* behind, responsible for security in his absence.

Finally, Hans pulled up in front of Castle Honsvang and ordered a halt.

"*Baseski!*" he called, at which command the senior noncom marched up to report.

"Take charge of the company. All except the alert platoon: breakfast, showers, full marching packs, weapons, basic load of ammunition, here, in one hour."

"Sir!"

*What an asshole.*

While his *baseski* ran the troops through their paces, Hans walked briskly to his own quarters. On his way, he passed one of the American renegades, the one he remembered as Meara. The grossly fat bastard was leading a nine-year-old brown-skinned boy, presumably his bed partner of the night before, by a leash, in the direction of the experimental slave pens. The child was crying.

Hans kept his face a mask, nodding no more than politely. Even so, he vowed inside, *You will be punished for this, swine.* He wondered why the filth didn't recognize him from the resemblance to his sister, then decided that the fat bastard was so self-centered he was incapable of recognizing most other people as human beings, let alone seeing familial relations by facial features.

Claude O. Meara removed the leash and pushed the boy into the pen with the rest of the experimental animals. A girl of perhaps eleven met the boy with open arms, glaring her hatred at Meara from over the boy's shoulder. Meara sneered and locked the heavy door, turning away to walk to the main lab.

There he found Guillaume Sands busily at work at his desk, manipulating a diagram of the true VA5H virus shown on a computer screen.

"Morning, Will," said Meara. "Any progress?"

Sands shook his head. "A little, not much."

"How soon before we're ready for more live tests?"

"Maybe ten days," Sands shrugged. "Maybe a little less."

"We're down to just the new batch, you know," Meara said, pointing generally at the crematorium and the pens.

Sands shrugged. Unlike Meara, he had no sexual use for children. Also unlike Meara, he took no particular joy in watching the victims die slowly. At least, unlike Meara, Sands never pulled up a chair to enjoy the sight of their suffering and death through the viewport. He didn't care that they did, either, of course. If a few people had to die so that that construct of utter evil, the American Empire, died as well . . . well, so be it.

## Honsvang, Province of Baya, 19 Muharram, 1538 AH (30 October, 2113)

Hans looked half dead.

"This isn't going to work," said Matheson. "Your idea of wearing the troops out to make our way easier is a good one. Unfortunately, it's also wearing *you* out, so badly that you're not going to be much use to either of us when the time comes. And if you take a break a couple of days before, so will the troops. Worse, you're wearing yourself out faster than you are them because you are, so to speak, working two jobs."

"But what can I do?" Hans asked desperately. "Both things are necessary."

Matheson sighed. He'd seen so many new officers like this. Hell, he'd *been* just like this at one time. Still, he was an old hand. His job had once been to mold young officers. That Hans was a member of an enemy army didn't change that.

"You've got to learn to delegate, young *odabasi*. You have a senior noncom, do you not?"

"Yes."

"Can he be trusted to lead some of the training?"

"Probably. The colonel says he's quite good. I haven't had a chance to see it yet."

"Then have him do so. You have an executive officer, don't you?"

"Yes, but he's an idiot," Hans said.

"All second lieutenants are idiots," said Matheson. "They become better through experience. Is he an idiot without energy?"

"Well . . . no. He seems more confused than lazy."

"Then unconfuse him. Give him some missions to accomplish on his own. Meanwhile, *you* sit in the ready room and watch the cameras. Snooze. Relax."

"I'll . . . try," said Hans, dubiously. "But I'll still have two jobs and only one me. I'm still going to be tired, if maybe a little less so."

"For normal fatigue," said Bernie, "up to a point, we have pills."

## Honsvang, Province of Baya, 22 Muharram, 1538 AH (2 November, 2113)

Hans was at Castle Honsvang, resting, it was devoutly to be hoped. Matheson and Ling had left this morning for am-Munch, Matheson taking the methane-powered car with him.

This left Hamilton and Petra alone. He still "owned" her for a few more days, and Latif still had his deposit against her return. With the mission upcoming and, in Hamilton's opinion, the really excellent chance that within a few days they'd all be dead, there was no question of, and less motivation for, sex.

*And besides,* thought Hamilton, *lovely as she is, I haven't the first clue as to whether she's been doing it because she wants to, really, or because it's the only job she knows.*

"Petra," he asked, "if we survive . . . make it through, what do you want to do with your life?"

*I can't tell him I want to spend it with him,* she thought. *In the first place, it's ridiculous. He's an important man and I'm just a houri, defiled and defiling. He could never stay with me or want me with him permanently. What do I tell him?*

Instead of telling, she asked, "What could I do? I can read but that's small beans in your world where all women can read. I know nothing but my . . . profession and that I would like to give up if I can."

"Well . . . of course you can," he said. "We have prostitutes where I come from but prostitution itself is illegal. They have even less of a position in my homeland than they do here. School? You can read, that's quite a bit. Would you like to go back to school?"

"Can you imagine me, at seventeen, sitting down at a desk too small, with my knees under my chin and surrounded by seven-year-olds?"

That was a funny image. Even so, he answered it seriously. "Maybe not in a regular classroom, no. How about if we hired a tutor for you?"

"I own nothing," she said. "Well . . . a little money I've saved hoping to buy myself back from Latif. But that's not enough for a tutor. Besides, I'll have to leave it behind. Asking for it would be too suspicious."

"I have money," he said. "Certainly enough for that. And there are programs, too, that help pay for such things. And my agency is going to owe you *big* if we pull this off." *Of course, if we don't, and the disease is released, we're all going to be dead. So the agency and the country will owe you* massively.

"Why should you pay for me?"

*Because I think I'm in love with you? No, mustn't say that. How about,* "Because we're comrades in arms? Because we're friends? Because it's the right thing to do?"

She thought about that for a while. Instead of answering, though, she admitted, "I'm terrified, you know. I might have talked big about striking a blow against this rotten system. But I'm scared to death. Do you know what they'll do to me if they catch me? My brother told me. They'll nail me to a wooden cross and leave me hanging there in agony for days. He's seen it. He's had to do it. Then, when they've extracted the last bit of pain they can from me they'll come with big iron bars and smash my legs so I hangthereuntilIsuffocate." Her voice grew high and a little shrill on the last few, jumbled, half-hysterical words of the last sentence. She really was terrified, he could see, and had been hiding it.

"I won't let that happen," he said. "Whatever the cost."

"If it happens, you'll probably be there on the cross next to mine." She bent her head as her shoulders began to shake.

He took her head in his hands and lifted it up to face him. There were tears gathering in her eyes, he could see.

"*I won't let it happen,*" he promised, again. "If it gets that bad, well, they won't take either of us alive."

"You swear to it?"

"I swear."

"I've got to tell you something," Hamilton said. "I loved a girl once. She was a lot like you in looks, though, honestly, she was just pretty where you're really beautiful. She had all the advantages you never did. But she wasn't spoiled by it. She was very brave right to the end."

"The end?" Petra asked.

"We were in the Army together. Her platoon was ambushed. I couldn't get to her in time. She was killed. In the end, rather than let herself be captured she asked for fire to come in on herself."

"What was her name?"

"Laura . . . Laurie Hodge. I took it really hard for a long time. I suppose that's why I got out of the Army; it just reminded me every day that I'd failed her, a woman I loved."

Hamilton's face grew very serious. "But I won't fail *you*. I couldn't live with myself if I did."

And that was as close as he could come to telling Petra that he loved her.

# Interlude

Nuremberg, Federal Republic of Germany,
11 September, 2015

The city was a better place for an artist than Kitzingen
had been. This was true not only in the scenes and people
there were to be drawn or painted, but in the ability to
sell her work as well. There was more for Amal, as well;
more culture, especially. This had figured into Gabrielle's decision to relocate a few years earlier, too.

Then, too, the EU was still growing jobs almost
entirely in the public sector. With the country graying,
young people leaving, and fewer paying taxes, Gabi
needed the improved sales. Worse, given a choice
between keeping up welfare payments and reducing the
size of the bureaucracy, Europe had no choice. She was

incapable of reducing either the number or the living standards of the bureaucrats. Indeed, she could not only not reduce, she had to expand. The bureaucrats were her most important supporters.

Mahmoud helped. He'd still not given up on getting Gabi and Amal to the United States. He called from Boston at least weekly and at least half of any given conversation was, subtly or openly, about just that. He was, in fact, nagging Gabi at the precise moment that the phone screeched and then went dead.

"Mommy," Amal called from the living room of their small apartment. "Mommy . . . something on television . . . something *bad*."

Gabi stood facing the television, tears coursing down her face and her little fist wedged between clenching teeth. The screen was split in three, each section showing a mushroom cloud over an American city. One of those cities was Boston and she knew now why the phone had shrieked and died.

The commentators were all as shocked as Gabi. People were bandying about inconceivable numbers of dead and dying. The bombs were apparently very old technology, very primitive, very powerful, and highly radioactive. Four million dead seemed likely, as each city had been caught during the work day, when the offices and buildings were most full.

*Thank God*, Gabi thought, even through her tears, her loss, and her pain, *thank God I didn't take Amal there*. Then, realizing what she'd been thinking, she amended, *Thank fate, in any case*.

Everyone was *sure* the United States would retaliate in some heavy-handed, murderous fashion. Thus, Gabi's art took a back seat for a while to her demonstrating, with other fair-minded people, against any such thing. Amal in tow, she was to be seen in Berlin, Frankfurt am Main, Hamburg, Munich. Wherever there was a gathering to remind the United States of its own responsibility for what had been done to it, there she was.

Nor was her voice subdued. Almost uniquely, she could point to Amal and say, "This baby lost a father and *she* is not crying out for a mindless vengeance." That voice could claim as well, "I lost my lover and *I* am not crying out for vengeance."

For a while, even, Gabi was something of a star. That stardom lasted until, eventually, everyone realized that the United States was *not* going to continue the game of mindless retribution, of the "eye for an eye" that left everyone blinded.

And after all, as the President of the United States said, "The perpetrators are all dead. Who is there to take revenge against?" That this was a lie was obvious to no one who wanted to believe it was true.

So, instead of revenge, the United States government reduced its aid to Israel and much increased the aid to Hamas, which had come out on top in the bitter feud with Fatah. It withdrew the last of its soldiers from Islamic soil. It accepted without demure a sudden, and serious, rise in the price of oil. It even changed the immigration rules to permit more immigrants from Moslem countries. It called off the pursuit of Osama bin Laden, which meant little in any case as Osama hadn't been heard from in years.

Of course, the President was only one woman, with one voice. There were other voices . . . carrying very different messages.

# CHAPTER FIFTEEN

We have the right to kill four million Americans—two
million of them children —and to exile twice as many
and wound and cripple hundreds of thousands.
                                        —Suleiman Abu Gheith
                                        Al Qaeda Spokesmen, June 2002.

## am-Munch Airport, 23 Muharram, 1538 AH (3 November, 2113)

Bernie Matheson—no, he was Bongo again—shuffled
like a proper *kaffir* in boarding the airship anchored near
the shabby, run-down terminal. Ling walked behind,
wrapped in a burka. Their bags were carried aboard by
a short coffle of slaves, owned by the airship line. As

chartering customers, rather, as the servant and presumptive slave of a chartering customer, there was none of the usual customs and security nonsense.

The flight engineer, Retief, met them at the hatchway. It really wasn't his job but he was doing a favor for the normal receptionist, the ship's purser, who was a bit late in getting back aboard ship.

"Welcome back, Mister Mathebula," Retief said. "Your quarters, and quarters for Mr. De Wet and his . . . guest . . . are prepared. We can leave in about two hours. Might I suggest a meal or, perhaps, a drink?" Retief's fingers indicated the direction of the cabin.

Bongo thought, *A frigging polite Boer? I hope we don't have to kill him.*

"You have booze here, *baas*?" Bongo asked. "I thought . . . "

"The locals almost never inspect international carriers, Mr. Mathebula. When they do, a minimal bribe is generally sufficient to get them to leave our stocks alone."

"Might take drink, *baas*. Old Bongo plenty scared flying. No like it."

"No need to worry, Mr. Mathebula," Retief answered. "The ship's captain and executive officer are both very competent and even I am qualified to fly the ship, provided I don't have to make any fancy maneuvers or landings."

"Thank you, *baas*. Bongo feel much better."

While Bongo and Retief spoke, Ling walked past them in the direction Retief had indicated. Neither Retief nor Bongo could help noticing how really delightful the sway of her hips was as she walked ahead.

◊   ◊   ◊

Later, in the cabin, Ling asked, in colloquial English, "What's this shuffling, 'Please don't beat yo' nigga, *baas*,' bullshit?"

"You're not Ling," Bongo said immediately. "Who are you and what are your qualifications?"

"*Zhong Xiao* Lee Gen, Celestial Kingdom's People's Liberation Army Air Force," Ling's lips answered.

"No surprise there," Bongo said. "But where did you pick up the language?"

"Mil attaché in Washington for a few years," Lee answered. "Masters at UC San Francisco before that. Fun times. The powers that be figured I'd be a good fit for this purpose, Lieutenant Colonel Bernard Matheson."

"Man, I am *so* going to push to clean out the infiltrators when I get home," Bongo said.

Ling's shoulders shrugged. "Push all you want. They don't all look like me or like this"—Ling's own finger pointed at her breast—"vessel. Besides, didn't it ever occur to you that you *want* a certain number of infiltrators, in case you need to send us a message you want us to believe? One of our problems is we *don't* have any of your people in our system, which means we have to be really unsubtle sometimes to get you people to pay attention. Unsubtle is not something my people are good at doing or being."

"Maybe so," Bongo conceded. "Whatever the case—"

He was interrupted by a steady *ding-ding-ding* and the announcement, "All passengers and crew, this is the captain. Lift off in ninety minutes. I say again, Flight Seven Nine Three, am-Munch to Slo, lift off in ninety minutes."

## Castle Honsvang, Province of Baya, 23 Muharram, 1538 AH (3 November, 2113)

Uniquely, the janissaries' weapons were left behind, locked in their barracks room. The men were going on an all-expense-paid night to paradise and, as Hans had announced, "There's no need to upset the houris."

Preceded by the first sergeant, who announced the name of each soldier before Hans inspected, Hans walked the lines checking uniforms. There was little to object to, predictably, as the janissaries were so eager to get out from under Hans' heavy thumb. They were even more eager to get at the houris, so eager, in fact, that they'd taken extra care to look perfect.

Hans stopped in front of one man and accused, "You've been over-trimming your mustache, soldier."

The accused soldier answered, "Sorry, sir. It's that we've been in the field so much lately, dirty and sweaty so much, that my skin underneath was starting to get inflamed."

Hans pursed his lips and seemed to think about it. "Well," he said, at length, "I won't pull your pass and send you back until the thing grows back properly. But I will hold you to letting it grow back."

Breathing a sigh of relief, the janissary answered, "Yes, sir. Thank you, sir. I promise I will."

*Now there's a fair officer*, thought Sig, the armorer, standing at the far end of the first rank. *And everyone was bitching about what a hard ass he was. I told them he was a good man.*

## am-Munch Airport, 23 Muharram, 1538 AH (3 November, 2113)

The airship's charter called for it to proceed north for a bit under seven hundred and fifty miles to Slo, in the Caliphate's northern provinces, there to receive a mixed cargo of high grade lumber and blond, blue-eyed female slaves to stock the higher class brothels of Cape Town and Jo'burg. Flight time, so the captain announced, would be approximately five and a half hours. Loading? Well, who could say about loading when picking up a cargo in a city of the Caliphate? If Allah wanted it to proceed swiftly, it would. If not, then not.

"Not that it makes a shit," muttered Lee with Ling's mouth, "what the flight time is, since we aren't going there."

The ship around them shuddered as mooring locks were undone. There came a rising, high-pitched whine as downward pointing, vertically mounted turbofans kicked in, raising the airship upwards on an even keel. Ascent under power was slow; the ship got about two thirds of its lift from the helium it contained.

Bongo checked the time. "Still a while to go." He reached into one of the bags dropped off by the airship's crew of slaves and withdrew a small earpiece which he mounted to one ear. "Hamilton, this is Bongo. Come in Hamilton."

## Highway 310, Northwest of ar-Rebchel, Province of Baya, 23 Muharram, 1538 AH (3 November, 2113)

Hamilton and Hans dug frantically in the deep shadows of the woods south of the 310 road to unearth the directional mines Hans had buried there before. There wasn't room for three to dig; Petra stood nervously watching.

"A little . . . fucking . . . close . . . to the fucking . . . road . . . isn't it?" Hamilton grunted.

"I needed . . . a sheltered place . . . where . . . Petra could see . . . the road . . . and . . . still be . . . protected . . . from the blast," Hans answered.

"All right . . . makes sense."

Hamilton's shovel scraped along something that didn't feel remotely like a mine. It was the protective cloth Hans had draped over the cache against the dirt and the weather. "I think . . . we're there," he announced.

In Hamilton's ear there was a beep, followed by, "Hamilton, this is Bongo. Come in Hamilton."

"Hamilton here, Bernie. We've just uncovered the mines. Fucking things look heavy. It's going to be a while."

"Right. We're just getting ready here."

## Flight Seven Nine Three, am-Munch to Slo, 23 Muharram, 1538 AH (3 November, 2113)

Watching Lee apply makeup to Ling's face struck Bongo as both odd and unsettling. "What the fuck are you doing?"

"Getting ready to seduce a member of the crew, to take him out of play," Lee answered through Ling's mouth. "It will work a little better, you'll agree, if I look seductive."

"Did they give you a female makeup course for this mission?"

The Chinese laughed. "No." He laughed some more. "Dude, you haven't figured it out yet, have you?"

"Figured what out?"

"I'm gay. When I say 'seduce,' I mean *seduce*."

"Fuck."

"Only if necessary." The Chinese reached into Ling's small handbag and, smiling, produced a tube of lubricant. "But if necessary . . ."

## Highway 310, Northwest of ar-Rebchel, Province of Baya, 23 Muharram, 1538 AH (3 November, 2113)

Petra stood over Hans, her submachine gun held in both hands. Not knowing any way to help, she felt both useless and frustrated. She said as much.

"Sis, you don't have to help," Hans assured her, as he lay behind one of the cylindrical mines aiming it precisely at a point in the road. "These things have to be set just right. Even Hamilton—and he's used to weapons—doesn't know how to aim them. He's doing the most he can just by lugging them to the firing positions."

"If you say so," Petra said dubiously. "But I'd feel a lot better if I could help."

"Fair enough," Hans agreed. "So tell me again how it's going to happen."

"Okay," Petra agreed. "One: once they're all set up and wired together, with the detonators in the hole, I go to the hole and wait. If I get tired, I take one of the pills Bernie gave each of us. Two: after you tell me the assault on the castle and lab is underway, I wait some more until . . . Three: when the column comes from af-Fridhav I wait until the lead truck is right there" her finger pointed at a boulder on the other side of the road—"and squeeze the first detonator. Four: even if that works, I press the second one anyway. I do it until the explosions begin. Five: I don't stick around, but crawl and then run toward an-Nessang. Six: there'll be a sedan waiting for me by the place John showed me. I get in back, lie on the floor, hold the bolt cutters to my chest, and cover myself with a blanket. Seven: you or John will come for me."

"Good girl! There's something else you can do, too."

"What's that?"

Hans handed her a reel of electrical field wire and said, "Run this back to your hole."

## Flight Seven Nine Three, 23 Muharram, 1538 AH (3 November, 2113)

The city lights of an-Nurber, fewer and fainter now than they'd been a century prior, spread out below the ship to the port side. The crewman being blown by Lee in Ling's body barely noticed. Arching his back and groaning with the orgasm, he held the woman's head and pumped into her mouth like a bull.

*You son of a bitch*, Ling's consciousness thought at Lee. *I'm a houri; I'm not a slut.*

*Quiet*, Lee answered. *This is for the mission.*

*My ass . . . and thank the ancestors you haven't given one of the crewman that yet . . .*

Yet . . .

The crewman stopped pumping, then half stumbled back onto the narrow bed in Ling's cabin. "Whew," he gasped. "That was *great!*"

"Lie down," Lee said. "Relax. I'm not done with you yet."

Obediently—who knew what delights this trim exotic body might hold—the crewman did, closing his eyes as he stretched out on the cot. Lee, meanwhile, rifled through Ling's bag as if for a condom, muttering, "Now where did I put that?"

What Lee withdrew, however, was not a condom but a syringe, an autoinjector containing a *serious* muscle relaxer. Removing the cap and placing it on the upper part of the syringe to arm it, he struck the thing into the crewman's thigh. The crewman barely got a yelp out, and that a yelp not inconsistent with sex, before relaxing completely.

"One down," Lee said aloud.

*Slut*, Ling thought.

*Nothing wrong with mixing pleasure and business.*

Deftly, Lee flipped the crewman over on his belly, then took a roll of high strength tape from the bag. With this he taped the crewman's hands together and behind him, taped the feet together, and then taped the mouth shut. Lastly, Lee ran the tape around the crewman's neck, then to the head of the bed.

"That should hold you."

Before leaving, Lee took the trouble to reapply Ling's smeared lipstick. She knocked on Bongo's door and, when it was opened, said, "Cockpit next."

Lee scratched at the cockpit door like a cat asking to be let in. Retief opened the door.

"May I help you, miss?"

"You may," Ling's sultry, breathy, desperate-sounding voice answered. "I haven't seen my master in two days

He'd kill me if I had sex with a *kaffir*. And the *kaffir* is too loyal, he'd report me if I tried. But I'm one of those with the kind of chip that makes me want to have it, to *need* to have it, every day. Won't one of you or . . . better still *all* of you, please, please help me?"

"Let the poor girl in, Retief," the unseen captain said. "We can surely help her in her hour of need."

*God,* Retief thought, *what a shitty world when we do things like this to beautiful women. Hell, what a shitty world when things like this are done to anybody.*

Bongo looked in on Ling's cabin to make sure the crewman was still alive. Force of habit and training had made Lee hook the needle of the autoinjector through the crewman's shirt.

*One won't kill him,* the agent thought. *Probably. That was the only guard on this deck, too. Time to go down and check on the ship's own loading crew. Better said, time to go recruit.*

The loading crew were colored slaves. As such, they didn't automatically rise and bow with deference when Bongo made his appearance in their cramped cabin. They seemed startled, though, when he spoke to them not with the pidgin such people usually learned, but with as clear a diction as any *baas*. That surprise was as nothing, though, beside what they felt when they noticed the silenced submachine gun in his hand and the pistol strapped to his hip.

"Gentlemen," Bongo began, "please sit and listen. I'd like to tell you a story about a man who died several hundred miles to the south of here, not quite two thousand and two hundred years ago.

"His name was Spartacus . . . "

◇  ◇  ◇

Lee heard a mental laugh from Ling. *Okay, you're a slut. But it just occurred to me that if these Boers knew what the sex was of the mind controlling my body, they'd all try to crawl out of their own skins with disgust.*

*That's half the fun of it,* Lee sent back. *I wonder how Matheson is doing down below?*

Matheson declaimed, arms thrust up and out with the submachine grasped in the left hand, " 'O comrades! Warriors! Thracians! If we must fight, let us fight for ourselves! If we must slaughter, let us slaughter our oppressors! If we must die, let it be under the clear sky, by the bright waters, in noble, honorable battle!' "

"This Spartacus fella, he say that?" asked one of the cargo slaves.

"That, yes, or about that, but in a different language," Bongo answered, with no less truth than the purpose required.

"And what happen to him?"

"He fought. He won many battles. In the end he lost." Bongo hesitated over telling the rest but, "His followers were all killed. Over six thousand of them were crucified."

All the slaves shook their heads at that. No they didn't want to be crucified.

"But we have some advantages," Bongo added, "notably, that we're much closer to Switzerland. And Spartacus lacked machine guns."

*Bang!* The hatch to the cockpit flew open with a single kick. Bongo . . . no, Matheson again; there was no more need to pretend . . . stormed in with his submachine gun in both hands, and a fierce gleam in his eye. Everyone, except for Ling's body, froze.

He saw that both pilot and co-pilot were in various states of undress, with Ling's body kneeling between the captain's legs, head bobbing and the captain's fingers intertwined in Ling's hair. Retief was sitting at a console, studiously watching a screen and apparently trying very hard not to pay any attention to the minor orgy going on in the cockpit.

"Take thees plane to Habana!" Matheson parodied, yet in a voice full of thunder. The slaves, the soon to be *ex*-slaves, given any luck, poured in behind him waving knives from the ship's galley.

Lee immediately punched the captain in the crotch, stood, grabbed the shocked captain by the hair, and hauled him out of his seat, tossing him to the floor. He deftly swung Ling's body into place and took control of the airship.

"Are you *sure* you can fly this thing?" Matheson asked.

"People's Liberation Army Air Force Precision Airship Drill Team," Lee answered, "2109 to 2112. Yeah, yeah . . . we do a lot of silly shit in the CKPLAAF. By the way, dude, your timing sucks."

## Highway 310, Northwest of ar-Rebchel, Province of Baya, 23 Muharram, 1538 AH (3 November, 2113)

"We've got the ship," Hamilton heard in his ear. He didn't bother mentioning it to Hans; both he and Petra would have heard the same news. "We're going low. The control for Ling says his people are painting a false image for Caliphate Air Control. As disorganized as these people are, there's good reason to believe no one will notice us dropping off their screens for a while, if at all. ETA is about ninety-seven minutes. If you need us to speed up or slow down, let me know."

"Wilco, Bernie," Hamilton sent back.

Hans was just about to hook up the detonators to the twin wires that led, one from the right most mine, one from the left most, back to the hole. He attached the wires and then laid the detonators on the ground. Petra looked at them nervously.

"It will be fine, Petra," Hans said, glancing up at Hamilton to suggest that he, too, offer some words of comfort.

Hamilton knelt down on one knee to bring his face almost parallel to the girl's. "Honey, Hans or I will come for you. I promise. And . . . "

"Yes?"

He looked very seriously into her eyes, just visible with the scattered moonlight coming through the tree. "Just . . . I love you. I should have said it before but it comes hard to me. Please, though, remember that."

In answer Petra threw her arms around his neck and kissed him deeply. She pulled back after half a minute, looked into his eyes, and said, "I never before knew it was possible to love a man who wasn't a blood relation. Now go before I start to cry."

With that, Hans and Hamilton raced for Hans' borrowed truck. Initially, both went into the cargo compartment, where Hans began to cover Hamilton with a tarp. Other things were in back, too, notably jars full of cyanide crystals, sulfuric acid, a bomb ginned up by Richter via Matheson, and their weapons and ammunition.

"This is the first time I'll have been in action." Hans gulped, holding the tarp over Hamilton and their arms. "I just realized that I'm more nervous than Petra is."

"Don't be," Hamilton answered. "I've been in the shit a lot. Trust me, you're a natural."

"Thanks," Hans said sheepishly. Still, the compliment *did* make him feel more confident, as it was intended to. "By the way, I really am sorry for punching you."

"Don't mention it. If you hadn't, we wouldn't have gotten as far as we have."

## Flight Seven Nine Three, 23 Muharram, 1538 AH (3 November, 2113)

The great white whale of an airship turned slowly to the left and southward as it descended. For as long as the deception held, Chinese intelligence would be portraying the ship as still moving northward at eighty-three hundred feet over ground level. In fact, it was moving the other way at under eight hundred.

Lee/Ling was at the controls, wearing a set of the night vision goggles Hans had pinched from the unit arms room perched atop his/her head. This was only a backup. Although the Chinese had killed all marking lights, and shut off all active navigation aids, the better to avoid detection, the ship itself had excellent passive limited visibility.

The captain and exec, along with most of the rest of the white crew, were down below, guarded by some of the former cargo slaves. Only Retief and three of the former slaves remained in the control cabin and for that there was a special reason.

Ignoring the flight engineer for the moment, Matheson asked, "How far down are you going to take us?"

"Just another fifty or sixty meters," Lee answered. "Any lower and people on the ground will be able to hear our engines. Any higher and we'll make a radar signal the Caliphate might pick up. Even at that height, though, there are places where we're going to appear on someone's radar screen."

"What can we do about that?" Matheson asked.

"Ourselves? Not much. My people back in Shanghai, the ones creating a false image of us proceeding north, are going to be trying to catch any time we appear on the radar and eliminate the trace on the screens. But they're not going to know we're there until after we've appeared. So there are going to be a few seconds every now and again when we will appear."

"Won't that cause the Caliphate to scramble fighters to investigate? I mean, in the Empire we'd be all over *any* unexplained radar signal like flies on shit."

"I don't think so," answered the Chinese. "Neither does the Ministry of State Security. Besides, you Yankees are paranoid. People in the Caliphate are just used to things going wrong. 'Will of Allah,' and all that. I think we'll be okay."

"She's got that right," Retief interjected.

"He," Lee corrected.

"He?"

Matheson explained. As he did, Retief began to laugh. "Oh, I can hardly wait to tell the captain he was being blown by a *man*."

Matheson didn't laugh, nor even smile. "Mr. Retief, I need to ask you a few questions. You need to think over your answers carefully."

"All right," Retief agreed.

"The man you might remember as De Wet—no need for you to know his real name—suggested to me that you have some . . . issues . . . with the slave trade."

"I do," Retief agreed.

"Enough for you to strike a blow against it? Before you answer that, you need to know that the primary purpose of the mission on which I am engaged is not to strike such a blow. It has, however, become the price we must pay to succeed in that mission."

Retief thought on that one, before answering, "I hate the trade. I hate my part in it. But I have family back home and they will suffer if I help you. That's what you're getting at, isn't it; you want my help?"

"How will they suffer?" Matheson asked. "Are you talking salary and finances or are you talking reprisal?"

"Both."

"What if I could guarantee you a diplomatic trade for your family, and guaranteed employment in the Empire?"

"You can't guarantee such a trade," Retief answered.

"Watch him," Matheson told the remaining cargo slave guards. He then turned away, walked to the empty copilot's chair, and sat down. His eyes closed.

"What's going on?" Retief asked.

"He's communicating with higher," Lee/Ling answered, while deftly tapping some control or other. "Shut up and let him do so."

## Castle Honsvang, Province of Baya, 23 Muharram, 1538 AH (3 November, 2113)

"I'm pulling up to the castle gate," Hans told Hamilton through the earpiece communicator. "Be very still."

"I understand," Hamilton sent back. He felt the brakes bite, heard their screech. The truck slowed and then shuddered to a stop.

"Evening, sir," the gate guard said. "You're back late."

"I was out looking for a place for a night exercise," Hans lied. "I think I found a good one, too."

"Allah help us, sir," the guard answered, rolling his eyes heavenward but then smiling to show it was a friendly joke. He turned around and lifted the crossbar from across the roadway. Without another word, but with a friendly wave, Hans guided the truck into the compound. Before reaching the castle proper, into which the truck would never fit, Hans turned right and drove toward the motor park. There he stopped, put on the emergency brake, but left the engine running for the moment.

"We're here," he whispered into his communicator. "There's a roving guard walking by. I may have to speak to him. I'll let you know when it's clear."

## Castle Noisvastei, Province of Baya, 24 Muharram, 1538 AH (4 November, 2113)

Sig the armorer sipped at something clear and cold and not strictly legal. Through a window he looked down at the other castle, brightly lit by security lights. He saw a truck pull in and though it was too far away to make out the driver, Sig thought it was the *odabasi*, no doubt returning from some late night foray to find some new training opportunity for the unit.

*And isn't that just like the boy?* thought the armorer. *When he could be here, enjoying the warmth of the women, instead he's out on a cold night looking for ways to make of our company better men. A fine lad, that he is.*

The first sergeant stopped by Sig's booth, a young houri in each arm, and said, "Not too much of that, you hear, Sig?"

"Never fear about me, *Baseski*. I never take more than Allah is likely to forgive me for."

# Interlude

Nuremberg, Federal Republic of Germany,
11 September, 2016

A glass of a clear liquor grasped in one hand, Gabi
switched channels from one covering a Moslem march in
Paris to another showing a similar celebration in Berlin.
*Ghastly*, she thought. *Simply ghastly to be celebrating
the murders of four million people. What kinds of terrible
oppression must those poor people have suffered to make
them so vindictive?*

It was all too distasteful. Gabi switched channels yet
again, this time to CNN International. That was, in its
way, far worse.

The big story on CNN was the rise of a new political
party in the United States, Pat Buckman's new Wake

Up, America Party was sucking voters and contributors from the Republicans and Democrats like the Sahara would suck moisture from a sponge. Worse, senators, congressmen, and state governors were likewise defecting. CNN's commentators were actually concerned that the lunatic might win the election in a couple of months. *And that just doesn't bear thinking about.*

Whether it bore thinking about or not, though, Gabi couldn't quite tear her eyes from the screen nor switch channels yet again. Why? Because the image was one remarkably frightening to the modern German soul. There was a march there, too. Instead of disarmed rabble chanting slogans, however, this march showed thousands of armed, disciplined men and women, in ranks, under what appeared to be their old officers and NCOs. They sang as they marched, past the old Iwo Jima Memorial, over the bridge across the Potomac, and on into Washington in complete violation of that city's ordinances.

And the police did *nothing*, so said the commentators. *How can that be?* Gabi wondered. *Don't they know, haven't they learned from* our *history, what that means?*

CNN said there were other marches taking place in the United States. None of those were in Boston, Los Angeles, or Kansas City, of course. Those cities had ceased to exist. But in Houston? In Chicago? In Nashville and Atlanta and a score or more others? Men and women marched and sang and chanted for *revenge*.

## 9 November, 2016

When the returns came in from Massachusetts, neither Gabi nor the commentators were all that worried.

With a sixth of the state's population—and the most liberal sixth at that—killed in the Boston bombing, it was only to be expected that there would be a serious swing to the right from those who remained. And besides, Massachusetts only had twelve electoral votes. (It would be fewer in coming years, so said the press, after the losses from the bombing came out of the official census.)

Still, Gabi had gone to bed with a sense of dread in her heart. California's fifty-five votes could not be known in Europe until the next morning. When she turned on the television that next morning to see the final results, her heart sank like a stone. Not only was that lunatic, Buckman, about to become President of the United States, he was doing so after carrying *every* state. Red State-Blue State: all wanted revenge. This had never been done since the uncontested election of George Washington, two hundred and twenty-seven years before. What a President might do with that kind of mandate was a frightening prospect. What this particular President would do was altogether terrifying.

## 1 September, 2019

Gabi had been surprised, along with nearly everyone else, when the Americans didn't attack the Moslem world within days of Buckman's inauguration. As years had passed, the world, outraged at Buckman's invasion of civil liberties within the United States, had forgotten about their earlier fears.

Then had come his request for a declaration of war and his ultimatum to the Moslem world.

And then, ten days later, the missiles had flown.

# CHAPTER SIXTEEN

It is permissible to set fire to the lands of the enemy, his stores of grain, his beasts of burden—if it is not possible for the Muslims to take possession of them—as well as to cut down his trees, to raze his cities, in a word, to do everything that might ruin and discourage him, provided that the imam (i.e. the religious "guide" of the community of believers) deems these measures appropriate, suited to hastening the Islamization of that enemy or to weakening him. Indeed, all this contributes to a military triumph over him or to forcing him to capitulate.

—Ibn Hudayl, fourteenth-century Granadan
theorist on the subject of *jihad*

## Castle Honsvang, Province of Baya, 24 Muhharam, 1538 AH (4 November, 2113)

The departing guard's boots echoed off the stone walls of the castle. He'd been politely interested in Hans' arrival, but no more than that. After a few words, and a quick but penetrating glance over the guard's uniform and equipment, Hans had sent him on his way.

Once the guard's footsteps had moved away sufficiently, Hamilton tossed off the covering tarp and stood or, rather, crouched between the cargo truck's bed and its cloth covering. He frog-walked to the back, by the tailgate, and handed down two submachine guns and two ammunition carriers to Hans. He had to wait a bit while Hans took from a pocket and slipped over his head and around his neck a crucifix on a rosary chain. He tucked the cross and chain under his uniform.

One of each of the SMGs and ammo carriers Hans slung. The others he draped from the vehicle's rear bumper. By the time that was done Hamilton was back with two rucksacks. He passed these down from the cargo bed of the truck to Hans' eager grasp. Hans set both sacks down very carefully on the asphalt and then helped Hamilton to dismount.

"They can't see us here?" Hamilton asked.

"No. The cameras are oriented toward the outer perimeter, for the most part. There are some inside, as well, but this is a dead spot. That's why I parked the truck here."

"How long until the next roving guard comes by?"

"Five minutes, no more. We must hurry."

Hamilton took his weapon and slung it over one shoulder, and an ammunition carrier over the other. He then gingerly lifted a sack. Hans felt his to make sure that it not only contained one jar of cyanide crystals and another of acid, but also the bomb he intended to set off in the control room.

The two raced on cat feet for the nearest door. Hans pressed a buzzer while Hamilton crouched down very low.

"Guard room," came from a speaker mounted above the buzzer.

"*Odabasi* ibn Minden," Hans said. "Open up."

"Immediately, sir." It was Hans' ensign's voice.

The door buzzed itself with the sound of a solenoid moving a bolt out of the way. Hans opened the door, said, "Thanks," into the speaker, and entered. Still crouching low, Hamilton followed. Hans shut the door quietly, then pointed. "Two barracks that way. They're marked. Good luck."

Both men then took night vision goggles from their packs and strapped them to their head. With a nod, Hamilton took off in the direction indicated.

He killed the hallway lights, then walked ahead to his target.

*These are men I am responsible for,* Hans thought, as he came upon the barracks room door for his own third platoon. *Men I took an oath to lead. And . . . they're good men, too.*

He heard another voice, an old and dying priest's voice. "What does the Koran say about lying to unbelievers? Turnabout is fair play."

*But these men never lied to me. If anything, they were lied to.*

"Not that. It's that it was permissible for you to lie under oath."

*Oh. I suppose so.*

Still, Hans hesitated at the door. His heart was pounding, yes, but not from fear. He was sick at the stomach, yes, but not from nerves. It was just that, *The only man I ever killed—helped kill, anyway—was that old priest. And now I'm supposed to kill nearly one hundred. It's a hard step.*

*But will it be any easier, knowing that two hundred children down below will be infected with a deadly disease if you don't save them? Take your pick, Hans. At least the men in that barracks room are adults.*

Sighing, Hans laid down the pack and removed from it the two jars and an oxygen mask with a small tank. Then, after placing the mask over his face, he opened both and set them down on the floor by the crack of the door. The door he opened gently until there was just about a foot of opening. He slid the jar of cyanide crystals almost through that opening. With two hands, carefully, Hans began to pour the acid onto the crystals. They immediately began to dissolve with a sound of crackling. He pushed the jar all the way into the barracks room and closed the door.

Inside, sleeping men began the process of dying.

On the other side of the castle, Hamilton felt none of the qualms Hans had. These were not, after all, his men. On the other hand, his heart was pounding just as Hans' was. And that pounding *was* from fear, if not fear for himself.

*If I fail in this,* he thought, *what becomes of Petra? If I fail, what becomes of the children down below? If I fail, what becomes of the world?*

*I must not fail . . . I must not fail like I failed Laurie.*

Repeating Hans' motions, Hamilton took out and prepared two jars. Likewise, he donned an oxygen mask—*be nice if it was impossible to absorb cyanide through your skin and eyes*—cracked the door, half pushed in one jar, and then filled it with acid from the other. He then pushed it in the rest of the way, and closed the door . . . just as the door for the other barracks room—the one for the headquarters platoon—opened and a robe clad janissary emerged from it.

"Who turned off the fucking lights?" the janissary cursed. "Get up to take a damned piss and you risk your life around this place . . . "

*Will he find the light switch? Probably. If he does, will he see me? Certainly. If that happens . . .*

Hamilton aimed his submachine gun at the greenish image of the janissary and pulled the trigger. The gun was suppressed; it hardly made a sound. The janissary, on the other hand, was not killed instantly and managed to get off a scream.

"Ah, fuck!" Hamilton exclaimed.

"Fuck," whispered Hans, as he heard a scream from the opposite side of the castle. He stopped on the stairs that led down to the ready room, wracked with indecision.

*Now, do I go help Hamilton or continue with the plan we already have? If I go back, the ready room may alert. If I go on, I can perhaps keep that from happening. Or not. Or fuck it all up.*

He waited that way for several long moments. Had there been more such screams, he'd likely have gone back. If Hamilton had asked he'd have gone back. As it was, it *sounded* as if Hamilton was still in control of the situation, and Hamilton didn't ask for assistance. Hans continued on down.

The path to the ready room led past the sealed pen in which the experimental slaves were kept, near the observation and cremation chamber. There was a light on in the pens. Hamilton looked in on the children. There were too many to count. Besides, lacking beds they lay on each other in a twisted tangle of heads, arms and legs. He could only hope they were all present and accounted for.

*It was only the one,* Hamilton thought. *Just one poor bastard who needed to take a piss. How many more in ten seconds?*

Already there were sounds coming from the last barracks room, men rising, questions being asked, the mechanical sounds of weapons being taken from racks.

*No time to fuck around.*

Hamilton re-slung his submachine gun and grabbed the last two jars. On the smoothly polished floor his feet scrabbled for purchase, to propel him towards the still ajar door. His speed picked up . . . too fast. By the time he'd closed on the door it was all but impossible to stop. Cradling the jars against his chest, he let himself fall backwards to the floor. *Ouch.*

He slid on back and side, closing to very near his target. His feet struck the bleeding corpse of the janissary he'd shot. That stopped him.

*No time to fuck around.*

Hamilton smashed the jar of cyanide crystals just inside the barracks room. He could see the scattered pile. The jar of acid he smashed too, just before the spot with the crystals began. Acid splashed. Crystals began to dissolve, releasing their deadly gas.

Hamilton rolled away from the door as fast as he could, rolled and rolled and rolled until he smashed against the wall opposite the barracks. He arose to one knee, unslinging his weapon as he did. His aim lined up on the door opposite just as the first janissary emerged, barefoot, yelping, and automatically stepping high to try to avoid the burning acid below. The poor janissary had a chemical hotfoot.

Hamilton put a three-round burst into the janissary's chest, causing him to fly back into the barracks room. The door swung back and forth on its hinges, fanning the cyanide gas emanating from the crystals on the floor.

A knot of three janissaries entangled themselves and their arms at the door, each trying to force his way through and all making it impossible for any. Hamilton fired again, a long and normally tactically unsound burst. The mass of tangled men didn't fly back this time. Instead, held in place by the common mass, they oozed downward, creating a small obstacle at the base of the portal.

*Long enough in this spot.* Hamilton tucked in one shoulder, his left, and rolled in that direction. When he finished his roll he took the prone, weapon still aimed at the door. Hamilton guessed there were perhaps nine rounds left in the magazine.

The next janissary out vaulted the bodies at the foot of the door. Hamilton fired and missed, fired and missed, fired and hit, spinning the janissary down, broken and bleeding.

*Six down, maybe forty to go. Change the fucking magazine. No time to fuck around. Gas, do your stuff,* he prayed, glancing at the door to the first barracks he'd poisoned.

◊    ◊    ◊

Originally, Hans had intended to take control of the ready room and give Hamilton time to thin the exterior guards, and possibly even to divert reinforcements from af-Fridhav. There wasn't going to be time for that, now. *Better to take control and make sure all the exterior entrances are locked, the mines armed. To Hell with subtlety.*

Hans knocked on the clear glass window beside the ready room door. The guards inside were already rising. "Open up!" Hans ordered. "Open up! The enemy is upon us."

The frightened *bayraktar* dutifully pressed the button to release the door bolt. Hans pushed the sprung door open with his posterior. With one hand he reached in to the delay detonator atop the explosive charge in his pack. He pulled the detonator, tossed the pack into the room, and then dove for safety, letting the door slam shut behind him.

The explosive was a two stage thermobaric device. When it went off it first spread a cloud of flammable dust throughout the room. This then detonated, creating an overpressure that burst the window even as it smashed the internal organs of every man inside.

The explosion didn't do any good things to Hans, either. Even with most of a wall between him and the blast, still the force of the thing stunned and deafened him. He thought one eardrum might be burst. He knew he'd been concussed from the way the world shuddered and shook around him.

Unsteadily, having to use one hand on the wall for balance, Hans entered the ready room and began to fire at any of the bodies that looked like they still had a spark of life to them. Compared to the overpressure of the blast, the overpressure from the muzzle was nothing.

Only one man emerged from the first barracks room. That one was blue in the face and clutching at his throat. He collapsed, gasped for a while, and then died.

From the other room they came out still, but more slowly and unsteadily as the gas filling the room took effect. Hamilton almost felt sorry for them as they staggered out, weapons sometimes in hand but fingers clawing at throats. He went through three more magazines that way, putting the suffocating janissaries out of their misery. He'd lost effective count of the number he'd killed, though more than fifteen bodies littered the corridor floor.

Hamilton felt the castle shudder. *That would be Hans' bomb, I think. No chance to take the perimeter guards out quietly now. Fuck. Going to make it difficult when we bring the airship in to load.*

Hamilton thought frantically about the implications of that. *No time to leave it to the guys inside to die at their own pace. Attack!*

Quickly he dropped the half empty magazine in his submachine gun and replaced it. He felt to check that his oxygen mask was still in place and feeding. Then he stood and charged for the door.

The men on the perimeter would have heard the blast; of that Hans had no doubt. Still stunned and staggering, he went to the control desk and pushed the *bayraktar's* body out of the way. With one finger he armed the mines in place around the perimeter, to include the newly emplaced directional ones the men had put in at his order. With another he fired the modular mine packs that sealed off all the roads and gates around the castle. These each sent out twenty-eight little bombs that dispensed seven metal threads upon landing and then armed themselves. Touch one of the threads, or disturb the mine, and it would leap a meter into the air and detonate, sending tiny bits of hot serrated wire in all directions. Then Hans killed all the interior lights.

Lastly, Hans cut off all communication between the castle and the outside world.

As soon as the sergeant of the guard felt the blast, he raced for the front door of the castle. Pressing the speaker button to demand a report, he heard only moaning and a muffled *pffft . . . pffft . . . pffft.*

"Crap!" he said aloud.

The sergeant then turned to the main gate where stood the same gate guard who had admitted Hans just a little earlier. Ignoring the guard, the sergeant picked up the phone and punched in the number for the *corbasi's* command post at af-Fridhav. Modular mine packs were going off around the perimeter. The sergeant had to assume all the mines were armed and live, now. *Shit.*

"Headquarters," came the answer.

The sergeant's voice was frantic. "This is Castle Honsvang, Sergeant of the Guard Bozkurt. We're under attack. The *odabasi* is in there. I don't know if he's alive or dead."

## af-Fridhav, Province of Baya, 24 Muharram, 1538 AH (4 November, 2113)

"Calm down, sergeant," said the colonel. "I'll be along immediately with reinforcements. The important thing

is not to let the enemy escape. . . . Sergeant? Sergeant?"
The line was dead.

"Bloodyfuckinghell!" the colonel exclaimed, before
shouting out, "Alert company . . . boots and saddles
. . . im-fucking-mediately!"

Thinking about what he'd told the sergeant, about how
the critical thing was to keep the enemy from escaping,
the colonel realized that the enemy was most likely going
to try to escape by air. How, he didn't know, but Switzerland was close and those brazen bastards were likely to
be in on this. The colonel then began to dial for air
support. *Though Allah knows how long it will take those
idiots to get out of bed, let alone get a couple of planes
in the air.*

The Caliphate's Air Force was filled with the lazy sons
of rich, connected, powerful men. All the janissaries had
contempt for them.

Briefly, the colonel considered delaying long enough
for the men to draw heavy weapons and the ammunition
for them. Ultimately, he decided that there just wasn't
time, that a faster response was better than a more powerful one.

## Castle Honsvang, Province of Baya, 24 Muharram, 1538 AH (4 November, 2113)

Sergeant Bozkurt heard the tone on the line change
from his living colonel's voice to absolutely dead. *Shit.
What the hell do I do now? Gotta think . . . gotta think.
What do I know and what don't I know?*

*One: I know there are enemies inside and that their
numbers are great enough to take down one hundred
and seventy or more guards, most asleep but probably*

*some of them alert. Okay, so myself and my fourteen men are outnumbered. Bad, bad, very bad.*

*Two: They might be a suicide mission but probably are not. If they were, they would have blown the castle sky high already rather than screwing around with retail work. So they intend to escape.*

*Three: If they intend to escape, they'll have some means, ground or air. I can't do squat about the air at the moment, since if it's coming it isn't here yet, but I can keep them from getting away by ground. And I can try to counterattack.*

"Corporals! Corporals of the Guard! Report!"

While those were assembling, the sergeant said to the gate guard, the only man outside the perimeter of mines, "I relieve you. Run like the wind to the other castle and bring the *baseski* and the others. Run, son, RUN!"

"Hans? Hans report!"

"This is Hans . . . ready room is taken down and the guards dead . . . exterior doors are bolted and the mine and mine packs activated. I'm . . . not in such good shape."

"Communications?" Hamilton asked.

"Cut . . . but not before they could have gotten word out. Petra?"

"I'm listening, Brother."

"Get ready. There will probably be a column coming from af-Fridhav soon."

Petra sounded more cold than nervous to Hamilton when she answered, "I'm ready."

Hamilton's goggled gaze swept the room full of corpses. He knew that the cyanide would pass through his skin if he stayed around long enough. He began to back out, careful not to trip over any of the sprawled bodies. "Hans, I'm finished here. We've got to get control of the scientists."

"Understood. They'll probably have heard or felt the blast. I suspect they'll head to the lab to try to ensure the survival of their work."

"Good thought. I'll clear their rooms, to make sure, and join you there."

Hamilton pulled several bodies away from the door, then exited and shut it behind him. No sense in letting the gas escape.

Claude O. Meara, Guillaume Sands, and John Johnston the Fourth met on the broad landing outside their suites of rooms. Meara, as was often the case, had a young boy on a leash. Sands and Johnston held flashlights.

"What the fuck is going on?" Sands asked.

"Explosion," Johnston said. "Felt like it came from the direction of the lab."

"*Merde!*" Sands exclaimed. "We must save our *work!*" He and Johnston ran for the broad staircase that led below, ever so slowly followed by the waddling Meara, tugging on his play toy's leash.

The night vision goggles on his head were not nearly as good as what Hamilton had become used to in the Imperial Army. Even so, they were better than the predecessor to that army had had up until about the year 2014. They still gave no depth perception, but that was something inherent in the very idea. The picture was a bit grainier than he was used to, but that could be lived with. They were sufficient for him to see by, to vault obstacles with, and to find his way to the three renegades' doors based on his memory of the diagrams Hans had drawn over a week earlier.

*Open. They're gone. Now where to? Probably the lab, just as Hans thought they would. Feets, don't fail me now.*

On his way down, Hamilton heard some pounding at the heavy wooden door that stood between two tall towers at the front of the castle. The door barely seemed to notice yet, so it seemed to him, Even so, given enough time even a soft pounding might cause the door to come off its heavy hinges. He checked his downward progress and made his way to the leftmost of the two towers that flanked the door. Looking down he saw two men holding up one end of a log. He estimated there might be enough space for another four that he couldn't see.

*Wish I had some grenades,* Hamilton mused. *Oh, well, no sense crying for what wasn't available.*

He turned a crank to slightly open a window, then pushed the muzzle of his submachine gun out the crack. Taking aim, Hamilton squeezed off two bursts—*pffft . . . pffft*—that sent the two men he could see sprawling in pools of blood. The pounding from down below stopped immediately. One other janissary, brave or stupid, showed himself as he tried to drag the bodies behind cover. *Pffft.*

*May not stop 'em but it will slow them down.*

Hamilton turned from the window and continued his progress to the cellar and the lab.

Hans, stunned or not, still beat the renegades to the lab area. He found a seat which he pushed off to one side. He then waited for them to arrive. He heard them, two of them anyway, long before he saw them. His submachine gun was already reloaded by the time Sands and Johnston arrived.

"Freeze, swine!" Hans said once the two were in his sights. When they had, he amended, "Get on your bellies, filth! Where's the grotesquely fat one?"

Meara stopped when he heard the voice. He stopped so suddenly, in fact, that the play toy bumped into his overly ample rump in the dark.

*My God*, Meara thought. *They've come to get me.*

His universe had always been centered on himself. He couldn't imagine any attack on the castle that did not have him as its prime target. *They'll put me in prison. I'll be beaten . . . people will be mean to me. I've got to get out of here. And to hell with the others.*

In his panic, Meara dropped the leash. The play toy wasn't important and would only slow him down. As fast as his lard encased legs would carry him, he began to waddle back the way he had come. Perhaps there would be time to get at his funds, or at least at his Swiss bankbook, before he made his escape.

It was a great surprise to Meara when an open palm slammed into his face, knocking him on his overstuffed rear to the cold floor. There, stunned, he lay quivering like the product of a Jell-O mold. Meara began to weep.

"I don't think so, you piece of rat-filth," said Hamilton.

# Interlude

Nuremberg, Federal Republic of Germany,
17 October, 2021

In 2006 there had been just over three million Muslims in Germany. By 2016 this had grown to five, even as the number of Germans in the country had dropped and the average age of those who remained had increased. By 2019, with the massive influx of refugees from the radioactive ruins of the Islamic world, there were ten million Muslims in Germany or roughly thirteen percent of the population. Their average age was younger. Worse, the percentage of those that could be considered radical had grown enormously, partly as a result of the American atrocities against them, but equally because of their second class status in Germany.

Then again, there were those who claimed that Muslims would be radicalized by any social order that didn't place them on top and everyone else beneath them, as the Holy Koran called for.

Gabi didn't, couldn't, believe that. *Fascist, racist nonsense*, she thought. *People are just people and will act well unless the iniquities and inequalities of society are too much to bear.*

Muslim society in Germany was also highly urbanized. In the largest cities, some of them, they even made up a majority of the population. Even where they didn't, they often had the numbers where young and belligerent males were concerned. Street fights had become common. Nor were Germans generally coming out on top, except in the case of those who sided with the Muslim street brawlers, such as Anti-Fascist Action, a German derivative of a Swedish movement with origins in the British Isles. As in Sweden and parts of France twenty years prior, there were places in Germany now where the police simply would not go.

In an effort to placate the Muslims and stem the violence, Germany had established Sharia courts under Islamic scholars for Muslim communities. Moreover, acting under orders from the Supreme Court, itself under the European Court of Justice (itself having taken in and taken over the personnel and duties of the European Court of Human Rights), local German courts had taken to using Sharia in cases involving only Muslims within Germany.

If this did anything to stem the outrage of Muslim residents, though, it was tolerably hard to see.

In Nuremberg, however, things were not so bad. Of the city's population of about half a million, fewer than twenty-five thousand were Islamic. There were neighborhoods Gabi and Amal dared not go, of course, as there were in virtually every European city. But they were few, small, and generally avoidable.

Too, Gabi avoided thinking about the implications of there being places within her own country that she and her child dared not go.

The *Christkindlmarkt* hadn't opened in several years. The last time it had, even Nuremberg's comparatively few Muslims had been able to shut it down . . . violently. This had, as in many parts of Europe, led to an expansion of Muslim representation in the *Polizei*. The practical effect of that, however, had merely been to give the imams and mullahs their own, state-funded, enforcement arms. If it produced greater peace within and around the Muslim community it was only because, having no place else to turn, moderate Muslims knuckled under to the rule of the mullahs.

Before Europe betrayed itself, it first made sure to betray those outsiders who truly wanted to become European.

The practice of French Muslims, to the extent that that wasn't a contradiction in terms, of engaging in gang rape of both European girls and Muslim girls who failed to dress the part—*tournante*, or taking one's turn, in French—had spread, too. But with the courts and police only interested in keeping the peace—as well as they were able, at least, within the German community—girls had little recourse. Germany's thirteen percent Muslims accounted for about eighty-eight percent of all rapes in Germany. This was perhaps not such a bad record. In Sweden, twenty years prior, they'd been credited with as much as eighty-five percent of all rapes, and that from a much smaller percentage of the population. Some argued that this showed that Germany was doing a better job of assimilation. It may even have been true.

Gabi refused to listen to those figures, too.

# CHAPTER SEVENTEEN

And even more honor is due to them
when they foresee (as many do foresee)
that Ephialtis will turn up in the end,
that the Medes will break through after all.
—C.P. Cavafy, "Thermopylae"

Castle Noisvastei, Province of Baya,
24 Muharram, 1538 AH (4 November, 2113)

The gate guard from Castle Honsvang, breathless from
his long uphill run, pounded on the great gates outside
the castle until his hands began to bleed.

"All right, all RIGHT! I'm coming," shouted Latif
from a window overlooking the near side of the gate. He
muttered, too, "Where did the damned gate guard go?
I'll have the skin off that lazy bastard's back for this."

In fact, the brothel's gate guard beat Latif to the gate by some seconds. All full of apologies, he insisted he'd only left to relieve himself. Latif said he'd take that under consideration, "Just before I have you beaten half to death and sold to a eunuch factory."

That sent the gate guard to his knees, begging for mercy and forgiveness, until Latif, realizing he couldn't open the gate on his own, said, "Never mind. Just stop blubbering and help me with this Allah-be-damned bar."

Together the two men lifted it, the gate guard doing most of the work, and admitted the breathless corporal.

"The men . . . from the security . . . company . . . you've got to rouse them . . . we are . . . *attacked*."

"Shit!"

## Flight Seven Nine Three, 24 Muharram, 1538 AH (4 November, 2113)

"Shit," exclaimed Lee/Ling. The eyes opened wide with shock and fear. "They've made us. Shanghai tells me there are two fighters lifting from ar-Ramstei even as we speak."

"Fuck," agreed Matheson, "what can we do?"

"Can't outrun them," Lee answered. "Can't fight them at all. Can't surrender."

"Set her down?" suggested Retief, a member of the team since Matheson had been able to get agreement—"from the highest authorities"—that his family would be traded for from the Boer Republic. "How good's their radar?"

Lee shook Ling's head. "Second rate. What they make for themselves is poor. What we and the tsar sell them isn't great either. Good enough to see us in the air, yes.

But good enough to catch us on the ground? Maybe not. The problem is that if I set down, some one of the locals *will* see us. And, given that, they might report it to the authorities. And there's no place around here that doesn't have some little town or other within view."

"Report us to the authorities?" Matheson mused. "Let me see the map."

Looking it over, Matheson saw one town a bit more isolated than the others in the area. "Set us down right next to that," he said. "I have an idea." He turned to one of the ex-cargo slaves and ordered, "Get me a couple of sheets . . . no . . . ah . . . three of them . . . and three checked tablecloths from the galley . . . and . . . ummm . . . a piece of rope or heavy string . . . say . . . ten feet worth. And bring me a sharp knife."

"Does this thing have a public address set?"

Matheson watched the ex-slave scurry off. *And that's what I'm counting on; that slaves don't usually ask—lack the self confidence to ask, really—too many questions of those who seem to be in authority.*

## Castle Honsvang, Province of Baya, 24 Muharram, 1538 AH (4 November, 2113)

The sergeant of the guard was neither a coward nor a fool. He'd been at the front of the battering ram, on the theory that fire, if any, would most likely come from inside once the door was down. When his men grasping the rear were cut down, he'd waited to see if any more fire came their way. When it didn't, he said a small prayer and walked out into the open, onto the blood-stained stones that marked where the enemy could fire, if he was still there.

*Apparently, he's not. Still, if I pull more men off the perimeter and some kind of aircraft shows up, as I expect it will, the enemy might be able to get away.*

*Fuck.*

## Highway 310, Northwest of ar-Rebchel, Province of Baya, 24 Muharram, 1538 AH (4 November, 2113)

The lights shone through the trees. Even before seeing the lights, though, Petra had heard the sound of the engines. With each meter closer, with each increase in the noise, with each glimpse of the headlights through the trees, the pounding in her chest grew.

For a moment she wanted to run into the little place inside herself where she'd hid during her rape, the same place that sheltered her during all the other abuses that had followed. And yet . . .

*John needs me not to hide . . . and so does Hans . . . and Ling . . . and those poor children down in the other castle waiting to be murdered. And perhaps even, too, my grandmother, long dead but with a bitterness and hatred in her heart for the masters who ruined her life . . . perhaps she, too, needs me not to hide but to fight.*

*And Besma? She'll never be able to strike on her own, now. I owe it to her to . . .*

Petra picked up a detonator in her left hand, wrapping her delicate fingers around it. With her right she flicked off the thick wire safety that would keep the squeeze lever from closing. Her right then took control of the other detonator. With her right thumb she flicked off the safety on that one.

"Wait . . . wait . . . wait," she whispered to herself as the column of trucks grew closer to the point she was supposed to set off the mines.

"Wait . . . wait . . . wait . . . " Petra scrunched down into her hole with just the top of her head and her eyes showing.

She misjudged it, just slightly. Or perhaps Hans had misjudged the proper spot to mark where she should squeeze the levers of the blasting machines. Whichever was the case, the mines detonated splendidly, all twelve of them, sending roughly eleven thousand half-ounce steel cylinders skipping gleefully along and across the road.

Men who had been sitting or standing up in the backs of trucks were scythed down with a collective moan, their organs and blood spilling across the truck beds and the road. Drivers and co-drivers, sitting up front, fared no better. As for the trucks, tires were blasted out, gas tanks were ruptured, lights and windscreens smashed. One truck, its front tires blasted off, went nose down to the roadbed, twisted to the right, and began a body-spilling roll that ended only went it struck a tree, broadside. Still another exploded in a fireball as the steel fragments not only spilled its liquid fuel but struck a spark off of the frame. Another of the five trucks struck went slightly off road until running head on into a tree. One, too close to a mine, was blown on its side. The last truck, with no living driver at the wheel, plowed into the truck before it.

Though there were men left alive in the kill zone, and even men left unhurt, there was no one left unshocked. It was a massacre.

Except, unfortunately for the lead truck. It had gotten *just* out of Hans' preplanned kill zone a quarter of a second before Petra finished squeezing the handle on the blasting machine.

The *corbasi* cursed himself even as he cursed at the driver to "Move, move, move, you fool!"

*Of course the filthy infidels had someone out to block the roads. I was an idiot. Idiot, idiot, IDIOT! And I've lost more than eighty percent of the men I brought with me. Shit. Should I go back and try to save any survivors? No . . . no. The important thing is still up ahead. And that ambush was thorough. There'll be a team of men there.*

"Faster, dolt!"

It was the worst sound she'd ever heard. Men screamed, wept, and begged for aid. And most of them, she suspected, were as blond-haired and blue-eyed as she was.

Petra covered her ears with her hands against the sound. In the process, a small device, no bigger than a hearing aid, was knocked to the dirt below.

She'd expected to take some satisfaction in striking a blow against the Caliphate. All she felt was a desire to vomit. *Their only fault was that someone took them young, just the way that someone took me. Poor boys. And yet, there's nothing I can do to help. Worse, if I don't get out of here John and Hans will finally come to the sedan I'm supposed to hide in, find that I'm not there, and come looking for me.*

*I'm sorry, boys,* she thought at the stricken men out on and around the smoky roadway. *I'm so sorry. But I can't help you.*

With that, Petra crawled out of the hole onto her belly, her submachine gun clutched tightly in one hand. She kept crawling, skinning hands, elbows and knees, and getting a little mud in the submachine gun, until the light from the burning truck was dim. Then she got up to a crouch, glanced all around like a hunted animal, turned to her right and ran.

She never noticed that she'd left her radio, ground by her own feet into the mud and dirt of the hole, behind.

# Flight Seven Nine Three, 24 Muharram, 1538 AH (4 November, 2113)

Perhaps a hundred people lived in the village below, crowded in behind a rickety and crude wooden fence. As the airship settled down just outside that fence, Matheson's voice came over the public address system.

"Infidels," he said. "Infidels, assemble to be counted and assessed."

Lee/Ling looked at Matheson as if to ask, *What the fuck does that mean?*

Matheson's answering glare said, *Who cares, so long as it sounds suitably impressive and threatening?*

Fearfully, the doors to the little shacks opened up and people began to step out.

"That's our cue," Matheson said to the newly armed and just liberated cargo slaves. "Follow me."

Each man, Matheson and the two slaves, had wrapped themselves in bed linen to simulate robes. On their heads they wore checked tablecloths held in place by short pieces of rope, tied in the back.

Matheson had his pistol strapped to the outside of the robes. The slaves carried his and Ling's submachine guns authoritatively.

Lee lowered the starboard side passenger ramp just in time for Matheson and his two escorts to debark. They walked over to the fence briskly. Forcing the gate open, Matheson demanded, "Who is the headman here?"

A stoop shouldered German advanced cautiously. At a distance of about six paces he got to one knee and answered, "I am, master."

Matheson swung his pistol in a broad arc, taking in the entire populace of the town. "Your people are needed for emergency work. Get them aboard. Now. On your head if so much as a single wretched soul escapes."

"But our crops—" the headman began to protest, pointing to where the airship had crushed the shoots in the fields.

"You will be compensated; that, or receive a tax remittance. Now cease your whining and get loaded. Bring your children. You will be gone too long for them to care for themselves. Food will be provided."

"Was that really necessary?" Lee asked, while awaiting word from Shanghai that the two hunting jets were gone.

Matheson shrugged. "If we'd tried to hold them there, some one of them might have doubted our official status and gone running to report. As is, they're convinced of it . . . even if some of them are still hiding in the village, they think they're hiding *from* the authorities. No chance then that they'll go *to* the authorities. Unfortunately—"

"Unfortunately, now we're stuck with them," Lee finished.

"Will that affect the flight?"

Lee shrugged Ling's shoulders. "Seven tons of emaciated Christians? I think *not*. It just seems unfair to risk them."

"To risk *what*?" Matheson sneered. "Lives lived in slavery aren't worth living. At least with us they'll have a chance at real life."

Lee/Ling stiffened. "Shanghai says the fighters are turning for home. Communications intercepts say they took off with the fuel in the tanks . . . and nobody had bothered to make sure the tanks were full when they parked them. How did these people ever get control of a continent?"

"Someone without the will to keep it gave it to them."

## Castle Noisvastei, Province of Baya, 24 Muharram, 1538 AH (4 November, 2113)

Latif went first to his office, just off of the entrance from where outside stairs rose above the mosqued courtyard, and entered the castle. The former gate guard of Honsvang followed as the brothel keeper waddled as fast as he could.

"There is a loudspeaker system," Latif told the janissary. "We haven't used it in years but—"

*We're fucked,* thought the janissary. No fool, he; he knew that if the thing hadn't been used in years then it probably couldn't be.

"—if the Almighty sees fit," Latif continued, "we can summon your comrades in a quarter of the time . . . a *tenth*!"

*We're* totally *fucked,* the janissary amended. *Still, one never knows. Perhaps, just this once, Allah will lend us his aid.*

Alas, it was not to be. Latif waddled briskly down the interior hallway, pushed open his office door, and sat down at the dusty desk holding the controls for the public address system. Pushing away some cobwebs he flicked a switch to power up the system.

And was rewarded with some crackling, and a fair bit of smoke pouring from the control box.

"Get your slaves to start knocking down doors," the janissary commanded. "And what do you have in this place for *arms*?"

That question spurred a thought. "Forget the slaves, except for those you send for arms," the janissary said. "I have a quicker way."

With that, the janissary left the office, trotted down the corridor to a spot near the center of the castle, took his rifle in hand and began firing the rifle methodically into the high ceiling. Janissaries began pouring out of rooms even as smashed plaster and bits of masonry poured down from above.

## Castle Honsvang, Province of Baya, 24 Muharram, 1538 AH (4 November, 2113)

It hadn't taken much to get the captive renegades to give him the combination to open the vault containing the virus. Hamilton had simply asked, "Now which of you does not want me to shoot him in the balls?" and they'd fallen over each other in their haste to volunteer.

The three renegades now sat, taped to chairs and facing away from each other. Their mouths were likewise taped. Hamilton and Hans had removed their shoes just before taping their legs to the chairs. For the nonce, Hans was occupied in the control room, watching the perimeter through the one closed-circuit television screen that was still useable, while keeping one hand poised near the switch to detonate diverse of the mines, if necessary. The slave boy liberated by Hamilton sat quietly nearby.

Not far away, in the lab, Hamilton spoke to the renegades while circling them slowly, not appreciably different from the way a shark might.

"I was taught this by Imperial Intelligence at Langley," Hamilton announced. "They called it 'musical chairs.' You'll see why in a moment.

"Here's rule number one: If any of you turn your heads to look at another, I will break one of your feet. If you understand, nod vigorously." Hamilton brandished a hammer he'd picked up in a closet off the main lab. If he hadn't found one, he'd have broken another chair to make a club for the purpose.

All three heads began bobbing like those of the children and whores the renegades had used and abused over the years.

"Very good. I'm now going to show you something. If it is part of the virus—of the virus project, rather—you will again, and without looking at each other, nod vigorously. If it is not, you will shake your heads to signify 'no.' If there is any disagreement I will smash one of each of your toes to bloody pulp. I'll then ask again. If there's any disagreement, I'll smash another. Again, in case it wasn't clear enough, if you try to consult, I'll break your foot. For starters. I can be a lot more imaginative if necessary.

"You see now why we call this musical chairs, gentlemen? It's because you *sing*."

Hamilton walked to a refrigerator and took a vial from it. He returned to the triangle of chairs and began to circle again, even more sharklike than before. "Is this part of the project?" he asked, with a calm all three scientists found utterly terrifying.

◇　◇　◇

Hans heard Matheson's voice in his earpiece. "What's the situation?"

"We've got the castle," he reported. "We've got the scientists. The kids are still locked up except for one who was outside. We've the keys for their pen. Hamilton is interrogating your renegade scientists. So far, except for a short-lived attempt to batter down the main door, the local security, what's left of it, is just concentrating on keeping us in. It makes me wonder if they haven't got something coming to keep you from evacuating us by air."

"They did, Hans," Matheson answered. "We ducked it. They might . . . probably will . . . be back in a couple of hours."

"A couple of hours will probably give us the time we need," Hans said. "Unless . . . oh, oh."

The *corbasi's* truck pulled up outside the gate and stopped. Armed janissaries began to spill off of the back, each man racing for cover behind whatever could be found. The colonel himself got out quickly, then hurried forward toward the gate until stopped by the sergeant of the guard.

"Sir, no closer," the sergeant said. "Whoever is in there set off the modular mine packs. The road's covered with the little bastards."

The colonel stopped immediately in his tracks, then crouched down low to present as small a target as possible. "What the fuck is going on in there? Where the hell is ibn Minden?"

"We think he's probably dead, sir—"

"Damn!"

"Yes, sir, he was a fine young officer. Anyway, there's been no sound of fighting for a while. The last was when one of them shot three of my men as we were trying to batter down the main gate. Whoever it was who shot them is probably up there still. But he can't see much of anything from the tower I think he's in."

"How are your men who were shot?" the *corbasi* asked.

"Dead, all three, sir."

"Dammit."

"I've sent for aid from the platoon that was on break up at the bordello. They should be along in half an hour or so, *inshallah*."

## Castle Noisvastei, Province of Baya, 24 Muharram, 1538 AH (4 November, 2113)

The still-cursing *baseski* formed the janissaries into four ranks, three of squads from the platoon and one of the company headquarters, in the reception hall above the castle's courtyard. Troops still filtered in, stumbling as they pulled up trousers and hopping as they tried to fit heavy boots to feet. None of them seemed actually *drunk*, the first sergeant was pleased to see.

Unfortunately, likewise were none of them armed, except for the one gate guard who had summoned them from their revels with sustained rifle fire. The *baseski* stifled a curse at fate.

Latif, hands clasped in worry before him, paced the hallway, likewise cursing. He'd sent two slaves, one to his own quarters and one to his guards, for whatever arms the castle might provide. He knew well enough how paltry these would be.

"Where are your stinking slaves with the weapons?" the first sergeant demanded, standing a couple of feet from the brothel keeper.

"Coming, *Baseski*, coming," Latif assured him.

Even as he spoke, the first of the slaves stumbled down the hall with an appreciable pile of weapons in his arms. He stopped next to the first sergeant and Latif. The sergeant took one glance at the pile and sneered.

"Shotguns? You have only shotguns in this place?"

"No, sir," the slave corrected. "There are two hunting rifles and also two automatic weapons."

"And where is the ammunition?"

The slave looked crestfallen. "You didn't *say* anything about ammunition," he said to Latif.

"Put down the weapons," the first sergeant ordered the slave. He then called out two names and ordered, "Go with this slave back to wherever he found these and bring all the ammunition there is to be had." The *baseski* shook his head with disgust. "Fuck! What does Allah have against me?"

## Castle Honsvang, Province of Baya, 24 Muharram, 1538 AH (4 November, 2113)

"God has turned his face from us," Hans whispered, as he watched the janissaries pour out of the back of the truck. "And what's happened to Petra? If these got through, are the others hunting her like an animal through the woods?"

He'd called for his baby sister many times on the communicator he'd snagged days before. She didn't answer. This ate away at him, causing a rise of nausea in his stomach. He was certain she'd have answered if she were still alive. He thought back to the day the tax collector had taken her away; felt anew—as fresh as if it were just yesterday—the humiliation of being unable to defend her.

Taking a last glance at the security board to ensure all the perimeter mines were still functioning, Hans checked his submachine gun, stood and walked out of the control room and toward the lab. He walked as if going to his death as, indeed, he felt he was and perhaps even should be.

"Boy," he said to Meara's toy. "Boy, follow me."

"Are there any other samples of this virus anywhere in the Caliphate?" Hamilton asked. He'd already placed every sample identified as virus or useful to creating the virus into the containment unit he'd been given back at Langley. Immediately, the three heads began shaking "no" in unison. From Meara flew tears, so hard did he shake his head.

Cleverly, Hamilton had asked mostly innocuous ques tions to begin. After a dozen of those, and three pulped toes each for the renegades, he'd *trained* them not to lie. From there he'd gone after the rest of the lab samples. Now his questions were oriented toward the spread of the danger.

"Bernie? Hamilton," he sent over his communicator. "High degree of confidence that there are no other samples anywhere in the Caliphate. How far out are you?"

"Maybe twenty-five minutes, John," Hamilton heard in his earpiece. "I'll send word to higher."

"It *would* be a good thing not to get nuked as we escape," Hamilton agreed, sardonically.

"Escape will be highly problematic," Hans announced, as he entered the lab.

At Hamilton's quizzical eyebrow the janissary added, "Petra didn't get them all. About twenty—at least that many—have joined the guards outside. Maybe worse, I suspect that the people I sent to the other castle are on the way back. We're about to be outnumbered about forty to one, and this time there's no surprise on our side."

"How truly good," Hamilton said.

# Interlude

Nuremberg, Federal Republic of Germany,
10 July, 2022

Gabi had done her best to raise Amal to be kind, sensitive, considerate of the feelings of others, tolerant, accepting . . . in all, a human monument to multicultural decency. She was also, and this had come rather harder to both mother and daughter, a good student. In her school, of course, she had friends of all stripes and persuasions; boyfriends, as well.

In fact, Amal had a *lot* of boyfriends. And why not? She was one of the, if not *the*, prettiest girls in the school. From her mother and father she'd garnered a meter, seventy-five in height . . . and she still had a couple of years to grow. Her baby-blond hair had darkened to a lustrous auburn not untypical of the province of Franconia. Her body was already that of a woman, enough so to set young boys to daydreaming in class, much to the detriment of their grades.

Between the height, the hair color, such features as she'd inherited from Mahmoud, her slightly darkened skin and light brown eyes, and her Arab given name, she could pass for an Arab or a Turk easily enough and was often taken for one. In the peculiar circumstances of Germany in the year 2021, this *could* be a problem.

"There's the slut now," whispered Abdul-Halim to his four friends, Taymullah, Mansur, Zahid, and Jabir. Of the five boys, two, Mansur and Jabir, were sons of German reverts to the faith. They were, if anything, more devout than the other three.

"Shameless," said Mansur. "The cunt should be veiled properly, her hair covered properly."

"It's the filthy Germans, polluting the world," added Zahid. "It will be a better place once it belongs to us, once the law of God replaces the nonsense they adhere to."

"And that is *our* job," said Taymullah, clutching a blanket in both hands. "As the imam said yesterday at the mosque, it is up to *us* to bring the word and the ways of Allah to this Godless place."

Amal was only human and thoroughly female. She enjoyed the admiration she received from people, men and women both, as she walked the street toward home.

Thus, it came as quite a shock to her, so much of a shock that she didn't even cry out, when five boys surrounded her, exclaimed, "This is our sister," dropped a blanket over her head and pulled her into a cellar.

Germans and German law had, long since, stopped defending Muslim women. Turks and Arabs, often terrified of retribution and having lost any faith that German law would protect them, simply turned away.

The "smiley," the cutting of a Muslim girl's face from one ear to the corner of her mouth in retribution for her dressing as a westerner, had been something of an urban legend in the early part of the century. Many had written and spoken of it yet no examples had ever been produced, no criminal cases had ever been launched.

Yet life can imitate art. Barraged with reports of the phenomenon, the urban legend had been adopted and turned into horrific reality. There were girls with "smileys," now, and in every corner of western Europe.

It was, after all, an excellent way to make a girl cover her face, in accordance with the *hadiths* and the *sunna.*

"You can't do this," Amal wept. "I'm not a Moslem. I've never been a Moslem."

"In the name of Allah we can do as we wish," insisted Abdul-Halim. "Besides, everyone is born a Moslem, that's what the imam says. It's just that some of them, like you, are apostate."

"You see," added Zahid, "there are only two kinds of women in the world. There are those who follow the law of God, and then there are sluts. Which are you?"

# CHAPTER EIGHTEEN

I will not blame Norwegian women for the rapes. But
Norwegian women must understand that we live in a
multi-cultural society and adapt themselves to it.
—Professor Unni Wikan, Oslo, Norway,
6 September 2001

## Flight Seven Nine Three, 24 Muharram, 1538 AH (4 November, 2113)

"There's the castle," said Lee/Ling, looking through
the airship's own night vision. "But . . . oh, oh . . . they've
got company and there's more on the way."

Matheson, who had more than a little time under fire
while praying for air support, answered, "Pity this thing
doesn't have a loaded bomb rack, or a 25mm pod."

The Chinese shrugged. "Nothing we can do about that. And the winds here are going to be a pure bitch when I try to hold her steady above the castle walls."

The black nodded, then keyed the earpiece he wore. "Hamilton, Hans, this is Matheson. Report."

"We've got problems here, Bernie. More when I can talk."

Matheson heard the *pffft . . . pffft . . . pffft* of a silenced submachine gun in his earpiece along with the louder ringing of bullets careening off stone.

## Castle Honsvang, Province of Baya, 24 Muharram, 1538 AH (4 November, 2113)

The *corbasi* had a simple, if inelegant, solution to the problem of the mines. He'd turned to the truck driver and asked, "Do you believe in Allah?" When the driver had, very nervously, answered in the affirmative, the colonel had said, "Go then, and drive your truck through these mines to clear a path."

Much to the surprise of both men the driver had survived the ordeal, though the truck was now considerably the worse for wear.

Through the broad, cleared path, the colonel and his remaining janissaries had poured, linking up with the dozen or so remaining to the sergeant of the guard. Not one for indecision, the colonel immediately detailed off ten men, five to each side, to watch the towers flanking the main entrance to the castle and keep anyone from shooting down at the gate. He then told the sergeant of the guard, "Get your men back on that battering ram. Make me a passage."

◇   ◇   ◇

Hamilton felt more than heard the steady pounding coming from somewhere upstairs. "They're at it again," he told Hans. "Watch these; I'm going up to block the door."

Hans nodded, causing his face to twist and his eyes to open wide with the pain. He looked at Meara, the pederast, and said, "I think it would be simpler just to kill them now."

All three of the renegade scientists began squealing their objections through the tape over their mouths.

Hamilton shook his head. "No, not just yet anyway. But if I can't stop the people at the gate, kill these and then *thoroughly* destroy everything in lab. Then put all the virus containers into the crematorium and toast it."

"What about the kids?" Hans asked.

"I'll leave that to you and your conscience," Hamilton answered, glancing at Hans' weapon.

"We're going to lose, aren't we?" Hans asked.

"I don't know. I think so."


"Do you think you can use a rifle?" Matheson asked of Retief.

"Yes, of course. I did my military service."

"Good. Where's the best place to shoot from?"

"From the airship? Out either port or starboard ramp."

"Fine. We use port. Come with me. Lee? Take us over the group around the castle but put them between us and the walls, with the port side facing the castle."

"How low do you want me to go?" Lee/Ling asked.

"How big are your balls?"

"Well, at the moment, they don't exist," the pilot answered. "But you know, even if I were here in my own body . . . well, I'm only Chinese. Small penis. Not like you Americans . . . *BIIIGGG* penis," he mocked.

"Just take us in as low as you dare."

That was more serious. "Roger."

"Can you bring us in quietly?" Matheson asked.

"With all the firing down there, I hardly need to," the pilot answered.

"Yeah, come in quietly anyway. Let me know when we're broadside. And give me those goggles; you don't need them."

"Take them," the pilot said.

*Asshole,* Ling whispered mentally. *That's my body you're taking risks with.*

*You knew it was dangerous when you volunteered,* Lee answered.

*I didn't volunteer. I was bred, chipped, and sold.*

*We all have these little issues,* Lee answered.

Matheson and Retief crouched to either side of the ramp hatchway. Matheson still clutched his submachine gun while Retief held an assault rifle taken from one of the freed slaves. Retief wore the goggles taken from Ling's face.

"How's the armor on this thing?" Matheson asked.

"Armor?" Retief laughed. "What fucking armor?"

"Silly me. Open the hatch."

Retief's hand reached up to a button set into the wall. He pressed it, causing the hatch to slide open with a *whoosh*. Cold air streamed in through the opening.

"Hamilton? Matheson."

◊   ◊   ◊

Hamilton eased the muzzle of his weapon out a window, hoping like hell that return fire wouldn't destroy his hands. He loosed a long, and almost certainly futile burst at the landing below. There was shouting and a single man cried out.

*Sometimes the law of averages works in your favor,* Hamilton thought.

"Hamilton? Matheson."

"I'm a little busy right now, Bernie," Hamilton answered, while dropping an empty magazine and inserting a fresh one.

"Yes, I can see. You're about to get a little, very temporary, relief. Look up."

The *corbasi* looked up and behind him. He wasn't sure why he did so, then or ever. He was, however, very glad that he had. At first, his mind refused to register the great, raylike shape that swung across the darkened sky without a sound. It was only when he saw the muzzle flashes that the threat registered.

"Duuuckk!"

"We're not hitting *shit!*" Matheson cursed.

This wasn't strictly true. Both men had fired into the covered alcove over the castle's main entrance. Normally, they couldn't have really expected to hit anything much. The stone walls of the alcove, however, caused bullets to ricochet. Several janissaries went down from these, even though only one was hit by a nonricocheting bullet.

Hamilton heard and answered. "I think you are . . . or did . . . or something. They've stopped trying to break through the gate anyway."

"If you say so. We'll be back. I'm going to try to buy you a little time from the people coming from the other castle."

"The other castle?" Hamilton asked. "Fuck! How close are they?"

"Too."

"Not too much further, boys," Sig called out to encourage the flagging spirits of men dragged from Paradise and thrust without warning into something they fully expected to resemble Hell. Worse, they expected to be thrust into Hell without anything so useful as a fire extinguisher . . . or even an antacid tablet. They were hanging back, as if reluctant. This was something Sig had rarely seen in janissaries.

About half of them were armed with something that could throw a bullet . . . in theory . . . if they'd had a chance to clean them . . . which they hadn't. For those, they had a totally inadequate supply of ammunition for everything except the four shotguns the brothel had held. The other half were armed with a mix of knives, swords, spears, whatever could be found that might be useful.

That, too, added to their already considerable demoralization. Despite his intentions, Sig's encouragement only made it worse.

Thus, when the airship passed to one side, and began to open fire, and the janissaries could barely return fire, half of them (and mostly the half with cutting implements) bolted into the woods.

"Come back, you stinking cowards," Sig screamed. "Back here, you filth," the *baseski* demanded. The fleeing troops paid them no mind.

"Well, Top," Sig said. "At least the ones we have left are good soldiers and true. Better those than a rabble."

The *baseski,* who was more observant than the armorer, disagreed. "No, the difference was that those who ran, ran because they felt outclassed and useless. But in running, they also took with them half the spirit, such as it was, of those who remained."

"Hans? Hamilton? Matheson. I think we delayed reinforcement of the garrison by a bit. But we've got a decision to make and I can't make it."

"What decision, Bernie?" Hamilton asked.

"I can have the airship continue to give you the little bit of fire support we have to give. You can't load like that. Or I can have the pilot bring us to the castle itself and you can begin to load. But—"

"But if you do that, the ship's going to be vulnerable while we load," Hans said.

"Worse than that," Hamilton added. "If I stay here watching the gate, I can keep them out even if they manage to batter it down. Or if not quite keep them out, keep them from rushing in and overwhelming us. But if I stay here, you can't hope to load everything, get the kids out, and guard the renegades."

"Well, as far as that goes," Matheson said, "I've got a considerable loading party here aboard the airship, if we have to use them."

Hamilton thought about that for a minute, then said, "Hans, be sure to get Petra where we told her to meet us. Bernie, bring the airship in and start to load."

The *corbasi's* first thought, when he saw the airship coming back, was that they intended to attack his men again. "Take cover!" he shouted.

He was surprised, then, when the ship continued on its way, circling the castle to the right, without firing so much as a single burst.

*Odd, that,* the colonel thought. *Or maybe not so odd. Maybe—no, certainly—that's their way out.*

He pointed in turn at the ten men he'd positioned to cover the twin towers flanking the gate. "You lot! Follow me!"

One of the janissaries shook his head, thinking, *I've had this shit up to here.*


The cross section of the airship was enormous. In these winds, it took a pilot of Lee's skill and experience to put it in position hard by the castle walls and hold it there. Even then, it was all he could do.

"Hurry, Yankee," the pilot said to Matheson. "We get a sudden gust from the wrong direction and we're paste."

"Roger," Matheson agreed. "Retief, you with me?"

The Boer nodded. "And otherwise miss the chance to do something absolutely right for once in my life? Let's go."

The ex-slaves, some of them armed from the airship's small armory and still others from the galley, followed Matheson down to the hold where the kidnapped Germans huddled in terror.

*Ask them to volunteer to fight?* Matheson wondered. *No . . . I wish but . . . no. Look at their faces, every one a mask writ in terror. I can use them for labor, but they're too beaten down and degraded to actually stand on their own feet. And this was a people that more than once made the world tremble? It's sad.*

Matheson still wore his makeshift robes and headdress. He was counting on the Germans being too terrified to notice just how threadbare his disguise was. He shouted, "You! You *Nazrani* filth. On your feet, all you men and the grown women, too." He waited a few moments for the captives to spring erect and ordered, "Now follow me."

Matheson, Retief and the cargo slaves led the Germans upward to the passenger deck. There, Retief opened the hatch and extruded the boarding ramp. Beneath the power buttons there was a small wheel coming from a maneuverable ball, an auxiliary emergency control, that he used to position the ramp on the pseudo battlements next to a tower. A collective moan escaped from the Germans when they realized that their new, temporary master intended to lead them out onto the pitching ramp and into the blackness.

"Stay here to make sure none of them escape," Matheson shouted to Retief. To the German serfs he repeated, "Follow me."

The *corbasi* and the ten men with him emerged around the corner of the castle. The colonel stopped in shock. The airship—it had to be some new technology from the infidels' pact with Satan to have penetrated so far into the Caliphate—was hovering there. Worse, so the colonel could see by the dim light, the ship was disgorging dozens, scores of soldiers.

*It must be a company of their Rangers*, he thought. *There's no hope of taking back the castle now, not with the few men I have left. And it will be hard indeed to knock down that airship. The thing must be armored to the gills. And I'm sure their Rangers are.*

*Still, I must try.*

He gave his men the order, "Try to hit the pilot or the engines."

◊    ◊    ◊

Gay he might have been; a sissy Lee was not. He held steady even as the first burst of fire passed through the deck of the cockpit and exited the ceiling above. Bits of plastic and insulation flew about the cockpit.

*Yeah, sure. You can be brave as Hell. It's easy for you to be brave and calm,* Ling thought, *but it's my body that's going to be shot, not yours.*

*Woman,* he sent back. *If it makes you feel any better, above all if it will get you to shut up, you can have my body if this one is killed.*

*Why would you do that?* she asked suspiciously. *Have they some way to preserve your consciousness and put it in a grown body?*

*No, they don't. As to why . . . because I really did volunteer, and you did not.*

*Oh. Look . . . I'm sor—*

*Just shut up and let me do my job.*

"Nice job, Hans," Matheson said as his gaze took in the three captive and bound scientists, the containment unit holding the virus, and the computers all stacked on a table. He turned to the chief of the villagers he'd seized, pointed toward the captives and ordered, "Take these men onto the airship. Now."

The village headman simply told six of the men in his party to do so. In an instant, so used to obedience were these Germans, the three scientists were being bodily carried, still taped to their chairs, up the winding staircase that led to the battlements above.

"These things, too," Matheson said, pointing at the computers and the cold storage unit containing the virus samples. "Get them onto the airship."

◇    ◇    ◇

Retief, with several armed ex-slaves still with him, saw
the janissaries down below open fire on the airship. *Only
a matter of time,* he thought, *until one of them gets lucky
and hits the pilot. Then we're all fucked. The cargo crew
can't shoot . . . probably never held a rifle before last
night. But I can shoot and they can draw fire.*

"On the battlements," he ordered the cargo boys.
"We've one chance to get away and that chance is the
airship! Try to aim, as best you can. Shoot slowly. I'll be
more deliberate."

His pistol was useless, of course. At this range the
*corbasi* could hit the airship . . . maybe . . . if Allah *really*
willed it. He didn't even bother. Nor was there any cover
to speak of. Thus, when the first burst of fire came from
above, the colonel's instincts, and those of his men, were
to go back around the corner of the castle. Under the
circumstances, men tend to follow their instincts.

Children will instinctively follow an adult. Even so,
these children had learned, if anything, never to trust an
adult who wasn't a parent. Thus, when Hans showed up
at the gate to their pen, opened it and said, in German,
"Follow me," the kids wouldn't. That none of them spoke
a word of German didn't help.

The little boy, Meara's play toy, spoke up, saying, in
his own tongue, "This is a good man. He saved me from
the man who used me. Follow him."

At first reluctant, then with growing willingness and
speed, the children massed at the exit, creating a traffic
jam that Hans was only able to sort out by physically
picking them up and moving them. In a short time,

though each second seemed to Hans to last hours, he had them outside in a loose gaggle. With his hands, Hans gestured for them to follow.

Much like the Pied Piper, albeit sans fife, Hans led the boys and girls out of their pen, past the crematorium, into the lab and to the exit that led to the tower stairs. From there, he selected a couple of older children, perhaps ten or twelve years old, he thought, and pointed upwards. He prodded the other children to follow until he'd established that as a natural direction of flow. He hoped that someone up top would meet them and guide them onto the airship. If not, Matheson would pick them up on his way out. For himself, he had other things to do.

*I was afraid of this,* Dr. Richter sent to Matheson.
*Afraid of what, Doc?*
*If we were running a bio war lab—and, of course, we are—we would have a failsafe, something to ensure the complete sterilization of the lab in seconds in the event of a failure of containment. I see nothing here to indicate that they've got that here—no pipes, no vents, no fixed neutralization agent dispersers, nothing.*

*How truly good,* Matheson sent back.
*No, Agent Matheson, it is not.*
*Do they send biological scientists to some special course to destroy, or to some surgical procedure to remove, their sense of humor, Doc? I know it's not good. What can we do?*
*Wait. Let me think.*

Retief scanned fearfully through the crenellations of the battlement. *I think maybe they've backed off for a while. I can't imagine why, though. All we've got is myself and some slaves who can't shoot. And these are janissaries, first-class troops. It's not like them to run unless they think they absolutely have to.*

"Give me your rifle," the *corbasi* demanded of a janissary cowering with him behind the castle's corner.

"Here, sir," the soldier said as he, more thankfully than not, passed over the weapon.

The colonel took it and, being very careful to expose no part of his body he didn't need to, eased the thing around the corner. When no return fire came he risked showing a bit more. When he had the forward half the airship in his field of view, he stopped. Moreover, for the first time he had the chance to look at the thing more or less calmly and carefully. He saw, however dimly, the South African markings on the thing. This didn't surprise him as the Americans, and he was sure they were Americans, wouldn't stop to scruple over using a false flag.

*Where would the cockpit be?* he wondered. *We put out a lot of fire initially and, so far as I can tell, apparently didn't hit anything. No matter. No doubt everything important is armored or has a redundant back up. What to shoot; what to shoot? The gas cells? I know this kind of airship, slightly. It gets a good chunk of its lift from its shape, not its buoyancy. And it has vertical thrusters. But it doesn't get all of its lift from those. If I puncture enough gas cells, it will start to fall.*

Slowly, adjusting his point of aim very deliberately between shots, the *corbasi* began shooting out the gas cells.

In the cockpit, Lee/Ling saw red lights start to appear on the control panel.

*How truly fucking good,* the pilot cursed, even as he increased power to the vertical thrusters and began to release more helium into the punctured gas cells.

"Matheson, this is Lee," the pilot sent over the communicator attached to his ear. "We've got a problem and you're going to have to hurry."

*Shit, Doc,* Matheson sent, *you've got to come up with something quick. We've not much time left before the airship either has to leave or it won't be able to.*

*Be calm, Agent Matheson, I've had to do some stubby pencil drill.*

*For what?*

*For whether the one source of massive heat we've got is up to the job.*

*What source?* Matheson asked.

*The crematorium,* Richter answered. *It's got its own fuel supply and oxygen source. It has to have. We can use it to increase the temperature of the lab.*

*You mean as in leave the door open and turn on the flame?*

*Precisely.*

*What if it has a fail safe so it won't fire up if the door is open?*

*Silly question, Agent Matheson. If it has a fail safe you break it.*

The nausea and the stumble-causing disconnect between eyes and brain were still pretty bad. And moving quickly only made it worse. Twice on the way to Hamilton's position Hans had to stop to vomit. Once he nearly fell over. Even so, Hans eventually clattered up the twisting stairs to Hamilton's position. He was nearly shot for his trouble.

"Jesus *Christ*, Hans! For God's sake announce yourself."

Exhaling forcefully—for, immediate stress-wise, the only thing worse than being shot is coming close to shooting a friend—Hamilton lowered his weapon.

"Sorry, John," Hans gasped, putting a defensive hand out. "I'm a little disoriented."

"Never mind," Hamilton conceded. "What's going on back there?"

"The children are freed. I don't know if they're aboard the airship yet. The airship's sinking. We've not much time."

At about the same time the janissary sergeant of the guard decided he should get back to the serious business of breaking down the gate. He opted to do it in the same way the colonel had, assigning men to keep the windows of the towers covered. The sound of the pounding down below quickly changed in quality, too—the earlier battering must have had some effect. The door was clearly weakening.

"I think it's about to give," Hamilton said.

"Yes," Hans agreed. "And that's why you have to go back, to get Petra, if she's still alive. I can hold the fort here. As long as I'm lying down and not moving, I can shoot."

Hamilton hesitated. "What about Ling?" he asked, cocking his head slightly.

Hans sighed. "Ling is important to me, yes. I might even be important to her. But it's mostly important that she be freed, if she can be freed, and have a decent life. This, you and your people can give her better than I can. And for Petra . . . you're her future. I'm only her past."

Hamilton stood for a moment in indecision. He called for Matheson, "Bernie, how much longer do we have?"

"Not much, John. And when you and Hans head to the airship, don't come by the lab; take the upper passages. It's going to be very warm down here."

"Roger," Hamilton answered. "Do we have a few minutes anyway?"

"That much, sure."

Hamilton reached out a fraternal hand to Hans' shoulder. "There's some solid furniture down below. If you're going to stay here, let's make you a fighting position facing the gate that can take a hit."

Nobody was hit racing through the cleared path in the minefields facing the castle's main gate. For this beneficence, Sig and the *baseski* both said a special prayer of thanks.

"Sergeant of the Guard!" the first sergeant bellowed as he passed through the checkpoint and took a crouch behind a concrete barrier.

"Over here, Top," the sergeant answered from his position in the alcove. The sergeant had to shout to be heard over the pounding of the battering ram. "We're almost through."

# Interlude

Nuremberg, Federal Republic of Germany,
10 July, 2022

The cellar was dark and dank and dreary. Cobwebs hung from the ceiling and the pipes and draped along the walls. There was an old moldy mattress on the floor, Amal saw.

"By the time we're through with you, you'll be glad to don the veil, slut," Zahid said, confidently, to Amal. The boy moved a small, silvery pocket knife in front of the terrified girl's eyes.

"Don't hurt me," she pleaded. "Please don't hurt me."

"We're not going to hurt you much," said Zahid. "We're just going to cut you from your ear to your mouth."

"That," agreed Taymullah, "or you can admit you're just a slut and let us all fuck you. Your choice."

That was no better a choice than being cut. Again, tears pouring down her face, Amal sobbed, "Please don't hurt me. I'll wear a veil. I promise."

"Your word's no good, slut," Zahid said. "Only way we can be sure you'll follow the law is if we cut you. Then you'll be too ashamed to show your whore's face."

"DON'T HURT ME!"

"We have no choice."

"I'll do anything you want; just don't hurt me," the girl begged, head hanging in hopeless and helpless shame.

Once more, Zahid flashed his knife by her eyes and then moved it as if to slash her cheek. He didn't cut her though. Instead, he brought the knife down to her shirt and began to cut it away.

The police car that took Gabi to the hospital didn't flash its lights or blast its siren. Instead, it went only as fast as the traffic would bear. It could have used its sirens and lights of course, but the woman sitting in back was so nearly hysterical that the two policemen up front thought that they'd only make things worse.

"What happened? What happened? What happened?" Gabi kept asking. Neither cop had an answer. They knew the woman's daughter had been hurt and was in the hospital, but that was all they knew . . . about the daughter. The policemen recognized well enough the artist woman who'd been so prominent in the papers and on television a couple of years prior.

One of the policemen helped Gabi to walk on unsteady knees from the patrol car into the emergency room. Surprisingly, a doctor and another policemen, this one in mufti, met them near the door. He led them to a small alcove, not too private but as good as could be procured on the spot.

"Your daughter was attacked," the doctor said, even before Gabi could ask a question. "She's hurt . . . badly, I'm afraid. And, yes, she was raped."

Gabi sank into herself, weeping and cringing at the thought of her sweet and innocent baby attacked by animals.

"We don't know who did it," the plainclothes policemen added. "She was in a neighborhood where this sort of thing happens a lot. Usually they leave German girls alone unless the girls have some connection with the Muslims."

Gabi said, between sobs, "My daughter . . . had an . . . Arab . . . father."

"That might explain it," the policeman agreed, "assuming she looked the part."

Gabi swallowed, forced herself to be calm, and asked, "There's more, isn't there?"

"Yes." The policeman looked at the doctor as if begging him to take this burden.

Hesitantly, the doctor said, "Ms. Von Minden . . . after they raped her . . . maybe before . . . maybe even during . . . they beat her pretty badly. She has several broken ribs and a broken arm. She's concussed. One knee is dislocated."

At each addition to the injuries Gabi shuddered as if struck. She looked at the doctor through her tears. "There's more, isn't there?"

The policemen put his finger to his cheek and drew a line down to the corner of his mouth. "It's a Moslem thing," he said. "They slashed her face open so she'll have to wear a veil for the rest of her life."

Gabi stood. Her fists clenched in front of her face. She felt feelings she should never have felt, thought thoughts she should never have had. But this was no abstract principle. This was her *daughter*, her flesh and blood, who had been hurt. She began to speak, coherently at first and then rising to a scream. "We should have gassed them . . . we should have gassed them . . . we should have gassed them . . . WE SHOULD HAVE GASSED THEM!"

# CHAPTER NINETEEN

But when it comes to this disaster, who started it? In his literature, writer al-Rafee says, "If the woman is in her boudoir, in her house and if she's wearing the veil and if she shows modesty, disasters don't happen."

—Sheik Taj Din Al Hilaly

an-Nessang, Province of Baya, 24 Muharram, 1538 AH (4 November, 2113)

Cursing herself for a fool, Petra ran toward the edge of the town. *I'm an idiot, an idiot, an* idiot! *I've lost my damned communicator and now Hans and John are both probably frantic.*

She stopped where the woods ended, looking right and left for any sign of people, especially policemen or janissaries. She saw none. Heart pounding, she released the folds of the burka she'd gathered up so she could run through the woods. She looked again for signs of people. Seeing none, and still gripping her submachine gun, she sprinted—as best she could, given the constraints of the burka—across the frozen field and for the shadows of the town. That few towns in Germany had streetlights anymore, an-Nessang not being among those that did, helped.

Breathless, Petra slammed herself against a wall and then crouched down, much like a feral animal. She listened for the sound of footsteps for a while and, after hearing none, stood and tucked her submachine gun in the folds of her burka. Even there, her fingers remained wrapped around the pistol grip of the weapon.

Trying to exude a confidence, a sense of right-to-be-there, that she did not feel, Petra walked out from the shadows in the direction of the car where she was to meet Hans or John. Her footsteps were brisk, her pace steady. A lone policeman, leaning against a lamppost, shivering and in the process of nodding off, nodded to her form instead. Politely, she nodded back and continued on her way.

Petra, raised first in a Christian town and then in a brothel, didn't know that any show of friendliness was overwhelmingly likely to be misunderstood as a show of interest, an invitation. The policeman, cognizant of his power and authority, cold and thinking perhaps of getting much warmer, followed her.

## Castle Honsvang, Province of Baya,
## 24 Muharram, 1538 AH (4 November, 2113)

The situation was about to get hot. Still, Hans crouched behind the heavy oaken table, reinforced by chairs and trunks and whatever was to hand, that he and Hamilton had set up to cover the gate once it fell off of its hinges or was otherwise smashed through. He wasn't too worried about a direct hit. True, the oak, even at two inches thick, wasn't up to warding off rifle fire. But the trunks and other pieces in front of and behind the oak should have been enough.

A direct hit wasn't going to be the only problem, though. The open foyer in which he hid was of stone. That stone would cause ricochets. And against those, Hans had no protection at all but his officer class torso armor.

He didn't expect a lot of protection from it but, even so, Hans took the crucifix from under his uniform and hung it plainly on the outside.

*Bam . . . bam . . . bam*, the ram battered at the gate. Hans heard a sound of wood cracking and splintering. *Bam . . . bam . . . crrraackckck* and the left-hand side of the gate popped open, followed by the right.

Hans didn't hesitate. As soon as the wooden gate was out of the way he opened fire, holding the trigger down until bolt locked to rear on an empty magazine. In the confined space of the alcove before the gate, perhaps no more than ten feet by twelve, Hans put just over one bullet into every two square feet. The half dozen janissaries holding the ram were cut down like harvested wheat. Except that wheat doesn't bleed or scream.

◊   ◊   ◊

"Goddammit, Matheson!" the pilot screamed. "I'm losing lifting gas like you wouldn't fucking believe and if you don't get your ass up and I'm leaving without you!"

"Calm down, Lee, I'm on my way," the black answered, as he prepared to close the door from the lab to the staircase. Already, with every burner in the crematorium on full blast, the temperature in the lab was inimical to human life. How high it would get neither Matheson nor Richter could be certain.

The fail safe proved to be a nonconcern. If the crematorium had such, it certainly didn't work. Matheson suspected that the burners worked only because they had no moving parts.

"Lee," Matheson asked, "are the kids loaded?"

"How the fuck do I know? My buoyancy is dropping so fast I can't even tell you what my weight is. Maybe they're on; maybe they're not."

"Roger. I'm on my way." Matheson hurried up the stone steps several flights before stumbling over a child who cried out.

"Shit. Lee, don't go anywhere. The kids are not, repeat not, loaded."

"Jesus H. Christ," said Lee.

"I'm getting them on their feet now. Just hold on."

"I'm trying to hold on, you dumb son of a bitch. I just can't guarantee I'll be . . . ah shit."

"What? What is it?" Matheson asked.

"Lost another gas cell. You've *got* to hurry."

"On your feet, children," Matheson shouted in Afrikaans, a language most of the boys and girls had at least some familiarity with. "Now up the steps."

"We tried, *baas*," one of the girls answered. "The way is blocked by the rest of us."

The agent thought about that for all of a second and a half before countermanding his previous order. "Lay down, kids. I'm going to have to walk over you."

Being walked all over was something, of course, that slave children were used to.

## an-Nessang, Province of Baya, 24 Muharram, 1538 AH (4 November, 2113)

Petra walked as fast as she could towards the car. Unfortunately, with the constraints of the burka, she couldn't outpace the pursuing policeman.

*Maybe I should just suck him off and send him on his way*, she thought. *That would be quickest and simplest. That's probably what Ling would do.*

*No*, argued another voice, though that voice was still her own. *You've spent your whole life until this evening submitting. Enough is enough. Girl, as your great-grandmother wrote in her journal, at the end there comes a time when you have to fight or it will be too late.*

"Fine then," Petra whispered to herself, her fingers reaching down to caress the journal, tucked into a belt underneath her burka. "I'll fight."

She slowed her pace and began to glance from side to side, looking for a deserted alley. After half a minute she came upon one, off to her right, with no lights showing. She turned down it. Behind her, the policeman's footsteps picked up as he closed for the kill . . .

## Castle Honsvang, Province of Baya, 24 Muharram, 1538 AH (4 November, 2113)

After throwing his weight against the door repeatedly, Matheson emerged onto the bleeding body of one of the former cargo slaves. The top of the man's head had been blown off and the body had been blocking the exit.

"Retief!" he bellowed.

"Here, Bernie," the South African answered.

"What the . . . never mind, you didn't have a communicator. But why didn't you move the body out from the door?"

"I figured the kids were safer down there than they'd be out here," Retief answered.

"Oh. Fair enough. But we've got to get them loaded *now*."

"Fine, but there's one little problem. The janissaries can bring the loading ramp under fire and I haven't been able to permanently drive them back."

"From where?" Matheson asked.

"Corner of the castle where we can't see but they can see the ramp and the airship."

"Really? Well . . . " Matheson took off at a sprint, or as much of one as his bad leg would permit, across the ramp. No bullets came in until he was nearly across, and those missed.

He threw himself onto the deck of the passenger compartment and then swung his body around to face back towards the hatch. He dropped his night vision goggles back over his face. Then, slithering like a snake up to the hatch, he paused to make last minute check of his submachine gun. Satisfied, he whispered a prayer, and then poked weapon and head around the edge of the hatch.

Just as a janissary exposed himself to engage the airship again, Matheson fired.

## an-Nessang, Province of Baya, 24 Muharram, 1538 AH (4 November, 2113)

Petra stood with her back to a wall. The alleyway was a dead end. A dozen feet before her, the policeman approached with a gleam in his eye that even the dim light could not conceal.

"I knew you would be waiting for me," the policeman said. "I could tell by the way you nodded."

"Yesss," Petra answered, her voice a throaty purr. "I knew you would follow."

Petra leaned her back against the wall, and spread her legs slightly apart in invitation. So excited and incited was the man that he began to fumble with his belt even as he walked forward.

When Petra judged he was close enough that even *she* could be certain not to miss, she raised the submachine gun, pointed it at his chest, and fired.

## Castle Honsvang, Province of Baya, 24 Muharram, 1538 AH (4 November, 2113)

Matheson saw the janissary spin and fall, and the rifle he bore go flying. His night vision was enhanced as much by the chip in his head as the goggles on his face. With those, he turned his head to look across the ramp to where Retief stood back from the wall with his arm across the door that led to the children.

"Send 'em now, Retief," Matheson shouted. "Send 'em *fast*!"

"You must hurry, children; do you understand?" Retief asked of the group nearest him. "You must hurry and run and get aboard and then get out of the way. Don't look down. Don't fear the pitching and swaying of the ramp. Don't pay attention if anyone else is hurt or falls off.

"Are you ready?"

Somberly, the children nearest him nodded, or said, "Yes," or even shouted it.

"Then go, go, GO!"

Off they flew, the foremost, as fast as tiny legs would carry them. Ahead the ramp bucked and twisted. Even so they ran for it. At the edge of the ramp two of the former cargo slaves waited. These helped the children, largely by shoving, or picking them up, or even throwing them onto the ramp as circumstances dictated.

Matheson stood now, on the airship's end of the ramp, encouraging the children on with shouts and open arms. Mentally, he did his best to keep count as the children passed: "One eighty-six . . . one eighty-seven . . . " He still had his submachine gun in his hand. Which helped him not at all when one of the janissaries below, perhaps enraged at his colonel's death (for it *was* the *corbasi* whom the agent had shot down), stepped out into the open and fired.

Hamilton had arrived at the tail end of the mass of children just as the gaggle began to move forward. He couldn't have them lie down, as Matheson had, to allow himself to pass, not if they were to have a chance to escape. Thus, he had to wait until the line moved ahead and the last children exited the door before he was able to get onto the battlemented roof.

Which he did just in time to see Matheson cut down.

"Bastards," Hamilton said. "Fucking bastards. Retief, get yourself and the cargo boys aboard. Now."

Hamilton waited until they were moving across the ramp and then mounted it himself. He walked halfway out, his lower body covered by the ramp's low sidewalls and his upper torso by the body armor provided by Hans. There he stood, stock still, and waited for a janissary to show himself. When the janissary did, Hamilton whispered, "This is for Bernie, you bastard," and shot the man down.

Then Hamilton turned towards the hatchway and walked aboard.

As he entered the ship, he looked down at Matheson's body and knelt beside it. Retief was already retracting the ramp and closing the hatchway.

Quite to Hamilton's surprise, the black man opened his eyes and said, "That was all very touching, to be sure, *baas*, but I'm not quite dead yet. And, if you can manage to stop this red shit that's leaking out of me, I probably won't be."

"You're a bastard, Matheson, you know that?"

"I didn't know you cared."

The pilot heard in his ear, "Take off now." He didn't have to be told twice. Applying full power to his vertical thrusters, he began to move the ship up and out from the castle walls.

*Where's Hans?* Ling asked, in his mind.

*How the fuck do I know, woman. He's not my responsibility.*

*I asked you politely*, Ling said. *Now tell me where Hans is.*

*Goddammit, fuck off. I'm busy.*

The pilot reached for the control to add gas to the central and main lifting cell. Rather, he *wanted* to do so but discovered that he couldn't move his arm.

*For the last time, where's Hans?*

◇   ◇   ◇

"She *what*?" Hamilton asked incredulously.

"She wants to know what happened to Hans. Who the fuck is Hans?" the pilot asked in Ling's voice. "If I don't come up with a good answer, she's not going to let me fly this airship. She's got me frozen. Look, I've got barely the horses to get up to Switzerland. Will you please tell her."

Listening in on the circuit, Hans asked, "Ling . . . can you hear me?"

"She can hear you . . . if you're Hans," the pilot answered.

"Then listen carefully," the man said. "I want you to release the pilot. It's important to me."

"Okay . . . she's unfrozen me."

"Ling . . . honey," Hans' voice continued. "Someone had to stay behind. I chose me . . . "

"Aiaiaiai!" the pilot screamed, then said aloud, "Goddammit, woman, I *felt* that."

"Ling . . . I chose me for a lot of good reasons. I'm sorry . . . . more than I can say. They're getting ready to rush me now. I have to go. I love you."

The last Ling heard was the *pffft . . . pffft . . . pffft* of Hans' submachine gun.

Down below, below the airship and even below Hans, the crematorium was fed from two tanks, each containing a mix of LPG, liquid petroleum gas, and oxygen. These tanks, for ease of installation, had been placed under the floor of the lab. That floor was growing very, very hot.

In those tanks under the floor, the oxygen-LPG mix was likewise growing very, very hot. Indeed, it was beginning to boil. This boiling was forcing more and more of the gas out through the crematorium's nozzles, lowering the liquid volume in the tanks and increasing the pressure on those tanks.

*For one minute give me control*, Ling demanded.

*Too dangerous*, Lee answered. *Besides, I don't know how to cede partial control. I don't know how you were able to freeze my limbs and still let me talk.*

*Neither do I. So what? Give me control. Please*, she begged. *Weren't you ever in love?*

*That's a low blow . . . Oh, all RIGHT! I wish there were some fucking way to give you only vocal control. But if there is, I don't know it. And do try to keep your hands steady on the controls, eh?*

Hans' hands and gaze were steady, steadier than anyone had a right to expect, given that the fire of his former soldiers was chipping away at the edges of the oaken table and wearing at its surface. Already bullets had made their way through, only to be stopped by his torso armor. Even if stopped, they hurt. Eventually—and probably very soon—a bullet would find its way to an uncovered spot. After that? Well . . . *After that I die.*

They were in the foyer with him now, he knew. More than a dozen but less than a score. *And I don't have enough ammunition left to deal with that number if they all lined up and just let me shoot them.*

Unconsciously, Hans reached for the dagger at his side and loosened the retaining strap. If he had to die—and he did, and was even "comfortable" with the idea—it wouldn't be without a weapon in his hand.

He heard in his earpiece, "Hans, this is Ling, not the pilot. He won't let me talk for long. But I wanted you to know that in all my life I never loved anyone but you and your sister. And you two I loved with all my heart. Goodbye."

Hans smiled, a last smile. *That* was warming. He then stood, fired once, twice, and a third time. His vision had narrowed under the stress. Whether he actually hit anyone he didn't know and, perhaps, at that point, didn't much care. He flung the empty submachine gun at a janissary aiming his weapon at him, causing the janissary to duck. Hans then pulled the dagger from its sheath, screamed *"Deus vult!"*— God wills it—and charged like a berserker, a force of nature in himself, right over the table.

Down in the lab the stone walls began to glow. Mortar, old and solid, likewise crumbled from in between set stones. Under the floor, the twin tanks of oxygenated LPG boiled and frothed furiously, albeit unseen. In the crematorium, the flames jutting from the burners were like flamethrowers pretending they were crossed swords. A mass of flame poured from the crematorium's open portal.

As the flames poured forth and the liquid volume inside the tanks dropped, the pressure on the tanks' walls increased. The tanks had a finite strength, and that strength was lessened by the heat. A small fissure appeared in the wall of one tank. Gas escaped, dropping the pressure suddenly. Under the lower pressure, and at the temperature the liquid was at, the boil became a storm. A massive quantity of the liquid suddenly flashed to a gaseous state, bursting the tank apart explosively. Gas and oxygen raced to fill every nook and cranny.

Some neared the flame pouring out of the crematorium's wide open door.

◇   ◇   ◇

Even within the night vision goggles, vision was tunneled down to nearly nothing. Still, Hans could see a janissary rise before him. He knocked the soldier down and jumped on his chest, pushing his dagger into the gap around the neck and bringing forth a furious spurt of blood.

Booted feet stood before him. Hans began to rise. He felt a blow, then another and a third. His armor kept them out, not least because the bullets were still unstable and did not hit point on.

Sig fired at the madman to his front without effect, so far as he could tell. In the unlit foyer he could make out no more than the silhouette of the body, except in the strobelike flashing of the muzzles of the combatants.

He saw rise before him something instinct told him was a monster. Sig was an old soldier, though, and was not ruled by instinct. A more careful look caused his heart to sink. "Is it really you, my *odabasi*?" he whispered.

There was no sense in denying it. Sig knew. He adjusted his aiming point upwards and fired.

Cas touched the flames. Boom.

The children were the first to notice. Their collective gasp and pointing fingers directed Hamilton's attention to the rear of the airship, toward Castle Honsvang.

What the children and Hamilton saw, initially, was a bright glow, originating at the lower levels and shining through the windows there. The glow spread upward. By the time the upper stories shone, it had expanded past the lower windows, engulfing the castle's base in flame. Inside that flame, one could not see. Yet above it, one saw the towers, the crenellations, the roof, all begin to rise in slow motion. The fireball, traveling faster, overtook most of that, reached apogee, and began to recede. As it did, roof and walls and crenellations and towers all began to return to Earth, following the fireball down. Some pieces continued upward, even so.

By the time the fireball was gone, and the rest fallen, there was nothing to see of Castle Honsvang from the airship. Nor was there anyone on the ground nearby left alive to see.

# Interlude

Grosslangheim, Federal Republic of Germany,
1 October, 2022

Amal didn't have to wear a veil at home. She wore it anyway because every time her mother looked at her face, Gabi broke down in tears.

They'd moved to Grosslangheim for protection. The boys had been caught early, but the judge, an Islamic judge, had released them on bail. About this the police could do exactly nothing except to advise Gabi to take her daughter someplace else for safety until the trial.

Not that there was going to be a trial. The boys had no sooner been released on bail then they'd fled, taking advantage of both the informal network of blood relations in Germany and the fact that German police had retreated from the Muslim neighborhoods, leaving them in the charge of German-funded Islamic police who were, in effect, an arm of the very mullahs and imams who counseled that the responsibility for rape fell entirely upon the female.

The police had warned Gabi this would happen and warned her, too, that despite the boys' practical immunity from prosecution, they would still kill her daughter, if they could, as a matter of "principle."

She'd thought of returning to her home town of Kitzingen but that, the police had also advised, was large enough and had enough of a Muslim community now that she and the girl would be in danger there as well.

"Better a small town," they'd advised. "One where there are none but Germans. You'll find a lot of us are abandoning the cities as they turn into foreign enclaves. No one will find you and Amal too remarkable. It will be better in a small town, too, since the welfare benefits are being slashed all over."

The welfare payments had become more important, too, as Gabi had found herself unable to sell much of her art. She, after all, concentrated on the human form and selling pictures of people had become a rather dangerous, as being against the *Sharia*, activity. Though she'd never encountered it, she'd had friends who had had their stalls and galleries ransacked by Islamic mobs.

In the end, she'd decided she must emigrate and take Amal with her.

# American Consulate, Zurich, Switzerland, 5 March, 2024

After the retaliatory nukings, only Switzerland, in all of Western Europe, had maintained diplomatic relations with the United States—now, since the occupation of Canada, rapidly morphing into the American Empire. Thus, it had been to Switzerland Gabi had had to go to apply for a visa to immigrate into the U.S.

She took her number, and waited impatiently for it to be called. Her initial application had been submitted months before, shortly after she'd realized that no place in continental Europe was going to be safe.

Once her number was called, Gabi proceeded to a private office where a consular officer invited her to sit while perusing her file.

"I'm sorry, Ms. von Minden," the official had said. "Your application has been disapproved."

"But . . . but *why?*"

In answer, the official began taking from the file documents and photographs, sliding them across the desk. Gabi saw herself in the photographs, standing on rostra while speaking to crowds, standing in crowds while carrying signs, signing petitions while being photographed.

She didn't understand. Her face said as much.

"We still take some immigrants from Old Europe," the consular explained. "But we don't really need them. We get plenty of high quality applicants from Latin America, India, Japan, China, Vietnam . . . all over. We not only don't need Europeans anymore, we don't really want them.

"I'm sorry to have to say it this way but . . . you're diseased, you see . . . politically diseased. You're in the process of losing your own homeland. You brought it on yourselves and it's become irreversible now. So ask yourself: Why should we accept into our country people with a history of destroying the country they live in?

"You're diseased, Ms. von Minden, and you're contagious. We had a long bout with the disease that's afflicted Europe, and it killed millions of us. Why should we allow any more contamination?

"Europe abandoned its future for a short period of comfort in the present, and you . . . you *personally*"—the consular's hand waved towards the pictures and documents on the desk—"encouraged this. Europe stopped having children, who *are* the future—because it was too uncomfortable, too inconvenient. Europe began taxing the future to buy comfort in the present. Europe let in millions of inassimilable, and therefore inherently hostile, foreigners to do the work that the children which you did not have could not do. And thus you have no future—you *sold* it—but only a past. Why should we let you take away our future? What do we owe you that we should risk that?"

"But my daughter? Her father was an American citizen!"

"We know. But he was not a citizen until well after your daughter was born. Thus, she is not a citizen. Worse, you raised her and she probably carries the same political disease you do. We don't want her either.

"For whatever it's worth, I'm sorry for you both."

# CHAPTER TWENTY

The grandchild, far from being incidental, is decisive. Civilization persists when there is a widespread sense of an ethical obligation on the part of the present generation for the well-being of the third generation—their own grandchildren. A society where this feeling is not widespread may last as a civilization for some time—indeed, for one or two generations it might thrive spectacularly. But inevitably, a society acknowledging no transgenerational commitment to the future will decay and decline from within.

— Lee Harris, "The Future of Tradition"

# Flight Seven Nine Three, 24 Muharram, 1538 AH (4 November, 2113)

The first thing Hamilton noticed when he entered the cockpit and stood beside the pilot was that Ling (he knew, at some level, that Ling was being teleoperated but still thought of the body as Ling's) was crying, tears coursing down her cheeks in an endless flood. Retief was sitting next to the pilot in the copilot's chair.

"I'm sorry if—"

—"I need you to set me down," Hamilton answered. "There's one of our team still on the ground, at an-Nessang."

"Not going to happen," the pilot answered. "I've lost so much lift that it's—no pun intended—up in the air as to whether I'll be able to make it across the lake to Switzerland. If I waste the altitude I've got I *won't* make it across."

"Fuck!" Hamilton exclaimed. "Parachutes?"

"Civilian airliners don't carry chutes," Retief answered. "Bad for passenger morale, don't you know."

"I've *got* to get on the ground," Hamilton insisted. "If things had gone according to plan I'd have driven away from the castle—"

"Things never do," the pilot said.

Retief thought about that for a moment, then said, "There *is* a way but—"

"What is it, man?"

"We've got the winches to hold the ship down when it's landed and the winds are high. But they don't have much cable to them."

"How much is 'not much'? Can they reach to the ground?"

"What's our altitude over ground?" Retief asked the pilot.

"About three hundred feet. It's staying pretty stable for now, since the ground is descending slightly."

"Not enough," Retief answered. "Can you make a thirty or forty foot jump?"

*Shit, my knees.*

"Not a lot of choice," Hamilton answered.

"Not a lot of time, either," The pilot commented, looking at the map on his navigation screen. "I'm having to balance lift from speed with loss of buoyancy from air pressure forcing lifting gas out. It's a *bitch*! Then again, I *am* the best. An-Nessang in . . . call it . . . oh, about five minutes . . . a little less."

"Fuck it," Hamilton said to Retief. "Let's do it."

"Any particular direction from the town you want to be dropped off?" the pilot asked, as Hamilton and Retief exited the cockpit.

"Right over it, if you can," Hamilton answered over his shoulder. "Maybe I'll luck out and find a soft roof about twenty feet below."

"Stand on the hook," Retief said.

Hamilton looked at the thing dubiously. Not that the hook didn't look strong; it was huge and solid. Rather, he was thinking of what it would do to his head if it ever connected on a free swing. Still, it was the only way down. Hamilton took off his armor—he was going to hit with more than enough kinetic energy as was; to allow that piece's weight to add to it was borderline suicidal—and passed it over to Retief. He then stepped off of the deck, placing one foot, and then another, on the hook. His hands wrapped around the cable. The cable was so thick that his fingers didn't touch his thumbs.

Hamilton threw his head back, then slammed his chin down to his chest, knocking the night vision goggles over his eyes.

"Let me down," he shouted to Retief, even as the latter opened the hatchway below to allow the hook to be lowered. Hamilton had to shout as the inrushing air drowned out normal sound.

The winch started with a squeal and a shudder. Fortunately, the Boer Republic of South Africa, whatever its other flaws, did maintain its equipment. After that initial shudder, the machine operated smoothly, lowering Hamilton into the blast. Unfortunately, however, the hook was free spinning to allow fixing at any angle on the ground. Hamilton spun and swayed without control. This was bad, very bad, as he needed to see ahead to mark his landing spot. The spin threatened to make him ill. It absolutely made him want to close his eyes but that would never do.

*Fuckfuckfuckfuck. How do I control this?*

Experimentally, and not without a certain feeling of terror, Hamilton took one hand off the cable—the hand opposite the direction of his spin—and thrust that arm outward. The spin reversed itself.

*Oh, oh. Too much.* He pulled the arm partway in, reducing the cross section. *There; that's better. And* there's *the town and . . . ohhh, shit, we're moving faster than I thought.*

Hamilton put both hands back on the cable and lifted his feet off of the hook. He began to scuttle his hands down the gable. After three such releases and regraspings, his left hand lost its hold and he fell.

"Ohhh . . . shshshiiittt!"

## an-Nessang, Province of Baya, 24 Muharram, 1538 AH (4 November, 2113)

Petra was slowly freezing solid. She was, in fact, certain she would die of the cold. Yes, she had her burka and, true, she was under a blanket. Yet there are some colds, and Germany's cold in the early autumn morning was one such, that no practical amount of insulation alone would help.

Intellectually she knew that she could start the car and get some heat that way. The keys were, after all, under the driver's seat and she had seen the car started before. It was just a matter of putting in the key and turning it. But an idling automobile was a guaranteed attention gatherer. Too, she could get out of the car and try to exercise to put some warmth back in her limbs. But if an idling automobile in twenty-second-century Germany was an attention gatherer, how much more so would be a woman in a burka doing jumping jacks? It was a formidable problem that she settled by simply remaining in the car and shivering as her limbs slowly went numb. The steel of the bolt cutters clutched in her arms didn't help.

Hamilton felt a wrenching pain in his left knee as he hit the rooftop and rolled to his left side. Almost, he screamed of it. For a brief moment, even, he felt the urge to cry over it.

That urge passed, surpassed by the greater need to find Petra and bring her to safety. He arose to hands and—*oh, my frigging God!*—knees, and then to both feet. His first steps were awkward. Very nearly he stumbled over. Still, by keeping his leg stiff he was able, if barely, to remain upright.

*First thing is I've got to get off of the roof.
Hmmm . . . no fire escape. There's that shedlike thing
though; it may be stairs.*

Hamilton walked over stiffly, wincing from pain, and
determined that, yes, the shed covered some stairs. He
descended one step at a time, careful to keep his left leg
stiff. At the bottom, he discovered a latched gate. He
opened and left, emerging onto a street he didn't recognize.

He had a fair innate sense of direction. *Hauptstrasse's
over there,* he thought. *And from there I can find the car
and, I hope, Petra.*

## Flight Seven Nine Three, 24 Muharram, 1538 AH (4 November, 2113)

"I hope to fuck we can shake them," the pilot said to
no one in particular.

"Shake who?" Retief, now returned to the cockpit,
asked. He noticed that the pilot's cheeks were wet, but
that no tears flowed for the moment.

"Shanghai informs me we've got four fighters inbound
in a couple of minutes. There are more after that."

Retief shook his head. "Shaking them isn't going to
happen. But they're going to have problems lining up on
us without violating Swiss airspace." Sitting in the copilot's seat, he reached for a headset and put it on. Then
he adjusted a dial on the control panel, flicked a switch,
and began to broadcast.

"Swiss Airspace Control, Swiss Airspace control: This
is South African Airship Lines Flight Seven Nine Three.
We are inbound to cross your borders bearing about
three hundred escaped slaves, mostly children, from the

Caliphate. We demand sanctuary under the laws of God and man. We are being pursued by jet fighters from the Caliphate. If you are still true Swiss, help us."

"Think it will work?" the pilot asked.

"Think it will hurt?"

"No, but those will."

As the pilot spoke a dual line of tracers crossed in front of the airship, to be followed by the sharklike image of a fighter.

A voice came over the cabin's loudspeaker. It was a woman's voice, throaty and, for some other man, inherently sexy. "Flight Seven Nine Three this is Swiss Airspace Control. We cannot cross the border to help you. But if you can make it halfway across Lake Constance we will escort. Moreover, if the Caliphate fires across that border we will engage them to defend Swiss sovereignty. Understand, you will be interned once you land . . . if you land."

"Swiss Airspace, Seven Nine Three. Roger. Understood. But we're not going to land; we're going to crash. And"—Lee stole a glance at his altimeter—"there's a good chance we'll crash into the lake."

"Then crash on *our* side, Seven Nine Three. We'll send some boats out. Best we can do. Good luck and Godspeed."

The pilot spoke. "You better do better than your best, Switzerland. Escaped slaves aren't all we're carrying. Call your foreign ministry. Right about now the ambassadors from the American Empire and the Celestial Kingdom are explaining just *why* it would be better for you to declare war on the Caliphate than let us fall back into their hands."

Speechless, Retief looked at the pilot and raised one eyebrow.

"I'll tell you later," Lee/Ling said. *Much later.*

## an-Nessang, Province of Baya, 24 Muharram, 1538 AH (4 November, 2113)

He was running late, very late. *Running late, my ass. I'm* staggering *late.*

Hamilton cursed at the knee, swelling now and badly, that held his progress down to that of a snail. He wondered at the absence of any policeman on the street. *True, it's just a small town and, true, it's nighttime. But you would expect at least* one *cop. And, between the goggles and the weapon, it's not like I* look *exactly normal. Then again, I expected to be able to sneak into town, or to drive in a janissary truck. For this and other things, O Lord . . . thanks.*

## Flight Seven Nine Three, 24 Muharram, 1538 AH (4 November, 2113)

Retief heard screaming from the rear, even through the many bulkheads separating the cockpit from the passenger compartment and the lounge holding the mass of children. The airship shuddered with the impact of light cannon fire.

"Christ!" The pilot exclaimed. "Go back and see to the damage. See to the kids, for that matter, the poor little bastards."

"I'm on it," Retief agreed, then pushed himself out of his chair, turned, and ran for the rear. He didn't make it before another burst of cannon fire hit the airship, not far from where he ran. The force of the blasts, coupled with the shuddering of the ship, knocked him from his feet, leaving him temporarily stunned on the deck.

Claude Oliver Meara lay on one side on the deck, taped and trussed to his chair like a Christmas goose. He'd shat himself when the cannon fire struck. This wasn't supposed to happen to *him*. What was wrong with these people? Didn't they understand that if he was unhappy, the world would be unhappy, that if he died the universe would end. Madmen! Devils sent to torment him!

Two children, one boy, one girl, crawled up to him. Meara recognized the boy as one of his favorite new toys. He breathed a sigh of relief; the boy was so grateful for his attentions he was going to free him! The children, their faces very serious, spoke to each other in a language he didn't understand. No doubt they were discussing how best to free him.

The girl produced a small pencil. The boy unlaced a shoe. Meara thought he understood the purpose of the pencil, to weaken the tape that bound him so the children could tear it. But why did the boy tie the shoelace loosely around his neck? Why did the girl put the pencil through the loop and begin to twist it?

Retief looked down at the buggy-eyed, blue-faced corpse with its tongue swollen and blackened. The corpse, still bound to its chair, was of the one he thought of as the "fat prisoner." There were two children nearby, coloreds, looking down at the grotesque, obscene thing with an odd mix of innocence, hate and pure satisfaction.

*No time to worry about that now. Later, maybe. If
there's a later and if it matters. Besides, there are enough
children hurt here not to worry too much about one renegade.*

He reached for an intercom button. "Retief here. It's
not as bad as it felt. We've got some kids hurt. Some of
them might be dead. And one of the prisoners is *definitely* dead."

"Can you toss them to lighten the load?" the pilot
asked. "Every inch might count."

"I *won't* toss the kids. I can toss the dead prisoner,"
Retief answered. "He's so fucking huge he might give
us the lift we need all on his own."

"Do it."

Retief, though no weakling, found it impossible to pick
up and carry Meara's obese corpse. After a couple of
attempts, he gave up the notion. Instead, he stepped
over the corpse and began to roll it, chair and all, towards
the back of the airship's lounge, to where the viewing
ports had been completely shattered. He had to kick
some of the clear material, a kind of double layered glass
with a plastic binder between the layers, out of the way.
Once that was done, he again went to Meara's corpse
and, with a great grunting heave, pushed it over the
stern.

It wasn't enough to give the airship much more lift
but for some reason Retief's spirit felt a bit uplifted.
There had to have been a reason those children had
strangled the wretch, after all.

## an-Nessang, Province of Baya, 24 Muharram, 1538 AH (4 November, 2113)

With a gasp of pain, Hamilton half collapsed against the black-painted auto. It was too dark to see if Petra was inside, and she was strong enough not to cry out.

"Petra, please tell me you're in there," Hamilton said, after wrenching the door open.

Still shivering, she tossed the bolt cutters aside and flew out from under the cover of the concealing blanket, scrambled over the backs of the front seats, and wrapped him in a desperate hug.

"I thought you forgot about me," she said. "I thought you and Hans were dead and everything had failed. I was expecting to be found and crucified. I had to kill a man."

"You had to . . . never mind. Honey, I've got some bad news and you ought to sit down for it. And besides, we need to hurry to the lake."

Hamilton had expected a scene. Petra didn't deliver. Instead, she simply asked, "My brother died a free man?"

"Yes."

"Then it is well. It's all he wanted; that, and to fight against our enemy. Ling knows?"

"Yes. She didn't take it well."

Petra nodded as she backed into the front passenger seat. "No . . . no, she wouldn't."

"Was she in love with him?" Hamilton asked.

"I think . . . maybe . . . she *wanted* to be. I think she could have been, in time. And maybe, too, she thinks she was."

Hamilton nodded understanding. He then reached under the seat, his fingers questing for the key. "Where are you, you little . . . ah, here you are." He put the key in the ignition, said a probably hopeless prayer, and turned it. Half to his surprise the car started immediately. He reached up, took the goggles off of his head and set them on the seat between himself and Petra. Only then did he turn on the headlights and put the car's automatic transmission into drive.

Over the sound of the engine, and coming from somewhere above, Hamilton heard the sonic boom of a fast moving aircraft.

## Flight Seven Nine Three, 24 Muharram, 1538 AH (4 November, 2113)

"Come this way, children!" Retief shouted over the crying and the roar of air rushing through shattered viewports. "Come to the center. It will be safer there. If someone's hurt, help them. Hurry! Hurry! Hurry!"

He was surprised by how well they followed his orders. *Maybe,* he thought, *just maybe, when you're born a slave you simply learn very young to accept the bad part of life and deal with it. Whatever the benefits now, it's still shitty.*

Retief arranged the kids as best he could on the deck of the lounge. They covered an area of perhaps twenty by thirty feet. He thought about moving the tables around them but, *No way; they're bolted down.* The chairs he could move, though, and he began to.

Without a word, Matheson, seeing what the Boer was doing, dragged himself over and lay on his side along one edge of the layer of children. His body, he thought, would be better than nothing for protection from fragment.

Retief nodded in approval. *Now there's a good man,* he thought.

He was dragging a brace of the chairs from the side to the center when he saw a sudden fireball in the night, the light reflecting off the waters of the lake, now below, to the clouds, above.

Wide-eyed, Retief asked, "What the . . . ?"

"Seven Nine Three? Swiss Airspace Control. We have been ordered to defend you. If you have any self-defense capability, go to weapons tight immediately."

"Switzerland this is Seven Nine Three. We've got nothing. What's your ETA?"

"Look behind you, Seven Nine Three. Hell, look around you."

The pilot saw nothing initially, then a sudden burst of light from somewhere behind lit up the world. In that light he caught a glimpse of a brace of fighters. He thought he saw a large red cross painted on each fighter's tail. Down below he was certain he saw several armed patrol boats leaving for the deeper water. Those definitely came from the Swiss side of the lake.

Lee, still in Ling's voice, said, "Switzerland . . . Seven Nine Three. Honey, for that I would consider changing my sexual polarity."

On the other end, a female Swiss Armed Forces radio operator looked at a microphone in considerable confusion, before answering, "If you're a girl, Seven Nine Three, and are as sexy as you sound, you'll do just fine."

"We'll talk," Lee/Ling said. "Later."

## Highway 12, Province of Baya, 24 Muharram, 1538 AH (4 November, 2113)

*Late, late, late . . . shit.* Hamilton drove like a madman. This was not, in itself, a problem; *everyone* in the Caliphate who drove, drove like a madman. But, what with castles blowing up, firefights, janissaries being alerted, dogfights overhead . . .

Seeing a road sign, mostly rusted through and in any case barely legible, Hamilton made a sudden decision. He slowed and jerked the wheel to the right, swinging onto another highway heading north.

Petra asked, "What are you doing?"

"Sudden rush of brains to the head," he answered. "All attention is on what's going on around and above the lake . . . that, and the castle. So what we're going to do—and, yes, it's a risk—is swing around af-Fridhav and come in from the other side. I *think* we're more likely to get away with this coming in from the east."

Petra chewed at her lower lip for a few moments before saying, "If you think that's best, I'll trust you."

*And doesn't* that *make my chest swell?* Hamilton thought.

## Flight Seven Nine Three, 24 Muharram, 1538 AH (4 November, 2113)

The shoreline swelled before him, all rocks and trees. The airship was in ground effect now, and still half a mile from shore. The pilot really didn't know if they'd make it. His control panel had become a Christmas tree of red lights from punctured gas cells and damaged or failing engines. Even if they did make it across, though, the airship wasn't going to land; it was going to crash.

*But there are degrees of crashing,* Lee reassured himself. *Some are worse than others.*

Calmly, or as calmly as one could expect anyway, the pilot brought the airship in closer and closer to shore. About a thousand feet out, he flicked a switch to dump the fuel. A sudden slight ballooning upward told him that had worked. He'd not been sure that it would, with all the damage the ship had taken.

He killed the main forward rotors, causing the ship to slow considerably. What little fuel remained in the system would go to the vertical thrusters.

Slowly . . . slowly . . . slowly the shore edged closer. The nose touched and began to crumple. There was still a lot of mass in the airship, and a lot of inertia. It was enough to half crush it. That mass drove the ship inexorably forward to ruin. At the last second, the pilot threw Ling's arms over her face.

And that was the last thing he remembered for quite some time.

## af-Fridhav, Province of Baya, 24 Muharram, 1538 AH (4 November, 2113)

Over the little tourist boats Hamilton stood with a set of bolt cutters in one hand. The boats were lit by the flames on the other side of the lake. The flames suggested to Hamilton that his worst fears were realized: The ship had crashed and burned, the people—including the freed children—were lost, and the virus somewhere at the bottom of the lake.

"Does that mean . . . ?" Petra asked.

"I'm afraid it might."

Her shoulders slumped and she seemed on the verge of tears. "To have come so far . . . "

Hamilton put his unencumbered arm around her and said, "But we're still alive. And we have to get away." *If we can get away. I was counting on our slipping through in the confusion . . . but if the airship's already down maybe there won't be enough confusion.*

"Damned right you do, asshole!" sounded in Hamilton's ear, startling him.

"Bernie?" he asked. "You're alive?"

"No, I'm speaking to you from the great beyond, *baas*. Of course I'm alive."

"But the fire?"

"The pilot dumped fuel to gain some altitude and reduce the chance of fire. I don't know what touched the fuel off, a tracer, maybe. Then again, there's been enough shit flying that it could have been anything. Now get your ass over here. There are Swiss medics and rescue personnel taking care of us, and a helluva fight in the air and on the lake. In the confusion . . . "

While Hamilton was talking, Petra looked at him as if he'd gone slightly mad.

"Oh, and Caruthers is here. He says move your ass."

Hamilton looked down at Petra and laughed. "They're *alive*! And we're going to stay that way, too. Hop in, Honey. Untie the boat while I cut the chain."

The boat's electric motor was virtually silent. At first, and for just under an hour, Hamilton followed the northern shore. The lights of the fight on the water and in the air receded. When he judged it was safe enough to do so, he cut the wheel hard port and set off into the lake.

His eyes scanned nervously about, as did Petra's. He kept his weapon leaning against the steering column. Hers she kept in her hands. She knew, intellectually, that it would be little defense against a patrol boat. That didn't matter. The comfort of the weapon was not in its ability to defend her. It was in its ability to make her a target to be shot rather than a victim to be taken, tried, and crucified.

*Or worse than crucified,* she thought. *Someone to be re-enslaved.*

"Get ready," Hamilton whispered. "There's something up ahead, a patrol boat, I think."

What he saw in his goggles she didn't know. That he moved the submachine gun resting on the steering column to a position across his legs frightened her. She grasped her own weapon all the more tightly.

"Ah shit," he said. "They've seen us."

Petra pulled the submachine gun to her shoulder. She couldn't see anything yet, not having goggles. No matter; when the enemy appeared, she would be ready.

"That won't be much use, you know," Hamilton said.

"Depends on the purpose," Petra answered. He understood completely.

The boat had four life jackets draped over the back. Hamilton pointed to them and told her, "Dump the burka and put one on. The water's cold but we might still make it if we swim for it."

"Or they might take us alive from the water," she answered. "No thanks."

He nodded that he understood that, too.

"If this were faster I'd try to ram them," he said. "As is, I doubt they'd feel the nudge."

Petra heard the first inklings of a heavy engine, somewhere up ahead. The boat that Hamilton had seen seemed to loom in the darkness. She aimed her submachine gun at it and was just about to pull the trigger when Hamilton began to laugh. That was odd enough that she lowered her weapon . . . and then screamed as the boat bearing down on them opened fire.

Hamilton saw immediately, as Petra didn't, that the patrol boat ahead was firing high. He immediately ducked low into the little stolen rental, dragging her down with him. For her part, her finger was still on the trigger of her submachine gun. The twin shocks of having fire pass overhead, and being dragged downward, caused her finger to tighten. The weapon fired into the bottom of the boat, three rounds before the thing further shocked her into releasing the trigger.

That was too late, of course. Water immediately began spurting up through the newly created holes.

"Ah, shit," Hamilton said, as a stream of icy water took him in the neck. The boat wouldn't sink; he was sure of that much. Between the walls of the hull it was sealed foam. Even so, as it sank its resistance to the water would increase to the point it would be faster—and with the boat rapidly filling, no colder—to swim.

The patrol boat in front of them suddenly leapt forward, missing the little pleasure boat by feet and rocking it dangerously. It might have capsized but that its center of gravity was already somewhat lower.

Hamilton struggled to put his rear on the seat and his hands and feet at the controls. "Bail!" he shouted to Petra, as the boat began moving ahead.

"Bail?"

"Use your hands . . . anything you can find, actually, to get the water out of the bottom of the boat."

Petra, being careful this time to put the safety on the submachine gun, bent over and began to scoop. That wouldn't do more than buy a little time, but it was better than nothing. With a naval battle developing furiously behind them, Hamilton pushed the little boat toward shore for all it was worth.

"Which isn't too bloody fucking much," he muttered. The water rising above his ankles sent a chill up his spine. Petra bailed even more furiously, crying with frustration that the water was still rising.

"Matheson!" he shouted aloud. No answer. *They might have put him under. Crap.* "Ling?" *Nothing. Probably hurt in the landing. Shit. I think I can haul Petra to shore . . . but we'll both be better than half frozen.*

"Get out of your burka and put on a life vest, honey," he said.

"Why?" she asked, still bailing.

"We're not going to get picked up by the Caliphate; that Swiss patrol boat will see to that. But we're going to have to swim for it."

"I CAN'T!"

"No matter, honey, I CAN."

Hamilton didn't put on a life jacket. It would have interfered with his swimming and hauling Petra to safety. Besides, he was a very strong swimmer and simply didn't think he needed one.

The top of the boat was almost flush with the water now, the little engine deader than chivalry. The firefight between the patrol boats behind them had ended, but without knowing who had won, Hamilton didn't think they should risk staying with the foundered recreation boat. *Odds are only fifty-fifty of being found by a friend if we stay here,* he thought. *Our odds of making the swim are a little better than that.* He could see the far shore in his night vision goggles but, with those giving no depth perception, he couldn't be sure of how far away it was. *No worse than fifty-fifty, anyway,* he amended.

"This is going to be really cold, Petra," he said, very gently. "Over the side now."

Nodding, she bent at the waist, put both hands on the gunnels, and stepped over into the water. Her mouth opened into a wide, round "O" with her silent scream.

Bracing himself, Hamilton eased himself over. *Oh, God, this is* cold. He moved his body to be almost parallel to the surface and said, still gently, "Grab hold."

Petra didn't move, but just clung to the side of the boat. Instead of telling her again, Hamilton took her hands, one by one, and placed them around his neck, interlacing the fingers. Twisting within the circle of her arms, he kicked away from the boat and began a slow, energy-conserving, breaststroke. Though she made no answer, Hamilton talked to Petra constantly to keep her awake and alive.

"You're going to like freedom, Petra . . . I can't wait to take you on a boat where no one's trying to kill us, honey . . . Babe, wait until you see the shopping in New York City . . . Love, scuba is just more fun than you can imagine . . . "

She never answered, vocally, but an occasional squeeze of her arms told him she was still alive and, in her own way, fighting to stay that way.

Hamilton couldn't really feel his arms and hands anymore. Petra's grip around his neck had relaxed to the point he'd had to switch from a breaststroke to a sidestroke, hooking his other arm under her armpits to hold her. At this point, her life vest had become critical to keeping her—and perhaps both of them—afloat.

He still talked to her, when he could spare a breath. His lungs were sacks of icy flame, containers more of pain than air.

Still, he pressed on. His sidestroke drove his right hand down, deep into the water. He thought he felt something solid brush his fingers but when he interrupted the stroke it was gone. He kicked to establish forward movement again, and resumed the sidestroke.

*And there it is again.* He didn't stop this time, but redoubled his efforts at moving the two forward. His next two strokes found nothing, but the third was interrupted by what had to be a rock. He stopped, and allowed his feet to sink. They, too, found solid ground beneath them.

With difficulty, Hamilton stood with Petra still caught fast in one frozen arm. He began to walk forward in a daze, barely noticing that the water level dropped beneath him, to waist, to hams, to knees, to ankles. And there, wonder of wonders, was a tree, growing right by the water's edge. He walked a few steps farther, to the sheer bank.

Hamilton bent and put his free arm under Petra's thighs and lifted her, placing her body on the dry land above the lake. He then crawled over her, and lay down beside her, covering her as best his could with his chest, arms, and legs. Eventually, the Swiss would find them.

"Welcome to Switzerland, honey," he whispered, as he drifted into unconsciousness. "Welcome to freedom."

# EPILOGUE

Zurich, Switzerland, 12 December, 2113

The reception was not exactly secret, even though it was held in one of the super-secret, underground forts, or *reduits*, that the Helvetian Confederation had maintained for over one hundred and fifty years, with a few short breaks. It was, in any case, secret enough that Hamilton didn't know exactly how he'd arrived in it.

The purpose of the reception? Switzerland, which had first crack at the computers in the castle, had discovered that they were on the target list. A little reception, and a few medals, seemed a small price to pay for not being exterminated.

Ling was there, bandaged in spots, with her arm in a sling, but wearing her new medal and holding hands with a tall brunette in the uniform of the Swiss Armed Forces. They didn't seem to be in love . . . exactly . . . yet. Lust, however, was written plain.

"It's good she found someone, though," Petra whispered to Hamilton. "Isn't it?"

"It can't be bad," he whispered back. "Speaking of which . . . " He looked over at Caruthers.

"The Han have agreed to release her to our care," Caruthers said. "For a price. Don't sweat the price; we've met it. She's scheduled for surgery to have her chip deactivated—too dangerous to remove it—next week."

"She'll be free then, at last," Petra said.

"You're both free now," Caruthers said.

"Speaking of which," Hamilton began to ask, "now that you're free and, thankfully eighteen, how would you like to be re-enslaved?"

Petra glared at him. Her features softened under the realization that Hamilton would never re-enslave her.

"What do you mean?" she asked.

"Well," he said, "I'm thinking about going back to the Army—"

"Big frigging mistake," Caruthers interjected. "You have a future with us, son."

Hamilton ignored him, except to say, "A future as a slave dealer? That's a filthy future." To Petra he repeated, "I'm thinking about going back to the Army. I could use a wife."

"A wife?" Speechless, she began to cry.

"A wife. If you would consent."

"But I'm . . . I mean I was—"

"A wonderful girl," he cut her off. "A girl whom life crapped on and who didn't let it turn her rotten."

"There's another option," said Caruthers. "And it wouldn't involve the slave trade."

"Would you *please* just butt out. I'm trying to pro-
pose here."

"Trying, shmying," Caruthers scoffed. "Stop being
melodramatic. She's going to accept; aren't you dear?"

Petra's head nodded, briskly. She was still crying too
much to speak.

"See? That's settled. Now instead of being a dumb ass
and turning your lovely future bride into a widow while
gallantly leading your men across the altogether too fire-
swept beaches of the English Channel in a few years,
why don't you stay here and become our chief of station?
I believe I once told you we like husband and wife teams.
And I can sweeten the deal," Caruthers added.

"How's that?" Hamilton asked.

"Well, the two renegades left alive spilled their guts.
We've got millions they'd been paid and secreted in
banks here. The Swiss government also turned over to
us the funds of the dead one, Meara. We could keep it
all, of course, but I convinced the DDDA that it would
be better put to educating and caring for those slave
children you freed; them and the farmers Matheson
grabbed. A man's got to be able to sleep at night, after
all."

"How is Bernie's recovery coming?" Hamilton asked.
He wanted to think before answering.

"He'll never play the piano again."

Hamilton looked confused.

Caruthers shrugged. "He couldn't play the piano
before, either."

"Asshole."

Caruthers laughed.

"What about the virus?" Hamilton asked.

"Which virus?"

"Which?"

"There were two, as it turns out," Caruthers said. "The one we inferred from notes left behind was intended to be a deception. The one they were actually working on was real though, real but useless."

"WHAT?"

"Oh, it's deadly enough," Caruthers said. "But what they were trying to do with it? Dead end. It *can't* be made to die out after a few mutations. We've got a vaccine for it in prototype. Inoculations probably begin next year."

"What about the renegades themselves?" Hamilton asked.

"Hanged side by side in an elevator shaft at Langley last week. Piano wire. No drop. I understand they cried a lot as they were noosed."

"Good," Hamilton said.

Petra wiped at her eyes and said, "John, there is a good reason to stay here."

"What's that?" he asked.

"I've told you of my best friend, Besma . . . the Muslim girl?"

"Yes."

"Before we left, I got a letter from her. Her husband had been displeased with her and had beaten her. She went to the courts and they told her it was her fault."

"So?"

"So . . . if we stay here, we could perhaps get my friend Besma and her children out of a slavery not much better than mine was."

"Let me think about it," he answered, then thought, *No, if you're going to be my wife, you get a say.* "You really think so?" he asked.

Petra wiped the last moisture from her eyes and answered, "I owe Besma a lot, John, and her life is Hell. I won't force you—I can't force you—but I'd appreciate it if we could stay here at least until we get her and her children out. And . . ." She hesitated.

"Yes?" Hamilton asked.

"Well . . . you tell me an invasion of the Caliphate is both inevitable and soon coming, right?"

Caruthers harrumphed.

"Oh, knock it off," Hamilton said. "Everyone knows it is." Turning back to Petra he asked, "So what?"

"Well . . . maybe from here, in the middle of the Caliphate, we could aid that."

"It's a thought, John," Caruthers said. "And then too . . ."

"Yes?"

"After deciphering those computers the Swiss are less enthusiastic about neutrality than they were. Another dozen or fifteen divisions suddenly emerging in the middle of the Caliphate would help an invasion immeasurably. You could be our man here . . . and then cross over to being the liaison with the Swiss later on."

Hamilton looked at Petra. "You realize, right, that this will delay your scuba instruction by years." It was his last, feeble shot.

"I can wait," she said. "When a continent of my people is enslaved I can wait for the other things."

Hamilton sighed. "You're a bastard, Caruthers."

"Does that mean you'll do it?"

"I don't see where I have a choice."

Caruthers sighed. "Nobody's had a choice in about a century, John. This whole thing? It's about giving people choices again."

"Speaking of which," Hamilton said, pointing with his chin at Ling and her new partner threading their way across the floor.

The pair, still holding hands, stopped directly in front of Hamilton, Petra and Caruthers. The Swiss girl seemed very shy, though Ling was forward, as usual.

After introductions, Ling said to Caruthers, "I wanted to thank you, you and your organization and the Empire, for getting the Ministry of State Security to release me."

Caruthers said, "You're welcome. After what you've done, you're more than welcome. I just wish the condition of release didn't include a covenant not to employ you ourselves."

Ling shook her head. "No thank you. I've had enough of being used . . . even if it was being used for a higher purpose." She looked very intently at Petra. "I'll miss you, honey."

"No, you won't," Petra answered. "We're staying here, John and I."

Hamilton nodded. "We'll be seeing a lot of each other, I think. And, maybe, too, you might do some work with us, if not for us."

"Only if you choose to," Petra added.

Ling smiled. "A wonderful thing, isn't it, choice? Maybe we'll work together, after all."

# AFTERWORD

*Warning: Authorial editorial follows. Read further at your own risk. You're not paying anything extra for it so spare us the whining if your real objection is that it is here for other people to read. If you are a Tranzi, and you read this, the author expressly denies liability for your resulting rise in blood pressure, apoplexy, exploding head or general icky feelings. Then again, if you're a Tranzi and haven't already suffered one of the above, it's unlikely this will bother you too much more.*

## A World Without Europe
(except as a geographic expression)

Brother, it ain't all bad.

What's Europe done for us, after all? Dragged us onto not one but *two* world wars? Inflicted on us murderous and repressive political philosophies from Jacobinism to Czarism to Fascism to Nazism to Communism? Carved up the world in such a way as to guarantee misery for the bulk of humanity for centuries?

Yes, Europe's done all that.

But then there were Greece and Rome, England and Switzerland. Leonidas' three-hundred and the even more admirable seven-hundred Thespians. Salamis and Platea. Horatius Cocles. The Parthenon and the Pantheon. William Tell and the Magna Carta.

Sempach and Stirling Castle. Roads, laws, engineering, science, philosophy. Democracy. Us.

Only a cold blooded, ungrateful bastard wouldn't shed a tear when only the barbarian foot trods the pass at Thermopylae. That, or someone like left-wing icon Susan Sontag, who said:

> "Mozart, Pascal, Boolean algebra, Shakespeare, parliamentary government, baroque churches, Newton, the emancipation of women, Kant, Balanchine ballets, et al. don't redeem what this particular civilization has wrought upon the world. The white race is the cancer of human history."

Note that the late Ms. Sontag once did apologize for that remark, but only to the cancerous.

This is probably as good a time as any to say that most Moslems in Europe today are not nuts. Anecdotally, I offer into evidence an achingly beautiful Turkish girl named Lale whom I met and chatted with once in Schiphol Airport, just south of Amsterdam, in 1999. Lale was Turkish only by parentage. She spoke German primarily and very little Turkish. She'd been a model for German magazines. She was dating or engaged to a German (I misremember which) and intended to *be* a German.

I don't think Lale was all that atypical. Many, perhaps even most, Moslems in Europe might like to become Europeans, insiders rather than outsiders, given the chance. It's not clear they are, or will be, given that chance.

But is Europe, *qua* Europe, going under? It's a very good question.

As of this writing (11 September, 2007) Brussels is the capital of the European Union. Brussels is ruled by the Socialist Party. Of the eighteen members of the Brussels City Council who are in that ruling Socialist Party block, ten are apparently Muslim. Does this prove Brussels is majority Muslim? No, not at all. If Muslims made up a majority this little tidbit wouldn't be so interesting. Rather, it shows that something considerably less than a majority is required to rule a political entity.

As Brussels, the capital of the EU, goes, so goes . . .

Well, we don't know.

Leaving aside a couple of fringe stands, there are basically four theories on the future of Europe. These are:

1. Differentials in birthrates condemn Europe to a) a Muslim majority and b) non-Muslim Europeans to second class citizen status and barbarism, more or less soon. This is Mark Steyn's position for a), and absolutely the position of the Koran, the Sunna, and the Hadiths for b).

2. The Europeans are nuts. However weak they may seem now, before they go under they'll go fascist, if not outright Nazi. The Moslems are heading for the ghettoes and the gas chambers, not rule over the Continent. I think this is, more or less, Ralph Peters' position.

3. Europe will become majority Muslim, but it will be okay so long as we've treated them well while we were the majority. This is basically the progressive position.

4. Problem? What problem? So long as I get my five weeks paid vacation yearly, guaranteed job security, universal health care, etc.—all of which are my right because I am in the position to rob the future for them—there is no problem. Let the future care for the future; I got mine. This appears to be the basic European citizen's position, with some not inconsequential dissent. (Note: for some of the dissenters, check the obituaries.)

So who's right? I don't know. Nobody does. All we can do is calculate the odds, while noting that 4 is the refutation of 2 and 1 is the refutation of 3.

Question One: if Euro and Muslim birth rates don't change, will Europe become Muslim majority?

Answer: Clearly, at some point in time, if we leave aside the question of Muslims assimilating to European culture. Let's try some rough figures. Assume, not unreasonably, that culturally European birth rates continue to hover around a low of 1.6 children per woman (it's actually quite a bit lower in some places), and that these women will have their children later in life, giving three generations in a century. (Remember, those are rough figures.)

What that means, over a century, is that 100 Europeans, half of them female, will have 76 children, that those children will have about 61 children, and that those 61 will have about 49 children.

Let's look at the other side. Assume 4.2 children per Muslim woman and *four* generations in a century, since they marry younger and have children younger. (Again, "rough," I said.)

Ten Muslims, half female, will have 21 children, who will have 44 children, who will have 92 children, who will around the end of that century have about 193 children.

From this point on, if nothing else changes, we're only arguing about the timing. When two populations have that much disparity in birthrates, and if that disparity doesn't change, and if the death rate of the second population doesn't change (the Peters gas chamber hypothesis), and if the assimilation rate (which will affect birthrate) doesn't change, then population B will at some point in time overtake population A.

There's an amazing amount of intellectual dishonesty floating about on the subject, most (maybe not all) of it on the progressive side. Yes, yes, some of that is just idiocy and some of it is the very human phenomenon of accepting without criticism that which we desperately want to believe. ("Communism's just never been done *right!*")

Example: in the book *Sixty Million Frenchmen Can't Be Wrong,* Canadian authors Nadeau and Barlow claim that half of immigrant men in France marry non-immigrant women, and that one-quarter of immigrant women marry non-immigrant men, for a total intermarriage rate of roughly 40%. (I'm indebted to world famous literary critic, Randy McDonald, for this little tidbit.)

End of problem, right? The Muslims of France, and Europe, will assimilate and all will be well, right?

Wrong. What Nadeau and Barteau did there (and what some seem desperately not to want to see that they did there) is an insupportable bit of sleight of hand. You see, the word "non-immigrant" does not mean culturally French, or assimilated, as they want you to simply assume. The word non-immigrant simply means born in France.

But what if those people born in France do not consider themselves French, have been unofficially ghettoized in a *banlieue*, have no loyalty to France, despise French culture, and loathe French liberalism and secularism? What if the immigrant, marrying a non-immigrant, is an Arab marrying another Arab in the *banlieues*? What if the non-immigrant, marrying the immigrant, is an unassimilated Arab, marrying his first or second cousin imported from Algeria for the purpose? What if the non-immigrant has done this several times, importing and marrying a girl, then divorcing her under French civil law and remarrying another import, while leaving the French welfare system (no great shakes perhaps, lifestyle-wise, but inarguably better than a poor village in Algeria) to pay to bring up his children who are legitimate under Islamic law?

Is that what's happening in France? It's not just hard to say, definitively; it's impossible. Why? It's impossible because the French go out of their way not to permit much in the way of such statistics to be gathered. They have some sound reasons for this; it isn't, or isn't entirely, that many of them wish to lull the people into that long cultural goodnight. (Though Sontag had her French adherents, as well . . . and likely still has. "The Left: getting rid of societal cancer one baby at a time.")

Yet there are some indicators we can look to, some questions we can ask. What are the odds of a culturally Arab girl, living in the *banlieues* outside Paris, controlled by her family from morn to night, not speaking French comfortably, burka-clad and veiled, and herself brought up in an unquestioning faith in the superiority of arranged marriage . . . what are the odds she meets and marries a culturally French, non-Muslim man? Perhaps by the romantic light of the burning Peugeots?

Yeah, pull the other one. Just because the French government has good reasons not to permit the collection of some important statistics doesn't also mean that there are not people trying to make up nonsense statistics to console or delude the French (and other Europeans) as they head into that long cultural goodnight. Why should they do this? Oh, perhaps they, as Susan Sontag did, simply feel that moral people will try to eliminate cancer where possible.


Statistics are an interesting thing. Their absence can be even more interesting. Example: it's common knowledge that France has about the highest birthrate in Western Europe, something near replacement level, about 1.82 children per woman or perhaps a bit over. This is often touted as something approaching proof that there is no threat of an Islamic majority in France and, by extension, Europe.

Question Two (and here's some more kitchen math): if 10% of the women of a country are bearing 4.2 children each, and the total for all women in that country is 1.82, what does that mean the other 90% are bearing?

Answer: a bit over a kid and a half. See Question One, above, for what this means.

◇   ◇   ◇

Then again, maybe they will assimilate, after all, and all those nominally Muslim births will become French, or Dutch, or Belgian, or—as with the setting for this book—German.

A couple of interesting anecdotes/tidbits:
From *Expatica* Magazine, 23 May, 2007

Wuppertal, Germany (dpa)—A 42–year-old man with ingrained traditional Turkish views was jailed for 54 months in Germany for the attempted manslaughter of his teenaged daughter after a row over family "honour."

The girl, 16, had been forced to marry and later rebelled. Witnesses described how her father lifted her over a fourth-storey balcony, with another family member prising apart her grip on the rail, and threw her down.

She survived the fall onto a garage roof. The family had accused the daughter of being "dishonourable" because she opposed her father's will, the court in the city of Wuppertal was told.

Passing judgement, a state court judge told the accused he lived in a "parallel world" dominated by Turkish concepts although he was *the third generation of a family that had resettled in Germany*. (The italics are mine. Fifty-four months for attempted *murder*? Oh, yeah, *there's* some protection from the law, for you.)

Or this one from that notorious neo-Nazi rag, *Der Spiegel*:

29 March, 2007
Paving the Way for a Muslim Parallel Society
But German law requires a one-year separation before a divorce can be completed—and exceptions for an expedited process are only granted in extreme situations.

When the woman's attorney, Barbara Becker-Rojczyk, filed a petition for an expedited divorce, Judge Christa Datz-Winter suddenly became inflexible. According to the judge, there was no evidence of "an unreasonable hardship" that would make it necessary to dissolve the marriage immediately. Instead, the judge argued, the woman should have "expected" that her husband, who had grown up in a country influenced by Islamic tradition, would exercise the "right to use corporal punishment" his religion grants him.

The judge even went so far as to quote the Koran in the grounds for her decision. In Sura 4, verse 34, she wrote, the Koran contains "both the husband's right to use corporal punishment against a disobedient wife and the establishment of the husband's superiority over the wife."

So much for the lure of liberalism, or for the liberal society's ability to assimilate the immigrants. They're supposed to respect a law, or want to be a part of a society, like this?

A few bits of wisdom from those who see no problem, perhaps somewhat scathingly paraphrased:

1. "But immigrant reproductive rates will drop. They always do. They're dropping in the countries the Muslim immigrants come from even as we speak."

This one's partially true, but mostly just tempting. There are a number of factors that go into female reproductive rates. Of those, the biggest single correlation with that rate isn't poverty, or religion, or culture, but the educational status of the female. Muslim girls in Europe are typically somewhat educationally deprived, on average. Moreover, while the reproductive rate in, say, Algeria, may be dropping, there is never any explanation given for why it must then drop in France. Could there be other factors at work in Algeria than in France? It seems likely, especially since the rate does *not* seem to be dropping in France. Perhaps this is because France provides free health care of a much higher quality than can be found in Algeria, along with all the other entitlements of the modern social democratic welfare state.

It does no good to say, for example, that "the reproductive rate of Catholics in America dropped," without at least looking at why this happened, and at the religious and cultural differences between, say, Irish or Italian or Polish Catholicism, Scottish or English Protestantism and, say, Algerian or Tunisian or Turkish Islamism. Hmmm . . . when *did* the Italian-Americans and Italian-Canadians let their women stop wearing burkas and veils? When did the Irish-Americans and Irish-Canadians cease their honor killings of girls who refused arranged marriages? Purdah was a Scottish institution, right? The English traditionally clitorectimize their females, yes?

2. "Europe's had a population drop before and survived it." This is very true and also very meaningless. It's worth noting that Europe did not at the time of, say, the Black Death, have another burgeoning population already on hand, within the borders, not subject to the Black Death, and, so, ready to take over. Nor was it then democratic, such that a change in demographics could be used to change law to both further change demographics and prevent assimilation. Nor was Europe then secular (since religion, too, seems to play some part in reproductive rates).

3. "But they're assimilating to our values even as we speak." In 1989, according to *Le Figaro*, 60% of Muslims

in France observed fasting for Ramadan. This year it will be 70% . . . and from a considerably larger group. This year saw parts of the United Kingdom assimilating to Muslim values, as non-Muslims were cautioned not to eat in front of Muslims during Ramadan. This year saw western newspapers violate their own codes of free speech lest they offend radical Muslims. They're not assimilating to you; you're assimilating to them.

4. "You're a racist bastard, Kratman." A bastard I may well be, but since when is Islam a race?

5. "There's no reason to believe that current levels of immigration will continue." This one's true, actually. As Europe becomes ever more indistinguishable from the Moslem world, ever less economically, its attractions for immigrants will probably lessen to near nothing. The technical term for this is civilizational extinction.

Ralph Peters thinks the Europeans will revert to type and crush the Muslims long before they become a problem. To this I think there are two answers.

One obvious answer is that Islam is already a problem, in many places (my Ouija board says Theo van Gogh and Pym Fortuyn will vouch for that much), and there appears to be no crushing in the offing. The other answer, perhaps in its way more obvious, is that one must have a commitment to the future to fight for that future . . . or to commit genocide for it. Where is the broad-based European commitment to the future? They don't grant themselves insupportable largesse from the public fisc because they're committed to the future? They have short work weeks and long vacations because they're committed to the future? They meet their self-imposed Kyoto goals because they're committed to the future? (Look, *I* think Kyoto is absolute bullshit, complete and utter nonsense, but that's not important. What is important is that the Euros don't think it's nonsense. They signed onto the treaty, and they *still* won't do something *they* consider critical for the survival of the human race.) They have an average of at least 2.1 children per woman because they're committed to the future?

On the contrary, the average, typical and normal European is committed to hedonism and the *sense* of security in the present and could care less about the future. This is the stuff death squads and *Einsatzgruppen* are made of? Puhleeze! Where are the children who will form those death squads? The Euros couldn't be bothered having them.

It might actually be much worse, or quicker, anyway, than I've described. One of the constants of mass psychology is that, for example, when the Huns show up, the Goths move on looking for greener pastures *without* any Huns. In the United States we can see this, in proto form, in California, where the population of the culturally Anglo are leaving in greater numbers than are coming in.

Be it noted, here, that outside of perhaps those of New England, California is our most "European" state. Note further that the phenomenon can be seen in multicultural Belgium where Rhode-Saint-Genese Mayor Myriam Delacroix-Rolin observed recently that the increase of Flemish speakers was driving out the French speaking Walloons from her village. Lastly, note that Bethlehem, with one of the oldest Christian communities (and majorities) in the world, is now majority Muslim. And no, it wasn't all birthrate differential. The Christians have, by and large, packed up and *left*.

In Europe, I would suggest that there will be two factors at work to drive young, productive and fertile people out. The first of these is that, as with the Goths and the Californians and the Walloons, when your homeland ceases to be your homeland, ceases to be comfortable and home*like*, there will be a temptation to leave. When your homeland becomes oppressive or dangerous, that temptation will grow strong. (America was settled, after all, by people, many of whom had this in their hearts and minds.) When tax rates reach a certain point (and the French government already takes over half, with the German not all that far behind), and one can make more, and keep more of what is made, somewhere else, forget temptation—buy an airplane ticket. "Go west, young man." More significantly, go elsewhere, young woman.

(By the way, Fascism, being at least as strange and uncomfortable as Islam, would cause approximately as many to flee. No help there.)

I began with talking about the odds. That's the way I think the odds lie. No, it's not a certainty but that's the way to bet it: Europe probably will fail to assimilate its Muslims. It will lack the will (and the children) to eliminate them. Muslim birthrates will remain fairly high, whatever may happen in the Islamic world, because they'll be able to feed, for a while, at the European social democratic teat, even while Europe will not be able muster the will to protect, modernize and educate Muslim women. Thus, at some point in time Europe is very likely to become majority Muslim.

I hope I'm wrong; but I think it's going to happen sooner even than Mark Steyn believes, precisely because, as Europe becomes both strange and even more overly taxed, young Europeans will begin to leave. The more leave; the fewer will be born; the stranger it will become to those who remain and the faster it will become strange. The more leave; the heavier the burden of taxation . . . the more will leave.

So is there anything Europe can do, anything besides the not-very-likely and even less savory return to Fascism predicted by Ralph Peters? Nothing seems very probable but, just for the sake of completeness, I'll offer a few suggestions.

1. Shit rises to the top. By this I mean there is a tendency for peoples to gravitate toward extremists. It's not clear Europe can do much about the tendency, but it could at least deport or imprison the extremists. Yes, I mean pretty much forever. They won't get better with age.
2. Go back and reread the fourth paragraph of this afterword. Then go read more of your history. STOP reading anti-European, racist, leftist cant. Oh, and stuff the anti-American nonsense. Then go look in the mirror and realize that, world view of the left notwithstanding, you are not a cancer. You have a history and a culture worth defending. You won't defend it unless you know it's worth it.
3. Besma (and Lale) need your help. Defend women, and especially Muslim women. If you want to assimilate them, reach out for the mothers and the girls who will be mothers. They need you and you are abandoning them to tyranny.
4. Intermarry. Don't convert when you do.

5. Stop the process of professionalizing your armed forces. Reinstitute conscription. The armed forces, left to their own devices, are all you have left, institution-wise, with the will and the means to assimilate non-Europeans. Let them do so. *Use* them to do so. And don't let your non-Muslim men weasel out of it.

6. Do not give up an inch in kowtowing to Islam. It only makes you seem contemptibly weak while making the more lunatic imams look correspondingly strong.

7. *Do* give Muslims in your countries a fair break for education and jobs. Perhaps you can (read: I think you should) tie this to honorable completion of military service.

8. Fix your economies. Cut regulation. Cut taxes. Cut the welfare state for those who neither sow nor reap. If you have to transfer income, transfer it to those whom you need to bear children. As a matter of fact, do whatever you must to get culturally European women to bear children in at least replacement numbers.

9. Stop or reduce immigration for a while. You can't assimilate Muslims as well when there's a continuing stream of new ones, full of old ideas.

10. Stop disgracing yourselves by tolerating intolerance.

Not that I think you'll listen.

So what's all this mean to the United States and our non-European allies? Three things, I think. One is that our own progressive movements—basically Marxist but also anti-white, racist (remember that "cancer of mankind" line) Euro clones, anyway—will be discredited even as they chant to each other at High Marxmass, "But it's just never been done right." I don't consider this bad. Another is that it's time and past time to begin writing Europe out of our strategic calculations. We cannot save them and, as written above, the odds are that they won't save themselves. The third is that, at some point in time, and if my reading of the odds is correct, we will need to watch immigration from Europe very carefully. Sometime in that progressive wave of continuingly reinforcing emigration, even the Euro left will begin to become uncomfortable and look for greener pastures.

Yet there is no reason to believe that the mere fact of discomfort, even when they vote with their feet, will take away the leftist, multicultural, Tranzi views that robbed them of their own homelands in the first place. After all, as mentioned above, we regularly hear the defense of communism, "But it's just never been done *right*." One would think that after perhaps two-hundred million political murders and negligent homicides committed by communism in the twentieth century people would realize that murder isn't a perversion of the system; it's a *feature*. But, no, "it's just never been done right."

This is the plaint of a movement and outlook incapable of accepting reality. It's never been done right because it can't be done right. It's like saying, "There's nothing wrong with Fascism; it's just never been done right." Some philosophies are just wrong (unworkable, false, dangerous, evil) from the get go.

Moreover, they will still think the white race is a cancer, even though they are themselves white. These are not people we should wish to have the slightest, tiniest, inkling of influence over our country and people. These are not people we should permit in.

It seems that ex-fascists can learn from their mistakes. I don't know that multiculturalists can.

# GLOSSARY

| | |
|---|---|
| Afwan | You're welcome |
| Allahu Akbar | God is great |
| Ave Maria | Hail Mary |
| Baas | Boss, Sir, Chief |
| Baseski | First Sergeant |
| Bayraktar | Ensign/2nd Lieutenant |
| Corbasi | Colonel |
| Dinar | From Denarius, a gold coin |
| Dirhem | A silver coin |
| Fil | A bronze coin of low value |
| Halawa | A confection made of crushed sesame, often sweetened with honey |

| | |
|---|---|
| Jizya | Special head tax on non-Moslems |
| Kreisskrankenhaus | District Hospital |
| Mahram | Legally permissible escort for a woman |
| Mutawa | Religious police |
| Mutaween | Plural of Mutawa |
| Nazrani | Christian |
| Odabasi | 1st Lieutenant |
| Pater Noster | Our Father |
| Shokran | Thank you |
| VA5H | Variola, Artificial, Version 5 (hemorrhagic) |
| Zakat | Mandatory alms tax on Moslems |

# ACKNOWLEDGMENTS

All the usual suspects: Yolanda who puts up with me, the 'flies, test readers Roger Ross and Dani Vogel and Sue Kerr, John Ringo, Toni and company, and—of course—the European Union, Transnational Progressivism, and Marxist-Leninism, without whose cooperation this book would not have been possible.

## GOT QUESTIONS? WE'VE GOT ANSWERS AT

# BAEN'S BAR

**Here's what some of our members have to say:**

"Ever wanted to get involved in a newsgroup but were frightened off by know-it-alls? Stop by Baen's Bar. Our know-it-alls are the friendly, helpful type—and some write the hottest SF around."

**—Melody L melodyl@ccnmail.com**

"Baen's Bar . . . where you just might find people who understand what you are talking about!"

**—Tom Perry thomas.perry@gmail.com**

"Lots of gentle teasing and numerous puns, mixed with various recipies for food and fun."

**—Ginger Tansey makautz@prodigy.net**

"Join the fun at Baen's Bar, where you can discuss the latest in books, Treecat Sign Language, ramifications of cloning, how military uniforms have changed, help an author do research, fuss about differences between American and European measurements—and top it all off with being able to talk to the people who write and publish what you love."

**—Sun Shadow sun2shadow@hotmail.com**

"Thanks for a lovely first year at the Bar, where the only thing that's intoxicating is conversation."

**—Al Jorgensen awjorgen@wolf.co.net**